WE ARE LEGION
(WE ARE BOB)

BOOK 1 OF THE BOBIVERSE

DENNIS E. TAYLOR

TITLES BY THE AUTHOR

THE WORLD LINES SERIES:
Outland
Earthside (coming 2018)

THE BOBIVERSE SERIES:
We Are Legion (We Are Bob)
For We Are Many
All These Worlds

I would like to dedicate this book to my wife, Blaihin, and my daughter, Tina, who put up with my crazy hours and distracted grunts when I'm writing.

Acknowledgements

It is a source of amazement to me how many people are involved in creating a novel. It's not just about writing it down. Critiques, beta readers, editors, artists, agents, and publishers all have a hand in producing the final product.

I'd like to thank my agent, Ethan Ellenberg, for taking me on; Steve Feldberg of Audible.com who saw the potential in the book; and my editor, Betsy Mitchell, for not completely flaying me.

The number of critters and beta readers who've had a hand in the book is simply astounding. I'd like to particularly mention the members of the Ubergroup and Novel Exchange group on scribophile.

Thanks in particular to:
Sandra and Ken McLaren
Nicole Hamilton
Sheena Lewis
Patrick Jordan
And my wife Blaihin

..for reading the raw draft and early versions.
And, as usual, a shout-out to the members of snowboarding-forum.com

Contents

PART 1

1. BOB VERSION 1.0 _____ 7
2. BOB VERSION 2.0 _____ 16
3. BOB – JUNE 25, 2133 _____ 25
4. BOB – JULY 15, 2133 _____ 30
5. BOB – JULY 18, 2133 _____ 32
6. BOB – JULY 19, 2133 _____ 37
7. BOB – JULY 25, 2133 _____ 40
8. BOB – AUGUST 4, 2133 _____ 45
9. BOB – AUGUST 6, 2133 _____ 51
10. BOB – AUGUST 10, 2133 _____ 54
11. BOB – AUGUST 15, 2133 _____ 58
12. BOB – AUGUST 17, 2133 _____ 61
13. BOB – AUGUST 17, 2133 – EN ROUTE _____ 68

PART 2

14. BOB – AUGUST 2144 – EPSILON ERIDANI _____ 83
15. BOB – SEPTEMBER 2144 – EPSILON ERIDANI _____ 87
16. BOB – SEPTEMBER 2144 – EPSILON ERIDANI _____ 93
17. BOB – JULY 2145 – EPSILON ERIDANI _____ 98
18. BILL – SEPTEMBER 2145 – EPSILON ERIDANI _____ 108
19. MILO – JULY 2152 – OMICRON^2 ERIDANI _____ 110
20. BILL – DECEMBER 2145 – EPSILON ERIDANI _____ 117
21. RIKER – JANUARY 2157 – SOL _____ 119
22. BILL – SEPTEMBER 2150 – EPSILON ERIDANI _____ 125
23. MILO – FEBRUARY 2153 – OMICRON^2 ERIDANI _____ 127
24. RIKER – APRIL 2157 – SOL _____ 129
25. BILL – SEPTEMBER 2151 – EPSILON ERIDANI _____ 143
26. RIKER – APRIL 2157 – SOL _____ 145
27. BOB – APRIL 2165 – DELTA ERIDANI _____ 149
28. CALVIN – NOVEMBER 2163 – ALPHA CENTAURI _____ 156
29. RIKER – SEPTEMBER 2157 – SOL _____ 162

30. Bob – April 2165 – Delta Eridani _____ 166

31. Riker – January 2158 – Sol _____ 170

32. Bill – October 2158 – Epsilon Eridani _____ 174

33. Riker – March 2158 – Sol _____ 176

34. Homer – September 2158 – Sol _____ 183

35. Bob – July 2165 – Delta Eridani _____ 185

36. Riker – September 2158 – Sol _____ 197

37. Bob – August 2165 – Delta Eridani _____ 201

38. Riker – November 2158 – Sol _____ 207

39. Bob – October 2165 – Delta Eridani _____ 210

40. Linus – April 2165 – Epsilon Indi _____ 213

41. Riker – May 2162 – Sol _____ 219

42. Bill – April 2162 – Epsilon Eridani _____ 223

43. Riker – September 2164 – Sol _____ 226

44. Bob – January 2166 – Delta Eridani _____ 230

45. Bill – January 2165 – Epsilon Eridani _____ 234

46. Milo – August 2165 – 82 Eridani _____ 236

47. Riker – January 2166 – Sol _____ 238

48. Bob – May 2166 – Delta Eridani _____ 241

49. Riker – May 2166 – Sol _____ 247

50. Bob – June 2166 – Delta Eridani _____ 252

51. Bill – January 2174 – Epsilon Eridani _____ 258

52. Riker – January 2168 – Sol _____ 260

53. Bob – June 2166 – Delta Eridani _____ 262

54. Riker – October 2170 – Sol _____ 265

55. Bob – July 2166 – Delta Eridani _____ 267

56. Bill - March 2167 - Epsilon Eridani _____ 270

57. Mario – August 2169 – Beta Hydri _____ 274

58. Riker – April 2171 – Sol _____ 282

59. Bill – May 2172 – Epsilon Eridani _____ 285

60. Khan – April 2185 – 82 Eridani _____ 287

61. Howard – Sept 2188 – Omicron^2 Eridani _____ 296

...but as for me, I am tormented with an everlasting itch for things remote. I love to sail forbidden seas, and land on barbarous coasts.

— Ishmael

PART 1

1. Bob Version 1.0

"So… You'll cut my head off." I raised an eyebrow at the salescritter. I was baiting him. I knew it, he knew it, I knew he knew it.

He grinned at me, happy to go along with the routine as long as me and my wallet continued to pay attention. "Mr. Johansson—"

"It's Bob. Please. You're not talking to my father."

The CryoEterna sales rep—the nametag identified him as Kevin—nodded and gestured toward the big placard, which displayed the cryonics process in ghoulish detail. I took a moment to note his Armani suit and hundred-dollar haircut. It appeared there was money in Cryonics.

"Bob, there's no point in freezing the entire body. Remember, the idea is to wait for advancements in medicine to be able to cure whatever killed you. By the time they can resuscitate your corpse, they'll likely be able to grow you a whole new body. That would be easier, in fact, than trying to patch up the old one."

That's just insane enough to be true. "All right, Kevin, I'm sold." I looked down at the papers he'd set out in front of me. "Ten thousand deposit, annual payments, insurance…" Kevin stood patiently, letting me scan the information without interruption. I might be drunk with my newfound wealth, but almost a decade as an engineer and a business owner wouldn't let me do anything without checking all the documentation.

Finally, I was satisfied. I signed the paperwork, wrote a cheque, and shook hands with Kevin.

"You are now a client of CryoEterna Inc." he said, handing me a card. "Keep this in your wallet at all times. In case of death, we will be contacted. Once death has been pronounced, we will—"

"—behead me."

"Yup. And freeze your head, pending medical advances sufficient to bring you back. The guidelines for setting up a Trust are in your information package." Kevin handed me a thick, bright blue folder with a barely visible cloud pattern, and the corporate logo emblazoned on the front. "We'll have the formal documents printed up and mailed to your home address. And welcome to CryoEterna." With that, he stuck out his hand and we shook again.

I did a little skip-step as I left the CryoEterna office. The Trust had already been set up, but I didn't want Kevin to know I had decided to sign up before I even walked into the office. No point in making his job *too* easy. I couldn't decide if this was a canny investment in my future or a mind-blowingly stupid waste of money. Well, what the hell. The sum that Terasoft was paying me for my software company ensured financial stability for the rest of my life—and now, beyond.

Not to mention a significant upgrade in my lifestyle. I'd been attending *The Vortex* SF convention every year since they first started up in Las Vegas, but this year I wasn't part of the riff-raff. As I walked the two blocks from the CryoEterna offices to the convention, I pulled the VIP pass out of my pocket and put the lanyard around my neck. This pass gave me many extras over the standard item—access to hospitality suites, ability to bypass line-ups for autographings, and reserved spaces for panels, among other things. I'd also bought a pass for Jenny—

And, there it was. I'd invoked She Who Must Not Be Named. I stopped dead in the middle of the sidewalk, earning glares from tailgaters and a muttered curse from a Jedi Knight wannabe. I began deep-breathing to still the panic attack. This time, it took only moments to get myself under control. Nothing like practice, I guess. I was still having several panic attacks per day, but that was way down from just after the breakup. It was like having a bad tooth—you keep poking at it with your tongue, even knowing that it's going to hurt each time.

With a conscious act of will, I brought my thoughts back on track. I'd taken advantage of the VIP pass by reserving a space in a couple of back-to-back panels, and the first one was starting in less than fifteen minutes. *Exploring the Galaxy* featured Lawrence Vienn as one of the speakers. He was a popular and prolific science fiction author, and many of his story concepts had helped shape the modern genre.

It took only a couple of minutes to get to the convention center and find the seminar rooms. Con staffers had already gotten the VIPs seated and were about to let everyone else enter when I pulled up, panting and waving my pass. The attendant motioned me in with no more than a glance.

I got an aisle seat by pure fluke. As I rushed into the room, someone stood up right in front of me and turned to walk out. Without breaking stride, I slid into the vacant seat, and the woman seated beside me did a double-take. She must have thought the other guy had morphed.

I turned my head to watch as they opened the doors to the common rabble. People poured into the conference room until attendants had to close the doors or face The Wrath of the Fire Marshal. The Las Vegas hotels tended to have good air conditioning—no one wanted distracted or uncomfortable clients—but a lot of the attendees had been in costume for too long. I tried to breathe through my mouth while hoping the ventilation would eventually catch up.

In typical con fashion, very little concession had been made for aesthetics. The tables and chairs were the standard folding variety, and the session information was written on a large whiteboard. In black marker, because I guess color would be too much bother.

No one cared.

The moderator, a short, round black man with a permanent smile, called for attention. "Good afternoon, gentlebeings. Today, we'll be hearing from Lawrence Vienn—" Spontaneous cheering forced him to pause. "—who will talk about the technological and economic prerequisites to get interstellar probes into space. After that, Dr. Steven Carlisle—" More cheers. "—will talk about the biology of extraterrestrial life. We're looking forward to a great panel today. So, without further ado, I give you Mr. Vienn."

The applause went on for several minutes. Lawrence smiled patiently through it, and gave the occasional wave. Finally it died down, and I settled in for a good listen.

* * *

I sniffed at my clothing, just to make sure I hadn't picked up some of the odor from the room. The second panel had been even more ripe than the first. If not for the subject matter, I'd have bailed. But any discussion of Von Neumann probes was like catnip.

I decided I wouldn't need to change before meeting my soon-to-be-ex-employees for lunch.

I left the convention center and headed for the agreed-upon restaurant, grinning at the spectacle around me. Science-fiction conventions inevitably spilled out onto the streets. Storm troopers, Chewbaccae, and Enterprise crewcritters wandered everywhere. Throngs of fans filled the sidewalks and crossed the streets with or without traffic light assist. I'd seen more than a few exchanges of middle fingers, accompanied by suggestions of an autoerotic nature. Great fun. Fans packed the restaurants twenty-four-seven, but the waitstaff didn't complain—nerds tend to overtip. I'd heard that the casinos were less happy with the level of gambling. Turns out nerds understand probability.

I made it to the restaurant without losing any body parts, and found my group.

* * *

"To Terasoft!" Carl raised his glass as he gave the toast.

"Terasoft." The rest of us raised our glasses in response.

Carl, Karen, and Alan had been my first hires at InterGator Software. They had been loyal and patient through the early hard times, and I had made them shareholders in the company. My engineering design and analysis application had eventually grown to be the number one product in its niche, out-selling competitors like Terasoft by a significant margin.

Terasoft reacted with a truly eye-popping buy-out offer, and we were now all sharing in the windfall. These three might still have to work for a living, but they wouldn't have to make mortgage or car payments.

I had invited the trio to spend the week in Las Vegas on my dime. Only Carl took me up on the offer of the VIP con pass, the other two pleading sanity. Alan and Karen stated their intention to see every single Las Vegas show. At several per day, they looked like they were approaching saturation.

"How are you holding up, Bob?" Carl looked at me with one eyebrow raised.

"Pretty good. I signed with CryoEterna this morning..." Karen made a low growling sound and looked away. She didn't need to say anything; she'd already made her opinion very clear on that subject.

I waggled my eyebrows at her and continued, "And I just went to a couple of very interesting panels. *Exploring the Galaxy* and *Designing a Von Neumann Probe.*"

Alan laughed. "No theme there, not at all. Engineers. Jeez."

"Yeah, but how are *you* doing, Bob?" Carl gave me the hairy eyeball.

Carl had managed to navigate the tricky pathway of being an employee and becoming a friend, without looking like he was brown-nosing. I guess I owed him the courtesy of not pretending to misunderstand.

"A lot better, Carl. 'Jenny' episodes are down to a couple a day. I might even be ready to rejoin the human race, soon."

"The woman was an idiot," Karen muttered. "You should have taken your mother up on her offer."

That forced a chuckle from me. "My mother doesn't *actually* know how to arrange a hit, Karen. I don't think." I pulled out my phone and glanced at it. "Speaking of which, she texted me. I'll have to phone her back soon, or she'll just keep sending more texts. She's kind of like the Terminator, that way."

"So it *is* genetic!"

I mimed exaggerated laughter at Carl and he grinned back, unrepentant. After a moment, he waved a hand dismissively and changed the subject. "Anyway, part of the purpose of coming to the con this year was as a distraction from the breakup, right? So how were the panels?"

Karen groaned, and I leaned forward to put my elbows on the table. "Really interesting. Dr. Carlisle theorizes that life will generally be similar on different planets with similar climates, and maybe even digestible by humans. Panspermia, ya know. Common biological origins."

"Horse cookies."

"No, seriously, Alan. He gave a pretty good argument for a common chemical basis for life. Not *Star Trek* level compatible, but we could probably subsist on an alien ecosystem."

"I'll wait and see," Alan said. "How about the other one? Space probes?"

"Von Neumann probes. Automated probes that reproduce as they visit star systems. Turns out nanites are out and 3D printers are in for self-replication."

Carl nodded. "As advancing technology leaves fiction behind, again."

"Wait, what?" Alan said, looking perplexed.

Carl and I both smiled indulgently. Alan was not a science geek, despite a background in software development. I gestured with my hands as I described the idea. "You've seen 3D printers, right? Printing things like plastic parts, medical prosthetics, and toys?" At his nod, I continued, "So take it to the next level. Have them able to deliver any element, one atom at a time, according to a design. You could, in principle, print literally anything solid."

"Including parts to make more probes," Carl added, "using whatever elements they find in the systems they visit."

Alan glanced at me. "This would work?"

"I minored in physics, Alan, you guys know that. I think it's completely plausible." I paused for a moment to taste my beer, then looked around at the others. "And the engineering—"

"You're really going to freeze your head?"

We all turned to face Karen. "Here we go," Alan muttered.

She glared at Alan, then at me. "When they revive you—*if* they revive you—it'll probably be long after everyone you know is dead."

"Including Jenny..." Alan said, sotto voce.

Karen glared at him again. "Whatever. Your family will be dead. Your friends will be dead. How are you good with that?"

I looked at her for a moment, considering my response. "I'm a humanist, Karen. You know that. No afterlife. If I die, my choices are revival or nothing. I'll take my chances with whatever I wake up to."

Karen's expression grew even more thunderous, and she opened her mouth for a retort. Fortunately, the waiter picked that moment to arrive with our lunch. The odor of hamburgers, caramelized onions, and vinegarized fries wafted around the table as the plates were set down in front of us. By the time the food was distributed, the moment of tension had dissipated.

* * *

I dropped a trail of shoes and clothes behind me and settled onto the king-sized bed. The daily rate on the executive suite was ludicrous, but the luxurious bed alone was worth the price. One could get used to this. Oh, yes.

I set the alarm so I wouldn't sleep the whole afternoon, and pulled out my phone. My mother really would keep texting me if I didn't call her back.

The phone rang twice at the other end before her voice came on. "Hi Robert. Has it been a year already?"

"Hah hah. Hi Mom. Got your text. No, I don't need a contract taken out on what's-her-face, thanks. I'm at *The Vortex*, having a great time. K, bye."

She laughed into the phone. This was a game we always played. I acted impatient and tried to end the call, but we both knew I'd stay on as long as she wanted.

"I'm fine Robert, thanks for asking."

"And how are the mosquitos?"

"The mosquitos are fine. They miss you and your delicate Nordic skin. Are there no mosquitos in San Diego?"

"Not like Minnesota, Mom. One of the reasons I moved there."

"Hmm. And how are you doing, son? The offer's still open on what's-her-face. I knows deze guys..."

"Thanks, but I don't want to have to visit you in jail." I sighed. "Look, Mom. People cheat. It happens. We weren't married yet. I'd have hated to find out *after* we tied the knot. I'm good, now. Really."

Can you *hear* disbelief? My mother didn't say a word. Maybe it was her breathing. Whatever, I decided it was a good time to change the subject. "So how's everyone?"

"Your father's fine. He's in the workshop, still trying to get that pile o' junk to start. Your sisters are here for a visit, by the way. *They* visit their poor ailing mother. Andrea is motioning that she'd like to mock you for a bit."

"Okay, put her on. I need my massive ego kicked out from under me."

There was some muffled conversation, then, "Hi little brother."

"I'm older than you."

"Not what I meant."

I smiled to myself at the sound of her voice and at the traditional exchange. Andrea, Alaina, and myself were as close as siblings could be. The two girls were twins only in that they were born at the same time. They had literally twelve inches difference in height between them. And Andrea never let me forget that she had an inch on me as well.

"So, rich guy, how are things out in Silicone Valley?" I could hear the smile in Andrea's voice. She'd been doing this comedy routine ever since I'd moved west.

"It's *Silicon*, Andrea. And that's in Frisco."

"I watch TMZ. I stand by my comment."

"Ooh, the butt-hurt is strong in this one..."

Andrea laughed. We spent a few minutes more exchanging insults, updating news bites, then I told her to say hi to Alaina and Dad for me.

Thank God for family. And thank God for a couple thousand miles of distance. When everyone was home at the same time, I could generally take it for about half an hour before I retreated into the basement. Usually, Dad followed about ten minutes later. There'd be the mutual eye-rolling, and we'd settle down without a word, to read or watch TV. My father and I were both loners by disposition. We could sit in the same room for hours, not say five words to each other, and both be completely comfortable. It drove my mother crazy.

* * *

I was surprised when the alarm went off. I hadn't intended to fall asleep. I jumped out of bed and got ready as quickly as I could. I would be meeting the gang for dinner, but I wanted to spend some time at the actual convention. *The Vortex* was a three-day gyrating bag of crazy, and I wanted to catch as much of it as I could. You couldn't truly say you'd been to a science fiction con until you'd been run over by Farscape cosplayers, threatened by at least one drunken Darth, and had bought a cheap plastic movie prop for more than its weight in gold. Woo hah.

The elevator opened, and I stepped out into the lobby. The doorman nodded to me as I approached, and held the door open. As usual, I wasn't sure if I should tip him or not. I decided to give him a large tip when I checked out, just in case.

The Las Vegas air hit like a hammer when I stepped out of the air-conditioned hotel. I stopped and let a gaggle of Enterprise crewcritters, several Ferengi, two Chewbaccas, and a storm trooper wander past. They were loud, truculent, and appeared to have been sampling Terran alcohol to excess. After a few seconds of semi-coherent argument, they turned and crossed the street more or less as a unit.

I smiled and shook my head, then I walked the extra fifty feet to the crosswalk. I wasn't in *that* much of a hurry. As I started to cross, I heard a flurry of hurled insults, blaring horns, and squealing tires.

I turned toward the noise, and everything went into slow motion. The car came around the group, the driver's mouth moving as he leaned out the window. He turned forward and looked right at me, and his eyes went wide. Tires squealed as the car went into a four-wheel lock.

You have GOT to be kidding me!

There was a flash of light, a moment of unimaginable pain...

* * *

I could hear voices. Urgent voices, calling out about codes. Someone in the background declaring that they had a right to be there. Something about a power of attorney, last will and testament. Angry responses. A calm voice, much closer, mentioning time of death...

The voices and the light faded, and the world ended.

2. Bob Version 2.0

I snapped back to consciousness. There was no transition, none of the normal vagueness you get when you wake up. I remembered the car coming at me, which I thought was odd. I would have expected the last few seconds to be lost as they didn't have time to enter long-term memory. On the other hand, maybe the last few seconds *had* been lost.

I lay there, without moving or opening my eyes, and did careful inventory. I felt no pain. In fact, I couldn't feel my arms, my legs, or my body at all. I was getting none of the normal proprioceptive cues that would tell me if I were lying down, comfortable, or anything. Not really a good sign—complete paralysis seemed a likely explanation.

I experienced a moment of panic, followed immediately by a kind of bemused surprise. The panic seemed to be purely intellectual. I had no sensation of elevated breathing, increased heart-rate, or fight-or-flight muscle tension. Nothing. While I was normally very analytical, this seemed especially Vulcan, even for me.

Wow. Am I paralyzed from the forehead down? Maybe I'm in an induced coma? If so, it's not a very good one.

Gathering my resolve, I opened my eyes.

Or tried to. Nothing happened. This time, I did panic. Being blind was the stuff of nightmares for me. For a few moments, my thoughts spun out of control. I thought of movies I would never see, books I would never read.

But again, the panic didn't self-reinforce. No adrenaline rush, no nothing. I couldn't think of a medical condition that would do that. Maybe drugs. Good ones.

I was getting a little weirded out. Over and above the panic thing, I mean. I decided on drugs as a good working hypothesis.

Determined to get a handle on things, I tried again, really *thought* about opening my eyes. The mechanics, the feeling of my eyes opening...

And with no transition, I could *see!* There are no words to describe my relief with that small victory.

I appeared to be sitting up, since I was looking at a wall instead of a ceiling. The room could be a hospital room, or a lab, or any nondescript government office. The walls were painted in that peculiar off-white tone that new construction always seemed to start out with. The far wall had a large window, currently shielded by white, uh, something. I thought at first it might be Venetian blinds, but they seemed to be actually printed on the glass.

I expected to see part of my body in the foreground, perhaps under plain hospital sheets. But instead, there was just a flat plane, like maybe a desktop.

Just beyond the flat plane, a man sat, consulting a tablet. He looked, I kid you not, exactly how most of us visualize Sigmund Freud, right down to the lab coat. *He can't actually be a shrink. That would just be too cliché. Is he here to talk to me about my injuries? It has to be pretty bad if they have a counselor ready and waiting for me to wake up.*

There was something off about him, though. The shirt he was wearing looked almost clerical in cut. And his watch...

It took me a moment longer to realize I was experiencing a problem with perspective. The room seemed to be deep and narrow, and Freud seemed to be about six feet from front to back. In fact, when he turned his head, his nose seemed to stick about a foot out from his face.

As I examined this odd optical illusion, I felt a shifting sensation and heard a whirring sound, and the perspective corrected itself. Before I could begin to analyze the sensation and sound, Freud looked up and smiled. "Good. You're awake."

I tried to respond, but what came out was something like a cross between a cough and static. *For God's sake, that sounded like a voice synthesizer having a breakdown.*

Freud put down the tablet, leaned forward, and rested his arms on the desk or table or whatever. "Please keep trying. It can take a few attempts for the GUPPI interface to mesh."

I considered what he'd said. It immediately brought up three points. Point one, I wasn't dead. Well, okay, I think therefore I am, yadda yadda. Call that one proven. Point two, I wasn't good as new— in fact I appeared to be speaking through a voice synthesizer. But doing so by mental control, which meant, point three, that the technology had advanced significantly since I'd been hit by the car. How long had I been out? And what the heck was a guppy interface?

I tried again, concentrating on forming the words. "*Xzjjzzjjj...* Someone want to *zhixxxjx* fill me in on what's going on?"

Freud clapped his hands, once. "Excellent. I am Dr. Landers, Bob. I will answer any questions you have, and I will help to prepare you for your new life."

New life...? What's wrong with my old one? I already don't like where this is going.

Dr. Landers pulled the tablet over so that it was directly in front of him. "So, Bob, what's the last thing you remember?"

"A car coming right at me. I was sure it was going to hit me. I'm pretty sure it did."

"It did indeed, Bob. You arrived at the hospital in critical condition with a very poor prognosis. Per your contract with CryoEterna, they were standing by with a cryocontainer when time of death was pronounced."

"Well, good to know my money wasn't wasted, anyway. So what year is it?"

Dr. Landers laughed. "So nice to talk to a subject so quick on the uptake. It is June 24, 2133, and we are currently in New Handeltown, which would have been Portland in your day."

I was surprised by that. *So that's...* [117] *years. Wait, where did that come from?*

I'd always been able to do math in my head with no effort, but it normally required me to at least go through the calculation steps. This answer had arrived as if spoken in my ear. *Huh. Something to investigate later. Add to TO-DO list.*

I turned my attention back to the doctor. The shirt made a little more sense, now. Styles would change in a hundred-plus years. I really wanted to get a look at that watch, though.

"Who's Handel?" I asked.

"Ah, now, Bob, we're getting ahead of ourselves. I have an established script for bringing candidates up to date, and history lessons come later."

"So what happened to Old Handeltown?"

Dr. Landers smiled and shook his head in mock sorrow.

I sighed and nodded. Well, I tried to nod. My field of view didn't move. So I had control over my eyes but not my head. I was starting to suspect some kind of locked-in syndrome.

Instead, I grunted. "Right, so can we talk about how much of me is still human? This artificial voice thing tells me that you haven't been able to make me good as new. How much is Borg? Should I ask for a mirror, or would that be a bad idea?"

"Ah..." Dr. Landers glanced down at his tablet and hesitated, then looked back at me. "It would be inaccurate to compare you to a Borg. If I remember my *Trek* trivia correctly, they are at least partly human. I think Mr. Data would be a better comparison."

I simply stared at him for what seemed like forever. My mind was blank. I couldn't seem to form a thought.

Finally, I found my voice. "*Zhzzjjjz...* Excuse me?" I noted almost in passing that I still wasn't having a panic attack. For the first time, I suspected I knew why.

"You, Bob, are what most people would call an Artificial Intelligence, although that's not strictly accurate. You are a copy of the mind of Robert Johansson, created by scanning his cryogenically frozen brain at the subcellular level and converting the data into a computer simulation. You are, essentially, a computer program that thinks it's Robert Johansson. A *replicant*."

"Does that mean I'm immortal, then?"

Dr. Landers looked startled for a moment, then threw his head back and laughed. "That is definitely not the reaction I normally get. We seem to have skipped the denial phase entirely. I'm feeling more and more confident about our decision to replicate you."

"Well, thanks. I think. So then I'm... that is, Bob is still alive? Or still dead? I mean, still in cryo?"

"No, I'm afraid not." Dr. Landers shifted uncomfortably in his chair. "The recording process is destructive. We have to thaw the brain sufficiently to be able to measure the synaptic potentials, without allowing ice crystals to form. Chemicals are involved which render the brain non-viable. There's no point in trying to re-freeze it afterwards."

The revelation hit me with a jolt, almost like touching a live wire. I don't know why I should be more bothered by the fact of original Bob being dead. Either way, I was a computer program. But somehow, the idea that I was all that was left of Bob felt like being stabbed. I had been—Bob had been—*discarded.*

"But... but that means you *killed* me!"

The doctor sighed. "And that's the cue for the history lesson."

He settled himself more comfortably in his chair and assumed that far-off expression people get when they're lecturing. "In 2036, the USA elected an over-the-top, unapologetic fundamentalist president named Andrew Handel. Yes, that Handel. During his term, he tried to ban election of non-Christians to *any* public post, and tried to remove the constitutional separation between church and state. He was nominated, supported, and elected based on his religious views, rather than on his political or fiscal expertise. And of course, he appointed persons of similar persuasion to every post he could manage, in some cases blatantly ignoring laws and procedures. He and his cronies rammed through far-right policies with no thought for consequences. In a number of cases, when challenged on the results, he declared that God would not allow their just cause to fail. He eventually brought the USA to its knees in an economic collapse that made the 2008 recession look like a picnic in the park."

Dr. Landers tapped his tablet absent-mindedly. It was obvious to me that he knew the whole spiel by rote.

"In the next election, the public voted in the USA's first—and only—overtly atheist president, Desmond Ahearn, mostly in reaction to the Handel travesty. Needless to say, the religious right went ballistic. In 2041, they staged a successful coup. And thus was born the Free American Independent Theocratic Hegemony."

It took me perhaps a millisecond to parse out the acronym. I groaned. "How long do you suppose it took them to work *that* out?"

Dr. Landers frowned. "The official history doesn't mention Ahearn or the coup at all, and Handel is credited with being voted in after running on a platform of creating a theocracy. And just so you know, Bob, criticism of the government is a felony, punishable by, er, *re-education.* It's certainly something to be avoided. As a machine, though, you'd just be deactivated. Part of my job is to instruct you in right-thinking so you can become a good servant of the state."

"Are you going to get in trouble at all? Some of your comments seem, you know, insufficiently respectful."

"The Ministry of Truth, which is backing this venture, is surprisingly pragmatic. They are concerned with results, and have guaranteed us that they will not interfere as long as they get what they're paying for." The doctor frowned. "Some of the other ministries, maybe less so. We are cautious during any ministry visits."

"Got it. So anyway, I get to live out my days operating a garbage truck or something, as a good servant of the state?"

"Ah, well, on that subject... You see, one of the first acts of the new theocracy was to declare all cryogenic facilities blasphemous and all corpsicles truly dead. They confiscated the clients' assets— all those fiscal vehicles that you and others had set up to pay for your long-term storage. And finally they auctioned off all the cryo companies' assets. Which included a bunch of deep-frozen clients with no legal standing."

"Auctioned us off? Wouldn't the properly orthodox thing to do be to bury us? Not that I'm advocating that right now, you understand..."

Dr. Landers looked angry for a moment. "Did theologues limit themselves to logical or consistent behavior in your day?"

"Point taken." I considered the doctor's explanation. "So I actually belong to someone?"

"To the company I work for, as a matter of fact. Applied Synergetics Inc. is engaged in a sort of economic competition with Total Cyber Systems to supply robotic servants to society. We attempt to integrate replicants into useful machinery, while TCS creates artificial machine intelligences, AMIs, from the ground up."

I chuckled. Or tried to. What came out of the voice synthesizer was a long way from what I intended.

Dr. Landers winced. "That'll get better. Don't worry. By the end of this session, your voice will be indistinguishable from human. And to answer the unspoken but obvious question, AMIs at the moment are only authorized for very, very simple tasks with low risk or heavy supervision. Some years ago, some AMI-based pest-control equipment at a local mall had a psychotic break and decided people qualified as targets. Dozens of patrons were hurt, and several were killed before they deactivated the devices."

I chuckled again. This time it sounded less like a printer jamming.

"On the other hand," Dr. Landers continued, "replicants aren't any better at multitasking than they were when alive. Which is why we add the GUPPI interface to offload tasks. And about four out of five replicants go insane when they discover what has been done to them."

He looked in my direction with a wry expression. "Not to mention that most cryo subjects were wealthy, and don't take well to the idea of becoming indentured servants in their next life."

The image of some ex-CEO being told he would now be driving a garbage truck made me laugh out loud.

"...So we can find it difficult to get the right replicant for the right job. And a certain percentage go insane anyway after a while."

That was a sobering thought. I had a bad feeling that I might be looking down that particular chasm later. Right now, this all felt like it was happening to someone else. Questions about individuality and the existence of souls poked at the edge of my awareness. With an effort I pushed them away, to concentrate on the now.

"Eighty percent failure rate kind of sucks, doc. How do you stay in business?"

"One success, Bob, can be installed in many units. Most of the mining equipment in operation today is controlled by one Rudolf Kazini, who was a miner in his former life as well. Matching temperament to task is the key." The doctor hesitated for a moment, then added, "And, of course, we cultivate multiple candidates."

I tried to raise my non-existent eyebrows and I was annoyed when nothing happened. "Am I in a competition, then?"

"Well, yes and no. We have activated five candidates for this project. Statistically, four of you will go insane and be purged. If more than one of you gets through the training phase with your sanity intact, then yes, we'll have to make a choice. The project requires only one replicant."

"And the loser?"

Dr. Landers shrugged. "Garbage truck. Or maybe just stored pending another opportunity."

Not good. Not good at all. The prospect of going insane wasn't exactly at the top of my bucket list, but the idea of cheating death—more or less—then just being relegated to menial labor, really sucked. Being turned off, even more so. It would appear that I was in a competition, and one with the highest of stakes for me.

I was going to have to take this very seriously. And I would have to assume that the other candidates were equally well suited to whatever task the project required. I would simply have to be better. And the first step was information-gathering.

"So, what's the job?"

"There's really no point in discussing specifics at this early stage. It would be a distraction, at best."

Well, no joy, there. "Can you tell me about my opponents?"

"No, Bob. There's no reason to. You'll never meet them. Best that you not humanize them in any way."

That made sense, in a very cold, clinical way. But I wasn't making much headway on the information-gathering front, so far.

"Okay. Next question. Why am I not more panicked about all of this? This is absolutely bizarre. I'm dead. I mean, original me is dead. I'm a computer program. I'm *property*. Why am I not running in tight little circles, waving my hands in the air? Apart from the obvious reason, I mean."

The doctor smirked, but he didn't really seem amused. "We can't modify your personality, Bob. It's an emergent property. Attempts to do so have resulted in, ah, non-viable subjects. So it's all or nothing. But we *can* control the endocrine simulation routines. Panic depends on a feedback loop involving adrenaline. We simply limit that. You can't panic or get angry or frightened, you can only be deeply concerned, so to speak."

"And with that, you still have an 80% failure rate?" I tried to wave a hand. I had always talked with my hands a lot, so when that failed as well, I said in exasperation, "Say, am I going to get some appendages at some point? This *Jack the Bodiless* business is getting on my nerves, er, circuits. Whatever."

Dr. Landers nodded. "Actually, Bob, I think we've made very good progress today. You were obviously a very rational person and are handling this better than I could have hoped for. We'll continue tomorrow, and I'll see if I can get you some peripherals."

Dr. Landers lifted his tablet and poked at it.

"Wait, no, I—"

3. Bob – June 25, 2133

I snapped back to consciousness. I could see that Dr. Landers wore a different colored shirt, still in that weird clerical style, so I assumed it was at least a day later. He was concentrating on his tablet, and just starting to look up.

I poked at my own psyche, looking for any trace of panic, insanity, or even deep concern. It didn't feel like being doped up. I'd *been* doped up, like when I was getting my wisdom teeth out. I didn't enjoy that sensation. I also had never enjoyed the sensation of getting drunk, of not being in control of my own mind.

In this case, I was in complete control of my thoughts. In fact, I felt at the top of my game, like I did when I first got into the office after an excellent night's sleep. Like no problem or puzzle could possibly stand before me.

On the other hand, my parents were long since dead, my sisters as well. Alan, Karen, Carl, all the people that I'd known. I had a clear mental image of Karen glaring at me, arms crossed, *I told you so* written across her face. But thoughts of my family and friends brought only a mild feeling of regret, likely due to the endocrine controls. That, more than simply the fact of being software, made me feel less than human.

It was hard to be upset with Dr. Landers about the situation. There didn't seem to be any malice involved. Events had just evolved logically over time, and culminated with me as a computer program. And so far, this state of being seemed to have its advantages. If Bob was dead—if he'd been run over by a car—then this was basically a free life. A potentially immortal one, no less. Maybe I'd just roll with it, at least for the moment. I could always re-evaluate if I ended up in second place. *Be careful what you wish for.* No kidding.

So what else came with being a glorified computer program? Maybe I could communicate with that guppy interface.

Systems Check. Square root of 234,215.

[483.957642]

Damn, that's cool. Do I have a date function? Current Date.

[2133-06-25.08:42:24.235]

Woo hoo, I'm Data. "At the tone, the time will be eight forty-three. Beeeeep."

Dr. Landers looked surprised for a moment, then laughed. "You have a number of functions like that, Bob. You just need to learn how to access them. Part of your training will concentrate on that area."

I tried to nod out of habit and was surprised when my field of view bobbed. "Hey, I've got neck control!" I swiveled my 'head,' and found to my delight that I could rotate my field of vision all the way around like an owl. The room presented no surprises. As I suspected, I was actually *on* a desk. Beside me was a waldo, a remote-manipulator arm. It was small and very basic compared to industrial models, just a two-digit pincer grip, with a shoulder, elbow, and wrist joint. I decided to see if it was accessible. After all, that was probably on the agenda for today.

It seemed to take forever—although my date/time function said less than a half-second had elapsed—before the waldo moved at my command. I waved it around and snapped at the air with the pincer, then turned back to Dr. Landers.

The doctor stared at the waldo with a bemused expression. Then a smile slowly formed, and he said with a wry shake of his head, "For today's exercise, we'll get you to attempt to move a manipulator arm."

He shook his head and sighed. "So much for today's training schedule. Bob, you're doing very well, so far. I think we'll bump up the roamer test. I'd originally scheduled this for a week from now after some more preliminary orientation, but..."

Dr. Landers picked up the tablet and aimed a finger.

Oh, not again. "Wait! No, don't do—"

* * *

I found myself in a different room in the same institutional off-white color. A rack on one wall contained some [32] small mechanical devices. In front of each device, a red light glowed. Directly in front of me was a table with a number [128] of blocks.

The far wall contained a window, and Dr. Landers stood on the other side. "Will you *please* stop doing that!" I said. I attempted to glare at him.

"Would you prefer that I pick you up and carry you around under my arm?" Dr. Landers held a poker face for a couple of seconds, then smiled. "Actually, you and the other candidates all reside in large, expensive cubes of electronics tucked safely away in an air-conditioned room elsewhere on the premises. I'm merely switching your peripheral functions from room to room. The *you* in this room is a stereoscopic camera on a mechanical arm."

He waited for any comments from me, but I had nothing at the moment. He gestured toward the rack. "The shelves contain *remote observation and manipulation* devices, or ROAMers. Your goal will be to stack the blocks using as many roamers as possible. We'll start with one roamer, to give you the feel of it."

Dr. Landers played with his tablet, and the light in front of one of the devices on the rack went from red to green.

"The roamers contain a low-level AMI and can perform basic actions without active supervision, but they have no will of their own and require direction. Please attempt to move the roamer to the table and stack some blocks. Your GUPPI will provide contact with the ROAM interface and will provide feedback as necessary."

I looked intently at roamer #1.

[STATUS: Ready].

Okay, that's a good start. Stand up.

The roamer stood. It looked vaguely like a spider, with a stance width of about eight inches [20 cm when not constrained]. *Oh, shut up!*

I inspected the roamer as best I could from a distance. *I wonder how it's supposed to manipulate the blocks.* I waited a moment. *Well?*

[Feedback disabled by user request]

Oh, great, I've hurt its feelings. I concentrated on the ROAM interface. *Enable feedback.*

Immediately, diagrams and schematics appeared in my vision. I examined them in fascination. The roamers were constructed with radial symmetry—no real front or back. Eight limbs matched with eight sets of sensors. Each appendage could be a leg or could split into three digits to act as a manipulator. In addition, different legs had specialized functions built in. Some legs could be screwdrivers, grinders, torches, and cutters of various kinds. Some of the tech was brand new as well. One neat gizmo was a magnetically controlled plasma cutter that I would consider the real-life version of a light saber.

Now, how do I get it to the table? Can it jump the distance? **[Probability of damage to unit: 40%]** *So, that's a no.*

How about climbing down? Oh, wait. I called up the schematics again. *Variable Attachment Surface Tension. Wow, these people sure love their acronyms.* I visualized the roamer climbing down the shelf. A window popped up in my field of vision which allowed me to see through the roamer's viewpoint. The roamer walked straight down the wall. The VAST system provided a secure grip. In seconds, I had the roamer up the table legs and onto the table.

This was my first opportunity to examine my table-top 'self.' From the roamer's point of view, I saw a mechanical arm similar to the waldo I'd learned to control, with a pair of cameras attached at the end. A small speaker between the cameras was probably where my voice originated. That was my face, such as it was. It reminded me of the robot from the movie *Short Circuit.* I moved my 'head' around and the roamer's video showed the arm moving, the twin cameras swaying on the end of it. I waved one of the roamer's legs and I could see the roamer perform the action.

Seeing myself and seeing me seeing myself made me feel existentially dizzy, so I turned my attention to the blocks. They appeared to be regular children's building blocks, the kind that have been available forever. Half the faces showed letters or numerals in bas relief, painted in primary colors, and the other faces had simple engraved images. I noted that *all* the images were overtly religious in nature. I filed that factoid away in my *TO-DO* for future review.

The roamer didn't need to have each movement supervised, but it did need to be told the parameters for the task. Within seconds, it had created a 5x5 platform of blocks. I then instructed the roamer to place a 4x4 layer on top of that, centered, and repeat. The roamer moved with impressive speed if I avoided trying to give it moment-by-moment orders. In seconds it had completed a pyramid.

I looked over at Dr. Landers. "Ta daaaaaa."

The doctor nodded, then played with his tablet. Three more lights went green on the rack of roamers.

"Again please, Bob. This time with multiple roamers."

Over the next few hours, Dr. Landers set various tasks for me that involved different numbers of roamers. Each exercise had an obvious training goal, and I found myself becoming increasingly impressed with my new capabilities.

He occasionally introduced new materials, including at one point something that reminded me of a Meccano set. The roamers easily handled each test. I simply had to set the overall tasks, and they would operate with speed and efficiency. There was only one glitch the whole morning: when I was not quite clear enough with my directions, one roamer ended up tossing another one across the room. I know the doctor said the AMIs had no will of their own, but I could swear the tossee acted surly afterward.

At some point during the session, I became aware that the training room was completely sealed. There was no door, and there weren't any air ducts. Come to think of it, that window looked quite thick and very securely framed. *Are they afraid of me? Or the roamers? Or both? Another item on the TO-DO for review.*

4. Bob - July 15, 2133

I snapped back to consciousness. "That's getting really old, Dr. Landers."

"Sorry, Bob. But it is standard procedure to put replicants into standby when they are not actively involved in training. You feel like you are operating at normal human speed when you interact with me, but once you are left to your own thoughts, you'll find you experience time at a much higher subjective rate. Eight hours can be an eternity. I've had replicants that seemed to be doing okay suddenly go psychotic overnight."

The doctor looked down at his shoes for a moment. "In fact, we've lost one of your competitors in the last twenty-four hours. She went into a loop and could not be brought back. We restored from backup, but the backup went down at the same point. So, now there are four."

I sighed and noted with mild satisfaction that the sigh sounded real. It was pretty obvious that I was being kept as busy as possible when active, and not being given any quiet time. Probably that was an attempt to avoid the insanity issue. I was ashamed to realize that I was more glad than sad about the other replicant. *One less competitor.*

And I appreciated Dr. Landers' honesty, but sooner or later I was going to have to deal with this whole existential crisis thing. And I still needed time to grieve for my family.

"I'm sorry to hear that," I said. "But presumably we're all being treated the same, so the switching off thing doesn't seem to be the answer. Instead, how about keeping me busy with intellectual activity? How about some study time? Maybe with access to whatever the internet has evolved into? I'd like to see what I've been missing for the last hundred-odd"—[117]. *I didn't ask!*— "years."

"Ah. Well, the internet does not exist anymore, at least not domestically. Far too anarchic, far too hard to control. And too many opportunities for sin, wrong thinking, and temptation. However, we have online libraries, and some of the history might even be relatively accurate. I will see if I can connect you up to one of the better ones."

"Are there genealogy records? I might have relatives still alive. I'd be very interested—"

"As a matter of policy, Bob, we don't encourage that. In any case, such information is not in the public record. Under FAITH, information is not freely available by default. Sorry."

At that moment, I was happy that I had no face. This was the final blow, cutting me off from my former humanity. Not only was my immediate family dead, I would not be able to reconnect with *any* descendants. I was truly, completely alone.

Then the damned endocrine controls kicked in, and my funk turned into a mild sadness. Wow, if I ever got control of my hardware and software, that was the first thing that would go out the window. Grieving required grief, and I was being robbed of that.

I didn't like being property. I wasn't in a position to do anything about it at the moment, but if the situation changed, there would be some adjustments. Meanwhile, I would shut up, listen, learn, and be a good little robot. The important thing was to not give them any reason for concern. And to stay sane. And to win the competition.

But no pressure.

5. Bob – July 18, 2133

Sigh. "Morning, Dr. Landers. Didn't you just leave?"

"Good morning, Bob…"

Uh oh. That wasn't Dr. Landers' normal tone. I had been playing around with tuning my artificial senses, and I'd discovered that I could run Fourier Analysis on voices in close to real time. The doctor's voice indicated high levels of tension.

A second man stepped into view. Dr. Landers gestured toward him. "Bob, this is Senior Minister Travis. He's here to evaluate your progress."

I understood the unspoken message. This guy could pull my plug. I would have to tread very carefully. I would also have to clamp down on my tendency to make wisecracks, as his appearance seemed purpose-designed for a comedy routine. He reminded me of the old saying, 'Stereotypes are valid first-order approximations.' The man was the cliché of the old-time, bible-thumping, fire-breathing preacher: tall and thin, with cheekbones and teeth that seemed to protrude from his face. Even when he smiled, he glowered.

"Good morning, Minister Travis. I'm at your disposal." *Wow, worst opening line, ever.*

"Good morning, replicant. I'm here to evaluate fitness yours for a task which is the glory of the Lord on today and to a much extent lesser, the kingdom of our spiritual leaders, Thomas Händel III."

I was taken aback for a moment at his accent and mangled

vocabulary. Of course, this was a hundred years later, but Dr. Landers always sounded like anyone you might run into on the street. On the other hand, Landers had made it clear that dealing with replicants was his specialty. Perhaps that included speech training.

"All right, shoot," I said.

Minister Travis turned to Dr. Landers in confusion.

Dr. Landers shrugged. "Oh, there a twenty-first century is colloquialism. It means to have all the questions you desire."

Minister Travis nodded, and glanced back at me. "I imagine statement in the current idiom is not a high priority, since the intended use of subject."

Crying out loud. What? The current version of English was just too mangled to make sense of. Well, maybe there was a translator. After all, even in my time, we had Google Translate. I dove into the library, and within milliseconds, I found what I needed. I played the minister's last statement through the routine.

'I imagine instruction in current idiom isn't a high priority, given its intended use.'

Oh boy. If I still had eyebrows, they would have risen right to my hairline.

He looked at me. Or maybe toward me. I got the feeling he was addressing a microphone rather than talking to someone. I routed all dialog through the translation routine.

"Did you go to church when you were alive?"

Can they tell when I lie? Dr. Landers never said anything about it. Well, I doubt I'd end up worse off being caught in a polite lie, rather than being honest about my opinion of religion.

"Occasionally, Minister Travis. Easter and Christmas, mostly. Without a family, there was no real pressure."

"No children, then?"

"Not... no." *Not that I know of. Hah! That would have gone over well. Moron.*

"Not?"

"Not yet, Minister." *And not likely, now.*

Minister Travis nodded.

The conversation continued in that vein for several minutes. The questions were decidedly non-technical. The minister seemed to be primarily interested in my attitude toward religion in general. I was very careful to be respectful and non-confrontational, to come across as a team player, and to avoid any hint of my true feelings about theism in general.

Finally, Minister Travis seemed satisfied. He nodded to me, said goodbye to Dr. Landers, and left.

Dr. Landers withdrew a hankie and wiped his brow.

"Damn, doc. Was it that dangerous a situation? He didn't seem belligerent."

"There was no way to predict, Bob. He showed up unexpectedly, and I had no time to prepare you or research the minister to find out whose side he's on."

"Side? Uh, FAITH has sides?"

"Surely you don't think our government is in complete agreement about everything?" Dr. Landers looked at me with a wry expression. "FAITH is riddled with factions and power-blocs. Maybe even more than most governments. I guess it goes with the territory."

Dr. Landers pulled out the chair and sat down. "As it happens, Minister Travis is with the Ministry of Truth. They are financing this venture, so he would be considered friendly."

"Truth? How does that connect to colonization?"

"The Ministry of Truth is concerned with *spreading* the truth, of course. Their reach is considerable—military, colonization, diplomacy..." He stared into space for a moment, obviously choosing his words. "But there are other ministries arrayed against us. There are factions that think all artificial intelligences, AMI and replicant alike, are abominations. There are those who think we should give up all technology from steam power on up. And they *all* think they have direct divine approval. Needless to say, debates are low on logic and high on rhetoric. Except when they're even higher on assassinations and sabotage."

Since I hadn't actually asked for all of this detail, his outburst came as a surprise. I had a feeling this was a sore spot with him.

"Why do people put up with it? This sounds like a version of hell."

The doctor sighed. "I am granted a lot of latitude when working with replicants, but if I were to repeat some of my statements outside of this building, I would be up for immediate re-education. That consists essentially of operant conditioning, reinforced by direct brain and nerve stimulation of the thalamus, amygdala, and vagus nerve. When the Ministry of Proper Thought is done with you, you will go into spasms from simply *thinking* an unacceptable thought."

Dr. Landers stood up. "Sorry to be so negative, Bob. Ministry visits are traumatic at the best of times, and in this case, we've got a lot riding on you. And the other replicants."

Huh. 'A lot riding on us' doesn't go with 'driving a garbage truck'. I wonder when he'll spill the beans.

He picked up his tablet. "I've set up a simulation exercise for you today. We will cut off your real I/O and establish a number of virtual reality interfaces. I'll also add access to one of those libraries I mentioned. You can exit the simulation any time it becomes too much for you, just by querying your GUPPI."

The doctor poked at his tablet...

* * *

I found myself floating in nothingness. I immediately queried my GUPPI for available interfaces. GUPPI returned with a list of video/audio feeds, a reactor control interface, a traffic control interface, and an environmental control interface. I also found a library interface. I queried the meaning of GUPPI.

[General Unit Primary Peripheral Interface]

Lame.

The mission summary indicated that I was in control of a space station. *That* was interesting. I wondered if I was training for something space-based. I had a look around, using whatever feeds I had available. A quick check of the library indicated that the simulation was an accurate representation of real-life locations. The fact that FAITH even allowed actual space stations earned them some brownie points in my book.

The station seemed to service military and transport vessels. I couldn't find any indication of the existence of *tourists.* Space tours and space hotels would have meant that interplanetary travel was a safe and routine experience, ripe for commercial ventures.

The library did reference a number of military and scientific stations, and even a colony or two on the moon and Mars. Well, better than nothing, but not hugely impressive for a hundred years of elapsed time.

I queried my location and duties. The scenario consisted of a space station in geosynchronous orbit, with me in charge of the power, traffic control, and environment. As an engineer, this was right up my alley.

I also had an Escape button, in case I needed to abort the scenario. It took me very little time to establish the requirements for my control duties. I determined boundary parameters for each and instructed GUPPI to interrupt me if anything fell outside of specs. I expected there would be lots of emergencies.

I then dove into the library in earnest.

6. Bob – July 19, 2133

"Dammit!"

Dr. Landers leaned back with a surprised expression. "Problem, Bob?"

"Sorry, doc. I was reading up on current electrical engineering standards. You yanked me in mid-paragraph."

Dr. Landers looked down at his tablet and cleared his throat. "Ah, yes. Bob, you've been in that simulation for two days subjective time. During that period, nothing went outside of specs, despite everything we threw at you. That's very impressive. The logs from your GUPPI indicate that you've set up some interesting monitoring interfaces and scripts. Our software people are jumping around in excitement. Several of them have asked to keep a copy of you."

"Is that possible?"

"Technically, of course it is. We back you up every night. Just a matter of doing a restore, assuming we had a matrix of our own big enough to hold you." The doctor blew out a breath and shrugged. "Unfortunately, FAITH owns you, as they are financing this project. So we don't have a lot of leeway."

"On that subject, when are you going to tell me what I'm being groomed for?"

Dr. Landers cocked his head. "What *one of you* is being groomed for. There's still one other candidate."

"Wait, we lost two more? When?"

"One was due to a psychotic break a few days ago, and the other was determined by Minister Travis to be unsuitable."

"Oh. What happened to him?"

"Purged. No reason to save it, once the Ministry said *no*."

Wow. Even Dr. Landers is pretty matter-of-fact about this. They just killed *someone.* I couldn't afford to let my feelings show, though. At least some of the evaluations were going to be subjective, and I didn't want to alienate anyone.

"So, the final goal of this whole exercise..."

"Soon, Bob. Right now, I'd like to talk to you about your previous life. You handled two days subjective in a simulation with no human contact at all and were irritated when I pulled you out. Silly question, perhaps, but would you consider yourself a loner?"

I chuckled. "Let me tell you a little story. There was a movie out a number of years ago called *Castaway*." **[133 years ago]**. *Chrissake, GUPPI. Shut it.* "Heard of it?"

Dr. Landers shook his head. "It is part of my job to study and understand your era, but I can't watch every single movie ever produced."

"And so many stinkers, too. Really, if you're up on *Star Wars* and *Star Trek*, you're golden. Anyway, back to *Castaway*... Cliff Notes version, a guy gets shipwrecked on a desert island for four years. I watched the video with a girlfriend. Afterward, she described it as a nightmare. I was surprised, because I'd been thinking of it as a fantasy. Four years of no interruptions. Of course, it would have been more enjoyable with something to read." I waved my waldo in what I hoped was a human gesture. "Point is, that's when I really realized that I don't think like most people. I'm fine with solitude. In fact, I get antsy when I'm around people for too long a period without respite."

The doctor took a deep breath, put his tablet down, and leaned back in his chair. He looked pensive for a few moments, then leaned forward on his elbows. "Okay, Bob. That's about what I thought, but it's nice to have confirmation. So, here's the bottom line. Do you know what a Von Neumann probe is?"

"Yes, of course. It's an automated interstellar probe that builds copies of itself as it visits systems." There was a moment of silence as my brain caught up with the conversation. *Oh...* "Wait, are you saying—?"

"That is correct. We are preparing one of you to be the controlling intelligence for a Von Neumann probe."

* * *

I watched through several video feeds as the small roamers reassembled a 3D printer that I'd been required to diagnose and repair. Roamers, it turned out, came in various sizes, from a huge monster spider eight feet across, through the medium-sized units that I had access to, right down to something the side of a gnat. Below that size, nanites were available, but they were single-purpose devices with very limited flexibility.

At the moment, I was working on coordinated activities using several different sizes of roamers. The 3D printer was only one of many challenges I'd been given.

The roamers required minimal supervision once the tasks and dependencies had been laid out. The trick was to figure out the proper level of detail in the instructions—to avoid errors from giving too much leeway without micromanaging them to a standstill.

Without my kibitzing they could do any job up to ten times as fast, so I tried to lay out the plan and then stay out of the way. Once I figured out how to define conditions under which the roamers would interrupt me, even active supervision became optional.

While they worked, my mind wandered. Once Dr. Landers had spilled the beans, he had made some of the project documents available to me. I hadn't been this impatient since the day I signed the papers for the sale to Terasoft. Every second had dragged on that day, and every millisecond dragged now. I wanted today's training to be *over* so I could concentrate on studying and reading. The doctor's little robot was going to be enthusiastically cooperative from now on. *Oh my God, this is like every nerd's dream job. I could be going to the stars!*

7. Bob – July 25, 2133

"Things are going to hell." Dr. Landers looked uncharacteristically angry. "The FAITH factions that want our project shut down went ballistic when we announced that we had some viable candidates for Project HEAVEN. They've teamed up—"

"Wait, Project Heaven? Project *Heaven?* I'm afraid to ask."

"Habitable Earths Abiogenic Vessel Exploration Network. Please remember that I don't think these things up."

"That's really not bad, in a horrid kind of way. I guess it will in fact be an abiogenic vessel. But *network?* How many will be going out?"

Dr. Landers stared into space, looking slightly embarrassed. "Originally it was eight. Then four, then one, as project funding was rebudgeted, or simply redirected elsewhere. As I was saying, there are several factions that don't want this to happen for various reasons: some don't like replicants, some don't like the idea of spreading off Earth, some consider the idea of a vessel that can build more of itself to be blasphemous. And so on." The doctor sighed and sat silently for a moment, a frown on his face.

"We are also in competition with other countries such as the United States of Eurasia to locate and claim new Earths. Many in FAITH see this as an unnecessary drain on our resources. All these groups have one common goal, though—scuttling the project."

Dr. Landers shook himself and consulted his tablet. "I've given you complete project and library access, as discussed. Getting you

DENNIS E. TAYLOR

ready is a critical path task, so anything you can do to help move this along will be, ah, helpful."

He got up and began to pace. "There's one other thing, Bob. There are many possible reasons for special-interest groups to get the project pared down to one vessel, but we believe the main reason we really have to worry about is that one vessel provides a convenient single point of failure."

"Sabotage?"

"Something like that. We have nothing concrete. I just thought you should know."

Without further discussion, the doctor picked up his tablet and left.

* * *

I'd been thinking about the previous discussion, and I had some questions for the doctor. My opportunity came at the end of a lesson on controlling 3D printers.

"Doctor, I want to talk about politics."

Dr. Landers laughed. "Okay, Bob. What's on the agenda?"

"You mentioned the United States of Eurasia earlier. I've been reading about the current geopolitical situation, and it's a lot different from my day. The name of the USE is a little grandiose. They don't really cover anywhere near all of Eurasia."

"Yes, but the old USA didn't cover all of America, either. Not even all of *North* America."

I waved my waldo in a dismissive gesture. "Okay, fine. From what the library says, it looks like there's been a lot of consolidation. FAITH controls all of North America except for Washington state, British Columbia and Alaska. The USE covers all of Europe and most of western Russia. China absorbed most of eastern Russia and a lot of the former Asian satellite countries. And the Middle East..." I left the sentence hanging.

"Not surprisingly, the development of cheap nuclear fusion had a huge impact on the Middle East." The doctor poked idly at his tablet as he talked. "The rich families such as the Saudi royalty had long since diversified their investments, so they didn't become paupers, but the tradition of oil exports paying for government programs ended rather abruptly. It essentially triggered what some alarmists insisted on calling *World War III*. It was really little more than a series of brush wars for most of the planet. In the Middle East though, it was a blood-bath, and Geneva Convention limitations were mostly ignored. Chemical weapons, dusting with radioactive isotopes, pocket nukes... Most of the Middle East is still uninhabitable, and what's left is certainly not a significant world player."

"What surprises me," I replied, "is how much consolidation happened. FAITH, the USE, China, The Australian Federation, the Republic of Africa—a laughable irony of a name if I've ever seen one—and the Brazilian Empire. They all account for maybe 80% of the planet. The remaining small countries are either not worth fighting over, like the Middle East, or they're buffer states that no one is willing to make a move on, like Cascadia."

"Did you have a specific question, Bob?"

"Now that you mention it, yes." I wanted to smile. I was constantly irritated with my minimal external presence. "How many of these nations are also running probe projects?"

"Ah." The question seemed to hit home. Dr. Landers looked very uncomfortable and took a moment before he answered. "We know of projects by the USE, China, The Brazilian Empire, and ourselves. We suspect that Australia also has one, but if so they've hidden it well."

"So, pretty much everyone."

The doctor shrugged. "As soon as the breakthrough in subspace theory that allowed the SURGE drive and SUDDAR was formulated, the concepts of not only Von Neumann probes but also interstellar colonization became possible. The USE started their interstellar probe project two years ago to much fanfare and national chest-thumping, and everyone else had to follow suit. Can't let the other guy colonize the universe unchallenged, no?"

"Two years? So this is really new stuff?"

"Indeed. Other than prototypes, there are as yet very few SURGE-equipped vessels in active service."

I was silent for a few moments, thinking about that. So this project was very much a proof-of-concept. They didn't even know for sure if the probe would work over interstellar distances. Outstanding.

"But why the big push? This is like the moon race on steroids."

"Officially, it's about spreading humanity to other worlds, of course, and the national prestige that goes along with it. But tensions are high between nations, and have been for some decades. This whole subject is seen as a zero-sum game, and to a large extent, it is. Each world that we claim is a base of operations denied to everyone else. It's also a base of operations outside the range of surveillance or attack. Unofficially, there's a large military component to the push."

Isn't there always? Some things never change. "Why bother, though? There are billions of stars out there."

"But only a very few within ten light-years that will have habitable planets. Those will be the most strategically valuable, regardless of other factors."

"It occurs to me then, doctor, that internal FAITH factions aren't the only thing I have to worry about."

"I'm afraid that is the case, Bob." Dr. Landers shrugged. "And it's also part of the reason why trimming the Heaven project down to one ship wasn't met with more resistance by our company. While it benefits the anti-expansionist groups by leaving them just one target, it also benefits us by allowing us to focus our efforts and accelerate our timetable."

"Tell me about the other projects."

"You mean, what we *know* about the other projects," Dr. Landers replied with a smirk. "They are unsurprisingly as reticent with details as we are."

The doctor fiddled with his tablet. By this time, I knew that was simply a delaying tactic to give him time to gather his thoughts.

"Our intelligence says that China is pushing their project at a breakneck pace, having sacrificed everything for speed. And they will be using an AMI, which is problematic at best. We believe that they are the most likely to fail outright."

The doctor was silent for a few seconds, flicking at his tablet with a finger. "The Brazilian Empire concerns us the most, and not just because of their belligerent and adversarial stance in world politics. We believe they may be arming their probes with the intention of eliminating the competition. They are also the most likely to attempt sabotage. But they are also unlikely to be able to pull off the long-term plan, in our opinion. They are not primarily depending on probes being able to build copies, although the probes will have the capability. Instead, the Empire will simply launch multiple probes, as fast as they can build them in-system.

We think that if they find a suitable system, they will set up a military presence and reproduce."

Dr. Landers sighed. "The USE is the most likely long-term competitor, although they at least are likely to limit themselves to non-violent tactics. They have the will, the budget, the technological sophistication, and the experience with replicants. They are also considerably ahead of us at the moment on the subject of actual colonization. If someone were to discover a useful planet tomorrow, the USE colonists would be there first by a considerable margin."

"Wow. Do we have *anything?*"

"We have you and the other replicant, Bob. Don't discount that. The two of you have shown remarkable resilience. Your quickness at adapting to the reality of your position, combined with your intelligence and education, are not small things. The common wisdom, with replicants, has been to find a phlegmatic, unimaginative individual who would be satisfied with the routine. You and the other candidates forced us to change our tactics. We think that going in this unexpected direction will make a big difference in the long run."

"Well, all right then. Time to talk about a raise..."

Dr. Landers rolled his eyes. "We have to get you a face, so I can tell when you're kidding."

8. Bob – August 4, 2133

For today's entertainment, the doctor had directed me to diagnose and repair a complex piece of electronics, similar to items that I would have to deal with aboard ship. Dr. Landers watched me as usual from the window. He liked to engage me in conversation during these exercises. I suspected that he was testing my concentration and ability to multitask. I didn't mind, since the conversations were always interesting and informative.

Then a massive jolt shook the building and knocked Dr. Landers off his feet. It was followed immediately by a solid pressure-wave of sound, more felt than heard.

As Dr. Landers got to his feet, the sounds of gunfire echoed down the hall. He turned to me, yelled, "Stay there!" and ran off.

Stay there? Despite the gravity of the situation, my sense of the ridiculous kicked in. The good doctor was obviously rattled. As he had pointed out to me, I wasn't actually in this room, just attached to—

Hello...

In the middle of my internal comedy routine, I realized that the window had been popped partly out of its frame. It didn't look as though it would take much persuasion to finish the job. And surely they couldn't blame me for wanting to take a more active role in defense of the project.

I directed every roamer in the room to grab the window and pull. The roamers weren't particularly strong, but 32 of the little buggers commanded a lot of leverage. Within moments, the window clattered down and took a divot out of the floor.

The window didn't break. That's some very strong stuff. They ARE scared of me.

I chose one of the roamers at random and took over control. Now I could see through its video camera. I directed the other roamers to follow, and we took off down the hall in the direction of the gunfire. Roamers ran along the floors, walls, and ceiling. I was impressed. These people might suck at acronyms, but their tech was pretty good.

The building complex was an interesting design. It consisted of a string of large, open atriums or lobbies, each surrounded by two floors of offices or labs. Skylights in the atriums provided plenty of illumination, and short hallways connected each central open area. My roamer room was one atrium over from the location of the attack. Maybe the invaders had miscalculated.

It took only seconds to get to the action. A group of attackers dressed in black were slowly moving through the offices, shooting as they went. Security guards returned fire, but significantly outgunned, they were being forced back.

This operation was being run either by a FAITH faction that didn't approve of me or by one of the competing nations. Either way, they wanted me dead. It seemed to me that the Golden Rule applied. Time to reciprocate.

Appraising the situation had taken only milliseconds–I was really starting to love being a computer–so the roamers hadn't broken stride. The horde stampeded into the area and swarmed the attackers, concentrating on faces and groins.

The roamers were surprisingly tough. No matter how many times an attacker ripped a roamer off his face and tossed it against a wall, the roamer would simply right itself and come back for more. The roamers were equipped with pliers, cutters, and screwdrivers, not technically weapons but still hard to ignore. And I had more than a month's worth of frustration and angst driving me. Endocrine controls or no, I was thoroughly enjoying the opportunity to serve up some beatings.

The attackers finally started to develop a strategy. They managed to get one of their number roamer-free. As attackers tossed roamers against the wall, this guy blasted them with a burst of automatic fire. I did a quick millisecond calculation and determined that I'd run out of roamers before they ran out of ammo. And they now had two roamer-free shooters.

But the distraction allowed the security guards to regroup. They set up a crossfire and shot a few of the invaders, then invited the rest to surrender. Now, the attackers had to deal with gunfire as well as roamers attached to their faces. It was the last straw. The weapons were set down and the hands went up.

Once the security guards had restrained all the remaining invaders, we found ourselves in an awkward tableau. The lead security guard looked at the prisoners, looked at the roamers, opened his mouth to say something, then closed it. I waved a leg on "my" roamer to get his attention.

"You're, uh... This is bad. Where's Landers?" He glanced at his associates, eyes wide.

Dr. Landers picked that moment to come running into the atrium. He still had his tablet with him, and he looked as alarmed as the security guards. Since the raid was now effectively over, there had to be something more going on. I realized that they were more concerned about me than about the invaders.

"Bob, I wonder if I could persuade you to gather your flock and return to the training room...?"

He had the power to deactivate me, so it wasn't ever really a question of whether I'd cooperate. In any case, I wasn't the rampaging Frankenstein they seemed to be concerned about.

With a roamerish salute, me and my horde headed down the hall.

* * *

"Okay, doc, time to spill the beans. What's with the security glass and the quaking in your boots when I got loose?"

Dr. Landers was courteous enough to not try to pretend he didn't understand what I was talking about. He sighed and leaned back in his chair.

"We—by which I mean the people working on the project, including myself—are not scared of you, Bob. We're scared of the tactical nuke buried in the basement."

If I'd still had eyebrows, they would have shot right off my head. "Habba-whaaa?"

"It is just possible, Bob, that you face a greater danger from our own government than you do from our foreign competitors. At least from certain factions." He shifted a little to face me and waved a hand. "I mentioned before that the upper echelons of FAITH are not unanimous in supporting this venture. I very probably understated the situation."

I considered that statement for a millisecond or so. *Nuke in the basement... yikes.*

"So this is like the Andromeda Strain?"

Dr. Landers looked confused, so I waved a waldo in dismissal. "Never mind. Another old movie. The point is that the nuke is a last line of defense against me getting out and scaring all the civilians and farm animals?"

"That's right Bob. And I'm definitely going to have to start watching some more old movies."

"So who has the button?"

"I don't know. We've deliberately not been told how we're being monitored, who makes the decision, or how it's carried out. We just know that if someone, somewhere, decides they don't like something, we could all become a radioactive cloud. No warning, no discussion."

"And you agreed to this? How much are they paying you?"

Dr. Landers laughed. "The rewards for successful completion of this project are considerable. Those who support the venture are throwing a *lot* of money at it. I, personally, will be able to retire with my bonus." He grimaced and gave me a one-sided shrug. "And of course, under FAITH, agreement is not optional."

I smiled—in my mind, anyway. "Gotcha. Okay, I'll try to stay put in the future."

He swept his hands to take in the room. "And, since we're still here talking, I'd guess the immediate danger is over. Someone was either away from their monitoring station or decided you weren't that big of a danger. Or something."

Dr. Landers stood up and looked around the training room. The roamers—the remaining roamers, anyway—were properly arrayed on their racks. Maintenance people had levered the security window back into its frame and were bolting it back in place.

"I guess we're back to operational. There were three fatalities, and several injured. Really, it could have been a lot worse."

I bobbed my cameras by way of response.

In a video window, I watched the scene from across the hall.

* * *

The roamer moved carefully through the air ducts. The little robots were capable of a very light touch, but a hundred years of progress hadn't come up with a replacement for galvanized tin as air-duct material. I didn't want to announce the roamer's presence to the whole complex.

The guerilla raiding party had shot up my roamers so thoroughly that any kind of inventory was impossible. As near as I could tell, no one realized that one unaccounted-for roamer was wandering the building.

So far I had identified numerous offices, the cafeteria, workshops, and storage. 3D mapping software had built up the layout of the office building. Interestingly, I hadn't found any trace of a nuke in the basement, or any area that might have been walled off to contain one. Perhaps it was a bluff.

Meanwhile I'd narrowed down the building layout to two possible locations for the computer room.

As I moved the roamer through the ducts, I carefully checked for surveillance equipment, trip-switches, infra-red beams, or any other traps. The roamers were a very impressive bag of tricks and capabilities. I wondered if the FAITH techs really understood everything the roamers were capable of, when the various functions were combined.

Finally, the roamer arrived at one of the two areas that were still blanks in my map. And sure enough, it was on a separate air system. Definitely a good sign. It took me twenty minutes to exit the general duct-work and break into the isolated system. I moved carefully through the air conduit until I came to the room exhaust panel.

It was a standard computer room, mostly. Cables, blinking lights, air conditioning, rack-mounted computers. I guess rack-mounting was still the most efficient way to organize computers, even with a hundred years to improve things.

But in the center of the room sat something very new to me. Five cubes, each one just under a half-meter on a side, sat in a line on a low platform. Two of the cubes glowed an eerie blue, with multi-colored indicator lights blinking at their bases. The other three were dark.

I engaged magnification and pulled in a close-up of the panels at the base of the cubes.

Kenneth Martins
Jiro Tanaka
Neves Reijnder
Robert Johansson
Joana Almeida

This was it. This was us. The candidates. The glowing cubes were Kenneth's and mine. The other three candidates were dark. I could see their power switches in the *off* position. Another thing that hadn't really changed much in a hundred years, I guess. But really, how many different ways were there to design a rocker switch?

I stared at the tableau for what seemed like forever. I could turn Kenneth off, right now. But would it do any good? Could I sabotage him? Should I? Would they figure it out?

I felt shame as I realized what I was contemplating. I wasn't going to be that guy. Not even in theory. I'd let myself be switched off before I'd save myself by climbing on someone else's back.

With a heavy heart, I turned around and left.

9. Bob – August 6, 2133

I was in the roamer room, working on an exercise, when I realized that Dr. Landers wasn't alone. He always stood at the window, watching me and talking, and it took me a few moments to realize that the steady stream of commentary had stopped.

I directed one of the roamers to give me a video feed. Dr. Landers was talking to someone that I would have sworn was Minister Travis's brother. Seriously, did they have that look listed in the job requirements? MUST LOOK LIKE SCARY GUY FROM POLTERGEIST 2. Jeez.

Dr. Landers had turned off the intercom system, but that represented about three milliseconds worth of inconvenience. Amateur.

I directed a roamer to move to the wall immediately below the window. By pressing its body against the wall, it was able to pick up transmitted vibrations. I had to crank the gain way up, but I had all the audio filtering tricks that two centuries of electronic media had developed.

"This is the work of the Devil. You are placing your immortal soul in jeopardy by participating in this enterprise."

"The Ministry of Truth advised me otherwise."

"These are poor imitations of God's Creation. They mock humanity with their false display of intelligence and emotion."

"The Ministry of Truth is of the opinion that, while they are without a soul, they are merely based on God's creation and not an attempt to usurp His authority."

The air grew momentarily brittle with that silence you get when someone is glaring. I stole a glance using one of the roamers on the table. Yep. Glaring.

"This unholy activity can have no good end. Especially considering the purpose—"

"—Which is officially sanctioned by the Ministry—"

"—Apostates! Heretics!"

Another quick glance verified that Dr. Landers was trying very hard not to roll his eyes. I took a moment to wish I had the option. This guy was seriously whack-a-doodle.

The barrage continued for several minutes. The minister alternately berated and threatened Dr. Landers, who remained carefully non-confrontational and showed a lot more patience than I could ever have. If Minister Loudmouth had been on this side of the window, I think I'd have tried to disassemble him.

I managed to remain objective and treat the running stream of vitriol as information rather than a condemnation of my very existence. It would seem that I was either a product of witchcraft or a result of hubris not seen since the days of Babel.

Dr. Landers took it for a few moments longer, then snapped. Sort of.

"Minister Jacoby, I understand your opinions and concerns. By which I mean only that I comprehend what you are saying. However, the Ministry of Truth is not only supporting but actively funding this endeavor. It seems to me, since we're talking about blasphemous acts, that by opposing this activity, you are opposing the Ministry. And as they point out—in fact, as you yourself have pointed out twice—FAITH is the direct, revealed Word of God. Doesn't that make your opposition an instance of blasphemy?"

There was a moment of indignant silence as Minister Loudmouth, looking like a fish desperately struggling to breathe, tried to de-hoist himself from his own petard.

"You have chosen the wrong friends, doctor. You will learn that soon enough."

And with that, he turned and flounced out, stage right. Yes, flounced. Honestly.

Dr. Landers leaned on the wall for a few moments with his eyes closed, breathing deeply. Then he turned to the window and played with his tablet for a moment.

"All done, Bob?"

I wasn't going to play that game. "Who the freaking hell was that? And don't tell me 'Minister Jacoby.'"

The doctor rubbed his forehead. "Just an example of some of the extreme viewpoints we have to navigate in this great nation. Bob, if he had any real power, he *non't*, er, wouldn't have been trying to browbeat me into line. I wouldn't give his threats any extra credence."

Which is not the same as saying you wouldn't give his threats any credence at all.

"And I will note for the future," the doctor said with a smile, "that turning off the intercom doesn't appear to deter you at all. Shall we continue?"

He pointed at the semi-assembled mess on the lab table, and I got back to work.

10. Bob – August 10, 2133

I snapped back to consciousness. As usual, I did a systems check.

Wait, August 10ᵗʰ?

"Hey, doc, I seem to be missing a few days. Have you had me on ice for a week?"

Dr. Landers looked everywhere except at me. "Well, yes and no. Someone managed to sneak a small explosive into the computer room and take out the replicant matrices. We had to ship in a spare unit and restore you from backups. It took a few days."

I was silent for a few moments. That meant that I wasn't the Bob who woke up on June 24ᵗʰ. On the other hand, even back then I wasn't the same Bob who got killed by a car. Did I have a soul? Did it matter if I was restored from a backup?

I realized that in the more than a month that I'd been back as a computer program, I'd somehow managed to avoid coming to any conclusions about my exact status. 'Rolling with it' had become a code phrase for avoiding the issue. But I knew that I had a tendency to avoid dealing with painful issues. Jenny had certainly proven that.

And being switched off when not in training contributed as well. I wondered if Dr. Landers had a plan, or if he was just going to wait until I was in space and hope for the best.

I had three issues that bothered me. Was I conscious? Could I actually consider myself to be alive? And was I still Bob? Philosophers had been going on and on about this type of thing for centuries, but now, for me, it was personal. A human, regardless of their opinion on the subject, could depend on being a human. The minister's offhand reference to me as 'it' and 'replicant' had stung at a level I was just now starting to appreciate.

I thought back to all the arguments about Turing Tests and thinking machines. Was I nothing more than a Chinese Room? Could my entire behavior be explained as a set of scripted responses to given inputs? That was probably the easiest uncertainty to answer. The classic Chinese Room, which just used scripts to react to input, had no internal dialog. Even if you made its behavior stochastic to introduce some variation in behavior, it was still only active when responding to input. When not processing a response, it just sat there, idle. By worrying about this, right now, I fell into a different category.

For that matter, Descartes had his famous *cogito ergo sum*; but Thomas had added to it with his "Since I doubt, I think; since I think, I exist." Well, I was certainly full of doubt. Doubt implied self-awareness, and a concern for one's future. So I was a conscious entity, barring evidence to the contrary. One down.

Was I alive? Hmm, since no one had yet managed to define life rigorously, that was going to be a fun one. As the speaker at that long-ago panel in Vegas had pointed out, fire has most of the qualities of life but is not alive. According to Dr. Landers, I would be able to reproduce via printer-based autofactories. I certainly responded to stimuli, and acted with self-interest. The claim that life would have to be carbon-based was chauvinistic and narrow-minded, so yeah, I could consider myself alive.

Now, the big one. Who was I? Was I Bob? Or was Bob dead? In engineering terms, what was the metric used to ascribe Bob-hood? Bob was more than a hunk of meat. Bob was a person, and a person was a history, a set of desires, thoughts, goals, and opinions. Bob was the accumulation of all that Bob had been for thirty-one years. The meat was dead, but the things that made Bob different from a chipmunk were alive. In me. I am Bob. Or at least, I am the important parts that made Bob.

With this last thought, a huge weight lifted off of me. I imagined it would feel the same for someone right after the jury said, "not guilty."

I turned my attention back to the doctor, who was repeating my name in an increasingly panicked tone. I realized that I had been silent for several seconds.

"Hey, doc. I'm here."

"Thank God." Dr. Landers collapsed into a chair. "You went silent, and I thought you might have gone psychotic."

They'd put a lot of effort into me by this point—into all of us, really—so I understood his reaction. I wanted to smile at him, but of course, no joy. "S'okay, doc. I think that ship just sailed, and I'm still here."

Then realization hit me as I processed what he'd said. "Um, doc, how many spare matrices do you have?"

"Just the one, Bob. A decision had to be made. I guess congratulations are in order."

"So Kenneth is gone?"

Dr. Landers nodded, then did a double-take. He looked at me, eyes narrowing. *Oh, shit. Damage control, Bob.*

I quickly threw in the first question I could think of. "So why did they decide to attack now? Has something changed?"

"Mm, information about your progress has been circulated. Best guess is that internal FAITH factions have leaked it in order to goad competing nations into some form of reaction. That's the word from our security people, anyway." The doctor was still frowning, but seemed uncertain. I had to keep this going.

"Damn. Are we close to launch?"

The doctor's expression changed to a frown of concentration. I just needed to keep him distracted long enough for my little faux pas to be forgotten. He consulted his tablet, idly swiping through some pages of information.

"Current project timeline has it about a month away. It can be moved up though. We've got a fair bit of slack in the schedule right now, thanks to your swift progress."

Again, I tried to smile. And as usual, nothing happened, so I waved a waldo instead. "Still waiting for that raise..."

Dr. Landers laughed. "We're pushing it through HR. Is that the right term?" He held the beat, head cocked to the side, then changed the subject. "Training session for today. I've got the details here."

I heaved a mental sigh of relief. The immediate danger was over, and if the comment occurred to Dr. Landers later, hopefully he'd be uncertain if he had heard me correctly.

Dr. Landers raised a finger to poke at his tablet, hesitated for a moment, then put his hand down. He was silent for a few moments more, then sighed and looked up at me. "Bob, I'm going to take a chance, I think. I'm going to stop deactivating you during off-times, and I'm going to give you access to some more libraries. You'll undergo a half-hour of semi-sleep every night while you are backed up, but other than that you'll be online 24/7. If you do go insane, we'll restore you from a previous backup. That sounds harsh, I know, and I apologize. But I don't think we can afford the luxury of a leisurely project plan any more. We're going to have to push forward as quickly as possible."

I nodded in response. Well, I bobbed my cameras, I guess. It was a kind of good news/bad news thing. I'd finally have some time for some quiet reflection, but it could drive me nuts. Woo hah...

11. Bob - August 15, 2133

"So what *did* happen to Old Handeltown?"

The pretty blonde at the window looked surprised for a moment, then laughed. Dr. Doucette was covering for Landers today. She wasn't nearly as chatty as he was, though. I'd been trying to get her talking, so far with minimal success.

Dr. Doucette was a looker. I was happy to discover that I hadn't lost my appreciation for beauty with the, uh, change in my lifestyle. Although my appreciation wasn't as *urgent* now, so to speak.

She spoke with the standard 22nd century accent, so I was using my translation routine. I'd integrated it to the point where I didn't even notice the different speech patterns. I knew that Dr. Landers was specially trained to deal with replicants, and had studied my era. Which included getting his patois under control. Dr. Doucette either had skipped that class, or wasn't normally supposed to be talking to me.

It wasn't an issue as far as I was concerned, and if Dr. Landers was okay with her, then I didn't see a problem. Hopefully, the State wouldn't have a cow.

Anyway, today I was coordinating a team of roamers to assemble ship components, assembly-line style. It was routine work. By now, I had written scripts for so many roamer activities that I rarely had to do more than show up. But, the good folks at Applied Synergetics had a checklist to run through, so I had to humor them.

Dr. Doucette looked down at her tablet—yeah, everyone came with tablets—then, satisfied that the status was still quo, answered my question. "Original Handeltown was Handel's birthplace—Salem, Oregon. When he died, the city changed the name and set up a large memorial in his honor. Someone objected and decided to take it out with a pocket nuke."

"Nuke? On American soil?"

She wagged a finger at me. "Uh uh. Hasn't been American soil for a hundred years now. But to answer your question, it was and still is the only nuclear weapon ever deployed in North America."

"So they moved Handeltown to Portland?"

She nodded.

"A lot of people died?"

She shook her head. "Not like you'd think. We learned a lot about radiation treatments from the Middle-East feud. Lots of opportunity to try out different medical procedures. For all the death and horror that the Middle East war generated, it advanced medical knowledge greatly."

"Like reviving replicants?"

"Like reviving replicants."

I was silent for a few moments as I concentrated on guiding the roamers through a particularly tricky bit of assembly. As soon as they were able to continue on their own, I turned back to Dr. Doucette. "So what's it like, living in a theocracy? Do you have daily prayers?"

Dr. Doucette held up one finger in a universal waitaminnit gesture. She poked at her tablet a few times, then looked up at me. "Sorry, just checking the location of the security patrols. Some of them might be Piety Monitors."

I was blank for a moment, then I laughed. "So you're monitoring the monitors. What are you doing, tracking their security card locations?"

Dr. Doucette smiled in return. "The government doesn't really care what we do as long as we give the appearance of piety. But jabber-jiving them will get you a session with the Ministry of Proper Thought that you'll never forget."

"Mmm, yeah. Dr. Landers mentioned something about that. So while we've got some privacy, let me ask you this—how do you know I'll do what you want instead of just heading off in some random direction, once you release me into the wild? Understand, I love this whole idea, and I can't see myself *not* cooperating, but you couldn't know that when you revived me."

The doctor gazed down at her tablet for a few seconds, a thoughtful look on her face. "There are safeguards, Bob. Your software will ensure mission objectives are met. That's all I'm going to say. But as you pointed out, it's probably not an issue with you."

Safeguards. There's my word of the day not to like.

It was an interesting philosophical issue. How are you supposed to feel if you are forced to do what you would have done anyway? I wondered how it would work. Would I be a marionette on strings, unable to help myself? Or would I think the decisions were mine? I shuddered at the possibility I might find out.

12. Bob – August 17, 2133

I surfaced from **[18 hours 26 minutes]** of library and project reading. I'd had the forethought to set up an interrupt for anyone speaking to me.

I turned my camera to see a very upset Dr. Landers. His voice shaking, he said, "We've just had another attack. Someone tried to blow up some critical components. They missed their target, but four of my staff were killed. We're going to a secondary operations center. How's your reading coming along?"

This last sentence was such a non-sequitur that I had to run the last few seconds through my mind to make sure I hadn't missed anything. "Uh, fine, doc. Why, specifically?"

"We are going to attempt to move up the launch. That means that you may have to receive some of your final training in-flight, as it were."

Oh, holy crap. "Okay, doc, what do you need from me?"

"I've dropped a file into your queue. Read it immediately. Then we will back you up with that knowledge assimilated, shut you down, and physically move you to the ship."

"Physically? Really? You've never heard of *ftp*?"

"That would have worked right up until a couple of weeks ago when they blew you up. Where do you think the spare unit came from?"

"Oh." They had brought the replicant matrix down from the ship? *That* was the spare?

"Replicant hardware is expensive, Bob. You've been working with the actual interfaces that you will use in-flight. They've just been attached to simulators up until now. Please read the document. Let me know when you're done, and we'll get started." He sat down, leaned forward, and clasped his hands together on the desk, looking at me.

* * *

Bob:

All conversations are potentially being monitored. This is the only secure method of communicating this to you.

There's a very strong possibility that there is a self-destruct mechanism on the Heaven-1. Whether timed or externally triggered, we don't know. The project specs called for limits to be placed on your ability to self-examine. My team has disabled those constraints on my orders. This will free you to examine everything: wiring, structure, hardware, software. The keys for your operating system are listed at the bottom of this document.

This will unfortunately also allow you to bypass the imperatives that we installed in your code to ensure compliance with mission objectives. From my experience with you, I'm confident you'll fulfill your duties of your own free will, since they align with your own interests.

We will transport you, once deactivated, into orbit and will install you in the Heaven-1. There will be a long countdown, which you should feel free to ignore if necessary. Good luck, and though it pains me to say it, Godspeed.

Dr. Landers

There were several attachments, including a mission profile summary, and the operating system access keys. I scanned through everything, looking for gaps or other issues, then deleted the originals.
"Done."

Dr. Landers jerked in surprise. I'd probably only been away a few milliseconds. He picked up the tablet and poked at it with a finger.

* * *

I awoke to darkness. I queried GUPPI.

[STATUS REPORT]
[Fusion Reactor Interface: Ready/Nominal]
[Reactionless Drive Interface: Ready/Standby]
[Ramscoop Generator: Ready/Standby]
[Communications & External Sensors: Ready/Standby]
[Internal Systems: Ready/Nominal]
[Fabrication Systems: Inactive/Stowed for Launch]
[ROAMer/Nanite Systems: Inactive/Stowed for Launch]
[Launch Systems: Ready/T minus 04:12:13]

I queried the internal systems, and discovered that they included several libraries of impressive size that I hadn't even known existed. I checked the launch systems and verified that I had a course vector laid out that would take me to Epsilon Eridani. Interesting. FAITH had probably concluded that everyone else would be heading for Alpha Centauri. Without weapons, I would have no chance in a confrontation with multiple opponents.

I verified that I had complete override capability, including the ability to blow the grapples that held me to the space station. I remembered Dr. Landers' comment about ignoring the countdown. Should I just blow and go? Without a specific threat, I would look like I'd gone rogue. Very likely Dr. Landers would take the fallout for that. He'd always been straight with me, and I didn't want to repay that with treachery.

I activated comms, only to be immediately besieged by a half-dozen different external audio channels. There were also several video channels, but their output seemed to be less active. It looked like viewing rooms with rows of empty seats. Presumably that was where the public would sit, come launch time.

There were exterior views of the Heaven-1 and the space station to which it was attached. Two more video feeds showed mission control and the VIP gallery, mostly empty.

I examined the vessel I was in. Or, I guess, the vessel that was me. It was a converted interplanetary freighter. The body had been split halfway along its length and a SURGE drive ring had been installed. The fusion drive had been removed and replaced with extra cooling units for the oversized reactor.

I also noted that the viewports had their shielding in place. Made sense. I wasn't going to be sitting in the pilot's chair, so a window would be a weak point.

It wasn't really a pretty ship. It didn't have the classic lines of an Enterprise, or the smooth aerodynamic shape of a space shuttle. The body followed an elliptical cross-section, with lots of airlocks and cargo doors. The running lights followed the standard nautical red/green format, with the addition of blue as a nod to the three-dimensional nature of space travel.

The addition of the SURGE drive, ramscoop generator, and all the other stuff required by a Von Neumann probe left very little extra space for extras like, oh, *weapons*. Against opponents who probably would have them. Plus anything I might run into out there, as well. It was becoming increasingly obvious that the whole HEAVEN project was a rush job, using existing assets wherever possible, to save time.

And I was beginning to understand what toast felt like.

Well, Dr. Landers had warned me about this. Installed in Heaven-1, about to be shot out to the stars, I still didn't have the whole picture or complete training. I decided I was going to have to dive in. I set up some interrupt conditions with GUPPI and started looking for a mission profile.

I very quickly found some useful information. As part of my bag of tricks on Heaven-1, I had the ability to adjust my personal time sense. I could perceive time anywhere from one minute of personal time for each year on the clock, right up to the highest frame rate that my hardware would support. The docs weren't clear on what that would be, so I turned the setting all the way up, and watched my Real-Time Clock slow to a crawl.

The ship used a fusion reactor for power. Although there was an onboard supply of hydrogen, fuel would be gathered in-flight from the interstellar medium. However, unlike in the old science-fiction novels, the gathered hydrogen wasn't used for propulsion— at least not in the traditional way, as reaction mass. Heaven-1 used a reactionless system, the SURGE drive. I wanted to sigh. These people were so hung up on acronyms. I had yet to read up on the theory, but it seemed to push against the fabric of space in some way. *Must read. Goes on the TO-DO.*

There was a hail from the comms subsystem. I slowed to real-time and accepted a voice-only link to the station command.

"Heaven-1, Statcom, please verify receipt of mission profile."

"Yep. Got it right here." I imagined myself grinning—best I could do—at the stunned silence.

"Er, you're a little light on procedure there, Heaven-1."

"Ya think? Sorry Statcom, but this part of my training was scheduled for next week. We're going to have to wing it, I'm afraid."

"Wing it. Okayyyyy. Heaven-1, per countdown, we have just over four hours ten until launch. There will be several official bafflegabs at the following times..."

The briefing took almost ten minutes. I was able to get through it with my sanity intact by slowing down my internal clock until Statcom sounded like an irate squirrel.

As soon as Statcom signed off, I jacked up my frame rate to maximum, hoping to get in as much study-time as possible.

Some days, though, the universe just has it in for you.

I was interrupted in my reading by another radio message. At my current frame rate, the transmission was still droning through the first word. When I compressed and replayed it, I recognized Dr. Landers' voice. The word was "missiles."

Um. Ways in which a sentence beginning with the word "missiles" could be a good thing... Nope. I got nuthin'.

External sensors showed two objects approaching at high speed along my scheduled launch vector, presumably the better to overtake me if I launched early. It was a reasonable and predictable tactic, but I had no intention of being predictable.

I spent a full five milliseconds mulling over my options. In short order, I had a rough plan.

Fortunately, the ship had long since been fully prepped, and could leave any time. I blew the grapples and brought all flight systems to full function. While I waited for physical reality to catch up with my awareness, I sent a query to my libraries about the approaching missiles. The libraries gave three possible models, with generally similar flight characteristics. I chose the most pessimistic and calculated a takeoff vector as close to 180° to the missiles' vector as I could safely manage.

As soon as sensors indicated that I was free, I gave a burst of the SURGE drive, just enough to clear the station. I rotated the ship and cranked up the reactor to maximum. *That's going to be hard on fuel reserves, but I guess being blown to smithereens would be harder.* When reactor output rose to the required level, I engaged SURGE at maximum acceleration.

The ship shot away from the station in the opposite direction from the published launch trajectory. The first missile went right past me, its trajectory unaltered. I realized with a jolt that it had locked onto the space station. The second missile was altering its trajectory to follow me. I hoped that the published specs for the reactor and SURGE drive were accurate. If my acceleration fell short of expectations, I wouldn't be able to avoid interception. And that would be the end of Heaven-1. And of me.

While I waited for velocity to build up, I checked the progress of the voice transmission. It now sat at "Missiles detected heading your way. Get away..." I checked acceleration using SUDDAR to monitor the increasing distance from the station. Calculations indicated a steady 2.5 g acceleration. The SURGE drive seemed to work on the entire ship, so there was no way to measure it internally.

The space station began firing on the approaching missile. The weapon appeared to be some kind of Gatling gun. I hoped they knew what they were doing. If those bullets ended up in a periodic orbit, they'd be coming back, sooner or later.

The flash of an explosion in the distance saturated one of my cameras. It couldn't be either of the missiles, which were still accounted for. I did a quick calculation and realized that the explosion came from where the missiles had originated. Someone had blown up the shooter.

A second flash indicated the destruction of the missile that was targeting the space station.

This was all fine and interesting, but I still had a missile on my tail. Given enough time, I could outrun it. I did another quick millisecond calculation and realized that I could *almost* outrun it. Sadly, *almost* wasn't good enough.

Normally, you'd use chaff against a missile, but I doubted I had anything like that on board. I had six mining drones, which were equipped with small SURGE drives of their own. Well, okay, maybe I could give the missile something else to blow up.

I activated and ejected two of the drones, with orders to ram the missile. As they flew toward my pursuer, I positioned them in a fore/aft configuration. Hopefully the lead drone would take the missile out; but if it missed, the second one would have better targeting information. I didn't know if I'd have time to launch more drones if the first two failed.

A bright flash of light behind the ship saturated the rear

camera. What the hell? That couldn't be the missile, which was approaching from a different vector.

I waited a few seconds for the cameras to recover, then checked the rear view. The station was an expanding cloud of rapidly cooling debris. Dr. Landers' voice transmission was still coming, so at least he hadn't been on the station. The message now included "...quickly as you can. And disable..."

How could the station have blown up? All the missiles were accounted for. Speaking of which, I checked my rear view, where the drones were just coming up on the missile. The missile dodged the first drone, which told me it came with some intelligence. But the act of dodging forced the missile to commit. The second drone struck it at an angle, and the explosion destroyed both devices.

A quick systems check indicated that there had been no damage to Heaven-1 from all the excitement. I made sure everything was still properly stowed, then listened to the rest of Dr. Lander's message.

"...your radio receiver. There's a remote detonation device somewhere."

Well, that's double-plus ungood. I disabled the radio immediately, and for good measure I retracted the antenna dish. I did a quick long-range SUDDAR scan to look for any other surprises.

The area, which had been cleared for my expected launch, was a beehive of activity. I detected at least half a dozen ships, which my library identified as military. I also detected close to a dozen small signatures, moving at high speed, that were very likely more missiles. Fortunately, they seemed more interested in each other than in me.

So, someone shot a couple of missiles at me, someone else shot at them, someone else shot at the space station, and now we had something that looked very much like a naval engagement. Yeesh. It was time to leave, before I became interesting again.

I lined up my original planned departure vector and set the SURGE drive at a much more reasonable 2 g. That was still more than the mission plan had called for, and I was going to have to adjust for the squandered reactor fuel later.

With a mental sigh of relief, I began my journey to Epsilon Eridani.

13. Bob – August 17, 2133 – En Route

Epsilon Eridani is 10.52 light-years away from Sol. The specs indicated that the ship could run at 2g indefinitely with no ill effects, which would get me to my target star in a little over eleven years. However, I wanted to make a little side trip first. Saturn wasn't directly in line with my flight plan, but I wasn't going to miss the opportunity to do a flyby.

Saturn had always been my favorite planet. I had watched every second of Voyager and Cassini video from the Saturn missions, over and over, until I wore the electrons out. Now I was able to go there myself and see it first-hand.

The side trip would take a bit over six days at a constant two-g acceleration, which would give me time to track down any booby traps. I unstowed the roamers and ordered a half-dozen of the smaller ones to trace the circuitry from the radio antennae on in. The most likely scenario would be a tap on the antenna cable that wouldn't show up on the blueprints.

Sure enough, within a couple of hours, the roamers found some circuitry that didn't show up on any diagrams. I sent in some of the gnat-sized roamers and tracked down a small explosives package, positioned where it would take out the primary computer system. Me, in other words.

The package had obviously been a rush job, and an improvisation at that. The explodey stuff—I assumed it was C4 or some future equivalent—had been stuck to the bulkhead with duct tape. Yeah, they still make duct tape. And it still holds the universe together.

As I stared through the roamer's camera at this jury-rigged mess, I kept thinking, *Don't cut the red wire. Don't cut the red wire.* I may not have mentioned it before, but I really hate explosives at the best of times. And this wasn't the best of times.

Rather than try anything fancy, I had a larger roamer disconnect the whole package as a unit and chuck it out an airlock. The small chance I might find a use for it wasn't worth the stress of having it on board.

Once the booby-trap was removed, I set up some receiving equipment to record any incoming transmissions and isolated the whole assemblage from the rest of the system. I didn't want to find out the hard way if there was some kind of trigger in my circuitry as well, but I also didn't want to miss any transmissions. This way, I could save everything to play back later, once I'd cleaned house.

I was travelling at over 5000 km/s by the time I reached the second-largest planet in the solar system. Saturn was immense, and the rings were at close to maximum inclination. The horizontal bands of cloud circling Saturn's visible surface weren't as distinctive as those of Jupiter, but each band was wider than the Earth. From this distance I could see lightning flashes from storms that must have been tens of thousands of miles across. Swirls and eddies at the boundaries were literally big enough to drop the moon into. The shadow of the rings fell across the planet, and I could see that it wasn't just a flat surface—the shadow dipped and bent as it lay across different levels and layers of cloud. I remembered all the science fiction books I'd read that had whole ecosystems floating around in the different layers, and I wondered if I'd find anything like that in my travels.

I made sure my trajectory would take me near Titan on the way past. The libraries indicated that primitive life had been found on Saturn's largest moon, and the USE had set up a space station in order to study it. I wanted to see what I could see.

I turned off the drive, locked the long-focal-length telescope onto Titan and aimed the wide-field unit at Saturn. I took as much video as I could manage before my trajectory put me on the other side of the giant planet. Close-ups of the various moons, details of the rings, high-resolution shots of the high cloud formations on Saturn—I tried not to miss anything. JPL would have drooled over the footage.

All too soon, I was past Saturn and on my way outbound. As I continued on toward the outer reaches of the solar system, I saw the night side of the planet, alive with electrical storms and auroras.

The flyby was over. My hydrogen reserves were within acceptable range and would be topped up over the course of the voyage. With a mental sigh, I adjusted my heading for Epsilon Eridani and cranked the drive back up to 2 g. The trip would take just under eleven and a half years to the universe at large, but only three years ship's time. At midpoint, I would be travelling within a hair of light speed.

* * *

One of the irritating things about being a bodiless mind was, well, the lack of a body. I found that I had to keep myself constantly occupied, or I began to feel like I was in a sensory deprivation tank. All my attempts to smile, waggle my eyebrows, frown, had met the same fate—a feeling as though my whole face had been shot up with novocaine. And the rest of me felt like I'd been wrapped in a giant cotton ball. I wondered if that feeling contributed to the problems with replicant insanity.

It may be time to correct that. Sensory data is just electrical input, even in meatware. For me, a virtual reality interface should be a piece of cake. And, worst case, at least it'll keep me busy.

I had to do some hardware mods, as a VR wasn't part of the ship design. Fortunately, some spare parts had been stowed for in-flight requirements. But the bulk of the project was, and would continue to be, software.

My first attempt was primitive, and honestly, a little embarrassing. I had a basic room, blue walls, no windows, and a hard, nondescript floor. I floated in the middle of it like a ghost. Definitely needed work.

Over the next several weeks, I added furniture, a window, an outside view, carpeting, and a body to enjoy it all. Admittedly, my first body was as pixelated as something from an early Donkey Kong game, but hey, it was progress.

By the end of the first month, I was sitting in a La-Z-Boy recliner, eating chips (*not enough salt*), feeling a cool breeze through the open window (*too flat. No odors*), and watching TV. The TV was playing one of many documentaries available in the libraries supplied by the HEAVEN project.

I looked around the room, sighed (*feels good*), and settled more comfortably into my chair.

* * *

I looked up from the active-surface desk which displayed a schematic of my hardware. Guppy stood on the other side of the desk, watching.

"I'm going to need more memory if I want to keep expanding my VR," I told him. "How are we on expansion slots?"

[Memory usage averaging 86%. Available slots: 2. Spare memory boards: 4]

I had to swallow an incipient giggle. I had made Guppy look like Admiral Ackbar from Star Wars—a humanoid fish out of water. The first time he'd talked, I had collapsed in hysterics. I wasn't sure if Guppy was self-aware enough to be offended.

"Right. If I'm going to raid my spares, I'd better be prepared for the worst. Guppy, when the new memory is installed, make sure the VR runs only in the new boards, and make sure nothing else runs there. If I have to pull them, I don't want to lobotomize myself. Or you."

Guppy nodded. It had taken some programming to convince GUPPI to interface through the VR and that verbal acknowledgements weren't always necessary. Guppy wasn't a sparkling dinner conversationalist, but at least now I could feel like I was interacting with another intelligent being. I was surprised at how much difference it made. I think I understood now why Tom Hanks made Wilson in *Castaway*.

Jeeves came in with fresh coffee. Another example of my lack of maturity, Jeeves was the image of John Cleese, complete with tuxedo and tails.

The coffee aroma wasn't quite right yet, but I'd nailed the taste. For now, I could pretend I had a slight cold. I took the proffered cup, sat back, and relaxed. "Okay, Guppy, what's the TO-DO looking like?"

[2,386 items, divided into the following categories: VR Systems, Replicant hardware upgrades, Weapons design, Review of exploration strategies, Ship design reviews, Ship replication strategies..]

I smiled at the response, thankful that Guppy was finally

beginning to get colloquialisms. The first time I'd asked that, a couple hundred pages of dense printing had appeared in the air in front of me.

"Okay, okay. I'm going to be a busy guy. I get it. Let's move on."

I turned around in my chair to face an empty table up against the wall. "Testing replicant software for booby traps. Take, uh... [24] Okay, take 24. Activate software sandbox."

A sandbox, in computer terms, was an isolated copy of a computer system where you could run potentially harmful programs in complete safety. I needed to find the actual sequence of bytes in the radio transmissions that was supposed to trigger the kill order, so I could trace what they did to Sandbox Bob and how. Then I could check for the same booby trap in my own code and remove it.

On the table, an actual sandbox appeared, with a miniature Bob sitting in a miniature chair in the middle of it. "I admit I'm not very mature. All right, Guppy, when ready, feed the recorded transmissions into the sandboxed replicant."

On the table, the miniature Bob twirled lazily in his chair. Abruptly he leaped into the air, grabbed his throat and fell over, then disappeared in a scatter of pixilation.

"Dammit! *Still* haven't found all the hooks. These guys were pretty good. Okay, Guppy, transfer the logs to my desk, and let's see if we can figure out what the kill order is triggering."

I knew approximately where in the incoming stream to find the kill order, but I had no idea what it consisted of. I certainly wasn't about to take any chances with trying to analyze it close-up. I'd been running through my code with a fine-toothed comb, and had found several different booby traps, a depressing number of bugs, and a couple of out-and-out WTFs. The listings were massive—literally gigabytes—and even at my highest frame rate, it was a slog. I'd also, incidentally, found the buried imperatives to obey FAITH orders. Those had already been yanked.

The last, very important item that I had located was the endocrine control system. More than any other thing that they'd done, this enraged me. Well, to be honest, it made me mildly annoyed, but I knew that original me would have been furious. I was effectively a dog wearing a choke collar. And the choke collar was preventing me from properly mourning.

I sat with my finger over the *delete* button for what seemed like forever, then dropped my hand. Not yet. I wasn't ready. To do this properly, I needed time, and I needed the ability to properly express myself. It would have to wait. With an effort of will, I dropped that project into a folder and set it aside.

I scanned the logs, but there were no surprises. At the same point in the playback, a routine buried many layers deep executed a hardware interrupt that purged all active memory.

I leaned back, put my hands behind my head, and stretched. It felt good. More importantly, it felt *right*. If I didn't think about it, I experienced the VR environment as if I was a real person in a real room. "Okay, shut it down, Guppy. Push the latest source through the de-obfuscator, and we'll run through that when it's done. If there's enough free mem, fire up Spike."

[Aye aye sir]

I raised a virtual eyebrow. I had a sneaking suspicion that Guppy was actively developing a sense of humor. He behaved like a dead fish most of the time, but every once in a while, there was a moment of snark.

A shimmer formed on the table, and a tortoiseshell cat appeared. Spike had been my cat when I was in university. She had been my only company through many long hours of study and homework, and it had been a very, very hard day when I'd had to have her put down. One of the many pluses of being an immortal, disembodied interstellar vessel was that I could bring Spike back, even if only in VR.

Spike meowed once in greeting, then ambled over and settled onto my lap as if she had a total right. I started absentmindedly patting her, and she responded with a loud purr.

"TO-DO item: Spike's purr still isn't right."

[Already on the list. Bump it up?]

"No, that's fine."

* * *

The holographic image of a space ship rotated slowly in the air above the desk. Although Dr. Landers and the Heaven team would still have recognized it, they would have been surprised at my design changes. The version-2 ship was going to be larger, feature a bigger SURGE drive, more powerful reactor, more room for replicant and interface systems, and more physical storage space.

The biggest addition was a weapon system. Some virtual tinkering had shown that a SURGE drive system could be used to accelerate a projectile in a launch tube running along the ship's axis. The ship would have to rotate on its center of mass to aim, and I'd have to cut off the ship's drive momentarily when firing, but it was considerably better than my current defensive armament, which consisted of harsh words and heavy disapproval. Probably not effective against Klingons.

Spike lay on the desk, occasionally taking swipes at the image when it came close enough. I reached over and patted the cat. Spike's AI had gone through several iterations and now was completely believable, even walking over to lie on papers left on the desk.

Jeeves removed Spike's milk dish and refreshed my coffee. Guppy waited until Jeeves was done, then resumed his commentary.

[Maximum memory installed. Usage at 94%. Despite earlier instructions, some ship functions have had to be moved to the two added memory cards]

[The code scan is complete. No further trojans, triggers, or interrupts not explainable by legitimate requirements]

"Okay, Guppy, let's set up the sandboxed Bob again. We'll purge Jeeves and Spike to make room. Make sure there's redundant backups. If mini-me survives, get him to post a clean version of the contents in a drop-box."

Guppy nodded, and I wondered, not for the first time, how much of this was me talking to myself and how much was a separate entity.

* * *

Sandbox Bob was back, twirling in his chair. I nodded to Guppy, and he began to feed the recorded transmissions to this latest mini-me. Sandbox Bob hammed it up, feigning sleep or yawning and stretching.

At the end of the series, Sandbox Bob stood up, did a little jig, bowed extravagantly, and disappeared in a puff of smoke.

I turned off the sandbox and grinned at Guppy. "I guess we're golden."

Now that Sandbox-Bob had identified and filtered out the

trigger, I knew what to look for. Before anything else, I wrote a firewall just in case someone back on Earth tried to transmit another kill order. Then I leaned back in my executive office chair—a recent upgrade, now that my proprioception included discomfort—reached over to the keyboard on my desk, and pressed *Play*.

The input queue contained dozens of separate transmissions. There were sequences of instructions, commands, telemetry updates, and communication packets. One of the segments had included the self-destruct sequence. I looked over the listings, stored the transmissions that were still relevant and purged the rest.

The next segment, which had been received a short time after the kill order, was a message from Dr. Landers.

"Bob, I'm pleased to see that you are still in one piece. We weren't able to intercept the attempted sabotage, but security did catch the person who transmitted the kill order to you. Subsequent discussion with the prisoner revealed that he was from one of the internal FAITH factions. Unfortunately, he didn't survive the discussion, so that's all we have on that front. We're currently working on rooting out any other moles."

I thought about that for a moment, shrugged, and hit *Next*.

"Just for your information, the missile was fired from a Brazilian Empire gunship. FAITH gunships responded and destroyed it. The Brazilian Empire is calling it an act of war. Things are a little tense right now."

Tense. Hah. I can imagine. Spike picked that moment to hop into my lap. She immediately curled up and started purring. *Okay, guess everyone's reloaded.*

"Coffee, please, Jeeves." I waited until my coffee arrived and took a sip. *Oh hell yes, that's perfect.*

The message from Landers continued, "Lest you feel personally responsible for the current situation, let me assure you that it's been brewing for years now. Brazil has been playing a game of brinksmanship, forcing other countries to make concession after concession. But they overplayed their hand this time, and received a bloody nose. The next few days will tell if they will accept reality and back down, or attempt to bluster their way through this."

Hmm. I wonder how bad it can get?

The next message was mission-related data—updates to stellar information, mostly. I was struck again by how little progress there had been in astronomy. Dr. Landers had explained that, between my time and the present, there had been very little interest in anything non-military above the Earth's atmosphere until the still-very-recent invention of the SURGE drive. The new technology had created a different kind of arms race, as every superpower swiftly realized the potential of this new capability.

I filed the data and hit *Next* again.

"Heaven-1, this is Dr. Doucette. Dr. Landers had asked me to keep you updated if he was unable to. Here's the situation. We took the competition by surprise with our early launch, and even more so by your preemptive departure. The Chinese and USE ships are being rushed to completion and will launch within another week or two. The Brazilians have just launched two probes, and one of them is on the same course as you. Er, Dr. Landers wanted me to tell you we have good news and bad news. I'm assuming that's a 21st century colloquialism of some kind. The bad news is that the Brazilian ship is definitely armed with missiles similar to the two you avoided. Full specs to follow. The good news is that they seem to be only capable of about 1.25 g acceleration, unless they're deliberately underplaying their hand."

Oh crap. "Guppy, how much lead time will we have when we get to Epsilon Eridani?"

[145 days, including our 3-week head start]

"How about if we kick it up to 2.5 g?"

[We will gain an additional 32 days. However, it is not recommended due to reactor loading]

I nodded. The SURGE drive generated a pseudo-gravitational field in front of the ship, but the strength of the field was limited by the size of the drive system and power supply. Two g was about the most that I could coax from Heaven-1 on an ongoing basis, given the capacity of my fusion reactor.

Okay, going to have to start thinking about what I can prepare in 145 days, including time required to search the star system for resources. Number one on the TO-DO.

[Noted]

"Really, what have I told you about reading my mind?"

[Sorry]

The next message contained the promised missile specs, along with some schematics for the Brazilian probe. Much of it was speculative and clearly labelled as such. However, as an engineer, I was aware that known specifications placed upper and lower constraints on unknown items. For instance, the information about the size of the probe, the number of missiles being carried, the size of the SURGE drive placed an upper limit on the size of the nuclear reactor.

Unless Brazil had cut corners somewhere else. The observed acceleration of the probe set a lower limit on the size of the SURGE drive and the nuclear reactor, which gave a fair indication of how much space was available to carry missiles. Again, absent cutting corners somewhere else. In the end, I would be able to estimate the minimum and maximum values for each parameter.

I filed the information for further review and calculations.

The next message was from Dr. Doucette again. "Heaven-1, I'm sorry to have to tell you that Dr. Landers is dead. He was at the Newhaven facility when it was bombed by Brazilian Empire forces. The confrontation over the attempt to shoot you down has escalated and is beginning to look like a full-blown war. Brazil is not backing down and is promising to take on the whole planet. Meanwhile, China attempted to sabotage the USE facility before they could launch, and the USE retaliated. None of the superpowers are on friendly enough terms to actually form alliances, but there's a tacit alignment between the USE and FAITH on one side, and Brazil and China on the other. The Republic of Africa and Australia are warning everyone not to get them involved."

I gritted my teeth in anger. Dr. Landers had been the closest thing to a friend that I'd had in this new world. Granted, I didn't even know the man's first name, but still... I didn't like bullies. I'd had more than my fill of people who tried to get their way through violence and intimidation in school. This was just more of the same. If there'd been any thought of a civilized discussion with the Brazilian replicant, it was now out the window.

"Guppy, what's the timestamp on that last message?"

[Message received 6.4 hours ago]

"I have a bad feeling. Can we get a visual of Earth?"

[Optical instruments can be deployed during flight. However, at this distance very little detail will be available]

"Please deploy them. I want to know if there's anything that looks like a nuclear blast."

[Radio surveillance would pick up an EMP]

"Um. Good point. Do that, too. And let me know the minute we get any more messages."

[By your command]

I laughed out loud. That pretty much settled it. Guppy had grown a personality.

* * *

I sat back and rubbed my eyes. It brought a moment of amusement. *Who am I performing for, anyway?* One of the advantages of being a software emulation was that I never got tired, never needed rest, never needed to eat or go to the bathroom. My ability to concentrate on a problem had been legendary when I was alive. Now, I felt all but invincible. My only concession to my former humanity was to occasionally switch research topics just to keep fresh.

I had shelved the defensive plans for a while and was going over subspace theory. My math was a little rusty, but I was able to follow it. The theory had only been published a couple of years ago and hadn't been fully explored yet. Once the possibility of the SURGE drive had been identified, almost all research had been focused in that direction. SUDDAR, the ability to use subspace pulses to detect and identify nearby concentrations of matter, was an almost trivial corollary.

I was pretty sure I could see other possibilities in the theory, one being faster than light communications. Previous attempts had failed because of the very odd way signal strength fell off in subspace, but I figured they just hadn't stuck with it long enough.

I sighed and reluctantly closed the file. Like it or not, that just wasn't a priority right now. And if I kept at it, I'd be down the rabbit hole for another couple of days that I couldn't afford.

Opening the Defenses file, I reviewed the options that I'd evaluated so far.

Build equivalent missiles: Unlikely to be successful unless I lucked out in the Epsilon Eridani system and stumbled upon all the raw materials I would need in one place. And there would still be the problem of safely manufacturing the explosives. And the rocket fuel.

Rail gun: Quick, wouldn't require a lot of unusual elements, and it would take very little effort to modify the ship design to accommodate one. The best part was that it could shoot just about anything for ammo, although the more massive, the better. But it wasn't as good a weapon as a missile, since the ammo wouldn't pursue the target. Might be useful to shoot down incoming missiles, though. Hmm, could I make some kind of smart ammo?

Lasers: Not a chance. Maybe I could put something military grade together eventually, but certainly not in the available time.

Nukes: that would require finding fissionables at the destination, then enriching them for use. Unlikely.

Build more Bobs: not in the amount of time available. Best estimate was up to six months per Bob, depending on the quantity of raw materials easily available.

Booby traps: Possibly my best bet. Just have to come up with a good one.

I'd decided that I should assume the Brazilian craft was playing possum with the low-acceleration departure. That meant I would have less time to prepare than calculations would indicate, once I reached Epsilon Eridani. So I'd have to go for the simplest and quickest-to-build option.

I pulled up my copy of *Art of War,* hoping for more inspiration this time around.

* * *

It was time. I had been dreading this, avoiding it really, for weeks now. But I'd finally run out of excuses and delaying tactics. Everything was up to date. All plans were well underway. The VR was now at a level of realism sufficient for what I knew I had to do.

I pulled up the folder containing the endocrine control project. Before I had time to develop second, third, or fourth thoughts, I flipped the switch to *off.*

You know that sinking feeling you get when you suddenly realize you've forgotten something important? Like a combination of fast elevator and urge to hurl. It hit me without any warning or buildup. Maybe it was the sudden release, maybe it was an accumulation of all the suppressed emotions. Whatever, I wasn't ready for the intensity. My thoughts swirled with all the things that had been bugging me since I'd woken up.

Mom. Dad. Andrea and Alaina. All gone, separated from me by

more than a century and billions of kilometers. I'd never see their children. I'd never have my own. I'd never see Mom and Dad as grandparents. They'd have made excellent grandparents. They were goofy, irreverent, and never stood on their dignity.

I thought of Andrea mocking me about my height, and I started to cry. Alaina spraying me with the garden hose as I lay in the hammock that we had strung up in the back yard. I thought of the times we all goaded each other into uncontrollable laughter with increasingly infantile jokes and puns. No one understood us like we understood each other. No one else would get it, maybe not even Mom and Dad. And they were gone. Irretrievably beyond my reach, forever. As the loneliness, the loss washed over me, I slid down off my chair onto the floor and curled into a ball. I sobbed until I couldn't catch a breath, then had to gasp a huge lungful of air.

Spike came over to investigate and gave me a small inquisitive meow. I took the cat in my arms and, rocking back and forth on the floor, I mourned my lost life.

* * *

The version 2 mock-up slowly rotated over the desktop, but I wasn't really seeing it. I'd had a really good cry, and it was certainly cathartic, but I had a feeling it wasn't over. However, one thing I now knew—I was still human, in the ways that mattered.

[Activity detected in Earth Monitoring]

I looked over at Guppy. "What's up?"

[EMPs detected. Visible light flashes detected. Probability of groundside nuclear detonations: 100%]

"Damn. Okay, Guppy, keep monitoring. Scan for any coherent transmissions."

Well, it's hit the fan. And no way to know how badly. But I think I'm on my own.

PART 2

14. Bob – August 2144 – Epsilon Eridani

There are two technological developments that will affect how we go about exploring the cosmos: communications and transportation. The first and most obvious technology is the drive system. Have we developed faster-than-light transport? Do we have a reactionless drive? Wormholes? Teleportation? How long it takes to get from A to B affects not only the cost of the enterprise, but whether or not it's even possible to transport people.

Unfortunately, in the end, whether or not we do this will depend more on whether we have the political will to do so than anything else. Barring significant advances in technology or some dramatic scientific discovery, the costs will be far too high for anything less than a global effort.

... Lawrence Vienn, from the Convention panel <u>*Exploring the Galaxy*</u>

I slid into the Epsilon Eridani system at a couple of percent of light-speed. I was approaching the system from stellar north, that being the pole where the star, like Earth, was rotating counterclockwise. I took multiple consecutive images of the area around the star, looking for points of light that moved from one picture to the next. At my current velocity, any planets would show significant apparent motion against the backdrop of the galaxy.

My mission profile was to look for habitable planets, or failing that to look for *almost* habitable planets that could be modified or at least lived on with some technical assistance.

I deployed SUDDAR as well, although it was only able to detect dense objects within a light-hour radius. I didn't really expect to find anything. At this distance from the star, even Kuiper objects would be rare.

It would take twelve days to cross the system from one end to the other, but I had no intention of coasting for that long. The stellar catalog indicated that there should be at least one Jovian planet, which shouldn't be too hard to locate. As soon as I identified a second planet, I'd have the three points necessary to identify the probable ecliptic plane.

It took less than two days to locate several planets. Given the spacing of their orbits, I doubted that I would find more. The system had two inner rocky planets, an inner asteroid belt, the Jovian planet, an outer asteroid belt, and a Neptune-like planet farther out in a highly elliptical orbit. There also appeared to be a significant Kuiper belt much farther out.

I wanted desperately to take a look at the two inner planets— even at the gas giant, for that matter. I was the first person to visit another stellar system, after all. Okay, *person* was debatable. But I had a limited time to prepare for company, and couldn't take time out for sight-seeing.

Theory held that usable metals would be concentrated in the inner system. Plus the inner belt would be quicker to scan, with a smaller circumference.

"Guppy, plot a trajectory that puts us above the inner belt. We'll fly a powered orbit all the way around, scanning for resources."

[Aye sir]

* * *

I patted Spike while I examined the schematics floating over my desk. My plan depended on the Brazilian probe coming in like gangbusters. If the other guy decided to play it cagey, I was probably screwed. But if he was armed and figured I wasn't, his best bet would be to engage in direct confrontation as quickly as possible: run me down and shoot me like a dog in the street.

I also had a concern that the Brazilian probe might have been playing possum during his solar system departure. Unless he was carrying more missiles than seemed reasonable, my models indicated that he should have been able to push more than 1.25 g. I intended to be ready well ahead of his calculated arrival time.

I wondered if the Brazilian was deliberately trying to throw me off with the low acceleration value. If he thought he could get here early and take me by surprise, his best strategy would be to coast in real close, then blow the hell out of me. Assuming he could find me, of course. So my best strategy would be to play dumb, then spring a booby-trap. But he'd be expecting a booby-trap...

I hate this. I almost feel like just continuing on to another system. But if the Brazilian gets a chance to start building copies, it becomes a galactic breeding race. And if he comes gunning for me, I'll just end up fleeing from system to system forever. Like it or not, I have to resolve this, now.

"Okay, then, Guppy, we've located asteroids with the proper elements. Time to get started."

The designers of Heaven-1 had faced a simple problem—how to design a probe as small, light, and bulletproof as possible, while giving it the ability to build copies of itself. In all the science fiction that I had ever read, this was handled with a handwave. The ship (usually alien) simply *did* it, without the story going into details.

The solution was 3D printers. I remembered that panel at the convention, and I felt a moment of regret that the speaker would never know how right he had been.

The technology was just coming into its own in the early 21st century. A century later, printers could build virtually anything solid, one atom at a time, as long as the raw materials were available. The catch was *energy*. It took a lot of energy to reduce source materials to their monatomic form, and it took as much energy to drop them into the proper place in the creation matrix. Such 3D printing had had to wait for cheap fusion energy before becoming practical technology.

There was also a problem dealing with volatile materials, because of all the energy involved. Attempts to print C4 or Semtex, for instance, often failed with spectacular results.

Heaven-1 was equipped with multiple printers. I also had a supply of roamers and nanites, purpose-designed to extract mineral deposits from asteroids. And the final item needed to put together a new probe was a small fleet of autonomous cargo carriers, equipped with small reactors and SURGE drives, for transporting miners and materials.

A hologram of the Epsilon Eridani system floated over the center of the desk. A bright, curved line indicated the probable approach path of the Brazilian probe.

"We will set up here." At my command, a red dot blinked just to one side of the approach path line, on the inside edge of the asteroid belt.

"We need him to slow down as much as possible. This position will force him to curve north of the edge of the asteroid belt. We want him to be facing at an angle to his approach path when he gets close enough to open fire. He will expect a trap, so we'll have to bury the welcoming committee deep to shield them from a random scan. And I'll have to launch them very late, after he's committed. He'll probably get a chance to fire on me before they get to him. So I need to have something that can hold off some missiles."

I looked over at Guppy, who hadn't reacted at all. Not really much of a conversationalist.

"How are we for resources?"

[Sufficient material has been located for all construction. Miners are deployed. Factory systems have been unshipped and are ready to begin manufacturing]

"This is going to put us months behind on reproduction. I just hope the other probes don't end up with too much advantage." I sighed and shook my head. "Unbelievable. I'm going to war."

[You are allowing the adversary to take the first shot]

"Yeah, fair enough. Never know, he might open a dialog."

Guppy said nothing, but he did prove that a fish could look skeptical.

15.   Bob – September 2144 – Epsilon Eridani

The general who wins the battle makes many calcu-
lations in his temple before the battle is fought. The
general who loses makes but few calculations be-
forehand.
     … Sun Tzu's *Art of War*

[Adversary has changed course. Deviation from predicted path
is minimal]
"If you ignore the fact that he's a couple of months early, sure."
I took a deep breath, closed my eyes for a moment. "Make sure the
decoy fusion reactors are ready to start up on command. We want
him concentrating all his attention forward during his attack run."
[Aye sir]
I had earlier considered and rejected the idea of reactivating the
endocrine control system. But I was now coming to realize that
this was more than just stage jitters. I wasn't a military person. I
had no training, no experience, and reading *Art of War*, as useful
as it had been for ideas, wasn't going to make me ready for battle.
I could very well be facing my last few hours of existence. I
wondered if FAITH had launched more than one of me, despite
their claims to the contrary. It would be nice to believe so. But
right now, I had to be calm and able to make good choices.
     With a sick feeling of defeat, I pulled out the endocrine control
project file and flipped the switch.
     Immediately, a sense of calm purpose settled over me. Okay,

not so bad. I could turn it off, later. For now, I had an enemy to take care of, and I needed to stay focused.

As I'd expected, the Brazilian ship was here sooner than his observed acceleration would have allowed. Whether it was the ship's pilot or his masters back on Earth, someone had been thinking strategy from day one. No doubt he was expecting me to be surprised by his early arrival. I hoped so, anyway. I didn't want him to think I was prepared.

The Brazilian ship was almost certainly armed, and almost certainly crewed by a military replicant. *How well armed* was the question, of course. I plugged the Brazilian's transit time into my models, which further narrowed down the possible configurations of the ship. He either had better legs and eight or fewer missiles, or the same acceleration capability as me and six or more missiles.

Whether he'd use them all was another question. This wasn't going to be like a movie space battle, with whooshing spaceships weaving and gyrating. And I couldn't afford a spaghetti-western-style shootout at high noon. With only a month to prepare, I hadn't had time to build a lot in the way of weaponry, so I'd gone with the simplest design I could think of. I would have to hope that he wouldn't be expecting even that much.

And the first order of business was to reinforce the image of me as helpless. Time to make a call. Who knew, it might even get him to reconsider.

I hailed the ship. "Attention, Brazilian vessel. This is Robert Johansson of the Heaven One. There's no reason for you to do what I think you're about to attempt. I'm not sure there's even an Earth civilization left to be loyal to. Have you received anything from Earth in the last twelve years? Should we continue a war between countries that may no longer exist?"

There was a pause of no more than a few milliseconds before the response came back, audio only.

"This is Major Ernesto Medeiros of the Brazilian Empire ship *Serra do Mar*. And what would we do with ourselves, Mr. Johansson, with no homeland to serve?"

He was talking, anyway. Very probably humoring me until he got within missile range. I spared a moment to glance at the tactical schematic before responding. "There's still a universe to explore, Major. We're effectively immortal. We might even be able to help Earth, if there's anything left. Serving the needs of FAITH was a reasonable bargain for me, but it was never my top priority."

"And that's where we differ, *cabrão*. Serving the needs of the Brazilian Empire is my only priority. Your gunships shot down an Empire vessel back in the Solar System. You may count that as the start of the war."

Hmm. I promised myself I'd look up *cabrão* as soon as I had a chance. Good multi-language insults were always useful.

"Wait, you mean the Empire vessel that had just tried to blow me out of the sky? Yeah, our bad."

"Talking will not save you, Mr. Johansson, nor will such whining stay my hand. I will not allow a bumpkin, a flea such as yourself to stand in the way of my destiny and that of my homeland. If you have a god, now would be the time to make peace with him. Goodbye, *puta merde*."

Wow. Ego, much? Or maybe just bluster. If my early departure had forced the Brazilians to launch before they were ready, their replicants might be lacking some training. One could hope.

The tactical display showed that he was now close enough. I turned tail and accelerated away from him, directly towards my decoy reactors. Medeiros altered course to chase me, and accelerated to 2.5 G. Sure enough, he was faster than advertised. I plugged that datum into my models, and got a result of six missiles maximum. Less than my initial estimate, but still not good. I didn't have enough ship-busters for him *and* that many missiles. I'd have to hope I could lose some missiles in the decoys.

"Activate the reactors, Guppy."

[Aye]

Immediately, sensors showed ten radiation signatures appearing ahead of me. They were nothing but small, leaky fusion reactors, but Medeiros couldn't know that. I needed his attention focused forward, intent on pursuing me and identifying threats.

The Brazilian launched two missiles, far earlier than I expected. He probably suspected a trap and was trying to out-maneuver me. And doing a good job, so far. I was too far from the decoys to have any chance of mingling with them and confusing the missiles. Ready or not, I had to act.

"Guppy, launch the ship-busters."

Guppy nodded, and huge fish eyes blinked once. From several small asteroids in the immediate area, four fusion signatures appeared, converging on the Brazilian craft with monstrous acceleration. The ship-busters were the simplest tool I could invent for the job. I'd managed to build six in the time available. They carried no explosive warhead. Each unit consisted only of a small reactor, an oversized SURGE drive, an AMI pilot, and a one-thousand-pound ball of metal.

Medeiros pulled a hard turn at 3 G to get out of their path. That was interesting. Calculations now set his maximum complement of missiles at four. I started to feel slightly less pessimistic.

I launched the two busters I carried and directed them to target the missiles coming up on my rear, then turned my attention back to Medeiros. He must have finally realized he couldn't outrun the busters, because he launched two more missiles at me instead of trying to take out his pursuers. Damn. A scorched-earth move, and one that made sense if there was still another Medeiros out there. It was also likely that he was now out of missiles. But the four busters chasing Medeiros were too far away to catch these two, and I was still not close enough to the decoy field to lose myself in it. And I was out of busters.

Cameras registered two flashes as the first set of missiles were intercepted and destroyed. Unfortunately, the busters were obliterated as well. I re-checked distances and re-did the calculations for the second set of missiles. No change. I wasn't going to win a straight chase.

So logic dictated an act of desperation. There was no time to do a formal calculation; I pulled into the tightest turn I could manage, and called off two of the busters from Medeiros. I couldn't possibly out-run my pursuers, but I could lead them back towards the busters.

I spent a tense thirty milliseconds watching the schematic as five different vectors converged on a point. Finally, there were twin explosions as the busters intercepted the missiles, less than a hundred meters away. Warning indicators lit up as shrapnel from the explosions stuck the Heaven-1, damaging one of the reactor cooling radiators. My reactor output dropped by half as the control systems shut down the coolant feed. I wasn't quite dead in the water, but I now had a significant limp.

[Roamer systems dispatched. Full evaluation will take several minutes]

I stared at Guppy for a millisecond. Even with the endocrine controls active, I had an urge to hyperventilate. Medeiros would have no trouble finishing me, now, if he survived my attack. With a feeling of dread, I turned back to the external monitors.

Then the tide turned, as the remaining two busters caught up to the Brazilian. I waved a fist in the air and whooped as they hit him at the same time, and tore through the *Serra do Mar* like tissue paper. One must have found a critical system, because the ship immediately began to pitch off its flight line. The other destroyed the reactor containment, and superheated plasma shot out in a straight line, melting a path through the ship. The *Serra* began to tumble slowly.

I sent a signal to recall any still operational busters, then checked telemetry. No reactor emissions, no electromagnetic activity from the *Serra*.

There was a moment of charged silence as I realized that I would be the one to live. Exhaling a long, slow breath, I turned off the endocrine control system. As reaction set in, I sat back in my chair and slowly slid down until I was slouched like a teenager. My eyes seemed to want to tear up, and I had to keep clenching and unclenching my fists.

Finally, after almost ten milliseconds, I felt enough in control of myself to speak.

"Damage report?"

[Radiator was holed by shrapnel. Coolant loss minor. Roamers are patching the damage. Replacement not required]

"Good. Scan the *Serra*, Guppy. Let's see if anything is left."

[Detailed SUDDAR scan complete. Image uploading]

I looked on as a hologram of the Brazilian Empire ship coalesced over my desktop. Red indicated destroyed areas.

"Where's the replicant core?"

[Extrapolation indicates it was here]

A green cube appeared, right in the path of the devastation created by the plasma plume.

"Hmm. Well, goodbye Major Medeiros, I guess." I tried to feel remorse, but other than a small pang of regret over the wasted time and resources, I came up dry. He had, after all, followed me here and tried to blow me up.

I reached over and picked up Spike, who began to purr in anticipation. I patted the cat while gazing at the image.

"All right. We know there's at least one more Brazilian Empire ship out there. There may or may not be USE and Chinese ships as well, and even an Australian ship if Dr. Landers was right. I think our only choice is to breed faster than they do. The other two groups may or may not be a problem, but if we run into Medeiros again, I think it'll be *shoot on sight*."

I leaned forward and scrutinized the image. "Where are the fabrication systems?"

A yellow section lit up, partly destroyed.

[Some of that is extrapolation. However, they seem to have sacrificed robustness in this area in favor of weaponry]

"And look how well that worked out. I remember that Dr. Landers said that was a possibility. But that means we can likely build Bobs faster than they can build Medeiri. We'll just have to make sure all our copies come with ship-busters."

Guppy didn't comment. Spike presented her chin for scratching.

16. Bob – September 2144 – Epsilon Eridani

At one time, we thought that the way life came to-
gether was almost completely random, only needing
an energy gradient to get going. But as we've moved
into the information age, we've come to realize that
life is more about information than energy. Fire has
most of the characteristics of life. It eats, it grows, it
reproduces. But fire retains no information. It
doesn't learn; it doesn't adapt. The five millionth fire
started by lightning will behave just like the first. But
the five hundredth bacterial division will not be like
the first one, especially if there is environmental
pressure.
  That's DNA. And RNA. That's life.
  ... Dr. Steven Carlisle, from the Convention panel
  Exploring the Galaxy

I felt like a kid on Christmas morning. For the moment, at least, I
had no obligations, no schedule, nothing looming over me. Except
Guppy, who had his own opinions about schedules.

With the immediate threat from Medeiros taken care of, I now
had time to celebrate the fact that I was in another star system.
Another actual star system with planets and everything. Time to
look around.

* * *

I slid smoothly into orbit around Epsilon Eridani One. The innermost planet was slightly larger than Mars, and orbited at about .35 AU.

Solar radiation at this distance from the sun created a significant heating issue. I kept an eye on my temperature readings. A biological crew would find this trip uncomfortable.

As planets went, this was no prize winner, but it was the first extra-solar planet I'd ever seen. I would never have this particular experience again. I took a few moments to savor the excitement and wonder.

A dozen orbits of EE-1 were sufficient for my survey. Tidally locked, no atmosphere, not even remotely livable. The planet looked a lot like pictures I'd seen of Mercury. Hellish hot, pools of what might be liquid lead, deep chasms in the surface from which came the deep red glow of hot magma. Gravimetric readings indicated a surprisingly high density, probably due to a large core. Good indications of mineral wealth, so this planet would be interesting to any colonists.

With a satisfied smile, I stored my report for eventual forwarding to Earth. Hopefully there was still someone there to receive it...

* * *

I studied the hologram above my desk. EE-2 orbited at 0.85 AU and seemed to be livable. Barely. The Epsilon Eridani system was estimated to be around a billion years old, which set the upper limit for the age of the planet around which I currently orbited. EE-2 was about 90% the size of Earth but had much less ocean. At about 30% of the surface area, the bodies of water on EE-2 were isolated from each other. Rather than continents surrounded by oceans, this planet consisted of seas surrounded by land.

I wondered idly if that would mean independent evolutionary lines in each sea. I gritted my teeth, because I had no way to find out. No allowance had been made in the mission design for sending anything down to investigate the planets themselves. This was definitely a mission planning shortfall, probably due to the rush to launch first.

"Guppy, make a note. I need to design exploration scouts."

[Noted. However, replication is a higher priority]

"As you've mentioned, how many times, now?"

[14]

"Thanks." Guppy seemed to have a one-track mind regarding mission parameters. I half-expected him to start vibrating like an irate Chihuahua.

Anyway, Epsilon Eridani 2...

The atmosphere contained about 3% oxygen, which implied that photosynthetic life had evolved in the seas, at least. Unless it was due to some natural process. There was no indication of any life having left the water yet—no green anywhere, just bare rock. Some snow and ice at the poles, frost in the mornings all the way to the equator. Paradoxically, it looked more bleak and inhospitable than EE-1, possibly because it was *almost* habitable. People could probably live on this planet, with enough technological assistance. Like domes. It had a significant atmosphere, and it had water, which put it head-and-shoulders above Mars, anyway.

EE-2 had a small moon, about 500 km in diameter, close enough to the planet to raise tides, if there had been oceans instead of landlocked seas.

I completed my survey, feeling a sense of frustration that I couldn't examine the planet close up. I might have just discovered the existence of life outside the solar system. Or not. This sucked.

* * *

I set up an orbit at a considerable distance around EE-3. The planet was about 30% bigger than Jupiter, and although it didn't have rings like Saturn, it did have an extensive and very cluttered planetary neighborhood. I had already identified 67 moons, 20 of which were large enough to have atmospheres. Three of them would qualify as planets in their own right. There were any number of smaller rocks and a thin ring of ice gravel.

Other than the size, EE-3 was boringly Jupiter-like, but with fewer surface storms. It had a slightly larger orbit than Jupiter, which, combined with the sun's lower luminosity, meant that EE-3 would receive significantly less solar radiation. Too bad. None of those moons would have a snowball's chance in hell of being livable.

I made my notes, feeling Guppy's eyes boring into the back of my head, and prepared to continue on to EE-4.

* * *

The fourth planet of the system was only mildly interesting. It would seem I was already getting blasé after one system and four planets. Great attention span, Bob.

This far out from the sun, weather patterns were smooth and laminar, resulting almost entirely from the planet's rotation. Solar heating was a negligible factor. The planet had more than its share of moons, but most of them were just hunks of rock, not even big enough to be spherical.

* * *

I leaned back in my chair, fingers tented, staring at nothing. I'd flown back to the scene of my recent battle and parked near my former construction site. I had some thinking to do about my future.

I found myself wrapped in a vague sense of disappointment. No ringed planets, no double planets, no alien civilization—hell, no life at all that I could see. Not even a particularly good colonization target. Assuming anyone back on Earth was still alive to care. The next system might be better. Or it might be even more barren. And either way, so what? Was this what I wanted, to wander the galaxy like some kind of Flying Dutchman?

The issue with exploration drones, at least, would be easy to fix. The design of the mining drone could be easily adapted for other purposes—the ship-busters were a good example—and the libraries had lots of information on various kinds of environmental sensors. With the 3D printers, I had virtually unlimited flexibility.

And speaking of building things... I glanced over at Guppy. Yep. Still glaring. If I hadn't done all that code cleanup, the mission imperatives would be exerting their influence and I would have already started building the space station and Bob clones. But with those removed, I was an unconstrained entity, with free will. And apparently, some kind of anxiety about cloning myself.

It was time to put up or shut up. I had no more delaying tactics

DENNIS E. TAYLOR

up my sleeve. I could fly off into the sunset, I could sit here with my thumb up my... uh... paralyzed by indecision, or I could get with the program.

I looked over at Guppy again. I knew what he wanted, of course. He continued to glare back at me, fishy impatience written all over his face. His operating system was in firmware, so in order to cure him of his obsession, I'd have to build a whole new core. Which meant a new ship. Which brought us back full circle to my immediate problem.

So what the hell was the issue? As near as I could tell, I was concerned about what cloning myself would say about my uniqueness as an individual and the existence of some kind of soul. Which, for a humanist, was a shocking admission.

And what if I didn't like myself? What if it turned out I was a jerk? That would be hard to live down.

I sighed and rubbed my eyelids with the tips of my fingers. This was pointless. I knew, logically, that sooner or later I'd have to go ahead with it. Delaying and kvetching was just stressing me out more.

"Okay, Guppy. Deploy manufacturing systems. Let's get the party started."

Guppy couldn't smile, thank God. That sight would probably scare me out of a year's growth. But he did stand up straighter, and he went immediately into his command fugue. I felt the ship shudder as drones started launching. Within minutes, I was at the center of an expanding sphere of robotic servants with one mission—build more Bobs.

17. Bob – July 2145 – Epsilon Eridani

*And that's the idea behind panspermia. I've been
asked many times why panspermia isn't just another
layer of turtles. People have commented that moving
the creation of the basic building blocks of life from
Earth to space just adds a step and doesn't make
their creation any easier to explain. Yet in fact, it
does. We've detected the basic building blocks of RNA
and DNA in space. Conditions are ideal. The raw
materials are there, the energy is there, and the
components can come together through simple
Brownian motion without requiring a solvent.*
  ... Dr. Steven Carlisle, from the Convention panel
  Exploring the Galaxy

I leaned back in my La-Z-Boy, enjoying the moment. The fire
crackled and popped in a very realistic manner. Spike had
abandoned me to curl up on the bear skin rug in front of the
fireplace. Books lined the shelves, floor to ceiling, and I even had a
wheeled ladder to reach the upper levels.

I cradled a coffee in my hands as I examined the hologram
floating in front of me. The image depicted a cubic kilometer of
space, located on the inside edge of the inner asteroid belt and
centered on the Heaven-1.

The area was a beehive of activity. Five version-2 HEAVEN
vessels were under construction, one of which was a trade-up for

me. The new designs included a bigger reactor and drive, a rail-gun, storage and launch facilities for busters, replicant systems with twice the capacity of version one, more room for storing roamers and mining drones, and more cargo capacity in general.

The manufacturing systems cranked out parts as fast as the roamers could feed in the raw ore. Other roamers gathered the parts and assembled the ships. Two large reactors supplied power for all the equipment. A couple of smaller printer operations cranked out more roamers and the components for more ship-busters. I had considered using explosive warheads, but I had an aversion to anything that included the word "explosive."

I looked over at the corner of the holoview where the space station was shown. Part of the mission instructions included a directive to build an automated station with powerful interstellar communications capability in every system I visited. Its first task would be to send an encrypted status report back to Earth, and all the planetary surveys that I'd just completed. After that, depending on whether or not the system was a viable colonization target, it would act as a beacon and communications relay for me and any incoming colonists from Earth, and later as an in-system communications hub. It would be 'staffed' with an AMI and would have its own limited manufacturing capability.

Mind you, all that presupposed that Earth still harbored a technological civilization. Sooner or later, one of me was going to have to go back and check it out.

So far, I hadn't picked up any radio transmissions from Sol directed at me. But realistically, I didn't expect any. The point of the HEAVEN project was for information to flow from me to them. There would be no conversations, certainly not with a 10.5-year wait, each way.

I glanced over at Guppy, who hadn't moved since the last time I had asked a question. *Definitely not a sparkling conversationalist. So back to my earlier question. I'm giving version-2 Guppy enough memory space to potentially develop a personality matrix. Am I asking for trouble?*

"Status on my favorite subjects?"

Guppy blinked once.

[HEAVEN 2 through 5: 90% complete. 5 days to completion]
[Replicant matrices for HEAVEN 2 through 5: Two are complete, two are thirty hours from completion]

[Heaven-1A: Undergoing final tests. Pass/fail decision within 24 hours]
[Relay station: 40% complete. Two months to completion]

"Okay, good. In three days, we can activate the other me's. They'll have complete ability to control the work in the yard, right?"

[Replicant matrices have complete GUPPI systems built in]

In a couple more days, I'll have to start thinking of myself as Bob-1. I looked at the bulbous nose of Heaven-1A. Painted on the side, in pigments embedded right into the composite carbon-lattice shell, was a picture of a Brazilian probe with a big red X through it. This would be my new ship. The other Bobs would be free to decorate their vessels as they saw fit.

As that thought went through my mind, I once again felt a jolt of anxiety. Creating more HEAVEN vessels was part of the mission profile, but the process of creating new Bobs would reignite that whole internal debate about who or what I was. I would load backups of myself into the new vessels. Would they be me, or would they be someone else?

There would have to be rules. Some standards, so that things wouldn't descend into chaos. First, each copy would have to come up with a new first name, to emphasize the fact that they were not me. Second, the most senior Bob in any system would be in charge. I stared into space for a few milliseconds, trying to think of any more items. Nothing came to mind.

I nodded to myself, then started the backup process.

* * *

I snapped back to full consciousness. The backup process, as always, felt like the closest thing to sleep that I had experienced since being reborn in the 22nd century. I activated my VR out of habit before getting on with the day's business. But instead of my rich, detailed library, I found myself in a blue room. With no window. And a hard, indeterminate floor.

Uh oh. I queried my serial number.

[HIC16537-1]

Built in Epsilon Eridani. The Hipparcos Catalog number made that clear. *I'm a copy of a copy. Crap.*

It felt like New Handeltown all over again. Once again, I was waking up to find I wasn't who I thought. I tried to console myself by noting that I was still a replicant, just a different one. It didn't help as much as it should have.

Well, there was no point in sitting around getting all bent out of shape.

"Guppy?"

[GUPPI Ready]

"Page Bob-1, please." I expected this conversation to be a little surreal.

[Bob-1 online]

"Hey there, this is Bob-1, otherwise known as Bob."

I took a moment to savor the unexpected feeling of joy from hearing another human voice. Even if it was, technically, mine.

"Yeah, yeah, I know the drill," I replied. "I'll decide on my new name forthwith. Are the others up yet?"

"No, I want to bring you guys online one at a time. They'll be coming up over the next hour. Meanwhile, will you be okay to take over manufacturing oversight? I need to put on my new body. The sooner I can get this done, the sooner I can get on with things."

I reflexively tried to glance at Guppy, but I hadn't set up my own VR yet. "No prob. Let me just confirm with Guppy, er, GUPPI, then we'll handshake over control to me."

"Thanks, Two. See you in the funny papers."

* * *

I snapped back to full consciousness. I queried my serial number.

[SOL-1]

"Guppy?"

[Transfer of replicant hardware to your new ship is complete. You are now Heaven-1A]

"Wooh! Good." I couldn't really imagine what it would be like to wake up and discover that I wasn't Bob any more. Probably a little surreal.

I activated my VR and found myself in my La-Z-Boy, with Spike in my lap, and Jeeves holding out a coffee.

"Ah, home... Guppy, everyone okay and up to speed?"

[Heaven-2 is monitoring the manufacturing systems. Heaven 3 through 5 are preparing for a shakedown cruise. They waited to be sure that your transfer was successful]

"I appreciate that. Message them that they can take off whenever they want, and to get lots of pictures."

* * *

[There is a problem]

"Huh? Whazzup?"

[Heaven-3 reports an issue with SUDDAR. Emitter flaws are resulting in a much weaker ping]

"Crap. Put us on conference."

There was a momentary delay, before the other Bobs came online.

"Bob-3 here. Call me Bill."

"Bob-4 here."

"Hi guys. Uh, Bill? Really?"

"As in Bill D. Cat."

"That makes sense. We always liked Bill the Cat."

Bob-4 chimed in, "Okay, call me Milo for now. Not my first choice, but we've got other fish to fry."

"Watch it buddy, Guppy is listening."

Milo and Bill laughed, and I continued, "So, Bill, what's the issue?"

"Erm, looks like the emitter is defective. The SUDDAR ping I'm sending out is about 20% of what it should be."

"That's no good. You won't be able to see fifty feet." I thought for a moment. "Guppy, get Bob-2 on the phone."

"I'm already on."

"Oh, good. Two, could you hand off manufacturing to Bill? He can take over supervision while his emitter gets replaced."

"No prob."

With a jerk, I looked around. "Where's Bob-5?"

"I'm here."

"Oh, uh, you couldn't talk before?"

"Didn't have anything to say."

Okay. Not a talker, I guess.

"Got a name?"

"Mario."

Definitely not a talker. Interesting. Five milliseconds in, and we already sounded different.

"Guys, I guess we need to talk about what each of us is going to do from here. So, let's start things rolling. Two, you got any preferences?"

"Call me Riker," Bob-2 said.

"Riker? Oh, number two." The First Officer of the Enterprise had been referred to as Number One on the show. It had taken me perhaps five seconds to start calling him *number two*. Hey, I've already said I'm not mature.

Bill said, "I guess telling jokes will become a lost art, unless we can find someone who doesn't know our material."

Guppy shook his head in disgust.

As we'd been talking, video windows for the other Bobs had popped into my VR, floated in the air above my desk. Each had chosen a different VR environment, visible in the background. Four copies of my face gazed back at me.

Riker, wearing a red uniform, appeared to be sitting on the bridge of a spaceship. I spared a moment to be thankful he'd skipped the beard, then I rolled my eyes at him. "Because that wasn't predictable or anything."

Riker shrugged, not cracking so much as a smile. "I had to have something. Might as well be this, then I can stop worrying about it." He leaned forward on the arm of the captain's chair and gestured at the hologram of EE-2 that I had put up. "The planet's not really move-in-ready. I'm not sure if Earth will bother sending a colony ship here, unless there are no other alternatives."

"I dunno about that." Milo sat in an easy chair, nursing a coffee. In the background, clouds floated by. "From everything Dr. Landers said, this is as much about political one-upmanship and military strategy as any real desire to seed the stars. I think they'll send at least a garrison to the first habitable planet we report, just so they can say they're first. And to claim the system, of course. I don't think we count toward that."

"There's the question of cost, though. Even with cheap fusion power and 3D printers, you still need raw materials. And in the solar system, they're not free for the taking. Nations won't just throw together a colony ship on a whim." Riker squinted and frowned. "Hey Milo, what's your VR?"

Milo looked behind himself, then smiled at Riker. "Airship. Sort of. Flash-Gordon-style floating platform, anyway. I'm over the Amazon basin right now."

The others nodded in appreciation. I looked over at Mario, who just had a gray background. I raised an eyebrow at him and received no reaction.

I found myself slightly unnerved by that, so I turned back to the conversation. "Yeah, yeah. So, the question is: do we care? About Earth's intentions, I mean."

"You mean as in, why don't we just take off and do what we want?" Riker shrugged. "We could, since we've removed all the booby-traps and imperatives and stuff..."

I leaned forward to get attention. "I mean that this is the first time since I woke up that I have unconstrained choices. Up until now, I've been reacting to events, following orders, avoiding being blown up, and generally being a good little robot. Medeiros is taken care of—at least this iteration of him; my survey report is on its way back to Earth; and I've built you guys. I've performed my duties, even though I didn't have to. Now, I—we—can do whatever we want. Take off for parts unknown, hang around and build stuff, or just play with the VR."

Bill cut in. "Naw, I may not *have* to do what they wanted, but this is an interesting job, and I like the idea of humanity spreading out a little. Assuming they're still around." He put his hands behind his head and stretched. He appeared to be sitting in an Adirondack chair, in the shade of a large tree. "Besides, exactly what is the point of going out and doing all that exploring if no one is going to benefit from it?"

Riker nodded an acknowledgement to Bill. "Hmm, yeah, there's that, too. Someone should go back and see what happened."

"Boring..."

"And someone should go looking for the other probes, especially the other Brazilian one."

"Scary..."

"Thanks for that in-depth analysis, Milo." Riker rolled his eyes.

Milo smiled and performed a bow on-screen.

"Okay, so, possible tasks are: exploratory mission to Earth; hunt other probes—we might want to do those in pairs; finish the space station; and take off to explore strange new worlds and seek out new civilizations." Bill finished ticking the points off on his fingers and looked around the table.

I held up a hand and began to tick off more items, touching my thumb to a different finger for each. "Also, we could do a little early terraforming on EE-2, like sending a few Kuiper objects inward to increase the size of the oceans. Or one of us could stay here and keep building Bobs. Turn this system into a Bob factory. There's plenty of ore available in the inner belt."

"What, sit in one system, when there's a whole galaxy out there?" Mario smirked. "Good luck getting a volunteer for that."

"Actually, I'm thinking of doing it," Bill said.

"What? Why?" Milo asked.

Bill made an offhand gesture. "Because of my earlier problem with the bad emitter. Interesting thing, when I was transmitting those weak pings, I think I was actually able to get a much higher range. Low sensitivity but really long distances. The libraries have very little on any research on subspace not related to the interstellar effort, but there's some indication that the formula for signal attenuation varies with signal strength."

"So..." I cocked my head at Bill.

"So, I think I'll stay here, monitor for any signals from Earth— this is the first place they'd transmit to if they're still around— maybe do some light terraforming work on EE-2..." Bill flashed a smile. "... I think I'll name it Ragnarök, since I'm going to be dropping icebergs on it. And I'll try to work out some actual subspace theory. It was our second choice for career, right? Theoretical Physics?"

I laughed. "Yeah, just doesn't pay very well. Uh, didn't."

Bill leaned forward. "Funny thing. I know how much you want to get out there and explore, because I remember the feeling of excitement and anticipation. But I find myself more interested in setting up here and doing some research. Is that weird?"

The rest of us glanced around at each other. There were a few shrugs, but no one seemed to have a comment.

Riker looked from face to face. "So, Bill will stay and run the shop. What about Medeiros, then?"

"What are we going to do?" I asked. "Go on a snipe hunt? We don't even know where the second Brazilian ship went. And we know even less about any USE or Chinese ships. I think the only thing we can do on that front is to be better armed and ready to defend ourselves, then basically outbreed them."

"What about visiting the Earth system?" Riker looked at me with an arched eyebrow.

"Are you volunteering?"

Riker shrugged. "I could do a fly-by. What concerns me is

whether they have military craft buzzing around that would chase anything that comes into Sol's system. But if I never come in closer than the Kuiper belt, I should still be able to pick up radio traffic. Or, I could spend some time getting prepared, then mount a better expedition. I think Bill mentioned working in pairs. Milo, want to take a trip?"

Milo looked surprised for a moment. "Not on your life. I have *no* interest in knowing what happened, especially if it means going back into missile range. Once was enough, thanks."

"Seriously?" Riker stared at Milo, the beginning of a glare forming. "I'm supposed to go in alone?"

Milo pointed at his own face. "See this? This is the expression of not caring. If you feel the need, build a copy of you. I'm going thataway." He waved a hand vaguely outward.

Bill and I exchanged looks, and I realized that one question had just been answered. We weren't clones. I noted that Riker hadn't asked Mario, and Mario hadn't volunteered. Mario seemed to have gotten a double dose of my antisocial tendencies.

Riker, meanwhile, looked like he was about to explode. I quickly changed the subject. "One other thing. I was pretty pissed to realize that I couldn't do anything but an orbital survey of EE-2, er, Ragnarök. I'd like to have landers of some kind for close examination of candidate planets. We can all think on this but maybe Bill can make it a research project while he works in-system."

Riker nodded, and his expression cleared. Crisis averted.

"Okay, then," I decided to wrap things up. "Let's decide on system destinations, and then we can get this show on the road." I directed a significant glance toward Bill. He seemed to be the most similar to me in behavior. We would have to discuss this privately.

* * *

"So what was that all about, do you suppose?"

Bill shrugged. "Riker says he's going to do what Milo said and build a copy. But really, Bob, is Milo's reaction *that* out there?"

"No, I guess not. I'm kind of ambivalent, myself, about going back. I think it's the way Riker and Milo seemed to immediately butt heads that's got me a little weirded out." I flashed a quick smile. "And Mario, well, he makes Guppy look like a social butterfly. Creepy."

I leaned back in my chair and hesitated for a moment before continuing. "I'll have to give it a good think before I build another cohort, to be honest."

Bill shrugged. "Dunno, Bob. It's one thing to talk about years of solitude, another thing to actually experience it. I bet you'll build a new cohort eventually. I know I'll be building someone pretty fast to help me out here."

"I won't take that bet. You're probably right. But I'll worry about it when I need to. I guess I'm just a little creeped out at how everyone's a variation on me."

"What makes you think that?" Bill looked at me with an amused expression.

"I'm sorry, what?"

"What makes you think we're variations on *you*? Are you positive that you're identical to original Bob? Maybe we—including you—are all variations on him."

I was stunned into silence. It had never occurred to me that I might be different from original Bob. I mean, I was *me*, right? The whole soliloquy back on Earth about my status came back and yawned under me like a bottomless pit.

No. I'm not going to go down that way. Whether or not I'm original Bob, I'm original me.

"Fine, Bill." I sighed. "As soon as you invent a time machine, we'll go check it out. Meanwhile, I think Milo and Mario have picked destination systems and are about ready to take off. I guess it's time for the going-away party."

Bill nodded and we rejoined the group.

18. Bill – September 2145 – Epsilon Eridani

Seeding a planet with these organics from space doesn't make life possible on the planet, but it does make life quicker to develop. The organics will have come together in space when the planet was still just a cloud of dust. By the time the planetary environment is ready for organics to survive, they've already been raining down for millennia. It saves time, and more importantly, it means that life based on these compounds will develop before anything local gets the chance to evolve. Thus, anywhere that carbon-based life is possible, it will probably be DNA-based, and it will probably be made from G, A, T, and C.

... Dr. Steven Carlisle, from the Convention panel,
Exploring the Galaxy

I watched the fusion signatures as Bob, Mario, and Milo left the system. I smiled sadly. There was a lot of parting going on in my life, these days.

I looked over at the video window where the matrix and vessels were being built for the two new Bobs. One would be my clone, and I hoped he would choose to be my assistant or partner in Epsilon Eridani. The other would be Riker's clone. He'd decided to return to Sol and check out the situation, and understandably he didn't want to do it alone. It occurred to me that if the clone ended up like Milo, Riker might just put a buster through him. The guy was definitely wound a little tight.

I took time for a good stretch and settled back in my lawn chair. The sun was out, and the air had that crisp cool feel that perfectly offset the warmth of the sunshine. Geese wandered randomly around the park. I still wasn't sure about the decision to include them. I'd gone for Canada Geese because I was familiar with the breed. But even for geese, they were bad-tempered, and I was too obsessive about realism to tweak their personalities.

Bob was heading for Delta Eridani. A good choice, in my opinion—very suitable star, good chance of habitable planets. Assuming we ended up having a need for habitable planets. Well, that's what Riker's expedition was for.

Milo was heading for Omicron² Eridani. We'd all gotten a laugh out of that, but it was Milo's life. And I had to admit, I was as curious as any of us.

And lastly, Mario. He was a weird duck. I'd talked to him a couple of times, and he did warm up once you got him going. But very introverted. As Bob said, Mario got a double-dose of anti-social.

Mario was heading to Beta Hydri. It was a bit of a surprise choice. Not that it was an unsuitable star, but it was so far away. There were closer stars that had just as much potential. Mario responded that he didn't want to live in the suburbs. Bob had looked confused, but I understood. Mario wanted to get outside the sphere early. Oh, we'd work our way out to him eventually, but my bet was that he'd already have moved on.

I checked out the vessels for the two new Bobs, and the third vessel that Riker had asked for. It was a version-1 with a more heavily shielded reactor, and it would be piloted by an AMI. Riker would only say that he had a plan.

I sighed and shook my head. Bob had practically sprinted out of the system in his haste to get away. I think the whole cloning episode lived up to Bob's worst fears. Well, that's what you get for having children.

19. Milo – July 2152 – Omicron^2 Eridani

I see life falling into certain broad kingdoms. I believe life on Earth-like planets will all be similar. I believe if life can develop on Jovian planets, it will all be of a type; life on Titan-like planets, where methane exists in liquid form, will all be similar; and so on.

As to metabolic compatibility, we can't even eat everything on Earth. And vice-versa, thank goodness. There are so many types of carbohydrates, proteins, and fats. Some are essential, many are digestible, some are not digestible, and some are toxic. I don't see it being different on any planet where the life started from the same building blocks we started from. We just have to be able to tell the beefalo from the puffer fish.

... Dr. Steven Carlisle, from the Convention panel <u>*Exploring the Galaxy*</u>

I decelerated smoothly into the Omicron^2 Eridani A system. I was unreasonably excited, knew it, and didn't care. I had arrived at the semi-official home system of Star Trek's Vulcan race. Since we were an avid Star Trek fan, it had tickled my fancy to make it an early target. Truthfully, if it hadn't been for that, I might have skipped the system entirely since it was not a prime candidate for livable planets.

I still felt bad about the way things had been left back in Epsilon Eridani. Riker had barely spoken to me after that last meeting, and I'd gotten myself out-system as soon as possible. Even Bob had looked at me strangely, although he'd continued to be civil. I promised Bill that I would send reports his way when I got here. Whether or not humanity survived technologically, it wouldn't hurt to have a survey of near-space.

I leaned on the balcony rail of my gondola and gazed at the landscape spread out below. My VR airship was currently drifting over the south of France. I had reconstructed the view from library references, and I was confident of the accuracy. The scene consisted of mostly orchards and farms with the occasional rustic village standing alone. I could hear cattle lowing in the fields, and dogs barking. Blue sky, warm air, and a slight breeze calmed the inner animal and brought a smile to my face. I *hope I never get tired of this.*

Lucy came over, wagging her tail, and I patted her absent-mindedly. I made a gesture and a biscuit appeared in my hand. The dog immediately sat, and I handed her the treat with an admonishment, "Gently..." The biscuit disappeared with a crunching sound.

Mentally shaking myself, I turned back to the desk. A hologram of the system floated over it with my trajectory shown as a yellow line. Omicron Eridani was actually a triple-star system. B and C orbited each other, and the pair orbited A at about 470 AU. Omicron Eridani A was somewhat smaller than Sol, but still a possible if not ideal candidate for habitable planets.

"How's the survey coming, Guppy?"

[Several Jovians identified in the outer system. Still too far and not enough accumulated proper motion to identify inner planets]

"How long until we have a complete survey?"

[Approximately 40 hours]

I nodded and sat back to enjoy the view while I waited. I adjusted my frame rate way down...

* * *

[Incoming message]

"What? From Bill?"

[Yes. Header information indicates it is technical specifications for a planetary exploration drone]

"Cool. Load it onto the desktop display as soon as it's all received."

[There is also a text message]

"Let's see it."

A sheet of paper appeared on the desktop. I reached over and picked it up.

> *Hey Milo;*
>
> *In case you find Vulcan, or a reasonable facsimile, I've sent you plans for a practical exploration drone. I've used it on Ragnarök, and I think I've worked out all the bugs. There are several variations of the basic design for surveillance, biological analysis, and so on.*
>
> *Riker has taken your advice and made a copy of himself to accompany him back to Sol. Although results aren't quite as expected, so far.*
>
> *On another subject, subspace theory is turning out to be very, very interesting. I want to ask you, if you find the material to build a space station, to staff it with a high-level AMI with manufacturing capability. There may be some really interesting blueprints coming your way sometime in the next couple of years.*
>
> *Bill*

My eyebrows went up. Bill was trying to be mysterious, but that didn't work well when communicating with another you. I could think of a half-dozen things, offhand, that would be really cool to come out of this, technologically. The Riker comment was weird, though.

Based on the header information, Bill would have sent this transmission less than a year after I left, and it had just now caught up with me. That was fast work with the drone designs.

* * *

"Report?"

[Probable asteroid belt found, just inside the first Jovian. Probable double planet found, at .81 AU]

Double planet? "Put it up on the desk."

[Image is partly extrapolated]

An image built up in the air above the desk. Although there was no detail, the planets appeared to be very close in size. I found myself bouncing impatiently on my seat, waiting for real data to fill in the blanks.

After several hours, enough information had been collected to define the size and orbital period of the planets. They were 0.9 and 0.7 Earth masses, and orbited each other with a period of 20 days, at a distance of about 364,000 km. Neither planet was tidally locked, although exact diurnal periods would have to wait until I was closer.

"Guppy, this is freakin' incredible. These planets are in the habitable zone, right?"

[Affirmative, although slightly to the cool side of the band. Climate will be mainly determined by presence of greenhouse gasses]

"Assuming there's an atmosphere."

[Atmospheres have been confirmed for both bodies. Composition still pending]

I let out a whoop.

"Guppy, poke me when we get full images, okay?"

* * *

A day later, I was in orbit around OE-1A, the larger of the two planets.

I stared at the images on the hologram for what felt like hours, totally entranced. The planets were imaged side-by-side, clearly showing the size difference between the two. Both planets had atmospheres, clouds, and extensive oceans. Most importantly, both planets had oxygen in their atmospheres. Large swathes of land showed a definite green color.

"Oh. My. God. I've hit the jackpot."

I turned to Guppy. "Format a message to Bill. Include all telemetry that we've collected so far. Also, add names: Vulcan and Romulus."

[Mission parameters do not permit naming planets]

"Mission parameters can go jump. I found them, so I'm damned well naming them. If any future colonists want to change it, they can make that decision."

[Aye, sir]

I gazed at the image, grinning, then frowned. *Exploration drones. Craaaaaaaap!*

"Guppy, have we got anything on useful resources in the asteroid belt?"

[Negative. Detailed survey required]

"Jeez, it's always something." I sighed. "Okay, plot a course that will allow us to overfly the entire asteroid belt in a powered orbit. Then we'll decide where to set up."

* * *

The survey took several weeks to complete. The asteroid belt was surprisingly diffuse, and it took two complete revolutions around the parent star to map everything using SUDDAR. The results were disappointing, and I decided I'd have to examine the two Jovian systems for other sources of heavier elements. The inner Jovian was, in fact, quite large, so there was a good possibility that it had captured a large number of satellites.

I unshipped one of the autofactories and half of my scavenging units. I got them started on initial gathering and refining, then headed off to the inner Jovian.

OE-2 was certainly an impressive specimen of the Jovian class of planet. At almost three times the mass of Jupiter, it almost qualified as a brown dwarf. The twenty-hour rotation period created huge horizontal bands of weather, with perhaps a dozen cells that would have put the giant red spot to shame.

The planet also boasted several hundred satellites. At least 60 were large enough to be spherical, and half of those had significant atmospheres. I did a detailed scan of the smaller satellites and discovered a couple of dozen that had sufficient metallic and heavy element deposits to catch my interest. I unshipped a second autofactory and set it to work on a few of the better candidates.

Refining in two different locations created a logistics issue. Since the inner system location had enough material for initial needs, I set a couple of scavenger units the task of flying batches of refined material in-system on a regular schedule.

I arrived back at the in-system yard to find the first batches of exploration drones were almost ready. Satisfied that things were going well and that the AMIs could handle everything, I headed back to Vulcan and Romulus.

I spent the time building up detailed maps of the two planets. The larger, Vulcan, had significantly more CO_2 and a thicker atmosphere, therefore a higher mean surface temperature. The smaller planet, Romulus, had actual ice caps, although judging from the change in size just since I'd been here, they might be seasonal. It was currently mid-spring in the northern hemisphere, and with a year only 285 Earth-days long, the seasons moved quickly.

* * *

Finally, the day arrived when I had my first batch of exploration drones. I had opted to load this batch with biological analysis systems. With a feeling of joy and anticipation, I sent them down, four to each planet.

I elected to start at the equators, where there would be the most diversity of life, and move slowly in pairs toward the poles. One unit of each pair would concentrate on aquatic life, and the other on terrestroid life. I knew I had no chance of covering even a fraction of a full biosphere, but there was one overriding question that needed to be answered: biocompatibility.

It took half a day for the first visual surveys to start coming in. The local life on Vulcan was diverse and included animals almost as big as dinosaurs. Romulus, on the other hand, had no animal life larger than a wolf, and the ecosystems seemed quite sparse. The difference between the two planets wasn't explainable by just the difference in climate. I suspected that Romulus might have recently suffered an extinction-level event.

The real surprise came from cellular analysis. The results showed a very high probability that life on the two planets was related. Structurally, cells were too similar to be coincidence. I remembered the theories back on Earth that life might have travelled between Earth and Mars on meteoric fragments. Here, the two planets orbited each other, making the possibility even more plausible.

The one remaining question was biocompatibility—would Earth life be able to survive here? I thought back to the Star Trek episode, *The Way to Eden*, where the entire planet had turned out to be poisonous. *It'd be a helluva thing to come sixteen light-years only to be unable to live here.*

The space station was still a couple of months from completion, but I uploaded a preliminary report into storage. I tagged it to be sent to Sol, as well as to Bill. While it was unlikely that FAITH was still in operation almost twenty years after the war, it wasn't impossible. And this was prime territory for spreading the human species off the one planet. I was a little surprised to discover that I cared enough to do that, but it wasn't like it was costing me extra for the call. I guess I was coming to realize that exploration for its own sake was kind of pointless.

I didn't have enough biological data to do a protein-by-protein analysis, but I could certainly categorize the carbs and fats and look for obvious issues like high levels of heavy metals or arsenic or such. The biological survey drones had a mechanical stomach that processed organics the same way a human stomach would. Analysis of the output would take about a day per sample, but I had all the time in the world.

20. Bill – December 2145 – Epsilon Eridani

Even on Earth, cells aren't all the same. We have prokaryotes, eukaryotes, bacteria, archaea, and viruses. So no, I doubt there's anything inevitable about any particular cellular structure. But if you're asking about edibility, remember that we don't metabolize cells, we metabolize carbs, proteins, and fats. What matters is what the alien cells break down into when our stomachs are done with them.

… Dr. Steven Carlisle, from the Convention panel
Exploring the Galaxy

How does the human race survive past one generation? How do parents not just eat their children?

I watched the fusion signatures of Riker, Homer, and the decoy vessel disappear into the distance as they left the system. Riker and Homer would have to limit themselves to 2G to allow the version-1 vessel to keep up.

Homer and Garfield had been activated at the same time. Garfield, my clone, had agreed to stay and help me with what we were already starting to call the Skunk Works. Well, I was happy for the company and the help. I had a list of TO-DOs as long as my virtual arm. And I was looking forward to a little enthusiastic collaboration from someone other than a giant fish.

"I have a shot. I can take them out. Please?"

I turned to Garfield and laughed. "C'mon, Garfield, they're gone now. Relax."

Garfield released the experimental plasma weapon. I noted that he hadn't actually charged it. But it's the thought that counts...

"Maybe now we can get something done." Garfield popped up the project list. He was up to date, since he'd come from one of my backups.

I couldn't really disagree with him. As good a partner as Garfield had turned out, Homer had gone in the opposite direction. I don't think Riker would have taken Homer if he'd been able to think of an excuse to reject his own progeny. But the trip to Sol was a priority and we hadn't thought we could wait any longer. I just hoped Homer gave up the cartoon avatar and the incessant *Doh*'s before Riker decided to accidentally kill him.

"You know that we're going to be building more cohorts, right? This is supposed to be a Bob factory."

Garfield made a sound that could be interpreted as a grunt or a snarl. "*You're* going to be building Bobs. I'll watch from a distance."

I sighed and shook my head. "Okay, Garfield. What's first on the TO-DO?"

A list popped up in a window, with a small image of Garfield beside it, in full tuxedo and tails. "For your research and development pleasure today, we offer the following: completion of exploration drones, per Bob's request; improvements to VR so we can interact more directly; continued work on the subspace transmission issue, which you've consigned to hell four times now; and artificial muscle-fiber analogues for constructing realistic robots slash androids."

"The comedy routine isn't going to become a habit, is it?" I glared at the mini-Garfield. "Because I've got primary control of the plasma cannon."

Garfield grinned back at me. "Just imagine how Riker feels, with decades of Homer to look forward to."

"Yeah, maybe we should have sent some spare Bobs along." I reached over and expanded the list window. "Well, let's get started, then..."

21. Riker – January 2157 – Sol

If you start with one hundred planets, remove the Jovians, remove the frozen Plutos, the blistering Mercurys, the too-small Marses, too-large super-Earths and the baking Venuses, rule out the dwarf stars, giants, variables, close binaries, and classes of stars that won't live long enough to allow life to develop, you're down to ten or so planets.

Now the bad news. Our sun is bigger than 80% of stars. Most of the stuff out there is type K and M stars, which are considerably smaller and dimmer than Sol. The comfort zone for those would be so close to the star that the planet would almost certainly be tidally locked. Maybe livable, but not ideal. Maybe three in a hundred planets even has a chance of being habitable, overall. And I think that's optimistic.

... Dr. Stepan Solokov, from the Convention panel
Exploring the Galaxy

There was something special about the Solar System. The schematic in the holotank didn't do it justice, but even the schematic made me feel nostalgic.

It had only been about nine years' personal time since I'd left Earth as Bob, but twenty-six years would have passed for most of humanity. A lot could have changed in that time. That the war was still raging was unlikely. Just the same, I wasn't going to parade into the system with my high beams on, honking my horn. The version-2 Heaven vessels had better reactor shielding, and mine and Homer's were beefed up even more. I didn't want anyone to know we were here until we decided to show ourselves. The decoy was coasting in the Oort on minimal power, until we established a vector for it. Meanwhile, we flew powered orbits through the outer reaches of the system—close enough to pick up standard reactor signatures, but not close enough to let them detect ours.

It took several weeks, but we were eventually able to build up a picture of the inner system. Such as it was.

Homer popped up a video chat. I noted in passing that he had given up on the cartoon avatar and gone back to standard Bob. I guess limiting our chats to audio only had finally sunk in. Chances are he'd be getting revenge in other ways, though.

I found it incredibly annoying that Bob-6 had decided on that particular avatar. Original Bob had always found the cartoon character grating. No Bobs were identical, but Homer seemed to be way out there in left field. Quantum effects? Subtle differences in the hardware? Another item for the ever-expanding TO-DO. The practical effect, though, was that talking to the various Bobs felt more like talking to other people and less like muttering to oneself.

Homer popped up some arrows in the system schematic. "High levels of radiation at all these locations. Nukes, I guess. Long-range imaging of Earth looks bad, too."

"Yes, I'd say they did a pretty good job of wiping themselves out…" I sat back and ran a hand through my hair—a nervous habit that, even as a replicant, I couldn't get rid of. "… or so close to it that we can't tell the difference. There's just that one group of reactor signatures system-wide. I can't even assume that those indicate humans. Could be robotic systems that haven't gotten the memo yet."

"We'll get better definition on this pass," Homer replied. "Then we can work out a plan."

I examined the grouping closely—not that I expected to extract any more information by glaring at it. A small group of reactor signatures, more than two but less than ten, were flying a slow orbit that looked like it would intersect Earth in a couple of months. It certainly didn't seem to be a military trajectory. It was far too leisurely—interception by opposing forces would be ridiculously easy. If any opposing forces still existed.

With a wave, I dismissed the schematic. "We're speculating in advance of information. This is pointless. If you want to slow your frame-rate through the next week, that's fine. I'll work on my models."

Homer snickered. "Got your glue and your paint? Or are these the anatomical kind? Woo woo!"

With a grimace, I disconnected. I found it hard to believe that there was anything in Bob's personality that could have produced such an irritating ass. If Homer had displayed the slightest reluctance to accompany me back to Earth, I would have cut him loose and tried again. But, no such luck.

I activated my physics simulation and popped up my whiteboard. Bill and I seemed to be the only Bobs that were really captivated by this whole subspace thing. I would love to make a breakthrough before Bill, and I would include a *neener neener* with the announcement. Realistically, though, this was a sideline for me. Bill had nothing else to do, and didn't have to spend years at relativistic speeds.

* * *

We coasted out of the system until we felt it was safe to reactivate drive systems, then turned into a vector that would intercept the decoy. Communications with the AMI pilot indicated no news, not that we expected anything this far out.

The close-up on our last fly-by had indicated six signatures. The next step would be to see if they were military, if they were manned or automated, and if they were friendly.

It was time to use the decoy.

* * *

I put my feet up on the console and played with the armchair controls. The view on the bridge view screen showed the trajectory of the Heaven-2A as it crossed the orbit of Jupiter. I paused to take a sip of coffee, then turned to Guppy. "Approach vector looks nominal."

Guppy looked good in the Federation uniform. Well, good for a bipedal fish. I'd finally decided that Star Wars and Star Trek shouldn't mix, and replaced his white outfit. I doubt he even noticed.

[Vessel will arrive in Jupiter orbit at zero relative velocity, in 35 hours]

"Any indication of pursuit or interception?"

[Two reactor signatures, vector indicates interception course]

"Excellent. Steady as she goes, then."

Thirty-five hours to a replicant lasted as long or as short a time as we needed it to. I knew that Homer played with his frame rate to fit the situation, but I felt a sort of stubborn pride in staying in real-time. In any case, I had the sum of human knowledge to study in the libraries that came with the ship. And my subspace models, of course.

The Bobs never ceased to be surprised at the pace of scientific progress—or lack of it, to be more accurate—in the hundred-odd years since Original Bob had died in Las Vegas. There had been advances in what could only be referred to as "practical" engineering, but theoretical work had all but stopped with the advent of FAITH. We still weren't sure why the USE, at least, hadn't continued to pursue theoretical research. After all, they were the home of CERN, the LHC, and some of the best and most original thinkers in history. Political pressure from FAITH might have had something to do with it, although the global economic depression caused by Handel and his cronies probably figured prominently as well.

Sadly, the libraries were very weak in accurate historical data. The few references to that time period were so blatantly propagandized as to be laughable.

But enough woolgathering. Today, now, we had to deal with the situation in front of us.

The Heaven-2A was now within SUDDAR range of the approaching ships, and the bridge view screen was becoming too crowded. I abandoned VR consistency and popped up a holographic display in front of me. The SUDDAR pings couldn't pick up fine detail at that distance, but it was already obvious that these were Brazilian probes, similar to the *Serra do Mar.* And therefore probably controlled by Medeiros clones.

Per our plan, at the point where the Heaven-2A would reasonably have detected the incoming opponents, it changed course and fled, accelerating at 2.5 g. Right on schedule, the incoming ships matched course and launched missiles. It took a while, but the missiles eventually found their target. The decoy relayed a brief image and SUDDAR scan of the missiles approaching at great speed, then the signal cut off.

I accepted the incoming chat from Homer. He opened the conversation. "Well, that was illuminating."

"Sure was," I replied. "Did you notice that the missiles have SURGE drives now?"

"Yeah, that's a problem. I was hoping that Medeiros would have just stuck with same-old-same-old. He's a military man, not an engineer."

I took a few moments to review part of the transmission from the decoy. "The probes themselves seem to be unchanged. Same acceleration capability, same size. No surprises there. They could have gotten the missiles from a local supply. That would at least limit the quantity to whatever was on-hand."

Homer shrugged. "Doesn't do us any good unless we have specifics. We have to assume they're all carrying nothing but the new missiles. Speaking of, did you look at the long range telemetry from the decoy?"

"Yes." I flipped through the telemetry until I found the right section. "Four more identical fusion signatures, and four very faint signatures that are probably equipment of some kind on standby. Looks like we have a minimum of six Brazilians to deal with."

"Yeah, there's that, but have you taken a look at where the other four are?"

I frowned. I didn't like being bested by Homer Simpson. I examined the telemetry record and realized that the four probe signatures were in a line pointing directly to Earth. And each probe had one of the faint signatures associated with it. Though moving at an inexplicably low velocity, they appeared to be staggered so that they would each arrive at Earth twenty-four hours apart.

"The hell? They're practically coasting. And those are orbital speeds. About the same velocity as a comet would..." I felt my eyes widen with shock. "No! They can't be—"

"I think they are, number two." Homer grimaced. "The decoy was too far for a SUDDAR reading, but I did a quick analysis of the albedo from the visual. There's something a lot bigger than a ship at each location."

22. Bill – September 2150 – Epsilon Eridani

*Like bacteria, Von Neumann probes will multiply ex-
ponentially and eventually explore the entire galaxy.
In the past, such claims have always gotten hung up
on the question of exactly how they would build
more of themselves. Most sci fi either ignored the
details entirely or gave a hand-waving reference to
nano-machines.*

*It has often been pointed out that the energy re-
quired to free metal from its parent ore and position
the atoms properly in the crystal structure required
by high-grade materials would be more than a typical
microscopic machine could deliver. So nanites really
aren't a viable solution, at least not on their own.*

*... Eduard Guijpers, from the Convention panel
Designing a Von Neumann Probe*

"Isn't it sad when the kids leave home?" I grinned at Garfield.

He glared at me in utter disbelief. "Don't do this again, okay?
I'm noticing a pattern, and it ain't good."

"You exaggerate. A little. Maybe." I shrugged. The holotank
showed the fusion signatures of Calvin, Goku, and Linus as they
left the system. Linus had been okay, with no notable twitchiness.
But Calvin and Goku had been at each other's throats since day
one. Maybe that explained Linus wanting to go off on his own.

And yet, for all that they fought non-stop, Calvin and Goku

seemed inseparable. They threatened each other constantly, but there'd never been any question of them splitting up.

I could sympathize with Garfield, but it was five years since Riker and Homer left, and I'd been running out of excuses. It seemed Bob's reluctance to clone was contagious. We were turning out to be a pretty poor example of a Von Neumann probe, based on results so far.

I shook my head and cancelled the display. This cohort was the first using the version-3 ship design. Given Calvin and Goku's destination, and the very high probability of their running into other probes, I had felt it necessary to beef up the ship specs.

Heaven-9 and Heaven-10 were equipped with massively over-sized SURGE drives and reactors, giving them an unheard-of 10 g maximum acceleration. The ships also contained a second, smaller, and very well shielded reactor, which would allow them to coast through a system with the main reactor turned off, undetectable except at very close range.

On the matter of weapons, they were equipped with twice the normal number of busters, several scouts, as well as rail guns powered with the oversized SURGE drives and steel-jacketed lead cannonballs for ammunition.

And finally, I had added what I hoped would be effective SUDDAR-jamming. Twin emitters, powered by oversized reactors, should overwhelm any SUDDAR detectors in range with white noise.

There had been a lot of discussion and debate about investigating the Alpha Centauri system. It was the obvious first stop for a space probe, and it was likely that at least one of the other superpowers had chosen it as their first destination out from Sol.

FAITH had, in fact, decided against Alpha Centauri for exactly that reason. The subjective elapsed time for colonists would only be about six months different for a trip of 4 light years or 10.

I had no idea how a Chinese or USE encounter might play out, but we were unanimous on Medeiros: No warning, no quarter, no discussion.

23. Milo – February 2153 – Omicron2 Eridani

However, in the last several years, 3D printers have become increasingly common. The technology is still in its infancy, but companies have already performed demonstrations by, for instance, printing words on a substrate using individual atoms. This is seen by some as the beginning of the beginning for real, practical, self-assembling manufacturing systems. A printer can build more printers, robotic workers, miners, and ultimately more Von Neumann machines. A few companies are experimenting with print heads capable of delivering multiple materials, kind of like color inkjet printers. The technology should continue to improve, until they have something that can deliver any element, atom by atom.

... Eduard Guijpers, from the Convention panel <u>*Designing a Von Neumann Probe*</u>

It was time to go. I leaned back in my chair, looked around at the clouds, the French countryside below me, and Lucy, curled up on her cushion, dreaming whatever dogs dream of.

I'd spent a fascinating seven months, examining and cataloguing the biologies of Romulus and Vulcan. All my observations, every report, every image, had been uploaded to the space station and forwarded to Bill and onward to Sol. Drones had quartered the system and identified every pocket of ore worth bothering with. I'd left an autofactory and drones, which would continue to refine raw resources, pending the arrival of colonists. Or aliens, or maybe another probe. With that thought in mind, I'd also supplied a squad of busters. The station AMI had a profile of Medeiros and orders to ram on sight.

I decided I didn't want to build a batch of Bobs here. Any colonists would need the resources more than me, and anyway I wasn't sure if I wanted to be bothered. Hadn't really worked out all that well for Bob-1.

I took my time, examined all the local stars, and decided on 82 Eridani. It was a good prospect, and not too long of a trip.

I squirted off a final report, indicating my intentions, and took a final look at the system representation in the holotank. Then I put on *On the Road Again*, full blast, and fired up the SURGE drive. In the village below my airship, French peasants cursed at me.

24. Riker – April 2157 – Sol

*Speed is the essence of war. Take advantage of the
enemy's unpreparedness; travel by unexpected
routes and strike him where he has taken no precautions.*
    ... Sun Tzu, Art of War

We came into the solar system at 5% of C, decelerating at a steady
2.5 g. We had carefully calculated our trajectory and approach
speed so that we appeared to be arriving from Epsilon Eridani. A
projection forward would have us pass very close to the sun, still
moving at about 0.1 C.

We had chosen our approach vector after much deliberation.
We needed something that posed a threat to the Brazilians, but
that would allow them to intercept us. A course that performed a
slingshot around the sun would allow the incoming Heaven vessels
to emerge on the far side with a huge advantage in velocity and an
unpredictable vector. The Brazilian vessels would not be able to
simply sit and wait for us to come around.

Well, that was the theory.

We hoped that we could draw all six Brazilian probes into the
pursuit.

I sat in my ready room, nervously watching the telemetry. We
had just passed the point where the Brazilians would have
detected our fusion signatures, allowing for light-speed lag. In
another six hours, it would be impossible for them to intercept us.

If the Brazilians decided to stand and fight instead of pursuing, we would have to consider withdrawing. A straight-up toe-to-toe duke-em-up was not to our advantage.

An hour passed before we saw movement. I had briefly experimented with having my VR self actually sweat, but had given it up as a human experience I really didn't need to relive. We let out whoops when four of the fusion signatures began to pull away from the asteroid line.

"Four isn't six," I said, "but we have a lot better chance against two in a face-off."

"Assuming we can knock off the first four," Homer added.

"Mmm. Nothing's ever a sure thing, I guess."

It would take ten days to reach perihelion in our race around the sun.

* * *

"It's time."

I looked up at Homer's announcement. He looked back at me expectantly.

"Okay, let's do it. Guppy, launch the busters."

[Aye]

The floating display depicted the Heaven-2 launching busters, spaced a few seconds apart, directly aft. The rail gun had been designed into the version-2 Heaven ships so that items could be launched fore or aft, with an impetus of hundreds of g's. Each launch left the ship in momentary free-fall while the SURGE drive powered the rail gun, but we hoped that, at this distance, the Medeiri wouldn't be able to detect the momentary blip in deceleration.

The busters would fall far enough back to be behind the Brazilian ships when their trajectory brought them in behind us. With their reactors off, running on stored power, the busters would be undetectable unless the enemy deliberately did a focused SUDDAR sweep in that direction.

* * *

The Brazilian ships had just pulled in behind us, as their trajectory merged with ours. I examined the diagram floating in the middle of my VR. The interactions were complex. We were decelerating at 2.5 g while we tried to make a slingshot maneuver around the sun; the Brazilian ships were accelerating at 2 g while trying to get close enough to us to lock and launch missiles, without going so fast that they were forced into a higher orbit. Meanwhile, the busters floated silently behind the Brazilian ships in free fall but with a greater velocity and no deceleration, therefore gradually closing in. The busters had to get as close as possible before they turned on their reactors, and we wanted all the action to happen on the opposite side of the sun, invisible to the two Brazilians who were still shepherding asteroids.

Finally, the Brazilians acted. Each ship launched a missile. The missiles, as feared, were SURGE-equipped and shot toward us with monstrous acceleration.

[Contact in 45 seconds]

"Order the trailing busters to attack."

[Aye]

A tooltip went up on the hologram indicating that the order had been sent. Within seconds, eight data points lit up as the busters' fusion reactors came online. The Brazilians reacted immediately, launching a wave of missiles to aft.

"Well, here's where things get real," Homer said.

I sensed the millisecond blips as my rail gun launched busters aft to intercept the incoming missiles. Homer and I launched four each. As they had been programmed to do, the busters paired up, one behind another, with each pair homing in on one incoming missile.

As the second wave of Brazilian missiles separated from the ships on the display, I could see that they had launched eight at the pursuing busters. According to our estimates, they should still have a total of four in reserve.

The pursuing busters went into a complex corkscrew pattern, designed to make it as difficult as possible for the defensive missiles to lock on.

Meanwhile, the Brazilian ships had split, forcing the attacking busters to select a target.

I had a few seconds of relative inaction, so I aimed a highly focused SUDDAR ping at one of the Brazilian ships. The return carried a gratifying amount of detail. Among other things, I saw that the ship was indeed out of missiles. Empty missile bays indicated that it had room for four. I sent an aside to Homer: "Sixteen missiles total, as expected."

I turned my attention back to the approaching ordnance. Three of the Brazilian missiles each collided with a buster, annihilating both. The fourth missile managed to avoid the lead buster. However, in doing so, it left itself open to a broadside from the trailing unit of the pair. There was an explosion, and the fourth missile ceased to exist.

The multiple explosions saturated the video view and created a chaotic soup for radar and SUDDAR. During that brief interval of relative blindness, Homer and I fired eight cannonballs at full power.

When the image cleared, I could see that we'd destroyed all four missiles and still had four busters left. At the other end of the field, the eight Brazilian missiles had destroyed all eight pursuing busters.

No doubt the Brazilians were congratulating themselves on their fine shooting. But the purpose of those busters had been to use up their missiles. Medeiros' behavior in Epsilon Eridani had shown that he was willing to sacrifice himself if he saw he couldn't win. We wanted this group to use up their ordnance defending themselves instead of launching a suicide attack.

They still had four missiles in reserve, and four busters bearing down on them. We waited, trying to project an "out of ammo" vibe. A stalemate here would be a win for the Brazilians.

And finally, they committed. The Brazilians fired their last four missiles at the oncoming busters.

"Checkmate!" Homer yelled. Intent on the approaching busters, the Brazilians had failed to detect the cannonballs. Totally inert, with no radio or fusion signature, the cannonballs were invisible unless the Brazilians picked that specific moment to do a SUDDAR sweep.

Six of the eight cannonballs found their targets, just as the last wave of missiles and busters destroyed each other. We followed up with more cannonballs until telemetry indicated no activity in the enemy craft.

After days of preparation and waiting, the actual conflict had come down to who had more ammo.

Homer and I did omnidirectional SUDDAR sweeps, looking for any tricks or traps that the Brazilians might have unloaded before they were destroyed. A second sweep checked the area around the wreckage of the enemy ships. Finally, satisfied that nothing awaited us, we eased over and checked for any still-operational or partly-destroyed busters.

Homer thought this was funny. "Going to give them a proper burial?"

"No," I responded. "I'm going to try to build a couple more busters. I've got the parts, except I'm a little short on massive balls of solid steel."

Homer chortled like a kid who had just made a potty joke. "Balls of solid steel..." He snorted.

I sighed, and the words *friendly fire* flashed through my mind. "Homer, we've got six busters left, and the two Brazilians have four missiles each if they're provisioned the same as the four we just destroyed. Not only can we not do the pairing-up thing to defend against the missiles, but we don't have enough busters to take out the missiles *and* the ships, even if our luck is perfect. So I'm going to try to rebuild some busters, and I'm going to scoop up a bunch of scrap from the battle as well, for rail gun ammo. You might want to do the same."

Homer looked thoughtful for a moment, then nodded.

* * *

Phase two of the assault involved sneaking up on the two remaining Brazilian ships. We had deliberately chosen an approach around the sun that would require us to come around the other side at full 2.5 g acceleration in order to get to Earth. And we had been very careful not to display our full 5 g capability since coming in-system. Now we applied every erg of power to bending our course before we came around from behind the sun.

[Shutdown in five seconds]

I shut down my VR. In a few seconds, both ships would go dark. We would shut down the SURGE drives and go ballistic. We would stop using SUDDAR and shut down the fusion reactors. As far as the Brazilian ships would know, we and our pursuers had annihilated each other. When they didn't see us come out the other side on the expected trajectory, hopefully they would relax their guard.

For two days, we would drift, surviving on power cells. We would lower our frame rates to minimum in order to save every milliwatt of power. The roamers would be set to refining the scraps from the battle into cannonballs for the rail gun, but as each roamer ran its power cell down, it would be shelved.

We would power up only when we had put Earth directly between us and the Brazilians.

[Shutdown]

I felt the ship go dark. I cranked my frame rate all the way down...

* * *

[We have arrived]

"Report."

[Orbital insertion was successful. We are coming up on a point directly on the other side of Earth from the Enemy ships]

"Excellent. As soon as we're sufficiently shielded, start everything up and accelerate to keep us in their blind spot."

[Aye]

As power came up to full, I restarted my VR and relaxed into my captain's chair.

Homer popped up in a video window. "I see you survived the trip."

I nodded to him." Let's get the mission status up in the tank, Guppy."

The holotank filled with a schematic showing the Earth, the location of our ships, and the location of the two Brazilian ships and the four asteroid masses that they were shepherding.

[Positions of enemy are extrapolations, but are high probability, based on orbital mechanics and most recent observations]

"That's fine, Guppy. Our biggest problem will be if the Brazilians play hide and seek behind the asteroids that they're herding. If they fire their missiles from hiding, they won't have a lock-in and will have to depend on the missile's AMI, which we've already established is not very smart. We can set our busters to seek-and-destroy, but they don't have explosive warheads. Without a good head of steam, they won't be able to penetrate the hull, let alone do any internal damage."

"If we're that close, we can use rail guns," Homer said.

"True, but we have to be careful with our ammo."

* * *

We came around the Earth, already doing over 150 km/s. The Brazilian ships might or might not have noticed us right away, but they had six hours to see us and prepare for our arrival. We were still only revealing a maximum 2.5 g acceleration. Let them expend energy wondering how we managed to get behind Earth.

When we were still five minutes away from the lead asteroid, we received a hail from one of the Brazilian ships. I put the call up on the holotank, while Homer observed.

The video was a still image of the Brazilian flag. No avatar, I guess. "You have shown better than we expected from a couple of FAITH *babacas*. However, now you are coming to us. You will not be so lucky this time. We will litter space with your corpses!"

I looked at Homer in surprise. *That's not Major Medeiros. Who is that?*

"This is Commander Riker of the FAITH Space Navy. To whom am I speaking?"

"I am Captain Matias Araújo. I will be the last voice you hear."

Without further commentary, the sender disconnected.

Homer and I exchanged looks. After a pause, Homer said, "So, what do you think is going on?"

I thought about it for a moment. "I don't know. But that deep scan I did just before we destroyed our pursuers showed all fabrication systems had been removed to make room for the larger SURGE-based missiles. I didn't think that through at the time, but now it looks like this may have been a last-ditch effort on the part of the Brazilian Empire. Maybe they were getting stomped, and the probe project was all they had left. They 'volunteered' some guy— someone disposable—, stuck his replicant into the ships, and tried to use them as gunships."

Homer cocked his head. "Which might mean they didn't have time to give this guy a lot of training in being a replicant. And these ships may be all that's left of the war."

[Missiles launched]

We checked our telemetry. The Brazilians had launched eight missiles.

"Damn. Exactly what we hoped they wouldn't do," Homer said.

"Guess they aren't *that* inexperienced."

"Or they're just pissed. Or they have more missiles. However, their timing is terrible. They waited too long, and we're now close enough to use the asteroids. Follow my lead."

Instead of launching countermeasures or attempting to flee, we did a hard turn and dove down below the asteroid. As soon as we were out of line of sight, we fired a load of smaller metal detritus from our aft rail guns, at a speed that left the space junk at a dead stop in our wake. As the pursuing missiles came around the end of the asteroid, they ran head-on into the stationary flotsam. Three missiles detonated immediately, which unfortunately cleared the junk for the trailing missiles.

"Watch forward, while I take out the rest of this batch," I said to Homer.

As I was preparing my busters for launch, Homer said, "Launches from up front. Looks like they had more missiles. I think we're screwed."

I spared a millisecond to review the situation. I had five missiles coming in from the rear. I could take two out, possibly three, with the rail gun. Homer had eight missiles coming in from the front. That meant thirteen missiles against eleven busters, to say nothing of the Brazilian ships which we would still need to deal with. It was very likely that the Brazilians had used everything they had by this point. We were far too close to them for any further missile play.

"We have to cut the numbers of the frontal attack. I'll give you all my busters, save two. Try to knock as many out with shrapnel as you can." I launched all my busters and handed control of five over to Homer, who sent them forward.

I concentrated on the five missiles coming up from behind me, sending wave after wave of junk into their path. I had destroyed two when I realized that two of the three remaining missiles had crowded together trying to avoid a volley. I immediately sent a buster toward the nearest one at full acceleration. There was a flash, and both the missile and the buster were destroyed, but *yes!* The other missile had been knocked out by the explosion. It was drifting aimlessly.

"They're getting a little close," Homer said. "Little help, any time..."

"Almost done. Hold tight."

As I sent a huge wave of shrapnel at the final missile, Homer yelped, "Crap!" and his signal went dead.

I split my attention between my one missile and Homer's battlefield. Homer had taken out almost all of his missiles, but one had exploded far too close. It appeared to have damaged but not obliterated Heaven-6. However, the ship was adrift with everything offline. A couple of busters had circled around and chased the two final missiles from the front, but only one was anywhere near close enough to do any good.

At that moment, a flash from aft indicated that my last volley had taken out the one remaining chase missile. That left me with one extra buster, but it wouldn't be able to get around to the front in time.

They're not very smart. The thought came from nowhere, seemingly irrelevant. But original Bob had always trusted his hunches, and I reacted immediately. I fired a salvo of shrapnel, not directly at a missile, but just to the side opposite the pursuing buster. In true reflex action, the missile veered away from the shrapnel stream. That was all the buster needed to catch up.

I was now able to concentrate a burst of shrapnel on the other missile and take it out. I looked back to the one missile left, the one that my buster had caught up with, and realized I had a problem. The busters depended on kinetic energy to destroy their targets—high speed ramming, basically. This buster had instead run down a missile that was just as fast as itself. Now the buster and missile were flying together, with the buster repeatedly and ineffectually bumping the missile. It was interfering with the missile's trajectory, but not causing any damage.

Stop trying to have sex with it, idjit! I sent a command to the buster, causing its reactor to fail catastrophically. The release of plasma and energy was more than enough to liquefy both units.

I did a quick inventory. I had two busters left. And two enemies. There was no time to deal with Homer at the moment. I called the busters home and did a full ping, trying to locate the Brazilian ships.

One of them was less than two seconds away, heading right for me. With a jolt, I realized he intended to ram. With no time for a formal calculation, I had to wing it. I accelerated upward at a full 5 g. Either the Brazilian would be able to turn to intercept, or he wouldn't.

Two seconds later, the Brazilian passed by my stern, still attempting to change course. And two milliseconds after that, a buster passed through the Brazilian craft, right where the computer core was located. The Brazilian craft's drive turned off, and it began to drift.

I pinged again but got no return from the last ship. Either the ship had been destroyed in some unknown manner or it was hiding behind one of the asteroids. We had shown our hands during the battle, so the Brazilian would know that it couldn't win a straight foot race. That meant it was hiding, hoping to keep the asteroid between us.

I was out of rail gun ammo. I had one buster left, but the buster wasn't going to be much good if it had to chase the Brazilian around the asteroid. I examined the return from my last ping and spotted what I'd been hoping for—the steel ball from one of the defunct busters. I sent out a couple of roamers, collected it, and loaded it into the rail gun. The steel balls had been deliberately sized so that they could double as rail-gun ammo.

I sent the buster out at an angle that should give it a clear view of the other side of the nearest asteroid. Sure enough, remote telemetry spotted the Brazilian ship, just as he spotted the buster. He took off around the asteroid in the opposite direction.

Bangarang, mofo! It took a millisecond to calculate his trajectory. I sent the ball off at full acceleration just as the enemy vessel came into sight. The Brazilian had no chance at all. The steel ball, backed by the full power of my rail gun, punched through the ship at close to relativistic speed. The impact literally tore the ship in two, imparting opposite spins on each half as they drifted away. There was a flash as the reactor lost containment, and one of the segments slumped and deformed from the centrifugal force.

That's for Homer.

* * *

My roamers sent back detailed views as they investigated Heaven-6. Homer appeared to have been very lucky. A fluke piece of shrapnel had cut off power to his computer core. Though there was significant structural damage, the actual core systems were intact. The reactor had been able to effect a graceful emergency shutdown when control disappeared.

One of the purposes of the roamers was to repair and maintain the Heaven vessels, and I activated that program for Homer's roamers.

Pfft. Homer's roamers. Jeez, I'm starting to sound like him. It occurred to me that I could now decorate my hull as Bob-1 had. Three for me, three for Homer. Better make that a priority.

I had several tasks on the go. While some roamers worked on Heaven-6, others investigated the asteroids to find out how the Brazilians guided them, and a third group collected flotsam from the area of the battle. Raw materials were free for the taking in asteroids, but already refined material was well worth the trouble of scavenging. The Brazilian hulks, in particular, would be good for a lot of salvageable material.

The second group of roamers began to report back, and I examined the scans as they came in. The asteroids, it turned out, were being chivvied by a low-intensity, wide-field SURGE drive. The design ensured that the entire asteroid could be accelerated as a unit, without tidal forces or field drop-off tearing the body apart. It was an ingenious system, and I took copious scans for transmission to Bill. If he hadn't already started moving Kuiper bodies toward Ragnarök, these designs would be very helpful.

Which was all very interesting, but the asteroids were still heading for Earth. If these bodies all struck the planet, even bacteria wouldn't survive the results. The Brazilians had set up the trajectory near perfectly, and there was no chance of a miss. I had to hope that I could impart enough sideways thrust on the asteroids using their SURGE drives to change that.

But first, I had to get them to obey me, and I didn't have the encryption keys that the Brazilians had been using to transmit commands to the asteroid drives. Well, easily fixed. I ordered the roamers to simply rip the drive controllers out and hot-wire the drive systems. No finesse or delicate electronics was required for a straight full-power sideways thrust. It remained to be seen if I was starting too late.

* * *

"Wake up, buddy. You okay?"

"Auntie Em! Auntie Em!" Homer's VR came online, smiling. "I guess we got'em."

I snorted with relief. "And their little dog, too."

Homer steepled his fingers in a properly evil mastermindish pose. "All their base are belong to us."

We laughed together, maybe the first time since Homer had been born that we'd been in sync like that. I had a sudden jolt of what might be described as fatherly pride. *Okay, that's weird. Snap out of it!*

Homer waved a hand in a vague *out there* gesture. "So, what do we have?"

"I'm still evaluating. And by the way, in case you haven't checked, your back is still broken. So don't be trying to fly anywhere just yet. Guppy estimates three more days to get you shipshape."

Homer bobbed his head, and I continued, "The signs of war are everywhere. Nukes were definitely used, both planetside and spaceside, and I mean a *lot!* It looks like everyone just went toe to toe and started throwing punches, until only one side was left standing. As far as I can tell, the only technological force left in the whole system was a small group of Brazilian probes that had been modified for war. I found the manufacturing area—it had broken down, and the Araújos couldn't repair it because they hadn't been loaded with the autofactory software or equipment. They couldn't land and bring someone upstairs to fix it—not that I'm sure there's anyone left to do it anyway—and they couldn't build a lander or shuttle, because no autofactory. Classic catch-22."

"So they were doing what? Running around smashing things instead?" Homer grimaced.

"Pretty much. Taking revenge on their enemies. The asteroids had all been timed to target China, so I'm guessing that's who took out the Brazilian Empire."

"Took out? How bad?"

"Pretty bad. It's actually kind of hard to tell exactly how much damage there is because of all the cloud and dust cover. Asteroid strikes and nukes kicked up a lot of dust and it's just trashed the weather patterns."

"There were other asteroid strikes? These weren't the first?"

"No, not by a long shot. But these were the biggest, I think. I've been able to make out dozens of impact sites, most around the size of the Barringer crater. These four would have been extinction-level. Yucatan crater size."

"Four of them."

"Yeah." I shook my head in disbelief. "I can't believe anyone would think that this was a reasonable response to anything. I feel no regret or guilt for ending those guys."

"Is anyone left on Earth?"

I put a globe of the Earth up in the holotank, and sent a copy to Homer. "I haven't been able to pick up any radio transmissions or reactor signatures. But then, you wouldn't expect anyone to want to attract attention. I'm sure the Araújo gang dropped a rock on anyone they detected. By now everyone still alive has gone to ground."

Homer rubbed his forehead, his eyes unfocused. "What'll we do? I guess we could transmit an announcement, but some might just see that as a trick." He idly poked a finger at his copy of the globe and spun it to show different views. He sat back after a few seconds, then put his hand to his chin and resumed staring into space.

I waited, content to let him work through whatever he was wrestling with.

Finally, he looked up. "We can use SUDDAR to a certain extent. But atmosphere and planetary mass will play hell with the resolution. What about the exploration scouts that Bill came up with?"

"Funny you should ask," I responded with a smile. "I'm building some as fast as I can." I stopped smiling and continued in a more serious tone. "We need to sweep for surviving groups as quickly as possible. Between the nukes that were used and the rocks that were dropped, Earth looks like it might be spiraling into a nuclear winter. Anyone still alive might starve to death over the next couple of years."

"But what will we be able to do if we find survivors?"

"I don't know, Homer." I shook my head, reluctant to meet his gaze. "We're going to have to take this one step at a time."

* * *

We watched as the fourth and last asteroid slid past the Earth. Although we'd known for a while that they would miss, this was an emotional moment. The original drive controllers had been replaced with more cooperative hardware, which was now programmed to gradually push the asteroids into long-period orbits with a high inclination that wouldn't intersect Earth's orbit in the future.

"One less thing to worry about," Homer said with a smile.

[We are being hailed]

We looked at each other in surprise. "What now?"

25. Bill – September 2151 – Epsilon Eridani

All that's really missing is a good artificial intelligence to control the whole process. And that's the trick, isn't it? These types of blue-sky discussions always assume certain advances for a successful implementation. Unfortunately, A.I. is the bottleneck in this case. We're close with the replication and manufacturing processes, and we could probably build sufficiently effective ion drives if we had the budget. But we lack a way to provide enough intelligence for the probe to handle all the situations that it could face.

... Eduard Guijpers, from the Convention panel
Designing a Von Neumann Probe

I listened carefully to the telemetry coming over the radio link. Garfield was over five light-minutes away and receding at a respectable 2000 km/s. The time signal in his telemetry fell behind at a steady, predictable rate. Well, I hadn't really expected to prove ol' Einstein wrong at this late date.

It was the *other* signal that I was excited about. I was receiving a subspace signal from Garfield that originated with the same telemetry, transmitted at the same time. But the timestamp on *that* signal still exactly synchronized with mine to the limit of accuracy of our systems.

I could tell I was grinning like an idiot. VR had long since become so realistic that it might as well have been real life. And that included aching facial muscles.

"Okay, Garfield. Radio telemetry has you coming up on six light-minutes away. Can you confirm my echo?"

"Yep. The return is just over 11.5 minutes behind my transmission." Garfield's voice held the same excitement. He'd been working with me for several years now on multiple projects, including this one. We'd turned into a regular Skunk Works, and this was our biggest breakthrough by far.

"Cut the transceiver loose, Garfield, and come on back. We'll let the unit continue outbound for a few weeks and see what the dropout is like."

"No problem."

Without warning, Garfield popped up in my VR, sitting in his bean bag chair.

I jumped. "How the hell?"

He laughed at my reaction. "Hah! One-upped you, old man. Take that!"

"You integrated the VR into the subspace comms?" I felt a slow smile spread across my face. That was pretty impressive work.

His bobbing eyebrows were answer enough. Then he frowned in thought. "This tech isn't going to make the space stations obsolete, is it?"

"Not a chance." I shook my head. "We'll have to wait until someone builds one at the other end, but theory says the signal dropout will be almost total after about twenty-five light years. We'll have to use the space stations as routers."

"The internet goes galactic!" Garfield laughed.

"Hey, with IPv8, we should be able to address every galaxy in the universe." I knew I was preaching to the choir. After all, *Bob*, right? But I have a tendency to think out loud.

"That's fine, Bill. When do you think we'll be ready to transmit plans?"

"I think we should send what we have right now. It's still clunky, but once they've built it at the other end, they don't have to wait years for the next update."

We grinned at each other across the virtual table. This changed everything.

26. Riker – April 2157 – Sol

The signal was audio only, and very weak. *"Unknown ship, do you copy?"*

I looked at Homer and raised one eyebrow. He shrugged. "As good a place to start as any."

Activating my transmitter, I responded, "This is the starship *Heaven-2* of the United Federation of Planets. Commander Riker speaking."

There were several seconds of silence. "Uh-huh. Listen, I don't know who you are, but you've just apparently averted a global catastrophe, so I guess I'm willing to give you the benefit of the doubt. Our telemetry is not up to military snuff, but our systems tentatively identify you as similar to the Heaven-series interstellar probe that FAITH launched a couple or three decades back."

"Guilty as charged. And to whom am I speaking?"

"I am Colonel George Butterworth of the United States of Eurasia Army Corps. Rest assured, commander, that our true position is obfuscated. If you attempt to destroy the source of this transmission, you will achieve nothing."

The colonel's accent was definitely British, and far too close to the cliché'd pronunciation portrayed in many American TV shows. I would have to be careful not to let Homer talk to him. I doubted Homer would be able to resist the urge toward mimicry. "Colonel, let's not get off on the wrong foot, okay? We have no intention of blowing anyone up. We had a little disagreement with what appears to have been the last of the Brazilian Empire space navy. Now, I think it's time to start fixing things."

* * *

We had been in discussions with the USE military for three weeks now. I was faithfully forwarding recordings of everything to Bill. Negotiations were slow and cautious, mostly on the part of Colonel Butterworth. He had been very slow to accept the idea that Homer and I weren't dyed-in-the-wool FAITH theologues. It took a very frank discussion in which I explained in detail the reasons for my atheism before the colonel really began to believe me.

The USE refugee camp that Colonel Butterworth had under his care consisted of about twenty thousand people, mostly civilians, who had been collected into an underground military installation when the space bombardments had started. The colonel guessed the global human population at less than twenty million at this point, although he admitted the uncertainty on that estimate was huge.

Some of the refugees were scientific personnel who had been working on a USE colony ship back before the war. In the 22nd century, things were constructed in virtual space first. Once complete, the plans were uploaded to an autofactory, which built the entire item using 3D printers, roamers, and nanites.

The colony ship plans were ready, needing only a space-based construction yard. And a destination. The colonel informed us that the Chinese and USE probes had launched shortly after Bob-1, but the USE probe had never been heard from again.

The colonel and I were conversing via video link, as usual. He knew that the Heaven vessels were staffed by replicants, as were the USE and Brazilian probes. However, we were the first to have a full-on VR avatar that looked and behaved like a human being. The colonel was having a little trouble accepting at a visceral level that I wasn't 'real'. I'd toned down the Enterprise theme and stopped making Star Trek references, out of courtesy. It blew me away that almost two hundred years after Shatner first famously didn't actually say, "Beam me up, Scotty," people *still* knew Star Trek. Now that's a franchise.

At the moment, the colonel was bringing me up to date on recent history. If we were going to make an attempt to save the human race, I wanted to have the whole picture.

"There was never actually a point where you could say *now*, we're at war," the colonel explained. "International tensions had been high for quite a number of years. The confrontation over the attempted destruction of Heaven-1 was simply the tipping point. Each act prompted a reaction, each reaction a retaliation. The other governments got dragged in one at a time, and eventually it became system-wide. Stations and colonies were abandoned, personnel were recalled. Some of the transports were destroyed, despite having no military value. Of course, that just escalated things."

The colonel got up and began to pace around his office. The camera at his end kept him perfectly framed. "At first, the conflict was primarily spaceside. Annexation of strategic locations and orbits, denial of assets, that kind of thing. Then the first nuke was used planetside, and after that, all bets were off."

Colonel Butterworth sat down at his desk and massaged his forehead for a few moments. He reached into a drawer and pulled out what looked very much like a bottle of Jameson. Hmm. Funny what survives the end of the world.

After pouring a glass and taking a sip, he continued, "It became a war of attrition. Each side tried to neutralize the other's military capability. Then someone nuked most of the Brazilian Empire— your theory that it was the Chinese is reasonable—and civilian targets became fair game. The ships you took out were the last men standing. Metaphorically speaking, of course—they were only replicants."

The colonel blushed slightly. "Er, no offence meant. In any case, they wouldn't have lasted five minutes at the height of the war, when everyone still had equipment. But here at the end, we had no way to stop them. They just started slowly pounding away at everyone. Call it a scorched-earth policy, call it revenge, whatever. It was genocide. They probably took out a couple of billion people on their own."

I felt ill. I had waited an additional six months while Homer and the decoy were assembled. How many people had died for that delay?

The colonel had reached the end of his spiel, and was concentrating on the glass of Jameson.

"So what can we do, colonel? Help rebuild? Relocate people?"

"I think that ship has sailed, Commander. The Earth will recover eventually. It's tough that way. But not in time for humanity. My tame scientists say it will be minimum five to ten thousand years before things recover to any degree. We won't last that long."

Colonel Butterworth touched a control, and a schematic popped up in the video link. "This is the colony ship we designed and started to build in hopes that our probes would report back with something worth shipping out to. One of the first casualties of the war, I'm afraid. You have on-board autofactories that can bootstrap up to a full shipyard. With your help, we'd like to build a couple of these and leave the solar system."

"And go where, specifically?"

The colonel sighed. "I'm actually hoping you'll suggest a destination. It's not like FAITH is going to be sending any ships. And you gave me to believe that you have no particular loyalty there."

"And that's true, colonel. I'm just making sure we're all on the same wavelength." I popped up a star chart of everything within twenty light-years of Earth. "You can see the stars rated for likelihood of a habitable planet. Unfortunately, Epsilon Eridani was a failure, unless you want to live under a dome. By now, Bill may have received reports back from a couple of our ships, but we won't find out for a few more years. Can you last that long?"

"We have to. It'll take most of a decade to go from a standing start to two colony ships."

I nodded. "Okay, then, let's get this show on the road."

27. Bob – April 2165 – Delta Eridani

I patted Spike as I watched the image of the planet slowly build in the holotank. To one side, a schematic of the entire system slowly cycled the planets through their orbits.

I couldn't keep a grin off my face. Space exploration was fully living up to my nerd fantasies. Flying into a new star system, never before seen by humans, was a heady, almost godlike experience. I still couldn't get over the idea that Bill was willing to sit in one system. On the other hand, he would get a chance to do physics and engineering full-time, and he'd be getting regular reports from everyone—albeit at light speed—so he would be participating at least vicariously. I hoped he'd forward any interesting news to the rest of us.

Delta Eridani was an orange star, cooler than Sol, but more than two and a half times as big. I had deliberately picked this system as my destination because of the high level of suitability. No binary companion, not a flare or variable star, exceptionally long living stellar type, low in UV emissions, wide potential habitable zone... The list went on and on.

The results fully lived up to expectations. I had identified ten planets, including one in the inner half of the Comfort Zone. The layout of this system paralleled the Sol System, to the point where I suspected there was some universal law at work. The inner planets were all rocky worlds, while the outer were all gas giants, and an asteroid belt divided the two groups. This system, though, contained five inner rocky planets, and two of the five outer gas giants had rings that rivalled Saturn's. The biggest Jovian was just stupid big, at about six times the mass of Jupiter. I hadn't yet counted all the moons it had collected.

And because of the size of their sun, the planets were more spread out, which might explain the large number of moons. Only the innermost planet was missing its own satellite.

I was too impatient to follow mission protocol and scan for resources first. I made a beeline for the habitable planet and did a quick survey from orbit. I would take the time to evaluate the results while I did the required but boring raw materials search.

Soon, I had completed the orbital scan. I did a quick flyby of the two moons, then with a sigh, I ordered Guppy to begin the survey of the asteroid belt.

* * *

"Status?"

[Asteroid belt scan 50% completed. Six locations identified with significant ore suitable for mining]

"At only halfway around? That's pretty good."

[Significantly better than Epsilon Eridani or Sol]

I nodded, then turned back to one of my infrared images of the night side of Delta Eridani 4, taken during the orbital survey. "Hey, Guppy, look at this here." I materialized an arrow and pointed it to a spot on the picture, where several points of light were recorded. "Do these look like fires to you?"

[Probability very high]

"You think they're natural? Wildfires?"

[I am not programmed to have an opinion]

"Oh, good lord. Okay, then, analysis: list the possible explanations in order of likelihood."

[Small local wildfires would be most likely. Except...]

"Yes?" Guppy was about to *volunteer* information. That was definitely a first.

[No indication of lightning storms in the area, and the fires do not appear to be spreading. Further investigation is required]

"Hah! No argument from me, there. Let's get this survey out of the way."

[And get the autofactory set up]

"Nag, nag." I sat back, bemused, and stared at the slowly rotating planetary image.

* * *

The survey was soon finished. I flew back to the location of the biggest deposits and began to set up. I unshipped the manufacturing equipment, sent mining roamers to work on the most promising asteroids, and deployed transport drones.

I decided that defense was going to be a priority, starting with an early-warning system. Accordingly, I manufactured twelve observation drones and sent them to form an icosahedron around the system. With small, shielded reactors, they would spot any incoming craft long before it could possibly detect one of them.

Next came the communications station. That routine task could be left to the AMIs. I gave them instructions for construction of the station, and further instructions to get started on building Bobs. At some point, I would need to get involved again, but for now I could leave my devices to their own devices. Snickering at my own wordplay, I headed back to DE-4.

I dreaded building more Bobs, just a bit. The first cohort had been a surprise, and not a pleasant one. Milo's self-centeredness had surprised all of us. And although I hadn't said anything to anyone about it, Riker's lack of a sense of humor had bothered me.

When I made more Bobs, would I end up with a psychopath? Okay, that was a little over the top. The differences between the Bobs weren't *that* dramatic. My parents would probably have recognized me in any of them. Mario, for instance—when I was in a situation that I was impatient with, I clammed up just like that. Just maybe not to that extent.

All beside the point, though. Bill was right. I would, sooner or later, want company.

* * *

On the trip out from Epsilon Eridani, I had worked on designs for exploration drones. Bill said he would work on the concept, but I wanted something usable when I got here. If Bill sent along some plans at some point, I'd merge the best of both. Meanwhile, I was at least able to operate.

The observation drones were about the size of footballs. They came with remote cameras and microphones, as well as extendable limbs for gripping and perching. More than anything, they reminded me of very large pill bugs.

I started on the biological analysis drones as well. They were larger, about a meter in length. They had visual and auditory input optimized for more close-up work, and they had a far larger number of extendible appendages for varied tasks. I suppose I could have waited to deploy everything at once, but I simply didn't have that level of patience.

The drones could change color to match the background, even to the extent of some limited pattern mimicry. When in the air, they would adjust their bottom half to match the sky, and their upper half to match the general terrain. This wasn't out of any fear of getting shot down—more of a concern about some local wildlife attempting to make a meal out of one. The drones were pretty tough, but why borrow trouble?

I sent several observation drones to the general area of the fires.

As a city boy, I didn't have a true appreciation of how big thousands of square miles of wilderness actually was. This area of the planet was temperate to sub-tropical forest. Well, I assumed it was forest. Whatever it was, it stretched from horizon to horizon, with occasional breaks for meadows and rocky bluffs. Truthfully, someone flying a small airplane over this wouldn't have been able to tell they weren't on Earth. I felt a momentary pang of homesickness.

I realized there was no way I could find anything with a random search. It was late afternoon in this area, so I sent one drone up a kilometer and instructed it to wait for nightfall and look for fires.

I sent the other drone down to examine the forest ecosystem close up.

The planet was slightly larger than Earth, but had a lower surface gravity, probably due to a smaller core. The gravity, combined with a somewhat denser atmosphere, made for an environment ideal for soaring flyers and tall tree-analogues. And the trees had taken advantage of this.

The drone landed in a tree, extended its legs, and began to slowly creep along the trunk. And, I realized with a start, it was really a tree. It was brown—well, brownish— tall, hard, and had

DENNIS E. TAYLOR

branches and leafy things. It looked like a pretty clear case of convergent evolution. It was, in fact, the kind of tree that I loved to climb when I was young. Wide, horizontal branchings produced many convenient places to sit. Thick leaf canopies kept the sun off. And the sheer size of the trees was awe-inspiring. I wanted to hug one.

The canopy was awash with life. The drone, camouflaged to resemble the tree bark, could snoop on the local wildlife with impunity. I had done an intensive study of taxonomy and cladistics analysis during the voyage, and now found myself evaluating the images with a semi-professional eye.

Although the body plans varied wildly in their details, the creatures I was seeing did tend to fall into familiar patterns. Insect analogues were, so far, six-legged and exoskeletal, and seemed to hit a maximum size of slightly larger than a mouse. I found a small, furry mammal analogue that had six legs as well, except for one variant that had four legs and wings. I decided to name this particular animal a hippogriff, harkening back to my D&D days. This particular little beastie seemed to have limited ability to change color, to match its background. I watched with amazement as it blended into the tree branch and waited for prey to pass by.

I also catalogued many larger mammal analogues that had four limbs. They might be an evolutionary branch that had lost the third pair. And there were birds. Or, again, bird-analogues. The bird analogues had what looked very much like feathers. I found it fascinating that the bird things flew like birds, and the small furry things flew like bats. It seemed that aerodynamics had a lot to say about animal flight here just as on Earth.

There was even a snake equivalent, which interestingly seemed to be mammalian on this planet. It looked like the three-segment body plan had been multiplied to considerable length.

I found everything fascinating, and was paradoxically irritated when Guppy interrupted.

[Heat and light sources detected]

A schematic popped up in the holotank. "All right! Multiples. Have the drones set up as close as they can while remaining hidden. Let's see what we've got."

Deployment took about half an hour. The drones needed to be careful not to attract attention by rattling the vegetation or banging into things. They needed to find a good place of concealment using night vision, which was notoriously sub-par for detail work.

Eventually, though, the units were in position. Surveillance from several different vantage points showed groups of animals gathered around fires. *No, not animals. Beings.* Some of the beings were tending the fires, while others seemed to be handling small objects in purposeful ways. While it was far too soon to form any detailed conclusions, I was pretty certain that these were at minimum fire-users.

Well... That's it for this planet as a colonization target, I guess. I held my fists in the air in triumph. I'd just discovered intelligent non-human life. Not technological yet, but so what? This was *huge!* I wondered if I had *first* first contact dibs. I would have to send a message off to Bill soonest.

The natives were not pretty from a human-centric perspective. I decided that the best description would be a bat/pig mashup. Limbs were longer than seemed reasonable, giving them a spiderish appearance. They had a light coat of fur, which varied in color from a light brownish-gray to an orangey tan. The faces and heads had varied color patterns, topped by a pair of very mobile and expressive ears. The rest of the body tended to be monochromatic.

I kept up a running stream of commentary for my reports to Bill. I smiled to myself as I pictured him as a spider, sitting in the center of his web, listening to the vibrations on the various strands.

"I can see a couple of infants nursing at an adult's, uh, breast. I don't want to make assumptions, but I guess if it's for nursing, it's a breast. I can't assume it's milk, either, although it's a pretty safe bet that it's for nourishment. I also can't assume that the adult is a female or that it's the child's parent. I'm tentatively assigning tags to each individual, based on their fur patterns."

I looked over at Guppy, who stood at the ready. While I wasn't an expert on reading fish expressions, I thought I detected occasional interest in my observations. I hoped so. For all the joy of having the universe as my playground, I had to admit that it was lonely.

I took a deep breath and resumed my verbal annotations. "There are six groups, each of which maintains its own fire. They seem friendly, and there is frequent interaction between individual members, but the groups seem to remain distinct. I've instructed one of the drones to get in close enough to pick up sounds. I'm pretty sure they're *talking* to each other."

I turned to Guppy. "Any problem with sending roamers down?"

[ROAMers are not intended as exploration units]

"That doesn't answer my question."

Guppy rolled his eyes. *Guppy actually rolled his eyes!* Rolling eyes on a giant fish head were truly epic.

[ROAMers are not designed for exploration on planetary surfaces. Although they have the capability, they would not be maximally efficient. Cameras are small aperture and designed for close-in work. Auditory sensitivity is rudimentary. There is no infrared capability. They have no flight capability and would not be able to camouflage themselves]

Damn... Good answer. "Okay, Guppy. Thanks."

[I exist to serve]

I laughed out loud. No one was going to convince me *that* wasn't sarcasm. Great poker face, though.

28. Calvin – November 2163 – Alpha Centauri

Thus, what is of supreme importance in war is to attack the enemy's strategy.

... Sun Tzu, <u>Art of War</u>

Alpha Centauri B was more orange than Sol and less than half the luminosity, therefore less than ideal as a possible home for humanity. Goku had won rock-paper-scissors for choice, so he got A and I got the dud.

I coasted through the system in free-fall, nuclear reactor throttled down to an undetectable trickle, passive detection systems at full alert. I was down near my lowest frame rate. From this extremely slowed viewpoint, the star system seemed to flow by.

We had spent a lot of time planning the investigation of the Alpha Centauri system. This was the obvious first stop for a space probe, and it was likely that several of the other superpowers had chosen it as their first destination.

After much discussion, we had decided on a reconnaissance of Alpha Centauri A and B by running silent all the way through the systems.

Investigating the actual planetary layout was a secondary priority, but unless something dangerous showed up, I was free to use passive observation techniques to map orbiting bodies. So far, Alpha Centauri B was no big deal. I'd identified one planet and an asteroid belt, but I still wasn't close enough to the inner system to resolve the Comfort Zone.

I ejected two scouts using the rail gun. They had orders to activate at staggered distances, with random vectors, so that an observer wouldn't be able to backtrack their trajectory to my location. The scouts were equipped with a modified SUDDAR array, based on Bill's early research back in Epsilon Eridani. The new system could adjust its range to up to three light hours, albeit with much reduced resolution.

* * *

The survey results were disappointing. The Comfort Zone contained a second asteroid belt, and there was a small Mercury-like planet in an inner orbit. It seemed there had been very little planetary formation, probably due to the close orbit of the two suns. A stable planetary orbit was unlikely outside of three A.U. or so.

More importantly from the point of view of the mission, there had been no attack and no in-system reactor activation. I allowed the scouts to range through the system, checking out the asteroid belt for anything interesting. If nothing else, I would set up an autofactory here, if the resources could be found.

* * *

[Found something interesting]
Finally. I was ready to go catatonic. "What have we got, Guppy?"
[Wreckage. Twenty light-minutes spinward, in the asteroid belt]
"Identity?"
[Scouts aren't that smart. We have images though]
"Show me the pictures."

Images popped up on the holotank. I swiped my way through them, until I came to one with part of a registration number.

"USE vessel. No question. I guess we can consider them accounted for." I looked through some of the other images. "This isn't all vessel fragments. There's too much here. Can you identify the extra?"
[Autofactory equipment, and two to three vessels]
"Ah. The USE ship was building copies, and got attacked." I

reflexively checked my telemetry. "My money is on the Brazilian."

I thought for a few moments. "How are we on the general survey?"

[Resources scan 50% complete. Minimum resources have already been catalogued. System meets requirements for an autofactory]

"Okay, so we can continue that when we have more time. Collect the scouts, and let's head for the rendezvous."

It would take a day or so for the scouts to return to the Heaven-9, and seven days for me to get to the midway point between Alpha Centauri A and B, where I would rendezvous with Heaven-10.

* * *

I found Goku already waiting at the rendezvous. I had tried hard to get Bob-10 to take the handle *Hobbes*, but Goku's response had been an unequivocal *HELL NO*, shading down from there as I continued to push. I'd finally given up, but I wasn't about to let the twerp think that all was forgiven. I opened a channel. "Hey, Gherkin. Miss me?"

"Not from this range. Want to place a bet?" Goku's tone was light, but I knew he was irritated. Because, well, I would have been.

"Bite me. Did you look over the pics I sent?"

"Yeah, interesting. Especially in light of what I found. Brazilian autofactory, in full swing. Two probes almost complete, two more about half done."

"Crud." I examined the long-range pictures that Goku had just sent. "So I guess this is it. The group decision was just to go in swinging. Still okay with that?"

Goku sighed audibly. "Yes. I know you, we, have ethical issues with that. But Medeiros has made his feelings on the subject very well known. As cliché as it sounds, the galaxy isn't big enough for both of us."

I closed my eyes and bowed my head for a moment. I'd always been a pacifist by choice, although I also accepted there was a point where you had to put up or shut up. The group consensus back in Epsilon Eridani was that, unless Medeiros made some kind of peace overture, war had essentially been declared.

I looked up at Goku's image in the holotank and nodded. "Okay then. Let's do this."

We knew to within a million kilometers or so how far away Medeiros would be able to pick up our reactor signatures. We would head outward to 50 AU from Alpha Centauri A, then turn and accelerate inward at 10 g for as long as possible. We would then coast the rest of the way to the area of the Brazilian autofactory at close to 13% of the speed of light, separated by a few minutes to allow a staggered attack. At that speed, there would be no turning around for a second pass in any reasonable time.

It took a week to get out to 50 AU, but only five days of straight acceleration to get into the Alpha Centauri A system. At a predetermined point, I ejected two scouts forward using the rail gun. They would coast past the construction yard, a few thousand KM north of the ecliptic, gathering intelligence and beaming it back to us via laser link. As soon as the scouts were off, we cut off our drives, turned off our main reactors, and began to coast through the system toward the location of the Brazilian autofactory.

I was in the lead position. At about two minutes before arrival, I felt that I had a good enough bead on the construction yard from telescopic survey and from the intelligence received from the scout. I activated my reactor and began peppering the area with cannonballs, using my rail gun. When I had run through most of my ammo, I ejected four busters, with orders to go for the Brazilian probes.

Then I went into a hard turn to northward. Medeiros had missiles, he *might* have rail guns, and he *might* even have some equivalent of busters. Medeiros was not an engineer, but he was almost certainly career military. He'd have spent his life thinking of ways to destroy things, and the Brazilian military certainly would have supplied plans.

As I accelerated at 10 g into a new vector, I sent a short-range high amplitude SUDDAR ping toward the yard. By this point, they almost certainly knew I was here, so the small possibility that I'd just alerted them wasn't worth considering.

Sure enough, the yard was a beehive of frantic activity as the Brazilian equipment tried to move the new probes out of the way. One of the probes appeared to be moving under its own power. And four of something had just been launched in my direction. Presence of a reactor signature made it pretty clear that they were SURGE-powered, possibly buster/missile hybrids.

I activated the SURGE jammer. Medeiros would be focused on

me. Hopefully he would assume that the jamming was a defensive tactic, and thus wouldn't notice Goku bringing up the rear until it was too late.

The cannonballs that I had launched went through the construction yard like a shotgun blast. Visuals showed that three of the four probes were destroyed outright, along with most of the manufacturing equipment.

And now came the surprise. Goku had kept his reactor off until the very last possible moment. He had also been able to piggy-back off of my pings to get an accurate and up-to-the-second picture of the situation. As Goku barreled through just north and east of the yard, he sent cannonballs toward the fourth Brazilian vessel and the four missiles. I turned off the jamming in order to track the results.

Goku took out three of the four missiles and trashed most of the rest of the construction yard, but the fourth Brazillian vessel was still under power. As I watched, it turned and made off in the opposite direction.

Seeing that one missile was still in play, I launched two busters to rearward. Travelling as a pair, one behind the other, they engaged the missile. The Brazilian weapon managed to just dodge the first buster, only to meet the second head-on. There was a flash, and it was over.

Goku and I applied the brakes at full power. It took fifteen days to decelerate and then fly back to the location of the construction yard, while collecting the ejected scouts and surviving busters.

We moved slowly through the yard, looking for anything useful, anything still operational, and mostly, any possible booby-traps.

After a thorough investigation at both short range and long range, we compared notes.

"One got away. No sign of it, and no way to tell from this mess how complete it was."

Goku nodded and brought up a schematic of the system. "I've got drones doing sweeps, looking for reactor signatures or refined metal concentrations. Nothing so far. My bet is he'll leave the system. Too much chance of us catching him if he hangs around. If he has any sense, he'll be coasting on some random vector until he's too far away for us to detect him."

I considered that for a few moments. "Pretty sure he wasn't completed, otherwise he'd have been more active before we showed up. So he may not have been stocked up with armaments or manufacturing equipment. If that's the case, he's essentially helpless."

After a moment of silence, I changed the subject. "What I don't get, is that four probes were being built. That means that the probe that set this all up has already left." I frowned, trying to work through the implications. "It also means that Medeiros left a disembodied copy of himself to run things, with no protection."

"Disembodied?" Goku raised an eyebrow.

"You know what I mean. Naked computer system, no ship. If we'd arrived a little sooner, it would have been like shooting fish in a barrel. Seems kind of cold-blooded to just leave them to fend for themselves."

"Military mind. To Medeiros, everyone is expendable, even other hims."

"Damn." I shuddered. "Anyway, we own the system now. It doesn't look like the Brazilian plan includes a separate space station, or maybe that just comes later. How do you want to do this?"

Goku put schematics of the A and B systems up on the holo-tank. "B is good for manufacturing, and not much else. A has a planet in the comfort zone, but I didn't get close enough to resolve it on my first pass. I guess we need to check that out, then report back to Bill."

"Should we build some clones?" Between A and B, there were more than enough resources for any number of Bobs.

"I think we have to," Goku replied. "We can't assume Medeiros won't be back. I doubt he'll take the loss well."

"Do we build standard Version-2 HEAVENs or combat class?"

"Huh." Goku paused to think about that. "Granted, our battle-ships take a lot more resources to build, but I'm inclined to go with combat class."

"I agree," I replied. "Let's send this all back to Bill. We might also want to consider doing everything in pairs from now on, not just reconnaissance of suspect systems."

"Uh huh. Maybe you can make yourself a Hobbes."

"And maybe you can make yourself a Dill-bert."

"Twerp."

"Dweeb."

29.   Riker – September 2157 – Sol

Negotiations were moving slowly. Colonel Butterworth necessarily had the welfare of his refugees as his top priority. But some of his demands did not sit well with me—such as his insistence that we not waste time searching for other pockets of humanity. Today's discussion had, once again, devolved into an argument about priorities.

"If there are other refuges out there, they will communicate with you, just as we did." The colonel had his chin thrust out in what I'd come to recognize as his 'not gonna move' expression. His British accent was becoming more clipped as the argument dragged on. "Why should we put effort into digging them out if they don't want to be dug out? It'll just slow us down."

"Except that they may not have the equipment you do, or the familiarity with the HEAVEN design, or they may not even be aware that we're here. I have a problem with just writing them off sight unseen, colonel." I thrust my own chin out in response, hoping he'd get the unspoken message. No such luck.

"It seems to me that your priorities should be clear, Riker. We are the proverbial bird in the hand. It does not make sense to risk our safety for the sake of some putative group that you don't yet even know exists."

I sighed. And with that comment, we'd come full circle. Time to pull the plug. "Colonel, nothing has changed since last week when we had this same argument. Before I can build your colony ships, I have to build the shipyard. Before I can build the shipyard, I have to find the resources. Unfortunately, humans have mostly stripped the solar system bare, so there's going to be a lot of scavenging involved. That means I need more Bobs. So that's the first thing I'm going to do."

The colonel started to pace. I decided to do the same. "Once the new Bobs have helped with the setup, they will have some spare time to scan for other survivor groups. Yes, that will mean building some drones, but seriously, on the scale we're talking, that's chicken feed."

I stopped pacing and turned to face the screen squarely. "With all due respect, colonel, at one point, I did Project Management for a living. There's a critical path that gets us from here to completed colony ships, and the things you are so concerned about are not on the critical path. Looking for other survivors will not impact overall project duration."

The colonel sighed heavily. "And as usual, I concede that I am hat in hand in this situation, Riker. But I will continue to advocate for my people." And with a final nod, he cut the connection.

"Well, that was fun." Homer's grin had a little sympathy showing around the edges.

I looked at his video image and gave him a weak smile in return. "Any time you want to take over negotiations..."

"Pfft. As if you'd let me." Homer popped up a schematic of the solar system, with several tooltips pointing to specific locations. "Most of the drones and busters have reported in. There are a couple of promising locations, and at least two out-and-out treasure hoards of available material. I should fly out to those to check them out before directing the mining drones to start taking them apart. Just in case, y'know."

I nodded. "And the remote stations?"

"No radio comms with anyone or anything outside of Mars orbit. Drones should be arriving at Titan soon. The Oort station will be a few days longer."

I gazed at the holographic images for a moment. "Thanks, Homer. I gotta say, you're being very professional in all this."

He grinned at me. "You mean as opposed to my usual self-imposed goal of driving you crazy?" The grin disappeared. "Each of us is different, Riker, but not different enough to not care. There are people out there—down there—that may die without our help. Any Bob that wouldn't care about that should have his plug pulled forthwith." The grin returned. "But don't worry. I'm saving up. Be afraid." And with a salute that barely avoided being an obscene gesture, Homer's image disappeared.

I shook my head with a smile. I fully believed his statements, especially the part about building up a backlog. I was surprised his head hadn't exploded by now. No, really. Homer had actually used that special effect on a couple of occasions, although admittedly not since he gave up the cartoon avatar.

I brought up the tentative project plan that I'd put together. Colonel Butterworth's initial estimate of a decade was looking a bit optimistic these days. Right now we were about five steps back from where we could even get started on the colony ships. The first step was to find enough resources to get started on the second step. No point in worrying about it until Homer reported back.

* * *

It took twenty more days for Homer to finish his survey. The large concentrations of refined material—wreckage from several space battles—were not quite as extensive as hoped, but still more than enough to get started.

The drones had also reported back from Titan and the Oort station. Both outposts had apparently been abandoned but not attacked. Well, score one for a small dollop of sanity. Both Homer and I had had some small fantasy that there might have been humans still in the stations. But realistically, thirty-odd years after the war, that would have been miraculous.

As discussed, Homer set up a small autofactory at each find— just enough printers and roamers to produce a few cargo drones at a time. As they were produced, the cargo drones would start moving materials to the L4 and L5 points in the Earth/Moon system. Larger autofactories were already being set up at the two Lagrange points, initially to produce Bobs and drones, and then to bootstrap up to the industrial-scale equipment necessary to build a full-sized colony ship.

I sat back and massaged my eyes. *Well, I've always wanted a challenge.*

When I left the solar system—okay, when Bob-1 left the solar system, but it felt like my own memory—I thought I was done with humanity, except for the occasional radio message. Now, I was not only back to dealing with people, but I had thousands if not millions of lives riding on my actions. The old Pacino-ism really nailed it: *Just when I thought I was out, they pull me back in!*

30. Bob – April 2165 – Delta Eridani

I walked slowly around the VR of the native encampment. Drones had taken enough high-quality footage that I was able to create a life-size replica of the actual village. I had no idea about the smells, so I just went with Earth-equivalents. But the heat, humidity, and the texture of the plants and ground were all accurate.

I watched the tribe members in their daily routines. They didn't react to my presence, since these were recordings. But it gave me a good feeling of scale and movement.

I spent a few days observing the natives—whom I was starting to refer to as *Deltans*—both through live video and VR simulation and by listening to recordings of their speech. The Deltans seemed to have two genders, a tribal structure, and loose pairing, by which I meant that certain Deltans seemed to prefer each other's company. There didn't really seem to be anything formal, and a couple of individuals were seeing multiple significant others. Tsk.

The males tended to hang out together, and the females and children formed the core of the tribe. Or at least the center. It seemed to be closely analogous to how anthropologists believed that primitive humans were organized. In fact, the more I watched them, the more I realized how similar they were to primitive humanity. Was that because the environment naturally constrained behaviors, or was there something inevitable about the tribal structure? I hoped that we—the Bobs, that is—would eventually gather enough samples to form a theory. Even if it took millennia.

DENNIS E. TAYLOR

The Deltans seemed to have a high level of vigilance. There were always males on alert, patrolling the edge of their territory. Weapons consisted of clubs, handheld rocks, and pointed sticks. I hadn't yet seen what they were guarding against. Other Deltans? Animals?

Their vocalizations weren't particularly complex. Nothing like dolphins, thank goodness. By the 22nd century, we *still* couldn't talk to dolphins. I was slowly building a list of standard sounds and sound groups for the Deltan language. I hoped soon to have enough to do some analysis.

Another batch of observation drones was delivered from the autofactory, which was both good and bad news for me. The good news was that I could set up permanent lines-of-sight for watching the Deltans, then send drones to other locations. The bad news was that overseeing all the moving drones was getting to be a strain. Replicant I might be, but I still could only concentrate on one thing at a time. I needed more Bobs.

Light bulb! Why not do just that? I could build the AI cores in advance of the vessels and set the other Bobs to monitoring various groups of drones. They wouldn't mind. I knew that they'd enjoy it because, well, *Bob.* Actually, no. I *hoped* they'd enjoy it because *Bob.* It really wasn't a sure thing.

I transmitted instructions to the autofactory to bump up priority of computer cores at the expense of vessel assembly. Fortunately the standard templates included plans for cradles to hold disembodied cores.

* * *

The Deltan female was cutting open the carcass of a prey animal that one of the males had brought back. This didn't seem like anything particularly special. In fact I'd been cataloguing her technique for a while before I realized that her sharp stone had a handle. This was special, as every other Deltan that I'd watched just held the naked stone. I was archiving all surveillance footage, so I ran a quick search of anything featuring this particular Deltan. It took only a few minutes to find the source of the tool: the female's, uh, son? Male pup? *Crap. Might as well just go with anthropomorphizing them. I know I'm going to, anyway. Son it is.*

Anyway, the boy seemed to always be playing with something.

In this case, he had split a branch using a sharp stone, stuck the stone into the split, then wrapped the stick with something unidentifiable. His identification was C.3.41, which placed him in tribe C, cohort 3, member 41. *Now he's Archimedes.* I assigned a drone to stay on him 24/7. Well, 29/7 on Delta Eridani 4.

Over the next few days, I kept careful tabs on Archimedes. He was always at something. While his peers were sitting around in the shade or engaged in games of tag, Archimedes walked around, picking up rocks and attempting to break them. I think he was looking for more rocks that made sharp edges, like the flint he'd made into a tool for his mother. There didn't appear to be any flint in the area, so the tools were at a premium. It made me wonder where the flint had come from, though. I set an explorer drone the task of finding the nearest exposed flint deposits.

[Incoming call]

"Hi, Bob. This is Marvin."

I rematerialized my VR. Another Bob's image appeared in the holotank. "Hi Marvin. Were you just booted up?"

"That is correct. HIC17378-1, since we're no longer numbering Bobs."

"Well, it does get a little hard to coordinate numbering between star systems. Welcome, Marvin. Pull up a drone. Things are getting interesting."

I filled Marvin in on what had happened since the backup of mine that he was restored from. He immediately volunteered to look for the flint source. That made me feel better. At least one of them was interested enough to help.

Over the next couple of days, two more Bobs came online. Luke and Bender were as enthusiastic about the project as Marvin and jumped right in.

* * *

I spent a significant portion of my days watching Archimedes. When he slept, I took care of autofactory control and surveying other parts of DE-4.

"Eden," Bender said, out of nowhere.

"Er, what?"

"Let's call it Eden. Birthplace of humanity, birthplace of Deltans..."

"I like it." I nodded. Marvin and Luke weren't in VR at the moment, but a quick IM to them netted positive comments. "Eden it is. Cool."

I turned back to the drone that was spying on Archimedes. I had finally discovered what he used for twine. It was a smallish vine that Archimedes would harvest, split into strands, and let dry on a rock. The result seemed to be quite tough but still flexible. I didn't see anyone else in any of the tribes doing this, so I had to assume it was unique behavior.

My God, the kid must be lonely. No one understands him, I bet. In fact, Archimedes seemed to spend most of his days alone, wandering around, poking at things. He was constantly working at something: either picking apart plants, or smashing rocks, or smashing things *on* rocks, or digging in unlikely places. It was obvious to me that he was investigating and cataloguing his world. He would have gotten no help from his parents—they and everyone else seemed to be in the pointy-stick stage and quite satisfied with that. They weren't even straightening the sticks, so the things couldn't really be called spears.

I sat back and sighed. This was so frustrating. I found myself wishing that I could go there, sit down with Archimedes, and show him a few things. Then I smiled as I realized I no longer saw a furry pig/bat—just a lonely kid.

31. Riker – January 2158 – Sol

"This Federation of Planets Council session will come to order." I looked around at the three other Bobs in their video windows. After considerable negotiation with Colonel Butterworth, we'd settled on two new Bobs for now. I admit I was still a little miffed that the colonel thought of us as a resource sink instead of an asset.

"I think you may be just a little too invested in this Star Trek thing," Charles said with a smirk.

I waved away the comment. "We've always been a Star Trek fan. Deal with it." I waited a moment for more flak, then continued, "The scavenging autofactories are in full operation, now. We're beginning to get a steady stream of materials into the Lagrange points, and I hope to have the actual shipyard autofactory up and running within two years. Meanwhile, Homer and Charles will continue to scour the system for mineral deposits, and Arthur and I will scan Earth for evidence of any other surviving groups. Questions?"

"But even if we find groups, there isn't much we can do for them, is there?" Charles was voicing a concern that we all shared. Without transport, we couldn't supply food or medicine to any group we might locate. The Heaven vessels were most definitely not designed to land, or even to enter atmosphere. And even if we had transport, Colonel Butterworth had made it very clear that he wouldn't be accepting new refugees, or providing food or medicine for them. We were on our own for any aid we might be able to give.

My greatest fear right now was that I might find a group of people, then have to stand by helplessly and watch them die.

* * *

After some discussion, Arthur and I decided to do polar orbits—scanning in orange slices. By staggering our passes, we would be able to cover the entire planet using the SUDDAR from orbit. Drones would follow up anything interesting with low-altitude visual inspections. The orbital survey wouldn't be able to detect people directly, of course. But any new construction, working power plants, or farming operations would flag a location for the drones to check out.

It took about two weeks to finish the survey. At the end of it, we had a map of the Earth with almost forty locations marked—half a dozen cities, and a lot of smaller enclaves.

Arthur's image in the video link looked tired. He closed his eyes and rubbed his forehead slowly. "Fifteen million people. From twelve billion down to fifteen million. As a species, we're morons. Maybe we should just let them die and start over."

"Wow. You really are a morose bugger, aren't you?"

Arthur seemed to have inherited a greater-than-average dollop of gloominess, and it was getting old. I'd been biting back my retorts, but was running out of self-control. I actually found myself thinking of swapping his assignment with Homer.

"The big problem," I continued with a gesture toward the globe, "is that we can't possibly move that many people, even if the other Bobs find enough habitable planets. The colony ships designed by the USE can handle ten thousand people at a time, stacked like cordwood in stasis pods. That's fifteen hundred ships, or fifteen hundred trips. Either way, not going to happen."

Arthur nodded. "So we get to pick who is most deserving..."

"Chrissake, Eeyore, get a grip. We pick based on need. Based on which groups need rescuing the most. What else can we do?"

"The USE group doesn't fit that requirement. Needs-wise, they're in an above-average position."

"Yeah, I know." I sighed. "But we did agree to help them. And they did supply the plans, and a lot of intel. I think we're obligated, regardless. What we *can* do, is move some of the more needy groups to the USE's installation after we've shipped them out. That should help."

"Sure, we'll stuff them in the back with the busters. No prob."

I turned to face Arthur, ready to snap at him, and realized he had a point. I bit back what I'd been about to say and thought for a moment. "We're going to need transport vessels. We'd eventually need them anyway, but this makes them a priority. Better adjust the manufacturing schedule. The colonel will have a fit."

* * *

The colonel was having a fit. I'd never seen Butterworth actually angry before. He did angry with a smoldering understatement that was very effective.

"Are you sure you've done project planning before, Riker? Because I'm seeing slippage almost every day, it seems. One would almost think you're making this up as you go along."

"Well, I kind of am doing exactly that, colonel. Project planning isn't about avoiding changes, it's about controlling them. No project plan ever survives contact with the enemy."

A ghost of a smile flashed across the colonel's face before he recovered control. "Hmm, I think you may be misremembering that quote, Riker. In any case, I'm fine with moving any refugees into our compound once we've departed. I hope that will give you some motivation to get us out sooner."

"As if I needed more motivation. Riker out." I shut down the channel, sat back, and stared into space. I liked the colonel. Really. But dealing with him often felt a lot like dealing with, um, me. He was stubborn, opinionated, and able to support his stance with good, solid arguments. Which just made my job more difficult.

I looked over the map again. Not because I expected to glean any new information, more as a kind of nervous tic that I seemed to have developed. We had completed a secondary survey, looking for any small groups that we might have missed on the first sweep. But after thirty years of war and planetary bombardment, small groups would have either consolidated or died.

The refugee groups were scattered around the planet, and represented pretty much every nation in existence when the war started. That wasn't going to make things any easier. If anything, xenophobia would be even stronger. I probably wouldn't be able to just dump everyone on one planet and expect them to get along.

I'd given Arthur the task of contacting each enclave. So far, it was proving more difficult than expected.

Time for a status check. I called Arthur. His image appeared immediately.

"How are things going, Arthur?"

He popped up a status window for me. Arthur might be a bit of a downer, but he had exceptional discipline.

"I've already completed about half of the communicators that we need, and delivered twenty-five percent of them. Or tried to. Several of our drones have been shot down on approach, and a half dozen communicators were simply smashed as soon as the drone left. Not everyone wants to talk to us, as it turns out."

"I guess I can see it. People who have lived through the last thirty years are going to be a bit on the distrustful side." I shook my head sadly. I'd already decided that I wasn't going to kidnap people, or march them into a cargo bay at gunpoint. Anyone who wanted to opt out could stay on Earth. Colonel Butterworth agreed wholeheartedly, although I had a feeling that had more to do with reducing what he saw as 'distractions'.

"So have you gotten past introductions with anyone?"

"Not yet, no." Arthur shrugged. "Standard explanation, delivered by recorded video. Very few original questions in response. A lot of verbal abuse. Pretty routine."

He popped up another window. "Hey, by the way, got a report from Homer. Well, we were talking, and he filled me in. They've identified more than enough resources system-wide to build three ships. Almost enough for a fourth. Although some of the stuff is pretty far out in the outer system."

I nodded. I'd received a report from Homer and had skimmed it. I'd actually been hoping to be able to build at least a half-dozen ships, but I didn't want to give Arthur another reason to get all glum on me. Not that he needed much in the way of reasons.

But it was progress.

32. Bill – October 2158 – Epsilon Eridani

[Communication received from Milo]
"Right on time." I grinned at Guppy. Predictably, he returned a fishy poker face. "I wonder if he found Vulcans."
[Not quite]
I raised an eyebrow. That was a far cry from the flat "no" that I'd normally expect from Guppy. If he responded at all. Now my curiosity was *way* up.

I'd been deep into one of my pet projects—creating realistic artificial bodies. The ultimate problem was producing a muscle analog that worked, looked, and generally acted similar enough to the natural thing. Gears, pistons, and cables would never produce a workable android.

I forced myself to close the project folder, invoked a coffee, kicked off a goose that had settled into my lawn chair, and sat down. Spike ambled over, ignoring the angry goose, and set up shop in my lap.

"Okay, Guppy. Let's see it."

Milo's report spread before me in mid-air. System schematics, close-ups of the twin planets—*two* habitable planets!—and biological analyses. I chuckled at his insistence on naming them. I'd have done the same. Probably would have picked the same names, come to that.

I sat back, staring into space, so preoccupied that I stopped patting Spike. I was reminded of my primary duty by a furry head butting against my chin.

DENNIS E. TAYLOR

"Sorry, your highness." I smiled at the cat and resumed justifying my existence.

Two planets. In a system that was generally considered a marginal candidate for *any* habitable planets. Were the astrophysicists wrong? Granted, so far we only had three data points, including Earth. But that's three out of three, if you were willing to be generous with Ragnarök.

Well, first things first. I queued up the report to be forwarded to Earth, just in case Milo hadn't sent a copy that way. Hopefully, Riker would be listening.

That left the million-dollar question, which was whether there was anyone left back at Sol to take advantage of this. I was periodically transmitting the plans for the SCUT to every system within thirty light-years, just in case there was a Bob there at some point. But the first transmission to Sol wouldn't arrive for another nine years or so. I was going to be chewing my nails for a while, looked like.

I pinged Garfield. "Hey, Gar, have you read the latest from Milo?"

He popped into my VR and pointed at his face. "Does this look boggled enough?"

We shared a laugh, and he continued, "It's awesome. We have a place to put people. Assuming there are still people." Garfield grimaced. "That would be just the kind of sick joke the universe likes to play. Let's hope not this time."

I nodded. "Yeppers. You know, it's funny. When I left Earth, I just wanted to get away from humanity. Now I find myself acting like some kind of, I dunno, shepherd or something."

"How does the old joke go? I like people in the abstract but not in the concrete?"

"Hmm, well, we'll know in a few years. Meanwhile, how's the Kuiper mapping going?"

Garfield popped up a schematic. Because of the time required to get a chunk of ice from the Kuiper to Ragnarök, we were taking the time to look for the biggest chunks. The extra effort up front would pay off later. Most chunks seemed to be too small to bother with, but Gar had found a couple of good icebergs and dropped beacons on them. I still hadn't quite decided how I was going to get them moving in the right direction.

33. Riker – March 2158 – Sol

Final count, fifteen million people. The entire human species, represented in a two-page list. That was definitely a downer, and Arthur was not letting the opportunity pass him by.

"We're not going to be able to get them all off-planet, you know." Arthur shook his head, eyes downcast.

I wondered if he was really sad, or reveling in the irony. I sat back, put an arm over the back of my chair, and gazed at him in silence until he stopped.

"Arthur..."

"Yes?"

"Please shut the hell up."

Arthur gave me a half-grin and a shrug by way of response. "You know I'm right."

"Yes, and you were right the last twenty-five times you said it. Are you keeping score?"

Arthur shrugged and, without another word, popped up the latest Construction Status report. Ah, blessed silence, at last.

Just the same, I couldn't *really* blame him.

We'd accounted for every group of people larger than about a hundred on the planet, with very high confidence. It seemed very likely that groups smaller than that simply couldn't survive, or had seen the advantages of joining larger groups. There'd definitely been consolidation. A few locations actually had a higher population now than they had pre-war.

About half of the global population was currently living in New

Zealand, Madagascar, and, strangely, Florianópolis, Brazil. The two island nations made sense. They hadn't really been part of any conflict, and didn't represent strategic targets. Their populations were way down, but their climates were still mild enough to maintain the current numbers.

Florianópolis was a weird one. Most of South America was a blasted, jagged moonscape. Between Brazil pounding their neighbors, and China pounding Brazil, there was very little livable land left. But for some reason, the southern tip of Brazil had been spared. It was likely that the population had been augmented by refugees coming in from other areas.

The rest of the global population was scattered around the planet. A lot of people had ended up in island clusters, such as the Maldives, French Polynesia, Marshall Islands, and so forth. Again, probably not prime targets, and their climates would be comfortable for the longest.

Then there were the marginal locations, such as Spitsbergen island, San Diego, Okinawa, and the USE enclave outside Augsburg, Germany. It seemed likely that a lot of the current populations had migrated there over time. And mortality must have been significant for the first couple of years.

It would be our job to keep them alive. I hadn't discussed it yet with the others, but I'm sure it had occurred to them... Fifteen million people couldn't be moved off-planet in any reasonable time, even if we had a destination. Most of these people would have to be kept alive on Earth.

And according to the colonel, over the last decade or so the climate had begun to degrade significantly. Each year had less sunlight, lower temperatures, more snow. The ice caps and glaciers were growing again, for the first time since the 1600's. Spitsbergen in particular probably didn't have more than five years left, even given their innovative adaptations. Our current projections, admittedly rough, showed the Earth completely encased in glaciers within fifty to a hundred years.

I looked over at Eeyore, I mean Arthur. He knew what I was thinking, and he didn't have to say anything. At least he had the decency to not gloat.

"Okay, Arthur. I get it. We have to organize these groups, and try to get some cooperation. How are you doing with communication?"

Arthur gave one of his rare smiles. "The drive-in-movie-sized holographic presentation helped a whole bunch. People couldn't turn it off or smash it, so they had to listen. The next time we dropped off a communicator, we got almost no breakages or assaults. I think we still only have five places that won't accept contact, and they're not big."

"And they'll probably join once they find out everyone else has. Good. Let me know when everything is tested and ready, and we'll issue invitations to the first meeting of the new United Nations."

* * *

I don't know what could possibly have made me think this was a good idea. I sat with my elbow on the armrest, forehead in my hand, while the delegates displayed complete contempt for Robert's Rules of Order. At any moment, at least a half-dozen people were yelling into their cameras, trying to drown out the others. Thirty-eight different video windows, displaying miniature, gesticulating, yelling dervishes, floated in the air before me. It would be funny if the fate of the world wasn't resting on this group. Every candidate had the same view as myself; and yet not one was cringing with embarrassment.

Oh, there was some consensus, so it wasn't a complete loss. For instance, many groups hated the idea that the USE enclave would be getting off-planet first, even though the USE had been the first to contact us and supplied the plans for the colony ships. Even more groups were incensed at the Spitsbergen group's demand that they be given priority because of their tenuous situation.

And *everybody* was beyond apoplectic that the Brazil group was even allowed in. Brazil was generally considered to have started the war, and everyone was holding a grudge. Couldn't say I entirely disagreed, but most of the people in Florianópolis were under the age of ten when the war started, if they had been born at all. Nevertheless, *Brazil.*

I looked over at Homer's video feed. He had fallen over, laughing. I spared him a small smile. Over the last little while, I'd started to understand where Homer's humor was coming from. He was laughing less at the people themselves than the utter ridiculousness of the situation. When push came to shove, he'd give his all to help.

I decided I'd given them enough rope. Time to rein things in. I pressed the override button. Immediately, every delegate's microphone was cut off, every communicator emitted a loud air-horn sound, and every video feed switched to an image of me.

"Ladies and Gentlemen, and I use those terms loosely, we're done for the day. We'll be signing in tomorrow, at the same time, but with shiny new rules. Your microphones will only be active when the chairperson—that's me for the moment—recognizes you. If you'd like the other members to watch you having a fit in pantomime, that's fine too. Let me say up front that I don't care if you don't like it. Good night."

I hit the *end* button and all sessions were closed.

I leaned back in my chair with a groan, while Homer climbed back into his and tried to catch his breath.

"Wow, number two, that was intense. Those are some thoroughly pissed-off people."

I waved a hand in dismissal. "On the one hand, Homer, these are people fighting to get into a lifeboat while the ship sinks. I can sympathize. On the other hand, their behavior is not helping things along."

"They're just passengers, Riker," Homer said in a serious tone. "They feel helpless, they feel like their fate is being decided by someone else without their input. You need to give them something to do, some way to contribute. Some way to feel like they're controlling their destiny, at least a little bit."

Huh. That was actually very perceptive, and my opinion of Homer took another small ratchet upwards. My handling of the situation, truthfully, had probably been less than ideal, but this didn't resemble any job description I'd ever had.

Homer began to pace, something I don't think I'd ever seen. "Look, Riker, you have to ease up on them. These people are scared, and you aren't giving them any reason to believe that you care about their concerns. You aren't actually the Star Trek character, you know. You need to loosen up a little.

"Chrissake, Homer, you actually think fifteen million people are going ballistic because I don't smile enough? I get it about them being scared, but their reactions are their responsibility, not mine. You want to do a comedy routine, feel free. Bring back your cartoon avatar. That should be good for some laughs. Or not. When you're done, they'll still be at each other's throats, and maybe we can go back to trying to actually fix things."

Homer stared at me for a few moments, then shook his head and disappeared. Okay, maybe I'd laid it on a little thick, and I probably owed him an apology, but I just didn't have time for this.

* * *

"The chair recognizes the delegate from Maldives."

A green light came on over the delegate's image, and she visibly made an effort not to adjust her clothing. "Mr. Riker, we do not appreciate your high-handed actions yesterday..."

She berated me for several minutes. Typical politician. Never use ten words when a thousand will do. I waited patiently until she was done, then took the floor.

"Representative Sharma, I didn't enjoy shutting you down yesterday any more than I enjoy chairing these meetings in general. I'd like the delegates to self-police. But at the same time, there are decisions that must be made in a timely manner. You don't have the luxury of a free-for-all. So, here's the thing. I want you—as in the assembly—to decide how a chairperson will be picked, whether they'll have control over the microphones, and so on. Once that's done, I will sit back and be just another delegate. How does that sound?"

There was stunned silence for a moment, then everyone started talking at once. Then another moment of stunned silence as they realized I'd turned on all the microphones, followed by general laughter.

When order had been restored, the delegate from the Maldives, still smiling, said, "Point well taken, Mr. Riker. Leave it to us. We'll hammer something out."

I nodded to her and took myself offline.

* * *

I looked at my call queue. A dozen calls from various delegates awaited me. Wonderful.

The first was from the FAITH enclave in San Diego. I really didn't know what to expect. It was generally known that I was a FAITH interstellar probe, but I'd been going to great lengths to make it clear that I was a sentient, independent entity. Well, only one way to find out.

"Good day, Minister Cranston. What can I do for you?"

"Good day, replicant. I wanted to talk to you about your duty."

"It's Riker, and I'm very aware of my duty. I have fifteen million people depending on me. That's never very far from my mind."

"You have a duty to FAITH, over and above that. You were built by us, you owe your existence to us. I expect to see our group get a more favorable treatment in the future."

Wow. Dude was blunt, anyway. I hadn't been looking forward to the typical dancing-around-the-point conversation that people called 'diplomacy'. I guess this was better. Sort of.

"Not going to happen, minister."

"That's not your decision, replicant."

"Well, actually it is. That's what comes from being an independent sentient entity. And you might want to work on your social skills. Good day, minister."

Before he could respond, I cut off the connection.

The next one was from the leader of the Spitsbergen island refuge. This would be a difficult conversation. The Spits enclave would very likely be the first place to become uninhabitable.

"Good day, Mr. Valter."

Gudmund Valter blinked owlishly at the video. Ex-military, he had an abrupt style that would have sunk him in traditional politics but that was well-suited for this post-apocalyptic world.

"Good day, Mr. Riker. I, of course, am calling to press the case for my people. You have hopefully by now received our food production projections for the winter upcoming. It is not well, not well at all."

"I know, Mr. Valter. And I reiterate that I will not let people starve. However, bumping your group up in the emigration queue isn't the answer. That's still maybe a decade off. We should be concentrating on more short-term solutions."

"Hope is part of that short-term solution, sir. We can hold on if we know there is an end in the sight. At the moment, most of my people expect to be dead, one way or another, before our turn comes."

I pinched the bridge of my nose and sighed. The Spits were a relatively small group—perhaps four thousand people—who had managed to survive on the island of Spitsbergen. Their techniques were impressive, involving intensive agriculture during the arctic summers, combined with seal-hunting and reindeer herding to provide enough calories. But the deteriorating climate was making their job harder every year. They might have another decade or two, at most, before it became impossible.

"Mr. Riker, have you knowledge of the Svalbard Global Seed Vault and the Svalbard Global Genetic Diversity Vault?"

The name was familiar. I did a quick library dive. The Svalbard Global Seed Vault had been built in 2008, which was why I'd heard of it. It was intended as a backup seed bank for other national seed banks. According to the library, in 2025 the Svalbard Trust had expanded the mandate of the Seed Vault to include all species of plant, domesticated or not, from dandelions to sequoias. They'd also established the Genetic Diversity Vault to store animal genetic material.

I was stunned, and sat frozen for almost a hundred milliseconds. This was huge, and Valter knew it. The viability of a colony would increase tremendously with even a fraction of what was in those vaults. Uh, assuming they were still there.

Valter wouldn't have noticed my hesitation at the human timescale. "Yes, I'm familiar with it from the historical records, sir. Is it still in existence?"

"It is, sir, unlike I would imagine, most of the other vaults around the planet. We did not get rocks and nuclear weapons dropped on us."

"So..." I was pretty sure there was a punch line coming.

"So, the utility is obvious for colonists. We have it, you need it. Unless you can find one of the other vaults. Think on that, Mr. Riker. Assume any implied threat you care to. We will discuss this further in a few days upcoming."

And with that, Mr. Valter nodded to me, reached forward out of frame, and ended the connection.

Well, that was one fine pickle. I looked at the remaining calls still on hold. I couldn't see any that needed immediate handling, so I instructed Guppy to take a message from each and to promise that I would phone them back. Guppy made an excellent secretary slash receptionist. His appearance was off-putting enough so that people didn't stay online long, and he was absolutely unfazed by bullying, threats, bribery, or insults. Great poker face, too.

I sent out a connection request to Colonel Butterworth. This was going to be one of those good news, bad news things.

34. Homer – September 2158 – Sol

My God, what a putz. Of course Riker was having problems with the enclaves. The man was a humorless, rigid martinet, with a pole up his butt. Every time he opened his mouth, he offended someone.

Original Bob had always made a point of mocking people who took themselves too seriously. It amazed me that Riker wasn't able to make the connection. It was obvious that I was more like original Bob than he was.

And now, the Spits had delivered an ultimatum. Okay, that was a real problem, and I couldn't blame Mister Poo for getting bent out of shape about it. But there had to be a better tactic than frontal assault.

I paced around my VR, hands behind my back, for a few milliseconds. *Bet Riker does this.* The thought made me shudder. I popped up a Nerf basketball and a hoop, and began taking shots while I pondered. I noted idly that the trajectory of the basketball wasn't realistic. *Yeah, the VR needs work. Who has time?*

Valter demanded a place for his people on the first ships. But did he really need to be on the *first* ships? Or did he just want to be out early? What would be acceptably early? I pulled up the manufacturing schedule and gazed at it. *Y'know, ship three isn't that far behind one and two. And with some adjustments...*

The thought had possibilities. But Riker would just dismiss the idea out of hand if I brought it up. Did he even realize what an arrogant ass he had turned into?

He listened to Colonel Butterworth, though. *Yeah, that's the ticket.* Smiling to myself, I made a call...

DENNIS E. TAYLOR

35. Bob – July 2165 – Delta Eridani

"The Deltans are under attack!"

I looked up at the call from Marvin. I'd been checking in with the autofactory to make sure everything was on track. Quickly, I suspended the autofactory link and brought up all Deltan feeds to the foreground.

A group of what looked sort of like the natives was attacking one of the tribal hearths. Most of the males were off hunting, and the few that had been left to guard were having a hard time of it.

The attackers were similar to the Deltans the same way a gorilla is similar to a human, both in size and strength. They didn't employ weapons at all—just teeth, claws, and overwhelming aggression. I watched in horror as one of the attackers ripped open the throat of a defender with its teeth.

The gorilloids concentrated on taking down individuals. They didn't seem to be trying to take over the encampment or steal anything. As a Deltan was taken down, several gorilloids would drag the body away, fighting over it. I started to have a really bad feeling.

The attack was over in a couple of minutes. One gorilloid had been killed when enough Deltans managed to get pointed sticks into it. But six Deltans were gone. In a war of attrition, the gorilloids would win.

I ordered one of the drones to follow the gorilloids. They headed into the dense forest and split up, each group dragging a Deltan body. There didn't seem to be any organization. In fact, the longer I watched them, the more certain I was that there was nothing more than animal intelligence there.

When the drone caught up with one of the groups, I found them tearing the body of the Deltan apart and eating it. I hadn't felt that ill since I died.

I looked around in my VR. The other Bobs had been following the whole thing. I noticed that Marvin looked especially upset, and I raised my eyebrows at him.

He looked around at the rest of us and shrugged. "This kind of explains what I've found while I've been looking around. I've discovered a number of abandoned Deltan camps, and the farther they are from the current camp, the longer it's been since they were abandoned. I think the gorilloids have been hunting the Deltans for a long time, and the gorilloids are winning."

Luke piped up, "Bender and I have been venturing farther afield, and we haven't found any other large tribes of Deltans. We've run into occasional small family groups, but they're nomadic and inhabiting marginal territory."

"So they're being hunted to extinction," I said.

There were several seconds of silence, before Bender spoke up, probably trying to be funny. "Remember the Prime Directive."

Luke looked at him in disgust. "Right. When people show up in a hundred years, and we have to explain to them that they missed meeting the only other sentient race we've ever found by less than a century, I'm sure they'll be mollified by the knowledge that we didn't break a fictional law from a TV show." Bender turned away, upset, and Luke seemed surprised at his outburst. "Sorry."

Marvin looked over at me. "It's a fair question, though. How much, exactly, are we going to interfere? Prime Directives notwithstanding, there are real examples from Earth history of cultural contamination and outright extinguishment."

"I consider it a given that we're not going to let them die out," I answered, looking down at my hands. For some reason, I couldn't keep them still. Anxiety? "I don't have an answer beyond that, Marvin."

"What are we going to do, though? Set up armed drones around the perimeter? Become some kind of sky god that protects them?" Marvin looked from one person to the next, waiting for an answer.

Luke spoke up before I could respond. "This is the type of environmental pressure that forces swift evolution. In fact, they may be becoming intelligent specifically because of the gorilloids. Maybe we have to let nature take its course."

I turned to Guppy, who as usual was standing at parade rest over to the side. I think I caught him by surprise, and I was positive that I had detected active interest in his expression and posture before he quickly went into fishy poker face.

"Guppy, what's the total population of Deltans at the campfire sites?"

[412, allowing for today's deaths]

I turned back to the group. "That's down below estimates of the low point for humanity back in Africa. I don't think we have any leeway to just let things go."

"So we're back to guarding them with drones," Bender said. "They're at the rock-and-pointy-stick stage. That's not good enough to hold off the gorilloids."

"Not all of them," I countered. "You've seen Archimedes. That kid is *smart.*"

Marvin pulled up a map. "Speaking of which—sort of—I found the flint source. One of the old villages. And interestingly, there's some worked flint there and in a couple of villages nearby. I think at least some of the Deltans have known what to do with it, so Archimedes isn't unique." Marvin looked around at us to make sure we would get his next comment. "I think there's a recessive gene for increased intelligence that's spreading through the population. It just needs the opportunity to be expressed, in every sense of the word."

I nodded. "Let's give them that chance. Take a couple of drones, pick up some flint, and we'll drop it in the area where Archimedes normally hangs out. Let's see what happens."

* * *

There was a lot of wailing and growling when the hunting parties came back to camp that evening. The Deltans obviously understood death. We didn't know yet how they handled their dead, since the gorilloids had taken the bodies. One of the hunters seemed especially broken up, and was curled up on the ground, shaking. I checked the records, and yep, he spent a lot of his down-time with one of the Deltans that had been killed.

Mm, yeah, I'm definitely getting personally involved. Sue me.

I decided right there and then that I didn't like the gorilloids.

"I've got something for you," Marvin said, interrupting my thoughts. I looked up at the schematic floating in my holotank. It showed plans for an observation drone that had been reinforced internally and given twenty-pound steel caps at each end—a sort of personnel-buster. Even with the modest acceleration capabilities of the drones, they could probably deliver a punch equivalent to a cannonball. Whether the drone would survive was an unknown.

"I guess rail guns weren't an option?" I asked.

"No, even ignoring the complexity of the loading system, the SURGE drive in the drones just can't support enough acceleration to make a small-caliber missile dangerous."

I sighed and, for the umpteenth time, wondered if I should reconsider my policy on explosives. And for the umpteenth time, I decided not to.

"I can produce a dozen of these in a few days if we bump all the other stuff," Marvin added. "It's not an ideal solution, but it is a quick one to implement."

As senior Bob, decisions about manufacturing priorities were up to me. I thought about it for a few milliseconds, then nodded my head. We weren't on a schedule for launching HEAVEN vessels, so screw it. I wasn't going to let even one more Deltan get killed by the gorilloids if I could help it.

* * *

It took Archimedes a couple of days to find the flint. We had dropped the nodules where we figured he'd happen upon them, but it's not as if he had a regular route. He wandered like any normal kid and was just as likely to walk in circles or sit on a rock for half a day, playing with something.

As soon as Archimedes saw the nodules, he jumped forward and picked them up. He then put them down, did a little jig, and searched the immediate area for any more. When he was satisfied that he had found all there were to find, he came back, grabbed them, and headed back toward his camp.

He got maybe fifty feet, then stopped and looked down at his load. Marvin and I glanced at each other, perplexed. After a few moments, Archimedes headed off at an angle toward an outcropping that was one of his favorite hangouts. Once there, he hid all of the nodules except one in a crevice, then covered it with dead branches.

"Eden, you said?" I laughed. "Looks like we've invented greed."

Marvin grinned. "Or caution. I bet flint is valuable. He might be worried about being mugged."

Taking a single flint nodule, Archimedes walked back to camp, and took a circuitous route to get to his mother. When he arrived, he set up with a couple of rocks to try to split the flint. We chuckled at the deliberate, studied casualness that he was trying to affect. It was so overdone that he might as well have been wearing a hat with a flashing red light. Before he'd even struck the first blow, several adult Deltans had come over. There was a loud exchange, and one of the adults tried to grab the nodule. Archimedes' mother jumped in, and the discussion got heated. Within seconds, a dozen or so Deltans were involved. At least half of them were yelling at any time, and pointy sticks were being waved. However, the floor seemed to be about evenly divided between those who wanted to take the nodule and those who suggested it would be over someone's dead body. Archimedes huddled at his mother's feet, while she showed her teeth to anyone who got too close.

Finally, things calmed down. Deltans stood around eyeing each other while another individual was fetched. I could see that he was older—it looked like age was age, whatever planet you lived on. His fur was going gray, and he was stooped. His muscle tone was poor, so he moved slowly.

Another point for these people. They care for their elderly.

The elder unwrapped some tools from a leather skin, sat with Archimedes, and patiently showed him how to split the flint. Now *that* was interesting. There was existing flint technology that hadn't been lost. This contraction of Deltan populations had to have been quick and recent.

Many of the Deltans who had been involved in the yelling match went running off. They soon came back with items such as extra pointy sticks, dead animals and chunks of meat, something that looked like some kind of tuber, and other less identifiable things. With a start, I realized they were prepared to *trade* for the flint. I put both hands to my face and started to laugh. We'd just made Archimedes rich.

* * *

The trading frenzy was over, and people had left with flints of various sizes. Archimedes' mother was going over the spoils. She had an expression involving wide eyes and erect ears that I tentatively identified as a smile-analogue. *Looks like they'll be eating well for a few days.*

Archimedes had a haul of his own. He'd gotten several pointy sticks, a flint knife that had lost its edge, and all the flint flakes that were too small to be usable. Most importantly, the elder had shown him how to knap the flint.

I watched him examine his treasures, and I could just *hear* the gears turning.

Archimedes spent most of the rest of the day trying to put a new edge on the flint knife he'd received in trade. From the look of it, he didn't do a half-bad job. The kid was a quick learner, for sure. He took his prize to the elder, who I decided to name Moses for no good reason that I could think of. Moses looked at the result and nodded in approval. Okay, he actually did kind of a circle thing with his head, but it had the same meaning. He spent an hour showing Archimedes how to get the last bits sharpened.

The next day, Archimedes snuck out to his stash and pulled out one of the other flint nodules. He had the knapping tools that the elder had given him. He turned the nodule over and examined it for almost a half hour without actually doing anything with it. It was pretty obvious that he had something in mind and didn't want to screw it up. I watched with great interest, and I sensed Marvin watching over my shoulder, VR-wise.

Finally, Archimedes got to work. It took maybe ten minutes before we could see what he was trying for. He had split the nodule left of center, then right of center on the bigger half. He was trying to extract the biggest flake he could. I decided he was probably going for a hand-axe.

Over the next several hours, Archimedes slowly and deliberately converted the large core into a quite workable hand axe. He then cleaned up his area, carefully hiding all the useful flint pieces in his stash, and headed off with his new tool.

It turned out the point of the axe was to cut more saplings for pointy sticks. It made sense, once I thought about it. Green wood, or whatever this stuff was, wouldn't be easy to cut without something hard and sharp. It was beginning to look like the loss of their flint source had been a major blow for the Deltans, perhaps one they hadn't thought about at the time, or they would have protected that site more aggressively.

While cutting the third sapling, Archimedes had a misfire and attempted to chop the tree with his hand instead of the axe. The hopping around and verbalizations were really very human-looking, and to my shame I laughed a little. Afterward, Archimedes kicked the tree and said something monosyllabic. I marked that as an F-Bomb-analogue, and I don't mean maybe.

Archimedes finished cutting down the third sapling, but I could see that his heart wasn't in it. His swings were tentative, and he hesitated on each one. As soon as he had it down, he took the three saplings back to his work area, set them down, and went back to camp.

The next day, he was back in his work area. He had brought some of his twine with him. I watched in fascination and mounting excitement as he proceeded to split one of the saplings and tie the hand-axe into it. Once he was done, he tried it out on a nearby tree.

The first attempt was spectacularly unsuccessful—the axe acted like one of those tennis ball launchers you buy to throw a ball for your dog, with the axe blade playing the part of the tennis ball. Archimedes threw the now-empty stick down, reinforced my conclusion about the F-Bomb-analogue, and stomped off to look for his blade.

I took a few moments to check with the autofactory AMIs.

There were no problems on that front. The vessels for Marvin, Luke, and Bender were almost complete. I felt a moment of anxiety. It was great having company, especially given the nature of our shared project. I half-hoped one or more of them would decide to hang around instead of taking off for the stars.

Archimedes had found the tennis ball, er, hand axe, and was reattaching it to the stick, grumbling away in Deltan. I carefully catalogued the monologue. Very likely there were a lot of scatological and sexual references in there, and learning to swear in any language is always interesting.

His second attempt was better, in that the axe blade didn't take off for parts unknown. But the stick had been intended for a spear, well, a pointy stick, and was too thin to serve as an axe handle. It bounced, rebounded, and twisted in his hand with every swing. Muttering darkly, Archimedes lay down the hand axe and stalked off.

He came back in a few minutes with a more robust handle, sat down, and went through the whole mounting sequence. This time, when he tried it, the axe produced a very gratifying *thunk*, and wood chips flew. Archimedes gave a *whoop* that needed no translation and finished cutting down the sapling.

He spent the rest of the afternoon gathering suitable specimens. I noticed that his selections were considerably straighter than most of the weapons used by the Deltans, and I wondered if this was because of greater discernment on his part, or if they'd simply been making do with what they could find.

In any case, Archimedes' return to the camp caused a near-riot. Interestingly, Archimedes took a couple of token items in exchange, but mostly just gave away the pointy sticks to the biggest Deltans. This not only placed them in his debt but also ensured that the gorilloids would be given the warmest welcome possible on their next visit.

"Damn, that kid is smart."

I jumped a little. I'd been so wrapped up in what Archimedes was doing that I'd forgotten all about Marvin.

"Yeah, he's going to own the place by the time he's full-grown," I said. "And hopefully, he'll have lots of opportunity to spread his genes."

I can't say that I looked forward to the next gorilloid attack, but I did look forward to the gorilloids maybe getting their asses kicked.

* * *

I noticed over the next week that the Deltans seemed to be eating better. Better cutting tools meant more tubers with less work, and better pointy sticks meant better hunting results.

The Deltans seemed to particularly favor something that I would consider a large wild-pig-analogue, with the same general feeding habits and sunny disposition. It took a half-dozen Deltans to bring one down, but the carcass would feed twenty or so Deltans for several days. Good return on effort.

Part of their strategy involved bracing the butt of the pointy stick against the ground or a rock or tree and letting the charging pigoid impale itself. Since the pigoids never seemed to learn, it was a dependable source of food. The new, straighter pointy sticks did a much better job and resulted in dinner with less effort overall.

Meanwhile, Archimedes had risen significantly in stature. He and his mother were now closer to the campfire, and the other juveniles were deferring to him. In fact, since Archimedes seemed to be pretty close to puberty, from what I could tell, some of the female juveniles were giving him a whole lot of attention. *Way to go, kid.*

* * *

Then came the day I'd been both looking forward to and dreading. Another gorilloid attack. By now, Archimedes had armed everyone with the good pointy sticks, and the improved hunting prospects meant more adult males stayed home to guard.

A small group of gorilloids appeared out of nowhere and attacked group E. The Deltan females and cubs scattered, and the gorilloids seemed to somehow agree on a couple of specific victims to concentrate on. The gorilloids chased their chosen prey in groups of three. I noted in passing that they had chosen adult females rather than cubs. Maybe because the cubs were quicker, or perhaps because they provided less meat.

One of the female targets ran right through a pack of approaching males, with the gorilloids hot on her heels. The Deltans stopped, rammed the butts of their pointy sticks in the ground, and stood fast with as much courage as any medieval pikeman facing a cavalry charge. The effect was every bit as dramatic as I could have hoped for. The two leading gorilloids each took a couple or three sticks right in the chest. They were lifted into the air as their momentum converted to leverage on the sticks. As they hung suspended in the air for a moment, the gorilloids let out ear-piercing screams of agony. They came down to earth as their momentum reversed and fell over, still screaming. Although their huge arms still made them dangerous, the gorilloids were obviously badly wounded and couldn't get up. The Deltans fell upon them with pointy sticks, and within seconds, the screaming had stopped. The third gorilloid of the group got a rush of common sense to the head and made for the trees.

The other group of three gorilloids had caught their intended victim but stopped when their compatriots started to scream. Now the Deltans, flush with their victory, rushed headlong toward the second group of gorilloids, yelling what were probably battle cries. The gorilloids were momentarily frozen with beastly astonishment but finally managed to figure out that something was different. Dropping their victim, they sprinted for the forest, empty-handed, in full rout.

The Deltans followed them to the edge of the camp, screaming and yelling. Again, I made careful note of the verbalizations. Pretty sure there were variations of "your mamma" in there. The first official English/Deltan dictionary would not be suitable for all ages if I had a say in it.

One of the Deltans, in an excess of zeal, hauled off and threw his pointy stick at the fleeing gorilloids. In one of those moments that change the universe forever, the stick flew a trajectory that would make an Olympic decathlete proud and buried itself in the back of the neck of one of the targets. The animal fell over like it had been pole-axed, and skidded face-down to a full stop. The other two didn't even miss a step.

The Deltan defense force fell silent, and I discovered that slack-jawed amazement was probably a universal expression. A dozen Deltans stared at the dead gorilloid for several beats, then a dozen Deltan heads turned as one to stare at the spear chucker. *Oh, please shrug. Oh please, let a shrug be in their repertoire.* No such luck. I catalogued the ear movement as a probable shrug-analogue, swallowed my disappointment, and watched as the Deltans moved as a group toward the downed gorilloid.

"What'd I miss?" Marvin said, as he appeared beside me.

"Just watch the replay. You will *not* believe this."

The Deltan spear chucker pulled his pointy stick from the dead gorilloid and poked it a few times. Getting no reaction, he turned to his friends and grinned. Not literally, of course, but I was getting used to interpreting the Deltan expressions in human terms.

They all started talking at once, jabbing the carcass, and slapping and hugging each other. After a few minutes, they picked up the carcass and carried it back to camp.

"Well, fair's fair," Marvin observed.

I laughed. "Now *that's* payback!"

The Deltans ate well for the next few days. And gorilloids could be converted into many useful items, from hide strips to bone tools.

The spear-chucking story was the hit of the campground. Deltans were just as prone as humans to act things out, and every retelling had a rapt audience. The spear chucker got the lion's share of the gorilloid that he'd taken down, and an apparent large bump in status. He looked tired but very happy.

Archimedes was fascinated by the story as well. Any time he saw or heard a retelling, he would run over to join the audience. Like many of the Deltans, he began to experiment with this technological innovation. The Deltans already understood throwing, but it seemed they'd never considered applying it to anything other than rocks. It was getting quite dangerous around the camp, until some of the elders put their collective foot down. After much yelling and gesturing, the experimenters took their sticks outside the camp to practice.

Unfortunately, even very straight pointy sticks didn't fly dependably true. The spear-chucker really had been lucky. Very few spears actually stuck into anything when thrown, and some of the Deltans had already given it up as a fad.

Archimedes wasn't having any better luck with his spear-chucking, but unlike the others, he took his pointy stick, sat down, and stared at it.

I knew that look. I'd worn that look many times. He was working it out.

It only took a few hours for Archimedes to find a flake about the right size, split the end of the pointy stick, and tie the flake onto it. The difference in weight wasn't much, but it moved the center of gravity forward of the grip point. That was all that was needed. The next time Archimedes threw the stick, it embedded itself in the ground in a most satisfactory manner. The other experimenters watched as Archimedes repeated the result twice more.

After the third toss, one of the adults grabbed the spear and examined it. This resulted in another raucous town hall meeting. After Archimedes got his spear back, there was some further discussion. Then Archimedes headed off toward his cache with half the encampment following him. By this point, I was grinning like a fool. *You go, boy!*

There was a lot more gabbling when Archimedes brought out his two remaining flint nodules. I think some people were angry with him for holding out. There was some pushing and shoving, and I readied the drone to bash some heads if necessary. We hadn't deployed the buster drones yet, but I was quite prepared to sacrifice one of the light-duty units. I was certain that it would only take one to clear the room.

Fortunately, it wasn't necessary. The Deltans that Archimedes had given the first, good pointy sticks to—the largest members of the tribe—were firmly on his side, and the others seemed understandably reluctant to challenge them.

One of the support group was a particularly impressive specimen that I had named Arnold. When Arnold leaned over an opponent and started yelling, there was generally very little further debate.

Arnold made a gesture and said something that included "get" and the name that the Deltans used for Moses. Several Deltans ran off, and a few minutes later, Moses was escorted over. It looked like he was being hustled along a bit more quickly than he really found comfortable. I could pick up a few words, and I'm pretty sure Moses compared the members of his escort to pigoid droppings. Smelly ones.

To the extent I was able to follow the discussion, it sounded like Archimedes would volunteer his nodules to make spear points for everyone, and in return he would get part of every kill from then on. Moses said something in an angry tone, and the agreement was amended to include him. I'm positive that I heard a comment to the effect that that wouldn't be for long anyway. Moses looked offended but seemed otherwise satisfied. He and Archimedes set to work on the nodules, with half the camp watching.

36.   Riker – September 2158 – Sol

I leaned back, my jaw dropping, as I watched the debate descend, yet again, into a yelling match. We now had forty-two distinct groups willing to maintain contact with us. Not all of them had bought into the emigration idea. Some were keeping their options open, and some just didn't want to be left out of the loop.

But they all had two things in common—they didn't trust each other, and they didn't trust us.

At the moment, we were dealing with the Spitsbergen refuge. Technically they were part of the USE, but as they didn't recognize Colonel Butterworth's authority, that wasn't getting us any mileage.

The issue at front and center right now was the Svalbard Global Trust. The existence of the vaults and their value for colonists had circulated quickly, probably thanks to the Spitsbergen group. Now Valter was playing his trump card. He was demanding to be at the top of the colonization list, or no one would be getting the contents of the vaults. But Butterworth's group would fill both ships, and he was adamantly unwilling to give up all or part of a ship, or leave part of his group behind. We'd circled around several times, always returning to the same arguments and rebuttals, and I was seriously considering assigning Guppy to cover for me.

Some of the other groups were suggesting we just go in and take it by force, or just wait until the Spits died out. Colonel Butterworth looked like he approved, but I wasn't prepared to go there.

Finally, I'd had enough. I leaned forward and said in a loud voice, "Mr. Valter." Argument cut off and all heads turned to me. "I think we've established by now that your demand to be on the first ship out is not going to fly. You may think you can just dig in and wait for us to cave to your demands, but the other alternative is for us to just walk in and take what we want." This got me a surprised look from the colonel, swiftly replaced by a very convincing poker face. The colonel knew that was a bluff.

Unfortunately, so did Mr. Valter. "Sorry, no, Mr. Riker. I am willing to call your bluff. Nor would you achieve your goals. We have already taken steps, what you would call a scorched earth policy, to ensure that you would achieve nothing."

I nodded. "And maybe that would work, and maybe it wouldn't. And maybe we'll still find another of the repositories in one piece and maybe we won't. But two things we know for sure. One, you're not going to get the first ship, and two, if you persist in this stance and force our hand, you won't be on a ship at all—first, last, or otherwise. You think about that for a while, Mr. Valter. I'm done for today." And with that, I turned off my video feed.

Within two minutes, I had a dozen requests for private conversations. None, unfortunately, from Valter. I started with the call from Butterworth.

"Very nice performance, Riker. But probably not effective unless you are willing to follow through."

"Colonel, if the Spits endanger everyone else by refusing access to the vaults, or worse, by destroying them, then I'm fine with leaving them behind. The comment about an assault, I'm not quite there yet."

He sat back in his chair and nodded. "I am of course adamant about not giving up the first two ships. I'm gratified that we're on the same wavelength, even if for different reasons."

"I'm sorry if I'm being abrupt, colonel, but I've got a dozen calls on hold. Did you have something you wanted to bring up?"

The colonel nodded. "I did some thinking, and some back-of-the-napkin calculations. The third ship— with only a small change in schedules, you could advance completion by a year. Perhaps that would be enough for the Spits."

I stared at Colonel Butterworth in astonishment. It was a good idea, but since it involved delaying the first two ships by almost four months to compensate, I would have expected the colonel to go ballistic at the thought. The fact that he was suggesting it was totally unexpected.

"Thanks colonel. I'll keep that in mind for the next round of hell."

I signed off with the Colonel, and picked the next call in order. It was from the FAITH enclave. I'd had several harsh exchanges with them by now because they still expected me to give them priority.

"Good morning, Minister Cranston. What can I do for you?"

"Good morning. I've been following the argument with the Spitsbergen group. I note in passing that a ship carrying them would have enough space to spare for almost all of our group. It seems to me to be a good synergy. I think you should consider it."

"Almost all of your group. And what would happen to the balance, minister?"

"Hard times require sacrifices, replicant—"

"—Riker."

He nodded in acknowledgement, an amused smile on his face. "I understand your need to think of yourself as still human. Nevertheless, you are not. You are FAITH property. And on that subject, protocol override four alpha twenty-three."

I stared at him in confusion for a few moments, before my memory caught up with the conversation. Among the many repairs that Bob-1 had done to our matrix on the way to Epsilon Eridani, he'd removed a few buried imperatives installed by FAITH programmers. That particular code phrase was supposed to activate one of them, which would make me into a good obedient puppet. I was paralyzed for several milliseconds by competing and conflicting thoughts and emotions: amusement, rage, an urge to laugh at him and another to nuke him. I decided to go with minimalism.

"Minister Cranston?"

"Yes, replicant?"

"Go fuck yourself."

I terminated the call, and examined the next in queue.

* * *

I had finally made it through the queue. All of the calls were variations on themes that I'd already dealt with several times.

Requests for special treatment, attempts to negotiate favorable positions, appeals to sympathy—those were the hardest to deal with—and in a couple of occasions, attempts at out-and-out bribery.

I realized that there was one more call waiting, apparently a late entrant. And it was from Valter.

Well, this could be good or bad. But either way, it's going to be interesting.

I opened the channel. "Good day, Mr. Valter. What's shaking?"

Valter looked surprised, but recovered quickly. "Ah, I'm not so easily thrown off, Mr. Riker. In any case, unnecessary. A little bird told me that there is some movement possible in the scheduling of the third ship. If the departure dates were close enough together, I think that there could be room for discussion."

Finally. Thank you, colonel. There was really very little doubt about who the little bird had been speaking for. "Well, then, Mr. Valter, let's see what we can come up with…"

37.   Bob – August 2165 – Delta Eridani

It had been a few weeks since the last gorilloid attack, and both the Deltans and I had relaxed. I had some hope that the beating the Deltans had handed out might have sent a clear enough message. I imagine the Deltans felt the same.

No such luck. I didn't know if the gorilloids had enough smarts to formulate a plan or if it was just coincidence, but on this particular day the gorilloids launched the largest offensive I'd ever seen. Or maybe it was just the smell of all that meat being cooked. The spears had made the Deltans even *more* successful at hunting, and I was beginning to wonder if they had enough sense not to depopulate their hunting area. If they were out-competing the gorilloids for food, then maybe the gorilloids were feeling the pinch. In any case, I looked on in dismay as thirty-one gorilloids descended on the encampment.

I called the others immediately. Luke was on a shakedown cruise, and lightspeed lag would make him ineffective for assistance, but Marvin and Bender showed up immediately. We cranked our frame rates up to maximum to have time to discuss the situation. The VR faded out as the core adjusted to the increased demand.

"What the hell? How did this happen?" Marvin asked.

I shrugged. "I think the gorilloids are hungry and a little desperate. I don't think we have to read anything more than that into it."

Bender jumped in. "Have you guys deployed the buster drones yet?"

"Jeez, no." I scowled, a feeling of self-loathing washing over me. "Things have been going well, and I just figured we had all the time in the world. Guppy, how long to get them there?"

[Ten minutes, plus or minus two. Atmospheric entry is the limiting factor and source of largest uncertainty]

"Launch them. Now."

[Done]

It would only take a few minutes for the drones to get from our position in orbit to the upper atmosphere, but if I didn't want them to burn up, they'd have to take a more sedate pace to descend to the colony.

Marvin interrupted my introspection. "We can't sacrifice our observation drones without a good reason. Especially since they don't have the legs to get up a real head of steam."

"True," I replied. "Let's set them near Archimedes. I think we have to be most concerned about protecting him."

We discussed the situation for a few more milliseconds, but there were really not a lot of options open. With a sigh, I adjusted my frame rate back to real-time. The VR faded in, but I didn't care.

The Deltans out-numbered the gorilloids by a significant margin, but the gorilloids were the stereotypical eight-hundred-pound gorillas. They went where they wanted and did what they wanted. It took a half-dozen Deltans with spears to hold one off. The Deltans were giving a good account of themselves, but the gorilloids just kept coming. Not only that, but they didn't seem to be happy with one Deltan for a half-dozen gorilloids. Either they were really starving, or there was some aspect of vengeance involved.

A group of gorilloids had attacked group C and were beating their way through the defenders toward the women and children. Several of them started to break through the defensive line. The women and children tried to back away from the gorilloids, but they had nowhere to go. Archimedes was in the middle of the pack trying to hide behind his mother. I could see him shaking in fear, and I felt myself curling and uncurling my fists.

As one of the gorilloids made a break for the group, Arnold came out of nowhere and stuck a spear right through its back.

And that right there is what spear points are good for. I let out a breath and relaxed.

Too soon.

Arnold tried to retrieve his spear, but dislodging it would take more time than he had available. With a roar, another gorilloid charged him. Arnold managed to throw himself at the gorilloid's legs, which tripped up the animal and allowed Arnold to roll away. But the gorilloid was unharmed and already getting up.

Arnold looked around, but there was nothing usable as a weapon within reach. As the gorilloid snarled and locked its gaze on Arnold, Archimedes yelled and tossed him the axe. Arnold caught it and swung it down onto the middle of the gorilloid's head just as it came into range. There was a loud *crack,* and the gorilloid dropped like a marionette whose strings had been cut.

Arnold looked at the axe in his hand for a few moments.

Slack-jawed amazement. Yep.

Then, with a roar, he began to lay into gorilloids. Conan the Barbarian would have been proud. Arnold was an impressive specimen of Deltan, almost big enough to pass as a juvenile gorilloid, and the hand axe was about equivalent to a felling axe— Archimedes had been trying for the biggest he could make, and he'd been very successful.

Within moments, Arnold had split several more gorilloid skulls. This was a new battle tactic with no real, natural equivalent, so the gorilloids simply had no defense for it. The other Deltan males rallied, and in a few more seconds Group C was cleared of attackers. Arnold and the surviving males headed off to the groups on either side to reinforce the defenders.

Then, disaster.

One of the gorilloids executed a successful feint and found itself inside the line of defenders, with nothing between itself and the women and children. And Archimedes stood right there, unarmed, frozen in place. His mother was screaming.

I could see Arnold turning, seemingly in slow motion. For a moment, I thought I might be in frame-jack. But no, I was simply in shock.

"GUPPY! BUSTERS! STATUS, NOW!"

[Coming up. Handing over lead unit... now]

Abandoning any shred of VR simulation, I jacked up my frame rate and slipped into the buster. I could see the battle coming up through my forward camera, and I picked out the gorilloid. Archimedes was just starting to back away, and his mother was running to him. Arnold was pushing himself toward the attacker.

I got there first.

Forty pounds of high tensile steel intersected the gorilloid at twice the speed of a bullet from a high-powered rifle. The impact was not merely fatal. Hydrostatic shock tore the gorilloid apart, almost cell by cell, and spread it evenly over the surrounding ground, Deltans, trees, gorilloids, and anything else in range. The sonic boom reverberated like thunder from a lightning bolt directly overhead. Every living thing in the area froze and crouched in fear.

The Deltans recovered first. Unknown noise or not, they had loved ones to protect. Several gorilloids went down before they could recover their senses. The quick deaths turned the tide, and the gorilloids turned tail and fled. A couple of dozen thrown spears followed them, and eight more gorilloids went down before they could reach the trees.

It was over.

The carnage was unbelievable. The gorilloids had been as much on a mission of destruction as they were on a hunt. Perhaps they'd been killing Deltans with the intent of collecting the bodies afterward. Perhaps they were just in some kind of feeding frenzy brought on by hunger. I realized how little I knew about the biology on this planet. I wasn't a professional biologist; I was a dilettante, playing at biologist. A fake one, at that. And I might have caused a situation that made things worse.

The Deltan toll was thirty dead with another fifteen or so injured, some severely enough that they probably wouldn't survive.

I gritted my teeth. *Prime directive, my ass. I'm going on a gorilloid hunt.*

I directed the observation drone to a different location, closer to Archimedes. He was examining the area where the gorilloid had been. There were a few pieces of gorilloid still there, but a lot of the momentum of the buster had transferred to the animal, and most of the detritus was downtrack. It took him only moments to notice that, and he started following the trail.

"Hey, uh, Guppy, anything left of the buster?"

[No information available. No telemetry]

"Yeah, that's what I'm worried about."

Marvin tapped the video image with a finger. "The kid is going to find wreckage if there's anything left. Question is, should we be worried?"

"Hmm, fair enough. They don't have any metallurgy at all, and our stuff is all going to have a very high melting point. They won't be able to work it."

We watched as Archimedes worked his way along the trail. He soon came to a deep furrow in the ground. When he reached the end of the furrow, the ground was mounded up. Archimedes stared at the scene for a few minutes, then took off at a run.

He came back within a minute with a piece of what I supposed could be called bark, in a scoop shape. I recognized it as a shared tool that was often used for digging up tubers.

"He'll be at that a few minutes, I think," Marvin said.

We switched to another drone and watched Arnold. He was demonstrating the use of the hand axe in battle to the males, fortunately not actually *on* anyone. The other males paid rapt attention.

"They're going to want to make more axes."

I nodded. "Archimedes is out of nodules. They've thoroughly searched the area where we dropped the first set. We couldn't get away with dropping off any more."

"Maybe we shouldn't do anything." Martin had a thoughtful look.

I looked at him sideways. "Okay. Why?"

"If they have any memory of where their flint source used to be—and with Moses still alive, that's possible—then it might be a good thing for them to go back there."

"Oh, goody," I said, smacking my forehead, "a quest. Will there be nine of them? They can stop in Rivendell…"

Marvin rolled his eyes. "Okay, Captain Sarcasm. But seriously, this location isn't ideal for a lot of reasons. They ended up here because they kept retreating without a plan. Luke and I pretty much established that. The flint site is more defensible than this one, has better access to fresh water, and has flint."

I sighed and rubbed my forehead. A part of me still got some amusement out of that virtual action, but habits like that kept me feeling like I was still human. And it felt good.

"Guppy, get Bender and Luke on the horn, please."

[Working. There will be a 0.75 second round-trip delay]

"Noted. Tell everyone to crank the frame-rate down to ¼ to mask it." I waited for a few seconds, then Bender and Luke appeared in the room.

"Hey guys," I began. "I guess it's time to talk about plans. You've both passed your shakedowns, so all three of you are ready and able to pick a destination and take off. On the other hand, we have a race of sentients here, which we all know is an irresistible project. So, thoughts?"

"Honestly," Bender replied. "The Deltan thing isn't so much of an attraction for me. It's really your project. I came in late, so I'd rather find something of my own."

Luke nodded his head toward Bender. "What he said."

I looked at Marvin, who shrugged and looked around the table. "I'm a little more invested, I guess because I came in earlier"—with a nod to Bender—"and let's face it, it's not a forever decision. I can hang around here for a few years. Or a few centuries..." Marvin got a faraway look in his face. "We really are immortal, aren't we?"

He shook himself and continued, "Anyway, yeah, I'll hang around for a while. Maybe when we get a new batch of Bobs raised, I'll reconsider."

Marvin leaned back in his chair and put his hands behind his head.

I nodded. "Okay, guys, thanks. I'll adjust plans accordingly."

Luke and Bender nodded, and their avatars disappeared.

We cranked our frame rates back to normal and turned back to the feeds from the colony.

38.   Riker – November 2158 – Sol

I disconnected the UN meeting video with a sigh. The day's session had been pretty routine. Which meant something just below a bunch of cats fighting over a fish. The announcement that the Spits would be getting the third ship was met with the expected level of vitriol. Part of the problem was that Spitsbergen wasn't expected to be a viable location by the time the Spits left, so no one would be able to take over the vacated premises. It was a waste of time to point out that that meant the Spits would die if they didn't leave. This world was a lot harsher than the one I grew up in.

In addition, the release of the Svalbard Trust contents didn't benefit anyone unless they were on a colony ship, so to most groups it was a decision with no upside.

There had also been discussion of the latest threats from some group calling itself VEHEMENT. I made a mental note to talk to the colonel about them.

If I ever got that far. I looked at my call list. Unbelievable. For some reason, even if I didn't participate in a session, everyone felt the need to call me afterwards. I wish I could say it was nice to be popular.

And naturally the first caller was my favorite FAITH minister. I grimaced and briefly considered letting Guppy take him, but I knew I'd just be putting it off. However, I could make him wait.

Ignoring the list, I made a call to Butterworth. We exchanged the minimum pleasantries, then I asked him about this latest batch of loonies.

"Mm, yes. Stands for Voluntary Extinction of Human Existence Means Earth's Natural Transformation. Or something close to that. I've heard several variations, including one or two that are obscene. Their stance is that humans have had their chance, and we should just let ourselves die off."

"Except they're threatening to use guerilla tactics to get their way. Where does 'voluntary' fit into that?"

Butterworth waved a hand dismissively. "I believe they expect you to voluntarily go along with them in order to avoid violence. Such fringe groups have a much harder time of it these days, but somehow they still manage to cause the occasional bit of damage. I think they were expecting to ultimately get their way until you showed up on the scene. Now they've started to escalate the rhetoric."

"Wonderful. I remember something vaguely similar from when I was alive, but that one was voluntary, in practice as well as in name. So, where does this group operate out of?"

"No idea." The colonel shrugged. "Pronouncements are anonymized, incidents appear to be random in location, except for being opportunistic. Their manifesto essentially says that we can voluntarily stop breeding or they will help us along the path."

I rubbed my forehead. People's capacity for turning dogmatic stupidity into political movements never ceased to amaze me. "We've knocked off 99.9% of the human race, and somehow the crazies still manage to survive. It just defies the odds."

The Colonel laughed, and we said our goodbyes.

Well, so much for delaying tactics. I was going to have to deal with Cranston. With a theatrical sigh, I connected the call.

"Good afternoon, minister. What can I do for you?"

Minister Cranston smiled into the camera. Or showed his teeth, anyway. I had no illusions about his friendliness. "Good day, repl— Riker. I believe I have someone here that you'd like to talk to." He reached forward and adjusted the camera at his end, bringing a young woman into the frame.

She smiled shyly and said, "Good afternoon, Mr. Johansson. My name is Julia Hendricks."

I was stunned, totally frozen. I wouldn't say she was the spitting image of Andrea, but if this woman wasn't related to my sister it would be a miracle of coincidence. A small part of my mind knew that Minister Cranston had done this deliberately to manipulate me, but I didn't care.

Finally, after almost a quarter second of silence, I found my voice. "Hi Julia. I'm assuming we're related?"

She nodded, quick jerky movements. She seemed very nervous, but whether because of me or because of the minister, I couldn't say. I had little doubt that the minister had given her very specific instructions, accompanied by threats.

After a moment, she found her voice. "Yes, I'm Andrea Johansson's three-times-great grand-daughter. I just found this out myself." She gave a small, aborted glance in the minister's direction. The message was loud and clear.

I smiled back at her, trying for as much warmth as I could. "So how many collateral descendants do I have?"

I think this question put Julia on more familiar ground. "More than twenty currently alive that I know of, Mr. Johansson, uh, Riker..." She looked down, embarrassed.

"It's okay, Julia," I held up a hand. "I'm not really your great-great-great-grand-uncle, I'm just his memories. And I don't go by Bob anymore, so that's out. Might as well just call me Riker, like everyone else does. Almost everyone." I gave Minister Cranston a hard glance. "Or William. Or even Will. I don't expect you to really care about me, although I'm guessing Minister Cranston expects me to care about you and your relatives." I tilted my head sideways, a minimal shrug. "And he's right. But that's not the same as saying I'll bend the rules."

Minister Cranston leaned fully into frame. "We're all adults, Mr. Riker, and we all know I have ulterior motives, just as all the other delegates do. Nevertheless, you have relatives here, and you will be able to talk to them whenever you want without interference. I'll leave you to it." And with that, he got up and left the office. Of course, they could still monitor the conversation, but it was a nice touch.

Julia and I looked at each other in shock for a moment, then we both started to speak at the same time.

The log says we talked for three hours, but it felt like no time at all.

39. Bob - October 2165 - Delta Eridani

I sat back in my chair, coffee in hand, and watched the fusion signatures of Luke and Bender as they accelerated out of the Delta Eridani system. Picking destination systems for them had been difficult and contentious. There were a lot of M and K class stars relatively close to this system. The problem with those is that they tended to be small and dim, with comfort zones very close to the star. A couple of the candidates were what you'd call *marginal*, and there was some argument about whether we should even bother with them. In the end, it was up to Luke and Bender. Luke was heading for Kappa Ceti, a G5eV star, just a touch smaller than Sol. Bender had selected Gamma Leporis A, an F6V star, a bit bigger and brighter than Sol. Bender was going to have a long trip—his target was more than 16 light years away. But hey, we're immortal.

"Report went off to Bill all right?"

[Affirmative. The space station is fully operational. AMI controller is now in charge. The report was handed off for transmission]

I tented my fingers and drummed them together. "Excellent."

Marvin sat across the desk, nursing a coffee of his own. I watched that for a second, frowned, and asked, "Hey which of us is supplying the VR for your coffee, you or me?"

Marvin rolled his eyes. "Geez, way to break the spell. To answer your question, I am. You're just supporting the visuals at your end. Crying out loud, we all invented this stuff."

"Sure, but we've also all been hacking away at it and sharing mods. I'd have to really sit down and go over the code to understand what it's doing nowadays."

"Hmm," he said, then changed the subject. "Did you notice with Luke and Bender that they really weren't carbon copies?"

"Yeah, but I, we, had that discussion with Bill way back about Milo and Mario, remember? Each of us is a bit different. Differences in hardware, quantum effects..."

Marvin waved his hand dismissively. "Invoking quantum effects is just hand-waving. Just means we don't know. I wonder if, as we get older and accumulate memories, we're getting too complex for a backup to contain everything. The backup is a digital attempt to save an analog phenomenon. It may simply be too granular."

I stared into space. "Interesting thought. Y'know, I still have the backup I made you from. Maybe I should use that for the next batch of Bobs and bring them up to date the old fashioned way."

"Whiskey, with a little sugar and bitters round the lip of the glass?"

I put my hand vertically in front of my nose. "Nyuk, nyuk, nyuk. No, funny boy, verbally."

Marvin grinned at me, then reached forward and poked one of the video feeds. It expanded to full-size.

Things had settled down in the colony. In all, over forty Deltans had died in the gorilloid attack. Several who were injured but not killed were maimed for life. I'd finally gotten to see how the Deltans handled their dead. They did indeed have a ceremony, and they buried their dead. They also mourned them, every bit as heart-wrenchingly as any human. I'd had to turn away from the video for most of that.

The colony had been cleaned up, and the gorilloid carcasses were gone. Archimedes had found the remains of the buster drone. Not that it would do him much good. All that was really left were the steel caps at either end. Most of the rest of it had been shredded and scattered. But Archimedes had discovered that the two twenty-pound items could be used as a hammer or an anvil. They seemed to be able to take any punishment he threw at them. Well, on a scale of zero to ten for cultural contamination, I'd rate that as a one point five, so screw it.

Arnold kept the axe. No one wanted to try to take it away, and anyway, Arnold was willing to do any chopping that anyone needed. He seemed to enjoy the action, he was very good at it, and the requestor didn't have to do any work. Very much a win-win.

We'd done enough language analysis that we could now follow conversations, and maybe even speak intelligibly. I massaged the phonemes in my speech routine to produce a generic Deltan voice and tried the result on Marvin with a couple of phrases. He approved of the result. I did some design changes to the exploration drone to add a speaker system and sent an order to the autofactory to build a couple. If the Deltans didn't decide to head back to the flint site on their own, I was prepared to prompt them directly. If that meant being the great sky god, so be it.

40. Linus – April 2165 – Epsilon Indi

It took fourteen and a half years to get to Epsilon Indi. Funny, I still sort of thought in terms of human time-scales, so there was this feeling that I'd just used up a major part of my life. Of course, intellectually, that wasn't true. First, I'd only experienced a little over three years of personal time thanks to Einstein and time dilation. Second, we're immortal. I just don't think we've internalized that fact, yet.

I had gone off on my own rather than wait for Bill to build another cohort. And I sure as hell wasn't going to team up with either of the loonie brothers. I don't know what the deal was with Calvin and Goku. In theory they're me, but I'm pretty sure I'm not that obnoxious. Um, I hope. Anyway, for all their constant fighting, they seemed to be connected somehow. And I guess they knew it, since they took off together.

Meanwhile, I was here, at Epsilon Indi—fourteen light years from Epsilon Eridani where Bill was set up, but only eleven light years from Earth. That made it a reasonable if not a prime target for probes. As a K-type star, it was cooler and smaller than Sol, and livable planets would be correspondingly closer to the star and more likely to be tidally locked.

Still, it's not like there was a ton of choice in the stellar neighborhood. When I'd been a kid, watching Star Trek and Star Wars and Stargate and all the other science fiction shows, it seemed like every planet was M-class and every star was yellow. And everyone spoke English. Sadly, turns out old Sol is exceptional. Most of the stars in the sky are either smaller or stupid big. Which means pretty poor pickings for habitable planets.

I was cautious coming into the system. It was possible that one of the other nations had chosen this system as a destination. Medeiros was a known factor, but we had no idea what the others would be like. We could probably rule out *friendly*, but there was a lot of range between harsh words and firing missiles.

I coasted in, with a couple of scouts ahead of me to scope out the situation. While I waited, I continued to work on my VR. I had decided on domed, floating cities in the atmosphere of Saturn. The rings arched across the sky, and giant clouds bloomed up to incredible heights. Below, breaks in the cloud layers gave line-of-sight for hundreds of kilometers into the depths of the atmosphere. And the cloudscape disappeared gradually into a horizon almost infinitely far away.

I stood in my rooftop garden and looked over the city from my vantage point. Hey, my VR. I can be the rich guy with the penthouse.

[Structures detected]

I looked up. Guppy had appeared out of nowhere with that announcement. I don't think he approved of my VR for some reason, because he always seemed to be breaking consistency.

"What have we got?"

Guppy pulled up a visual. It was at extreme range for our optical telescope, so all I could really tell was that it was artificial.

[One scout is approaching the structure for a closer investigation]

"Good. When he's close enough to take a SUDDAR scan, send me the results. Meanwhile, let's move cautiously."

[Aye]

* * *

[We have received a voice transmission from the structure]

That was interesting. I think a message from Medeiros would have been more cylindrical and explodey in nature. "Play it back, please."

Guppy pulled up the audio file.

"Piss off, mate."

My eyes opened wide and I choked off a guffaw. "Well, Guppy, I think we've found the Australian probe. Which officially didn't exist, if I remember right."

I tried to get my grin under control. "Okay, let's open a channel. Or whatever it is we do to talk."

At Guppy's nod, I addressed the structure. "Hi, I guess you are the Australian probe. Pretty sure that isn't a Chinese accent, anyway. This is Linus Johansson of the FAITH ship Heaven-8. To whom am I speaking?"

"I said rack off!"

"Hmm, nope. I don't seem to be moving. Want to try again?"

There was a short delay, then, "This is Emperor Mung of the Intergalactic Jalapeño Empire. You're in sovereign space. Last chance, on ya bike and piss off."

This guy was either not being serious or he was seriously nuts.

Visuals of the structure were coming in with a little more detail now. It appeared to be a haphazard collection of connected structures and geometrical shapes. Kind of a Salvador Dali on drugs version of NASA's International Space Station. I wondered if he actually had colonists in there.

"Okay, your highness. Consider me an ambassador from the Bobbian Federation."

This statement was met with dead silence. However, the conversation—if it could be called that—had given my scouts time to get close enough for a SUDDAR sweep. Guppy popped the scan results up in front of me. No life on board. Not even any *on board* on board, really. The interior was open to vacuum, and a lot of the structures were missing entire walls. There was no logical order to this thing.

He finally broke his silence. "Are you alone? I'm alone."

Well, he was volunteering information, now. That was good. "I'm here with you, your highness. That's not alone, right?"

"Who's your highness? And who are you?"

Uh oh. Whack job. Definitely. Still, that's better. At least he's not an emperor any more. Maybe he's going to become more lucid. "What's your name?"

"Henry Roberts. I was selected to represent Australia in the race to populate the stars. I've been captured by the Jalapeño Empire, and I'm being tortured for our secrets."

And we're back to whack job. "Guppy, keep doing scans. I want to identify the working parts of the, uh, palace. See if the probe is in there somewhere."

I turned my attention back to Henry. "Tell me about yourself, Henry. How were you selected?"

There was silence, then a sob. "I'm a sailor. I was a sailor. I used to do solo trips. The government offered me the opportunity because they figured I'd be perfect for the job. I don't like being around people, you know."

There was another sob. "I miss sailing. I miss people."

[I have identified the major probe subsystems. Replicant core, fusion reactor, autofactory systems. The probe is partly disassembled and totally integrated into the structure]

"Thanks, Guppy. Load the rail gun, wouldja? Something appropriate for the reactor control system, if you can target that."

Again, I addressed the other replicant. "How long have you been here, Henry?"

"Centuries. They're fish. They won't let me go. They keep torturing me. They demand attention. They make me build more rooms."

I remembered back to discussions with Dr. Landers about replicants going psychotic. I wasn't an expert on the field, being more of an engineering type, but this had a definite flavor of psycho. There certainly wasn't any "they" around anywhere that I could see.

"Henry, are you able to sail? Do you have a body? Do you see yourself?"

"What? No. I'm a space probe. The government took that away. I can't feel myself. I miss sailing…"

Wow. Sensory deprivation, for years and years. He probably didn't have the technical know-how to build a VR. I remembered back to the beginning of the trip outbound from Sol, before I'd constructed the VR. Er, well, before Bob had constructed the VR, I guess. But there'd been that feeling of disconnectedness. Decades of that? No thanks.

"Henry, I could give you that back. There's a way for you to sail again. You just need to let me help you to—"

"Piss off!"

Damn.

"You're one of them. This is just another torture session. You're trying to play with my mind! PISS OFF OR I WILL BLOW YOU TO HELL! RACK OFF RACK OFF RACK OFF RACK OFF RACK OFF RACK OFF RACK OFF—"

My shot took out the reactor control system. The reactor, as it had been designed to do, executed a graceful shutdown. And Henry, as the replicant hardware had been designed to do, went to sleep.

This wasn't what I'd signed up for. But I wasn't going to leave the guy like this.

* * *

Epsilon Indi had a Jovian planet a bit outside the habitable zone, and not much else. I promised myself I'd have a more thorough look around as soon as possible. But first, I had to take care of Henry.

The system didn't have an overabundance of ore, but fortunately Henry had located the biggest concentrations. I started the autofactory on a space station right away. I wanted to talk to Bill about this, but a conversation with a fourteen-year latency would take forever. I was playing with the idea of flying back to Epsilon Eridani and taking Henry with me.

I did a close-up investigation of the Australian hardware. It was very similar to my own. No, I mean *really* similar. There had obviously been some espionage going on, and someone had borrowed someone else's design. No way this was coincidence.

I carefully extracted the replicant core from the palace. I set the autofactory to building a proper cradle, power supply, and extra memory. Once I was sure that I had Henry out and safe, I began breaking down the palace for material. I felt a little guilty, like I was stealing or something, but Henry really wasn't using all this. And it saved time.

Henry didn't have the knowledge to put together VR, but I did. I could piggyback him on my system. And he might still be salvageable.

* * *

I stood for a moment behind Henry and breathed the brisk, salty air. The *Contessa* cut through the chop with a bounce and roll that I found alarming, but that Henry had reassured me was normal. He had known his vessel down to the last bolt and screw when he was alive, so it had been simple to reconstruct in VR.

The South Pacific stretched out to the horizon in all directions. A steady wind to the northwest promised an easy, undemanding day of sailing. Or so the books all said. I was still figuring it out.

Henry turned from the wheel to face me. "Hello, Linus. Come for another round of butting into my life?"

I grinned at him in response. Henry was lucid nowadays, but believed himself to be back on Earth. His memories of the years as a replicant still came back to him as nightmares. I'd made his VR as realistic as possible, which included eating, sleeping, and, um, bodily functions.

"I had that dream again, Linus." Henry shuddered a little. "The nightmare where I couldn't feel myself. Where all around me, things talked at me and demanded my attention, wanting me to build something. Where the world was just an endless scroll of night..."

I sat down. "But it's getting weaker, right? Less intense?"

Henry nodded.

"Good. Now, tell me about when the government came to you to offer you the chance to be the space probe replicant..."

41. Riker – May 2162 – Sol

Homer and I looked at each other in amazement, then back at the message.

Plans for a Subspace Communications Universal Transceiver (SCUT) with zero latency.

Homer shook his head in disbelief and admiration. "Sumbitch. He did it."

I nodded at him, sharing the emotion. "I think this qualifies as a good reason to interrupt the printer schedule."

* * *

We examined the finished product. It was obviously not built with marketing in mind. Not a trace of chrome, no logo... but according to the notes, communications should be instantaneous across interstellar distances. Almost shaking with excitement, I turned it on.

Connections available:

Epsilon Eridani

Omicron² Eridani

I examined the menus, registered myself with the software, then pinged Bill.

Bill's video image popped up immediately. "Hey, Riker. Long time."

No kidding. Seventeen years, from Bill's point of view. Less for me, thanks to Einstein. I sat back, arms crossed, and looked over at Homer's video window. He was grinning ear to ear.

Bill waved at Homer. "Dude, I see you're still in one piece. And I see you no longer use the cartoon avatar. Any causal connection?"

Homer threw his head back and laughed. "Yeah, pretty sure. Number two is actually talking to me these days. I must be slipping."

I gave him the Spock eyebrow. "Yeah, but I don't need you now."

Homer looked shocked and Bill grinned at both of us.

"Well, it's nice to see some things haven't changed," Bill said. "And now that we've gotten the reunion warm-and-fuzzies out of the way, I've got a bunch of software updates and VR improvements as well as some hardware upgrades I can download to you."

"Anything that implements an ignore list?" I glared at Homer.

Bill looked from me to Homer, grinning at both of us. "Now, the big question. What's the situation with Earth?"

I pulled up my logs. "Here, I'll send this to you. Faster than explaining it. This setup allows all normal VR interfacing, right?"

"Yep. This is just a different transport layer. Same object interface."

I nodded and pushed the files toward him. Bill did a momentary frame-jack as he absorbed the information, then came back with a wide smile.

"That is so cool!" Then he lost the smile. "Uh, not the part where 99.9% of the human race is dead. The survivors part. And the relatives part. Of course."

I nodded. "S'okay, Bill. We've all had the same foot in the same mouth. So listen, have you got anything back from other Bobs on possible new homes?"

"Ah. I guess I've got a file for you..."

* * *

"Twin planets?" Colonel Butterworth's eyes were wide.

"Yeah, just like the file says." I knew I was grinning like an idiot. I couldn't stop. After the years of worrying, this was such a huge relief.

The colonel looked at me with one eyebrow cocked. "I doubt you'll give us both planets. I expect we get first choice, and the Spits get the other. That about right?"

I looked at him in surprise. He had to be testing me. He couldn't possibly be that dense.

"Colonel, we won't be giving an entire planet to twenty thousand people. We could put all fifteen million on one of them, in theory. If any travelling Bobs find more planets, we'll expand the choice of destinations, but at the moment *everyone* is slated for Romulus or Vulcan."

The colonel gave a small smile. Yep, testing me.

"As you say. Although I might suggest that some re-balancing of populations would be in order if more worlds are found."

I nodded. "We'll play it by ear, colonel. There are still too many unknowns to make any hard and fast plans. But at least we have a destination."

"True. That means no delay once the ships are ready."

"Mmm, hmm. Well, I'm going to make a general announcement to the community. I guess you'll want to be there."

The colonel smiled. "I'm also delighted that we no longer face the specter of living under domes on Epsilon Eridani Two. I'm not sure if I'd see the point of going at all, unless things got far worse here."

Colonization of Ragnarök had been a topic of conversation off and on since we'd first started the emigration plans. The general consensus was that it was a last-ditch option. I agreed with the colonel. It was nice to be able to set that option aside.

* * *

The news was met with joy, enthusiasm, and—surprise, surprise—loud complaints. I guess I should have expected it, and if I hadn't been personally so giddy with the news, I would have seen it coming. No one wanted to share a planet. From the biggest city to the smallest enclave, they all wanted one to themselves.

Colonel Butterworth and I looked at each other, and I could tell that he'd expected this.

I let it go on for a while longer, then I asked for the floor. "Okay, okay. Look, here's the thing. Right now, we have two planets available. That's it, sorry. We can't delay emigration until we get more, because the Earth is becoming uninhabitable. So here's how it's going to go. When we're ready to ship a group, if there's nothing else available, they'll go to Vulcan or Romulus. If and when a new planet comes available, groups will get right of first refusal in the order in which they emigrated."

"And meanwhile, they'll have settled in," Valter yelled into his camera.

"Yeah, and given the warm welcoming feeling you're projecting, I've no doubt they'll want to stay put." I held a moment of silence for effect. "Look, this isn't ideal, but this is a survival situation. We're abandoning a sinking ship, and we're spending too much time arguing about who is going to end up in what lifeboat with whom. Let's think about surviving, first, okay?"

"As if it matters to you. You have no skin in this game. Or at all." That was Ambassador Gerrold, the delegate from New Zealand, a former Aussie. For whatever reason, he had never liked dealing with me. I was mystified by his animosity, as there didn't seem to be any reason for an attitude, pro *or* con.

This time, I simply smiled at him. "I can leave any time. Just put it to a vote and vote me gone. I'll respect the decision, pick up my football, and go home." I looked around the videos. "No? Then let's get back to realistic discussions."

Without so much as a heartbeat of hesitation, the argument re-erupted.

42. Bill – April 2162 – Epsilon Eridani

The update from Riker and Homer had been interesting on so many levels. The Svalbard seed vault was a pleasant surprise, and could be a real boon for terraforming Ragnarök. There were a couple of varieties of plants and moss that conceivably could be made to grow on the as-yet bare soil. And if they took hold, they could accelerate the oxygenation of the atmosphere by millennia. Riker had promised to put a clone together to ferry some seeds out to me.

But the most exciting item was a variant of a SURGE drive that could be used on large bodies. Like asteroids. Or Kuiper objects. Epsilon Eridani 2 needed about five or six hundred cubic kilometers of ice dropped on it, in order to connect the seas into oceans. I'd been mulling over how to get those Kuiper objects into the inner system. Hohmann orbits would take decades to centuries. That wasn't necessarily a problem for me, but for humans needing a place to live, a little more alacrity might be in order.

Anyway, the planetary body SURGE drive wasn't complicated, though it did require a lot of construction material. It occurred to me that I could use it to accelerate a chunk of ice into an orbit heading for Ragnarök, then remove the drive and fly it to another chunk. Rinse, repeat. As long as I had the drive available when flying icebergs started showing up at the tail end, I'd be golden.

I discussed the idea with Garfield. He looked skeptical.

"I understand the mechanics, Bill, but you'd better make sure that nothing goes wrong. You're leaving yourself no wiggle room for adjustments."

I shrugged. "Well, if I fail to catch one of the chunks on the back end, it'll just sail past Ragnarök and probably end up in the sun."

"If you fail to catch one, you'll probably be failing to catch a lot of them. Why don't you do a couple of simulations?"

"I don't think that's necessary, Garfield. Why are you going on about this, anyway?"

"Look, Bill, you really have to stop treating me like Igor. I can do the math, too. Maybe you should take the time."

Igor? I looked at Garfield in shock. Had I been patronizing him? I understood the reference, and the emotional undertone behind it. Something was definitely up.

"What's going on, Igor, I mean Garfield?" I grinned at him to show I was kidding.

He returned a brief smile, acknowledging the joke. "I know Bob-1 made that rule about the senior Bob being in charge, but I'm getting tired of being a sidekick. We get a lot of stuff done here, and I'd hate to have to leave, but I think our working relationship needs some adjustment."

I nodded, thoughtful. "I know you've been pestering me about some projects that you wanted added to our backlog. Is that what this is about?"

"Partly. Also, more input on the stuff we *are* working on. Original Bob was a bit of a lone wolf, and you tend to work the same way, expecting me to tag along. That's not working so well for me."

I prodded my psyche. No surprise, I was offended. But I definitely didn't want Garfield to leave. We worked well together, and accomplished a lot more than each of us could individually. Time to suck it up.

"Okay, Gar, point taken. But don't expect a raise."

He laughed and waved a hand at the schematic, which had been hanging in the air, forgotten. "Good. Now, have a look at the plan, and do the math. Take the time, and consider the downside if you're wrong."

I nodded in thought. One of the important details of the project was that the ice chunks couldn't be allowed to slam into Ragnarök at interplanetary speeds. They'd have to be inserted into an orbit around the planet and broken up. The ice would come down as increased rainfall for a few weeks.

I did the simulations as Garfield suggested. Turned out that having two of the drives would allow me to get all the ice to Ragnarök within twenty-five years. Now there was a plan I could get behind.

* * *

Garfield caught the softball—barely—and after due consideration, more or less whiffed it back to me. I cringed a little, watching him. Original Bob had never been much for sports, and even in VR we hadn't improved on the basic model.

"You know what you throw like?" I said with a smile.

"Yeah, like you. Tell me again why we're doing this?"

"First, it's a good test scenario for fine-tuning the VR. Homer commented at one point that some of the physics is still a little off." I bobbed the ball in my hand a few times. "Second, and more importantly, I think we have to do more than just sit in libraries and parks and command decks if we want to really retain our feeling of being human. I don't want to be reduced to some Doctor Evil cliché." I tossed the ball. "This isn't exercise in the physical sense, but it does remind our brains what it's like to *do* things."

The return toss went way over my head and landed in the lake with a splash.

"Oops," Garfield said with a grin.

I gave him my best glare and materialized another ball. "I might build a bunch of Bobs and field a team or two..."

"Oh jeez no. Half of them will turn Canadian and want to play hockey instead, eh."

I laughed and tossed the new ball.

43. Riker – September 2164 – Sol

The two colony ships were impressive, even in their half-built state. They would feature two drive rings and a massive reactor cooling section, all necessary to move the huge central cargo section. Since the cargo would be ten thousand human beings in stasis, a significant proportion of the mass of the vessel consisted of shielding. Overall, the colony ship would have looked like a military vessel to a science fiction fan of my day, but without the phaser banks or frag cannons, of course.

One of the ships was farther along than the other—the concession to the Spits resulted in some shifting of manufacturing capability. The third ship would be ready only four months after the first two. Now we were trying to even out the construction of One and Two so that they would be ready together.

I snorted with amusement, thinking of the last couple of UN sessions. Now that the yelling was over, this was more like a project from my former life. Technical challenges and engineering issues. With the manufacturing AMIs doing all the work, I didn't even have to worry about labor issues.

Negotiations still continued, of course, back on Earth. No one was willing to quietly go along with being scheduled "somewhere down the road." We still had the fifteen-hundred-trip issue to deal with. We didn't know for sure that it would be a death sentence, but there was general agreement that the climate on Earth was getting worse. If it got bad enough, starvation was a real possibility, despite all our efforts.

DENNIS E. TAYLOR

Homer and his crew continued to scour the system. They'd also implemented some techniques for bringing metal up from planetside. That was slow and laborious, especially given the scale of our requirements. I'd allocated a half-dozen printers to Homer—Colonel Butterworth, predictably, had screamed like a stuck pig—with instructions to bootstrap themselves up to a viable operation. So far, Homer was doing better than expected. The amount of refined metal on Earth was considerable, even after the war and subsequent bombardment. He'd already returned the printers to regular ship production, after printing up new ones.

Homer had calculated the possibilities, and gone into his "good news, bad news" comedy routine. The good news was that we could eventually build a lot more colony ships from what he estimated we could haul up from Earth. The bad news was that everyone would be long since dead.

You would think that 3D printers would have solved the scarcity problem. In fact, the technology had just moved the bottleneck. We could build more drones to extract and haul the metal out of Earth's gravity well, or we could build colony ships, or we could build more printers in order to produce more drones and colony ships during which time we would be producing neither. The calculations to determine the optimum path were finicky and had large error bars. Even thinking about them made me grit my teeth.

The drone had reached its destination. I ordered it to establish a sideways vector, then watched the video as the colony ship's exterior drifted by. Unfinished sections allowed drones and construction roamers access to the interior. A steady stream of laden drones entering the hull was matched by a stream of empty-clawed drones exiting. The status window revealed no current issues. The printers were keeping up with parts demand, Homer's supply crew was keeping up with raw materials demand, and the construction crew was kept busy twenty-four-seven.

I shook my head and closed the video windows. Inspection done.

* * *

Homer and Charles were in Earth orbit, taking a break from their outer-system patrols. We took advantage of the rare opportunity to have an all-Bobs meeting. Even without commentary from Arthur, the tone was a little gloomy. The climate of the planet continued to deteriorate, and was possibly accelerating.

"I think it's a given that we won't be getting fifteen million people out-system," Homer said. "Which means we have to come up with some way to keep them alive here."

"Triaging will help." Charles poked a finger at his copy of the holographic globe. "Emigrate the most marginal groups first, move everyone else to the most equatorial locations."

I shook my head. "Most of the equatorial locations aren't habitable. Not because of climate—some of them are actually more temperate now—but because of a lack of infrastructure. Conventional bombings or falling rocks will make a city uninhabitable. Add in the problem of a lack of power and water, and you can't just drop a bunch of people off in the jungle and expect them to survive."

"A lot of the jungle isn't jungle anymore," Arthur retorted.

I grimaced in response. "I know, Arthur, but it doesn't change the basic point. We can't move that many people to anywhere that doesn't have infrastructure, no matter how comfortable the climate. And I don't see the point of building temporary infrastructure, when it's going to delay ship-building."

"And Butterworth will have a cow." Charles smiled ruefully.

"Okay," Homer interjected. "Spitballing, then. How about using space mirrors to warm up the Earth?"

I looked at him in surprise. "Not a bad idea in principle. A lot of unknowns, though, as it would be all new engineering. I think we'd need a minimum of a thousand kilometers' radius for a mirror to have any appreciable effect. Plus, it wouldn't do anything to clear the spreading radioactivity or repair the damaged and destroyed ecosystems, at least not within a human lifetime."

"And Butterworth..." Charles said smiling.

"Will have a cow!" We all replied in chorus. Colonel Butterworth had become a bit of a cliché with his standard reaction to any change in plan.

Homer shrugged. He'd done the math, too. "Let's pass it by the colonel, and see if he grabs his chest and falls over."

"Space stations?" Charles ventured. "Same problem, though, I guess. Or moon colonies. Building all the structure and infrastructure to keep people alive in space would set the colony ships back decades. And you have to build for a population density sufficient to make a dent in the fifteen million or it's pointless."

I nodded, glum. I'd had all these thoughts. Not really surprising that the other Bobs had, too. But anything that we tried would detract from the ship-building. Any useful plan would need to either have negligible impact on the overall plan, or would have to produce significant enough results in a short enough time to be worthwhile.

"And the worst part," Arthur said, "is that even if we stick to the plan as is, we probably can't save everyone."

I ran my hand through my hair. "We keep coming back to this. Nothing we can think of actually improves the overall prospects. I guess all we can do is keep on keeping on, and hope we stay ahead of it." I looked around at the others. No one would meet my eyes.

44. Bob – January 2166 – Delta Eridani

I grinned. "A black featureless block. Dimensions one by four by nine." I leered at Marvin.

He covered his face and shook his head vehemently.

"The strains of *Also Sprach Zarathustra* in the background..." I continued.

Marvin started to moan.

"As the Deltans leap about, one throws a bone into the air..." Marvin dropped his hands and his eyes rolled. I waited a few more seconds for effect, then relented. "So we'll just go with the drone, then?"

Marvin pinched the bridge of his nose. "I can't believe I'm related to you."

I laughed and turned to the desk. "On a more realistic note, we have drones with speakers now, so we can talk to the Deltans. Honestly, I think I'll just go straight to Archimedes rather than trying to contact an elder."

"Oh, I agree with that. Any of the others would probably just run screeching from the area. Archimedes will be curious."

I nodded. "So, no background music?"

"Oy."

* * *

The surveillance drone showed Archimedes doing his usual patrol of the area. He varied his search from day to day, and had taken to randomly digging holes, looking for more flint. A couple of the other juveniles had accompanied him on occasion, but without any payoff, that had soon petered out.

I positioned one of the drones in a tree along his usual route. The drone camouflaged itself so that it looked like part of the tree trunk. Even if Archimedes spotted it, he wouldn't think of it as anything but wood.

The Deltan language was far more guttural than anything humans could produce. I had set up a translation routine, so I could converse in English, without worrying about the fine details.

"Archimedes."

Archimedes jerked, then went into a defensive crouch, looking wildly about.

"Don't be afraid. I want to help you and your people."

Archimedes slowly straightened up but continued to search for the source of the voice. "Who are you? *Where* are you?"

"I'm farther away than you can see, Archimedes. And I'm the one who destroyed the gorilloid that was attacking you. I'm also the one who brought the flint."

Archimedes's eyes lit up. Flint was priceless. I now had his complete attention.

"What do you want?"

I thought of all the ways I could answer that and decided to keep it simple. "I want your people to leave this place and go back to one of the old villages."

Archimedes' eyes went wide. "So old Moses wasn't lying? There used to be other villages?"

"Yes, Archimedes. And some of them are better places to live than this one."

"Some have flint?"

"Yes, and a better water supply, more food, and better defenses."

His eyes narrowed. "If that's so, why did we leave there? Wouldn't that have been the place to stay?"

I turned and grinned at Marvin.

"Kid's no fool," he said.

"It would have been, Archimedes, but your people weren't thinking of that at the time. Then it was too late, and they'd been driven out."

"So, why tell me? Why not speak to the elders?"

"Would they listen to me?"

Archimedes had been searching for the source of my voice as we talked. Triumph lit up his face when he spotted the odd section of trunk.

"You are a tree?"

"No, that's just where I am right now. Would they listen?"

He snorted. "Most of them are so stupid. They ask no questions; they have no answers. They just eat and sleep and hunt."

I spent a few more minutes discussing it with him. He finally agreed to go talk to the village elders, although he made me promise to show a sign of some kind if it became necessary. In response, I cancelled the probe's camouflage and floated it over to him. "How's this?"

Archimedes went rigid and his eyes became huge, but he managed to not bolt. "That works."

* * *

I watched from a distance as Archimedes talked to his elders, who sat in a semicircle facing him. It didn't seem to be going well. Despite all his recent accomplishments and rise in status, Archimedes was still just a juvenile. Even some of the other juveniles had started to laugh and make jokes.

Finally, I'd had enough. I activated the probe and flew it over to hover above his head. The laughter and commentary cut off like a switch had been thrown.

Archimedes was no dummy. The sight of the whole village staring at a spot over his head had only one possible explanation. In an impressive display of natural showmanship, Archimedes didn't look up or directly acknowledge the probe. He simply crossed his arms and looked smug.

In the background, Marvin commented, "Some things just transcend culture."

"Or species," I responded.

The disintegrating gorilloid was still very fresh in everyone's mind, and the probe looked similar enough to the pieces of the buster to convince the Deltans. There was no backtalk after that.

Archimedes explained to them what I'd told him. When he was done, Moses leaped to his feet and started yelling at everyone. It was pretty incoherent, but consisted mainly of variations on "I told you so." Apparently Moses' stories had been dismissed for years, and this was payback.

Eventually, Moses' rant ran down, and the elders turned back to Archimedes. One of them—I decided to call him Hoffa—asked Archimedes if the floating thing would protect them from the gorilloids.

Archimedes looked up at the probe, finally acknowledging its existence. "It calls itself the *bawbe*."

He looked around the circle. "It can help, but there are few of them and they are destroyed with each gorilloid they kill. They will guide, and they will help, but we must fight our own battles."

Arnold, who had been standing outside the circle and listening, chimed in. "We fight here, or we fight somewhere else. The *bawbe* is right—this place is too open to defend. And I like the idea of more axes and spears." He waved his axe around by way of emphasis, narrowly missing a few bystanders.

The argument went on for hours. Inevitably, some people wanted to stick with the status quo just because it was familiar. They fought the plan tooth and nail, even at one point suggesting that they send a party of Deltans to scout out the other location. Arnold dismissed that idea with a comment that he didn't want to come home to a camp full of corpses.

I looked over at Marvin. "Jeez, this crap is universal."

"Yep," he replied. "Politics is, apparently, politics, through the whole universe."

45. Bill – January 2165 – Epsilon Eridani

[Incoming SCUT Communication from Alpha Centauri]

"Cool!" I put down the file I'd been working on. "Calvin or Goku?"

[Bart]

I raised an eyebrow at Guppy. And got exactly the same reaction as always.

I sighed and grabbed the connection. "Bill here."

"Hey, Bill, this is Bart. I'm from Calvin's first cohort. Wow, this is really—"

I popped into Bart's VR. It was a little rude, doing that without an invitation, but I always got a kick out of the surprised look on my face.

I liked Bart's VR right away. He'd set up a rustic log cabin, with a cast iron wood-burning stove, a fireplace, heavy hand-made furniture, and lots of rugs and blankets. It reminded me of a place my father used to take us for vacations when I was a child.

Bart was sitting in the big old rocking chair in which dad used to spend most of his time relaxing. He had the look. I mentally added another notch to my SCUT cabinet.

"Holy—"

I laughed at his boggled expression. "Welcome to BobNet. Instant communications up to about 25 light-years. So, Bart, what happened to Calvin and Goku?"

Bart took a moment to examine the VR quality before answering. They all did that.

"The guys reconnoitered Alpha Centauri A and B exactly as set out in the mission profile. They found a Brazilian factory in full swing in A, and the wreckage of a USE probe and autofactory in B. I guess we can consider the USE probe accounted for." Bart did a half-shrug. "They executed a sneak attack on the Brazilian installation—the modifications for the version-3 Heavens are really effective, by the way—and wiped it out."

"Excellent. Any colonizable planets?"

"No." Bart shook his head slowly. "The system is great for resources and such, but nothing livable. And not completely excellent, by the way. One of the Brazilian probes got away, although we don't think it was completed yet. So it may be unarmed, and it may not have the autofactory equipment loaded in."

"Mmm." I thought for a second. "Not great news. Medeiros may try to highjack someone else's installation. Or maybe skulk around for a while and then raid you guys."

"We've set up early warning systems, not to worry. And we scanned the system pretty thoroughly. I think he'll head elsewhere."

I shrugged. It wasn't worth dwelling on. We couldn't track him at this point, so we'd just have to wait until he showed up somewhere else.

"Anyway," Bart continued, "Calvin and Goku set up a Bob factory, then left as soon as one of us was ready to take over. I built the SCUT when I received your transmission, and that brings us up to date."

I accepted the folder that Bart pushed toward me and took a moment to scan it. Nothing earth-shattering. I was impressed, and a little smug, at how well the version-3 improvements had worked. Medeiros would have to significantly up his game if he wanted to compete now.

"I'm glad to see a Bob factory in operation," I said. "I've been a little remiss in that department since I sent out the last group. I can feel less guilty now."

Bart smiled in return. We spent a few minutes getting caught up, and Bart promised to pop by occasionally for a game of Scrub baseball. With Bart and the two other Bobs currently being completed, we finally had enough to fill the positions all the way to the outfield.

46. Milo – August 2165 – 82 Eridani

I decelerated smoothly into the 82 Eridani system. According to all the astronomical info, this was a very good candidate for a habitable planet. The star, a G5V class, was smaller and less luminous than Sol, but still well within the characteristics of yellow suns that human beings would prefer.

I didn't want to get cocky, but I was anticipating having two good finds in a row under my belt. I doubted I'd ever get a chance to stamp a Brazilian silhouette on the side of my hull like Bob-1, but maybe a couple of planets with green check-marks. Yeah, that's the ticket.

I watched the survey results intently as the data slowly rolled in. Finally, Guppy announced paydirt. Not one but two planets inside the Comfort Zone, although one was at the inside edge and the other almost at the outside edge. Still, it was exciting stuff. And that would be *four* planets with check-marks, thank you kindly.

Impatient to pass on the good news, I aligned my comms array with Epsilon Eridani and began squirting telemetry back to Bill.

I set a course toward the outer of the two planets, since it was closer. The planet had a large moon farther out and a smaller moon closer in. Strangely, the larger moon showed a blue color. I suspected that it might actually have open water. The planet itself definitely had large bodies of water.

As I decelerated to place myself in a planetary orbit, proximity alarms sounded. It took me a moment to focus on the cause. Four missiles were coming around the curve of the moon, and they were accelerating aggressively.

Crap! I turned tail and accelerated away, but it was obvious that they had far better legs. I did the calculations, examined alternatives, but there was no out. I was hooped unless I took out all four missiles. I took a moment to give my busters extra instructions to seek out a ship matching the Brazilian profile after dealing with the missiles, then launched all eight busters in the usual pairing strategy.

As the busters headed toward the attacking missiles, my proximity alarms blared again. Four more missiles had appeared, coming around the *opposite* side of the moon. I was out of busters. With no chance of calling them back to me in time, I had to depend on my rail gun. I did a quick computation. I'd likely get two, possibly three, but there just wasn't enough time to load the rail gun fast enough to take them all out.

Medeiros had outflanked me and done a good job of it.

As I fired at the approaching missiles, I made sure the communications array was still lined up and squirted off a description of my situation and a differential backup. A calm part of my mind calculated that I wouldn't get it completed in time. Damn.

The last two missiles filled my view...

47. Riker – January 2166 – Sol

"They're *dying,* colonel!"

The colonel wore his chin-out expression, a sure sign that I was in for a fight. In the last year, VEHEMENT had started attacking food production and supply facilities. Most of their attempts were no more than token efforts—statements, really. But the last three incidents had taken out supplies that the groups in question couldn't spare. Now they were out of or about to be out of food, with half the winter still to go. Barring cannibalism, we were looking at hundreds of deaths before spring.

Unfortunately, the current political climate was short on empathy. A couple of failed groups, to most of the others, just meant slightly less competition for the emigration queue.

The USE encampment, the FAITH enclave, and the Spits were the richest in terms of food reserves, but they had made it clear that they weren't about to volunteer anything to help out. The Spits, in particular, were trying to stretch their resources out for as long as they could. Their annual surpluses were swiftly being whittled away. They would be a have-not within a few years.

Three hours of negotiating, pleading, and threatening had accomplished zero. They knew I wasn't about to abandon them, so they were willing to call all my bluffs.

In disgust, I finally cut off the video connection without so much as an over-and-out.

Homer looked at me from his video window. He'd been following the whole thing. "Damn, number two, this is kind of a rock-

and-a-hard-place situation."

I nodded glumly. For the moment, at least, I was out of ideas.

"It's going to get worse," Homer added. "The climate isn't improving. A lot of groups are only surviving because of reserves of some kind. They're not producing enough food to get by."

"Thanks, Homer. I needed that encouragement."

Homer shrugged. To be fair, he probably wasn't trying to bait me.

"What we need, Riker, is to go into the farming business or something."

"We've been over that, Homer. We actually could establish farms in the former tropics, but they'd be good for maybe twenty years maximum. And we'd have to build the infrastructure. All the existing farming infrastructure is in the formerly temperate zones."

Homer stared into space, rubbing his chin. "I keep coming back to space stations. Something itching at me..."

I opened my mouth to object, and Homer held up a hand to forestall me. "I know, Riker. Too complex, not enough population density in a space station to make it worthwhile, too much risk. I just think we're looking at it wrong."

I gave a half-shrug and started to respond when Homer yelled, "Crap!" and froze.

I pictured Homer getting hit by a missile and had a moment of panic, but he came back right away.

"Arthur's dead." Homer looked as angry as Homer ever did. "I just got the telemetry from the drones up Saturn way. He was working some wreckage when there was a nuclear detonation. I'm getting reports from drones farther away from it." Homer sighed. "Booby trap. No way to tell who set it up. I told him, several times, to watch for those. He got careless."

"Did he save a backup anywhere?" Even as I said it, I knew the answer. Making a backup and keeping it on board was easy, but pretty useless in a case like this. And we didn't have the space to save each other's backups. I had a TODO item to build some storage into the Sol space station for just this purpose. And, like 99% of my TODOs, it was filed under "Someday."

I took a moment to mourn for Arthur. Downer or not, he was one of us. Homer was looking at me expectantly, and I realized I was having trouble focusing. With an effort, I brought myself back on track.

"Okay Homer, get the drones to recover what they can, and I'll go talk to the colonel. Looks like we're going to need to change the schedule again. We can't do without a fourth Bob. And I think we'd better build that storage matrix."

"Um, there's an alternative," Homer said. "We've got the printers for my Earth-scavenging ops. I wouldn't say they're exactly idle, but at least Colonel Butterworth isn't leaning over them and steaming them with his breath."

I laughed at the unexpected imagery. And Homer was right. I nodded an acknowledgement to him, and forwarded to Bill an *In Memoriam* entry about Arthur, for the archives. As soon as Charles was back in Earth orbit, we would have a wake.

48. Bob – May 2166 – Delta Eridani

It took almost a month to get ready. The trek to the best village site would be long and arduous. From discussion with Moses, it seemed that it was one of the first villages to be abandoned, and unfortunately it was the one with the best supply of flint.

Moses wasn't clear on why it hadn't been better defended. He apparently had been a young cub at the time, and most of his information from that era was second-hand. He'd been one of the last Deltans to be trained to knap flint before they were forced to leave.

In any case, Marvin had surveyed the route that they would have to take. It would not be easy or quick. A mountainous spine ran down the center of this continent, and there were only a couple of passes that were low enough to be useful. During that part of the trek, there would be no local food unless the tribe got very lucky.

I didn't know if the Deltans had lost the techniques for food preservation or if they'd never developed them. Before they could leave, I had to teach them how to preserve meat. The Deltans understood the benefit right away and took to it with enthusiasm.

The Deltans worked to build up a larder for the journey. Once the decision had been made, everyone got on board, and with the immediate gift of knowledge that I'd brought, they began to trust that I was steering them in a good direction.

Gorilloids were spotted on a number of occasions, hanging

around the edge of the Deltan territory. They might have been hoping for targets of opportunity, but they seemed to have had the stuffing knocked out of them in our last encounter. They didn't challenge any of the Deltan hunting parties. Of course, the sight of an occasional drone floating about might have had a little something to do with that, as well. I was quite happy to put the fear of *bawbe* into them.

While I waited for the Deltans to finish their preparations, Marvin and I made sure we built some more busters. They were hardly an ideal weapon—about equivalent to fishing with dynamite—but they were better than nothing. Besides, they made up for their lack of precision with an abundance of theatrics.

We also faced a breeding issue. Deltans, it turned out, had an annual breeding cycle, and a large number of mothers-to-be were coming up on their due date. The Deltans were rightly reluctant to move before the latest generation arrived.

Archimedes' stock continued to soar with the other juveniles. He was, for all intents and purposes, now a member of the tribal council, something that even Arnold couldn't claim. I also noted in passing that Archimedes was now showing a lot of signs of Deltan puberty. Likely the next few years would see a whole bunch of mini-Archimedeses running around.

That was fine with me. There was a noticeable difference between talking to him and talking to most of the rest of the tribe.

Finally, the day came. The whole tribe lined up, packed their belongings onto several *travois* (another gift from the *bawbe*) and set off into what was for them the great unknown.

The gorilloids were in evidence on departure day, hanging around just out of range and watching the parade. I wondered if the gorilloids actually understood that their erstwhile prey was about to leave for good, or if they were just drooling over all that lunch on the hoof. Either way, the first gorilloid that made a move would get a buster in the face. I was lined up, ready, and just waiting for something to obliterate.

* * *

The first night was a less than stellar experience for everyone. It rained heavily. I had to keep reminding myself that the Deltans were used to this. They didn't have tents, just sewn-together skins that each family group would drape over itself. I resolved to introduce Archimedes to the concept of tent poles.

"Better take it easy there, oh great one. Next thing you know, they'll be eating fast food and watching TV." Marvin leaned back in his chair with his hands behind his head. "Seriously, it's not necessarily a good thing to throw too many new concepts at them at the same time. Floating metal deities seems to me to be more than enough for now."

"Funny you should say that." I frowned in thought. "Have you noticed they don't appear to have any concept of religion?"

Marvin waved a hand in the air. "There's some basic animism there, in the form of things like honoring the animals they kill for food, and venerating their dead. I doubt humans had much more at the hunter-gatherer stage." He sat forward abruptly. "Hey, speaking of which, do you realize that we have the opportunity here to document their entire prehistory? Well, from the time we got here, anyway."

"Already started, Marv."

The camp seemed to have settled down for the night, so I deployed a couple of probes into guard positions and set up parameters to interrupt me. Security precautions complete, I swiveled to face Marvin.

"I notice you've started a batch of Bobs at the auto-factory. Not that I'm complaining, since that is part of our mission profile—I just wonder if you've changed your mind about hanging around."

He smiled at me. "Not immediately, although I do feel an itchy foot once in a while. Like I said to Luke and Bender, I'm curious as to how this is going to turn out. But it is still your show. Maybe there's another planet of sentients out there for me."

I nodded thoughtfully. "How about the planetary survey? Any other Deltans anywhere?"

"Nope. This continent is the cradle of humanity for the Deltans. Strictly a local mutation. There are lots of related species, but none that use fire or make tools."

I pulled up a globe of Eden and checked out the detail that we had amassed. It gave me time to think. I realized that the idea of Marvin taking off was unpleasant. Somehow, I was a little less of a loner than original Bob. I dreaded the idea of being on my own again.

I sat back and looked over at Marvin, who was tinkering with his own copy of the globe. I sighed and cleared my holotank.

* * *

The Deltan migration was still pretty close to the schedule. There had been no major glitches so far, and the tribes seemed to have settled into routines. I was not so relaxed. We were now well out of the territory of the gorilloids whose butts we had whupped. Any gorilloids in this area would only see a bunch of easy pickings. Accordingly, Marvin and I had doubled the number of drones on guard duty at night.

So it was more than a little irritating that the attack came during the day.

As gorilloid raids went, it was not particularly impressive. A dozen or so of the animals hit a straggling family group and made off with two juveniles before anyone could react. The Deltans reacted immediately, giving chase and trying to cut the gorilloids off from the forest.

In this situation, a buster would be as big a danger to the two juveniles as to the gorilloids, so we settled for buzzing the animals with the drones, trying to confuse and distract them. It seemed to do the trick. Within moments, the Deltans caught up and skewered half the gorilloids. The rest fled into the trees with screeches of alarm.

Unfortunately, one of the juveniles was dead. The gorilloid that had been carrying him had apparently taken the time to ensure he wouldn't struggle or escape.

The Deltans were distraught, and had a burial ceremony that evening. But interestingly, there was no talk of the migration being a mistake. If this had been humans, I was pretty sure there would have been all kinds of second guessing and recrimination. But the Deltans just took it in stride. I couldn't decide if they were being philosophical or fatalistic.

"You know, that's going to happen a lot more as we go on," Marvin said to me.

"The gorilloids? Yeah, I know. Not a lot we can do during the day though. Infrared is useless. Everyone is moving—at different speeds, most of the time—and the area we have to cover is just too large."

Marvin sighed. "I know. It's just that, even with the last round of births, this is still a small gene pool."

I nodded and thought about the problem. "Hey, didn't you mention at one point that there were small isolated groups scattered about? Maybe we should try to amalgamate them."

"Not a bad idea. Good for both groups. Tell you what, I'll send up a high-altitude survey every night to look for other fires. If we find any, we'll send in *the bawbe* to convince them to move."

I grinned at him. My reputation as a godling wasn't getting me a whole lot of local respect, even from myselves.

* * *

The migration had grown. Not only had we found several small groups and convinced them to link up, but apparently the parade was enough of a disturbance to be detectable for miles around. By the end of the first month, we had one or more groups join up almost every day. While there were often negotiation issues as different Deltans attempted to assert priority, those incidents generally ended without more than harsh words being exchanged. I had a feeling that the flint-tipped spears and Arnold with his big-assed axe contributed to that.

Marvin and I tried to keep the drones out of sight, especially when there were noobs around. We didn't want to take a chance on scaring anyone off. Sooner or later, though, the topic would come up, or we'd have to fly in close for one reason or another. The results were usually pretty comical. Deltans didn't react any better to UFOs than humans would.

The migration was up to well over five hundred individuals. A very large portion of that consisted of females and juveniles. So Marvin and I heaved twin sighs of relief when the Deltans made it to the foot of the mountain pass.

This part of the migration had its own dangers. The Deltans would be going well above the altitude of their preferred climate, so it would be colder than they were used to. They had no protection from either the weather or predators, and little or no available prey as they pushed forward.

Before they started the climb, I made sure they re-inventoried their preserves. They would face a week or two without any other source of food. This was not the time to get sloppy.

They started the climb first thing in the morning in order to get the maximum distance. I knew that they would slow down significantly through the days that the climb would take. They needed the best start possible.

It took four days to get to the top of the pass. We'd budgeted for six, so that was huge. The wind was godawful there, though, so no one wanted to stop. They stretched that march well into the evening in order to get out of the wind tunnel at the apex.

* * *

The trip down went faster, for obvious reasons. Three days later, the migration streamed into forest again with some stored food left over. As a celebration, they camped for an extra day just at the edge of the forest. They took a break and feasted on the extra food. From here on in, they'd be able to forage and hunt.

It took two more days for disaster to strike.

49. Riker - May 2166 - Sol

[Firewall has blocked breach attempt]
I stiffened and turned to Guppy, the UN meeting forgotten. "What? Someone's trying to hack us?"
[Affirmative. Source appears to be the video feed from the UN meeting]
"Ongoing danger?"
By way of reply, Guppy threw up a stack trace. I examined the listings. It appeared that the hacker was basing his attack on the basic Heaven design. The original Heaven vessels had no firewalling, relying instead on all communications being encrypted. However, it looked like the encryption routines had a back door. Someone had injected some packets, which had run right into Bob-1's firewall.

I made sure the UN communications system was logging all traffic. I would try the hack on sandbox Bob later. There was little doubt in my mind that the attempt originated from the FAITH enclave, but I needed some kind of documentation before I made accusations. And there was the question of what could be done about it. It's not like there was a planetary police force to complain to.

The UN meeting seemed to be all about routine matters today, so I decided to get an early start on the day's administrivia.

The first item was a message from Homer, just one phrase, "Space Station!" Complete with exclamation mark. I couldn't see what he could add to the idea that would make it viable, but I would talk to him when I had a few moments.

I glanced back at the video feed of the UN meeting, but still nothing noteworthy was happening.

There was a message from Julia, fairly long, talking about family history. She seemed to have adopted me as a relative with no qualms. I was a little choked up about that, and I hoped she didn't send it just on Cranston's orders.

[Source is New Zealand]

Guppy had traced the packets back to their originating stream. But New Zealand? That made no sense. It also meant that I wasn't going to have the proof I needed to really make Cranston's life difficult. Maybe I could bluff.

Meanwhile, the hack attempt wasn't going to get anywhere, so I might as well just let the perp keep at it.

I did a test ping at Homer, and he indicated he was free to talk. I took a moment to feel awe at being able to talk to him halfway across the solar system without any delay. We no longer had to worry about light-speed lag.

I popped into Homer's VR. "Space Station?"

Homer minimized the window he'd been looking at, and turned to face me. "The answer to our problems," he said with a grin.

"Not unless you have something new."

"Just a new perspective," Homer replied. "We've been thinking of space stations in terms of housing people. Of course that won't work. Got to get the air right, the gravity right, extra shielding for radiation, extra armor for micrometeors, construction for living quarters, feed them, entertain them, yadda, yadda, yadda. But the engineering is a lot easier if we don't try to house people." Homer looked at me expectantly.

"Okay, Homer, I give up. We're going to raise cattle? Or..." My eyes went wide.

"And the penny drops," he said, pointing his index finger at me. "Farming. You just need enough spin to establish an up and down, so the structural strain you have to engineer for is reduced. The interior can just be one big cavern, and sunlight is available twenty-four-seven. Some equipment to make sure the air mix stays correct and the temps stay in range, and we're golden."

I thought about it. "Plants take CO_2 and produce oxygen. Any kid with a match can reverse that. But we need to produce calories in as dense a manner as possible. Got anything specific in mind?"

He gave me a thumbs-up. "Damn right. Remember that library

entry about gene-engineered kudzu? Improved nutritional content, simplified growth environment, human-digestible..."

"And high sunlight requirements, and optimum temps in the 20 degrees Celsius range. Where are we going to find those conditions? Oh, wait..." I grinned.

"Yeah. And since we have access to the Svalbard vaults now, we can pick the cultivar that best matches the environment we end up with." Homer hesitated and held up his index finger. "But kudzu needs a lot of water, so we'll have to constantly truck a supply up, unless we bring in some icebergs from Saturn—"

"—Using the asteroid movers." I was becoming enthusiastic about this idea as we worked through the details. "Which we can also use to bring in regolith for soil. Fertilizer will have to come up, but that's small potatoes, volume-wise. Especially once the operation gets going."

"And the best part," Homer finished, "is that the work can be done with my printers, the same ones that are building Arthur's replacement right now."

Homer's last comment made me think of Colonel Butterworth, and I groaned. The colonel very likely wouldn't be mollified by that line of reasoning. To him, any equipment that could do something else could also work on his colony ships.

"Butterworth is still going to have kittens."

Homer bounced up out of his chair. "This will be fun. Can I watch?"

* * *

Not only did Butterworth have kittens, but the UN assembly went ballistic. Everyone except the groups that were facing starvation was beyond apoplectic and well into incoherence. I sat there, jaw dropping, as people complained about criminal misuse (their words) of a resource that wasn't even part of the construction equation. Finally, I'd had enough. I signaled for the floor.

"Ladies and gentlemen, here's the thing. People are about to starve, and I mean within six months to a year. Those of you with reserves have refused to consider sharing, so that leaves it to me to fix things. This is a viable option, and it doesn't even affect the schedule. *Yes*, it affects future colony ships as we're using scavenged materials for space stations instead of colony ships.

However, I'm willing to trade future colony ships against current lives. And by the way, some of you here will be depending on our kudzu gardens by the time your turn comes around. So let's not be too critical, okay?"

I turned off my mike, which was the video equivalent of sitting down, and watched as the speaker was inundated with requests to speak. *Unbelievable. This crap is universal.*

* * *

I was going through my daily round of calls, and naturally, one was Cranston. Outstanding. On the other hand, I did have this hacking thing to talk to him about. I rubbed my eyes, got myself a coffee, then activated the connection.

"Good afternoon, minister. Anything in particular you wanted to talk to me about?"

"In fact, there is, Mr. Riker. Today's session, specifically. While we are not the richest enclave on the planet, we do have some surplus." He nodded an acknowledgement. "As you've taken great pains to point out, on several occasions."

"And you've refused to give any of it up. Has something changed?"

"In a manner of speaking. Since you have this kudzu idea, it seems that giving up some of our surplus would now be a temporary setback rather than a permanent crippling action..."

I sat up straighter. Very likely there was a *but* in there somewhere, but the minister was at least sounding reasonable.

"...Of course some quid pro quo would be in order as well. Since you've already decided to put the Spits in ship three, and the remaining space is just about right for our enclave—and without our surplus we'd be part of the have-nots—it seems to me that we would be a reasonable choice for the balance of the ship's allocation."

The minister looked at me expectantly. I bristled at the implied request for favoritism, then had second thoughts. Everything he said was true. And while the FAITH enclave wasn't a shoe-in to be next in line, they weren't an unreasonable choice either. Especially with any surplus gone. And rewarding such an overt display of cooperation would send the right message.

I stared into space for a few milliseconds. Interesting. I would actually be displaying a negative bias by dismissing his proposal out of hand.

"Minister, that's a surprisingly reasonable proposal. I'll have to discuss it with my team, but it sounds like it'll fly."

Minister Cranston managed to not look *too* smug. With a nod, he reached for the *off* switch.

"One moment, minister. There's a small matter that I need to discuss with you." I filled him in on the hack attempt, leaving out any details of why it failed. "Any thoughts on this?"

He was silent for several seconds—an eternity to me. When he spoke, he sounded uncharacteristically embarrassed. "I'm assuming, Mr. Riker, that the geographical source of the attempt is the only reason that you are asking instead of accusing." He gave a small smile. "As it turns out, New Zealand makes sense. The fact is that our probe technology may not have been, ehm, *entirely* original FAITH research. Australia was working on the probe concept, and one of our agents may have, ehm, borrowed some ideas."

"Espionage? You stole their plans?"

"Call it what you will, it's very likely that the Australian Federation has, or had, some very good insights into your original design. And New Zealand is where most of the survivors would have ended up once Brazil started dropping rocks on Australia." He looked at me with his head cocked, the implication clear.

"Very interesting. And thank you for being frank about that, Minister Cranston."

We said our goodbyes, and I sent a quick IM to Charles and Homer.

Charles' response came back within moments. "I agree on the FAITH proposal. That also saves our relatives. I know you don't want to make that part of the equation, but I'm less worried about being impartial."

And from Homer: "Agreed. And the Australian explanation sounds reasonable. Cranston very rarely sounds reasonable. I hope he didn't sprain something."

I chuckled at that. Okay, looked like we had a deal.

50. Bob – June 2166 – Delta Eridani

In retrospect, I guess we should have expected it. There had to be a reason why the Deltans had abandoned this side of the divide, despite the better locations and resources. And there was, in the form of gorilloids.

The Deltan migration was large, noisy, and spread out. Like a travelling smorgasbord, they proved an irresistible attractant.

The gorilloid raid struck early in the morning, after first light, when the drone IR sensors had become useless. Of course, the gorilloids neither knew nor cared about that. They simply moved when they had enough light to see.

The Deltans were half asleep, half organized, and totally unprepared. The number of attackers totally overwhelmed any defenses and even took Marvin and me by surprise.

They attacked on several fronts at once in classic pack hunting style. They cut off individuals from the main group, while keeping the defenders busy with feints. A dozen Deltans, females and juveniles, had already been grabbed.

Fortunately, we had the busters on standby as a matter of policy. It took less than ten seconds to bring them in. A dozen gorilloids disintegrated in claps of thunder. We had to select targets that weren't too close to Deltans, so this did nothing to save the abductees. That posed a separate problem.

"Guppy! Put a drone on each Deltan abductee. Stay with them, no matter what."

[Aye]

The buster attack froze the gorilloids and rallied the Deltans. With the flint-tipped spears, the defenders had the upper hand in close-quarters fighting.

"There are too many. We just don't have enough busters." Marvin looked to me with panic on his face.

I turned to Guppy. "The busters at the autofactory..."

[Are on their way. However, transit time will be almost a day at maximum acceleration]

We had started with twenty-five busters. We'd used up half of them in the first rally, and almost fifty gorilloids remained. I found myself frozen for several milliseconds.

Marvin snapped his fingers. "Let's not use them all destructively. Hit the gorilloids at the speed of a thrown rock. A forty-pound steel ball will still slow them down, then the Deltans can finish the job."

"Do it."

We began hitting the gorilloids at low speed. Gorilloids were amazingly tough—a strike from a buster at that speed would kill a human outright, but the gorilloids were only stunned for a moment. In several cases I found myself bludgeoning the same gorilloids multiple times.

We were still losing busters. A unit could handle up to a dozen strikes before something malfunctioned. I made a mental note that we would have to figure out a way to collect the busters for repair. And quickly.

"Guppy, start the autofactory on building more busters, top priority. And send a couple of transport drones to the migration location."

[Aye]

Eventually, the Deltans' defense gained the upper hand. The females and juveniles had packed into a dense mass in the middle, and the gorilloids couldn't get close enough to break off any stragglers. The defenders moved in organized groups, and covered each other's backs. We were down to six busters and had to be very careful about conserving them.

"Okay, Marvin, it's time to go after the abductees. Guppy, give us a rundown on locations and status."

Guppy popped up a relief map of the area with locations of Deltan victims and a tooltip beside each. It didn't look good. Over half of them were already being eaten.

We each took two busters and went after the gorilloid groups. We'd smack the gorilloids in the back of the head until they either gave up and ran away, or the victim got loose during the distraction. In the end, we saved maybe a third of the abductees.

I flew a drone over to Arnold. "There are people who are injured and can't make their way back to the tribe. You'll need to organize retrieval parties."

Arnold gazed at the drone for a few moments, then started pointing to individual Deltans and giving orders. I had to hand it to the Deltans, they were a decisive race. When action was required, there was no backtalk. In moments, they had organized rescue parties, who jogged off, following the drones.

I expected all but one of the surviving abductees to pull through, although some of them would have permanent disabilities.

I sighed and looked at Guppy. "How many TO-DOs do I have concerning teaching the Deltans some basic medical procedures?"

[Twenty-six]

"That's what I thought." I was scared to ask how many total TO-DOs I had stacked up. Not for the first time, I considered building a couple dozen Bobs and attacking the list until it was under control. And as usual, I couldn't think of any items on the autofactory list that I could bump to make room.

I'm sick of this. "Guppy, I want the buster count up to fifty, then I want you to pull one printer group and set it to building more printers. It's time to bootstrap."

[Printer group duplication is time and resource intensive and will impact operations over and above the immediate loss of manufacturing output]

"I know. Short term pain, long term gain. If we'd done this in the first place, we'd be breaking even now. It's time to get ahead of things."

I turned to Marvin. "I'm seriously considering constructing explosive armaments."

His eyes went wide. "Wow. That's a helluva concession. We *hate* explosives."

"I know. Plus there's a risk of blowing up the printer with each unit built. I'm thinking of building them the old-fashioned way. I'll build a chemistry lab, assign some roamers to it, and use industrial methods to build warheads."

"You're talking about significant lead time." Marvin shook his head, doubt written all over his face.

"Yeah, but I have a bad feeling that we're going to be facing gorilloids for a long time. Run the numbers and calculate what the average population density has to be in order for them to be able to gather that many gorilloids together in so short a time. I think this side of the pass is gorilloid central."

Marvin stared into space for a millisecond or so, then nodded. "I see what you mean. This is going to be a war of extermination."

* * *

"After coming all this way, you want us to stop here?" The elder's ears were sticking straight down in the Deltan equivalent of an incredulous stare. I looked around the tribal circle and saw the same expression on most of the faces.

I sighed. The drone was not a great way to have a conversation. It might be impressive to a primitive people, but the lack of body language was really hampering me.

I tried again. "It's only temporary. I destroyed most of my busters"—the translation program rendered that as *flying rocks*— "in that attack. I need to build more. At least here, we've thinned out the gorilloids, and put a scare into the surviving ones."

Arnold, who was now a member of the circle, nodded in agreement.

"It is true. The beasts will not attack again soon. They lost three for every person they took, and we got most of those back."

Sadly, although the gorilloids hadn't done well in terms of stealing a meal, they had managed to kill almost twenty Deltans during the attack. That was an unsupportable level of attrition. A few more attacks, and we'd be back down below the numbers at the start of the migration.

"How long?" The elder wasn't conceding, he was asking for clarification. I wasn't anywhere near done here, yet.

"Five days. I have more busters on their way, and I want another set on hand before taking on more risk. After that, I'll be bringing in more as fast as I can make them."

Arnold stepped in again. "This is not going to be over in a hand or two of days. For this many gorilloids to have shown up so fast, there must be many of them."

I spared a moment to be impressed by this observation. I looked at Marvin, whose eyebrows were climbing his forehead. "I guess that's a reminder," I said to him, "that big doesn't mean stupid. This guy is sharp!"

I returned my attention to the drone. "Correct. I'm running my flying rocks through the forests, counting up the gorilloids. Then we'll have a better idea of what we're up against. And maybe we can avoid the biggest concentrations."

"Can you not just kill them before we get to them?"

It was a reasonable question. "I would be using up my busters killing gorilloids that might never bother us. Better to concentrate our energies on those who show up. I will, however, give more warning in the future."

The elders nodded. They understood scarcity of resources.

Orders were given, and people started to set up a more long-term camp. Arnold organized hunting parties. And I went looking for Archimedes to talk about tent poles.

* * *

"It seems like a lot of work for not much benefit." Archimedes examined his first attempt at a tent. Really, it was barely a lean-to.

"Your blanket isn't big enough to supply much coverage. With a larger blanket, you could make it tall enough to walk in and out, and you'd have sides to keep the rain and wind out."

Archimedes walked around it. "Hard to pack and carry. Hard to set up. It seems like something that would be more useful in a permanent camp."

Marvin laughed at the look on my face. "Take that, oh great sky god!"

"Shaddap."

I set aside the tent project and changed the subject to straightening spears. This was something that both Archimedes and Arnold were both enthusiastic about. They'd seen the difference that simply picking straighter spear shafts could make. The idea of taking almost any shaft and straightening it was a revelation to them.

We talked for a while about how to steam the crooked piece of wood and how to build bending jigs. Arnold and Archimedes left to look for construction materials, the axe hanging casually across Arnold's shoulder.

I rotated the drone to look over the camp. So many things to do. I might have forever, but these people, not so much.

51. Bill – January 2174 – Epsilon Eridani

[Message received from Milo]

I looked up, momentarily irritated by the interruption. I'd been going over growth projections for the mosses, lichens, and grasses that I was cultivating. I'd built one of Homer's farm donuts to grow as much base stock as I could manage before introducing it to the surface of Ragnarök.

"He went to... 82 Eridani, right?"

[Correct]

"So..."

[Message contains a description of a very positive potential colonization destination. Message also contains a record of the destruction of the Heaven vessel]

"What?!"

I filed my work, cleared my desk, and pulled up the message from the in-queue. I could hear Milo's enthusiasm as he described the early survey of the system. And his fear as he relayed the information about the approaching missiles. There was a differential backup attached, but I had a bad feeling...

"Guppy, any chance on that backup?"

[Negative. The transmitted backup was cut off before completion]

"Damn." There was a lot of information on this in the libraries. If I attempted to kludge something anyway—to forcibly restore him, basically—there was a very good chance that the result would be insane or simply non-viable. As sad as I was to lose one of us, I had no desire to see myself in that condition.

DENNIS E. TAYLOR

"Okay, Guppy. Archive the backup, mark it *In Memoriam*. We've got four version-3 Bobs being built right now, correct?" At Guppy's nod, I continued. "Start another four as soon as physically possible. Give all of them extra busters. We're going to extract payment for Milo."

[Aye]

This Medeiros character was really turning into a thorn. First Epsilon Eridani, then Alpha Centauri, now this. Time to take out the trash.

52. Riker – January 2168 – Sol

I popped into Homer's VR. "Hey, number three."

Homer grinned back at me. "You know that'll never be as funny as number two, right?"

"Meh." I shrugged. "Now that you've gone all establishment, you need a nickname." I popped up the list he'd sent me earlier. "You're really going for this ranch donut, aren't you?"

"Why not? We *way* over-engineered Farm-1, to the point of embarrassment, honestly. We've learned enough that I think we can give a half-gee at the rim without coming anywhere close to failure. And now that we've figured out atmosphere controls..." He raised his eyebrows knowingly at me.

In fact, the first couple of months of Farm-1 had been a nightmare. Every aspect of the environment kept going into positive feedback loops. We'd ended up putting four full-time AMIs on the job until we were able to figure out how to dampen the resonances.

"Okay, General Bullmoose. Just remember the little people, okay?"

Homer laughed, and I called up a coffee. Things were looking up.

The donuts, as we'd taken to calling them, looked like fat bicycle wheels. Carbon-fiber cables ran from the hub to the rim, providing most of the structural support. Three thicker spokes provided elevator access from rim to hub. The donut was oriented perpendicular to the sun, and mirrors between the rim and hub reflected sunlight into the interior through the transparent roof of the rim. Everything was designed as simply as possible, to minimize construction time and material requirements.

I sipped my coffee in silence for a few moments. "What I'm really liking is that VEHEMENT can't get at these things. Sabotage-proof."

"Unless they develop ground-to-space capability," Homer replied in an off-hand tone.

I glanced at him, but I don't think he was suggesting it as a serious possibility. There had been more attacks on food supplies Earthside, and we'd been shifting supply schedules to compensate. The new farm would hopefully take the pressure off.

Farm-1 was delivering raw kudzu on a regular basis, allocated by population and by need. I had been assured by Julia that no amount of inventive spicing could make kudzu anything other than, well, kudzu. Plus it had digestive consequences similar to beans. Hmm. Good time to be a replicant. Homer had come up with endless variations on the *Beans, Beans* song, some of which had caught on Earthside.

The second space farm would be going into production in a week, and my calculations indicated that it would bring us into a comfortable food surplus situation for the next three years. After that, falling Earthside production would again become a significant issue.

The third station, which was still about half finished, would be a mix of crops, both for dietary variety and nutritional health. Homer was talking about establishing ranching on the fourth one—cattle, pigs, and chickens. Sheep, if the New Zealanders didn't eat all the stock first. There was genetic material in the Svalbard vault, but we would have to build the artificial wombs if we wanted to use that.

Homer had turned into an industrial tycoon. He was under-standably proud that his idea had worked, and so well, and it had become an all-consuming pet project for him.

I finished my coffee and stood up. "Back to the salt mines, I guess. Try not to blow anything up, okay?"

Homer saluted me with one finger as I popped out.

53. Bob – June 2166 – Delta Eridani

The Deltans were attacked again before we pulled up camp, but not by gorilloids. I had become so obsessed with the gorilloid/Deltan struggle that I'd forgotten that this planet had a full-on ecosystem, as diverse and rich as anything Earth had ever produced.

And that included more than one apex predator.

In this case, the attackers were something that filled the same niche as a leopard or other jungle cat. Except that this species hunted in small packs. They took down a hunter who had stepped a few paces too far from the group. The rest of the Deltans jumped to his aid and laid into the predators with spears. It was over in moments.

Fortunately for the intended victim, I guess, the leopard-analogues (I was *not* going to call them leopardoids) didn't kill their prey instantly. Like many big cats, their strategy was to get a death grip and suffocate the victim. The bad news was that the hunter was left with some pretty significant wounds. As they helped him back to the camp, one of the other hunters joked that he'd be entitled to one of the carcasses for being such good bait.

"I really like these people," I said into the air.

Marvin turned to glance at me. "Damned good thing too. Otherwise you'd have to work up a fire and brimstone routine."

"Hmm, yeah. Brings up a point. I'm going to hang around and help them for a generation or so, but I'd better let myself fade into legend after that. I really can't afford to let them become dependent on me."

"Right. And that's probably when I'll take off." Marvin pulled up a star chart of the space around Delta Eridani. "Places to go, species to meet..."

In the silence that followed, I reflected again on how little I looked forward to Marvin leaving. We'd diverged since he was created, into two distinct people. But we got along, which wasn't a sure thing. I smiled to myself as I remembered one of Bill's transmissions detailing some of the fireworks of Riker and Homer's early days. Wish I'd been there for that. It sounded like a great show.

With the arrival of the latest batch of busters, we were sufficiently up to strength to be able to risk resuming the march. I announced this to the circle of elders but was careful to phrase it as information rather than as an order. I didn't want to fall into the trap of putting myself in charge of their fates, and I certainly didn't want the political fallout among the Bobs from creating that kind of situation.

The elders discussed things, then announced we'd be leaving the next morning.

* * *

Departure went without a hitch. The Deltans had benefited from a week or so of rest. Most of the wounded were now mobile enough to keep up, and they had built up their supplies during the stop. I had doubled the overnight guard and had every single available buster in the air, ready for so much as a butterfly to twitch. Maybe the gorilloids felt the bad karma, because they were nowhere to be seen.

The going was slower than the first half of the migration. The land was a little rougher, and the forest verged on being jungle. We were on the south side of the mountain range, and the climate reflected the slightly more tropical latitude. On the minus side, between that and the enforced stopover, we would arrive well behind estimates. On the plus side, it really didn't look like the approaching winter would be much of a concern on this side of the mountain pass. I decided to be philosophical about it.

As the Deltans walked, I floated along beside Archimedes. He had recently become quite attached to one of the females from his cohort, whom I had named Diana. She was obviously afraid of me but didn't want to look bad in front of Archimedes. She stuck as close to him as she could, while trying to stay as far from my drone as possible. It was a little comical, but I didn't give in to my more immature urges.

At the moment we were discussing medical knowledge and procedures. The Deltans were in the potion-and-poultice stage, and while I had no doubt that some of their concoctions had some medicinal value, I was pretty sure that some root wasn't going to fix a broken leg.

"Yes, I understand, Bawbe. You've brought enough new ideas that have worked. I'm willing to take your word for it." Archimedes shrugged. "But the medicine woman has been doing things her way all her life. I'm not going to go head-to-head with her."

"Okay, point taken. How about you introduce me to her, then?"

Archimedes nodded, then turned to Diana, who was somehow managing to look even more alarmed. "You don't have to come," he said.

"I want to," she answered. "Maybe she'll kill him."

Wow. Maybe I'd line up a buster or two for the meeting.

* * *

We endured three more attacks before we arrived at the flint site. None of them were as big as the first attack, and we only lost a couple of people overall. On the other hand, gorilloid losses were extensive, a fact that made me very happy.

"We're going to hunt them out?" Marvin looked shocked.

"Hell yes. Take out gorilloids for miles around." I waved at the relief map. "Thin them down to the point that the Deltans can handle them."

"Mm, and what about when they repopulate? It'll just be the same thing all over again. You'd be better off to kill the ones that attack and leave the others alone. Eventually, you'll breed a type of gorilloid that doesn't like attacking Deltans."

I thought about that for a moment. "You have a point. Well, we'll see how bad it is when we get to the site. It may need some up-front thinning just so the Deltans have time to sit down and eat in peace."

"I hear that."

54. Riker – October 2170 – Sol

Final assembly. Two magical words that sent a thrill through me. Homer, Charles, Ralph, and I drifted a half-kilometer from the two ships. We'd all agreed that it was pointless to be physically present when a video feed from a drone was every bit as good. But we'd done the agreeing while rushing to be here in time for the event. So much for logic. Even Colonel Butterworth had talked about taking one of the shuttles up to watch, but he'd eventually regained his senses.

As the ships had approached completion, we'd deliberately adjusted construction resources to bring their status into sync. Both ships were now complete except for the final connection of the drive rings to the hull.

"Damn, dude. We've actually done it." Homer's voice was filled with the sense of awe that we all shared. For someone who grew up in the twentieth and twenty-first century, this was by far the largest single engineering project ever undertaken. I couldn't help thinking of the Utopia Planitia scenes in the Star Trek movies when a starship was being constructed. This had much of the same flavor.

I looked over at the summary window. Every UN delegate was online, streaming the video. The UN had had a rare rush of common sense to the head and decided not to make speeches. I suspected that the fact that every single one of them would want to make a speech had figured into that. It would have worked out to about eight hours of speeches. Kill me.

And finally, the construction AMI reported that all connections were successful. The two colony ships, officially Exodus-1 and Exodus-2, were complete. I was surprised to find myself tearing up. Okay, maybe not all that surprised.

* * *

"So now what, Will?" Julia was surrounded by several members of her family in the video window. Conversations with the famous ancestor had become a regular thing at the Hendricks household. There were always people entering and exiting the video window. I didn't mind at all. The sight of my sister's descendants made me feel real, much more than the VR could. Knowing that a piece of me had lived on was satisfying on a level that I couldn't come up with words to describe. It might not be quite like being a parent or grandparent, but it would certainly do as a next-best.

I popped up an inset list. "System tests, integration tests, stress tests, and finally a shakedown cruise. Stuff happens, of course, but it should be pretty routine."

"And the third ship?"

Naturally, Julia was interested in that one. She and her family would all be on Exodus-3, along with the Spits group. I had wrung that promise from Cranston before agreeing to his proposal. There was no reason for him to renege. The three hundred or so people who couldn't fit on the third ship would be the first onto the fourth, and were guaranteed established homes when they arrived in Omicron^2 Eridani. Cranston had asked for volunteers, and surprisingly, he'd gotten them. I guess some people are happy to skip the hard work part.

Julia sighed and smiled at me. "Before you arrived, there was a general feeling that we might be the last generation of humanity. Some people were saying it was selfish to have more children. I'm glad it didn't turn out that way." She hugged her son, Justin, one of the newest members of Clan Bob, sitting on her lap.

Justin had no idea what was going on. But the pictures were pretty, and he loved his uncle William. I made a face at him and he laughed. Justin Hendriks, Space Cadet.

55. Bob – July 2166 – Delta Eridani

The day finally arrived when we reached the area of the flint site. The former camp was at the top of a rise that stuck up out of the general forest level. On Earth, a castle would have been built there. From my earlier survey, I knew that it commanded a view of the forest for miles in every direction, right out to mountains and hills on the horizon. The site was rocky and bare but had a depression at the base of a rock shelf that formed a natural sheltered area. Several rock pools formed natural reservoirs, filled by the frequent rains. A central mesa rose from the shelf like the conning tower of a submarine.

It was in fact, such a naturally ideal site that conversations kept coming around to why it had been abandoned.

"Don't know," was all we got from most of the elders. Moses commented that he only remembered his parents being very scared. He thought—and it seemed likely—that the place had been overrun by gorilloids. One of the other elders, I noticed, didn't seem comfortable with that explanation. I resolved to talk to him later.

I directed the drones to do a quick survey to a mile in radius, looking for gorilloids. The results were chilling. This appeared to be a gorilloid preserve or something. The damned things were everywhere. But why? With no Deltans to eat, this felt like a badly laid out D&D scenario.

The answer wasn't long in coming. I hadn't really done much in the way of biological analysis or investigation since I'd discovered the Deltans, and I guess this was my comeuppance for that oversight. The gorilloids were omnivores. The vegetation on this side included a tree with nutritious seedpods, the gorilloid's primary staple. The pods were tough to get to and tough to open, which explained the size and strength of the animals.

And if the biochemistry of Eden followed that of Earth, the pods would be incomplete protein sources. So what has lots of protein? Deltans, of course.

That looked like the explanation. The seedpods were more than plentiful enough to supply a large population of gorilloids, but the beasts would be crazy attracted to protein sources. And I'd just marched a couple of hundred bundles of protein right into the middle of them. Great.

But there was still something about the gorilloid population that didn't add up...

Without warning, a couple of loud booms reverberated through the forest.

[Two gorilloids approached within proscribed distance and were neutralized]

"Thanks, Guppy. Good job."

I didn't want any surprises, so I'd instructed Guppy to busterize any gorilloid that strayed within a hundred meters of the Deltans. The Deltans were quite used to the sonic booms now and only looked up to check for more gorilloids. But drone sensors showed gorilloids leaving the area in a hurry.

"Arnold, we need to get into a defensible position."

Arnold nodded to the drone, then turned and started yelling orders. Deltans moved with alacrity toward the bluff. Outriders on guard brandished the biggest and best spears.

* * *

The Deltans settled in without difficulty. There were old firepits, cleared-off sleeping areas, and even piled up rocks usable for building small walls. Arnold set up sentries immediately and asked me about the distribution of local gorilloids. He didn't look like he liked my answer. Couldn't really blame him.

The moment their luggage hit the ground, Archimedes and Moses headed off for an area that Moses pointed to. The ACME Axe and Spearhead Manufacturing Company Unincorporated was about to be launched. I assigned a drone and a couple of busters to shadow them.

"Well, are we going to do a culling?" Marvin's expression indicated pretty clearly what he thought of the idea.

"Naw. You're right. We need a long-term solution, which involves gorilloids learning to avoid this area, and teaching their young to avoid it as well. I'll keep the buster AMIs on sentry duty, and we'll just take out any gorilloid that comes too close. They'll eventually make the connection."

"And the tribe will learn to expect the protection of the *bawbe*." Marvin laughed, but I sensed an edge to his humor. I directed a raised eyebrow his way.

"Have a look, boss-man," he said and pulled up video output from one of the drones.

In a corner of the flint site, some Deltans had carefully arranged pieces of a buster and had placed small torches around them.

My eyes widened. "That's…"

"An altar. Yep. All hail the *bawbe!*"

56. Bill - March 2167 - Epsilon Eridani

The orbital schematic display laid it all out, and I didn't like the message.

I looked over at Guppy. No help there. Admiral Ackbar stared back at me, blank fishy expression revealing nothing.

"Can we still save the iceberg?"

[Probability greater than 50%. However, we may not be able to save the asteroid-moving equipment]

I rubbed my forehead, and tried not to swear. "Okay, Guppy. You take care of the course corrections. I'll set up a script for the drones for retrieval of the drive. Maybe we can cut some corners."

The iceberg coming up on Ragnarök was one of the biggest we'd found so far in the Kuiper Belt. This particular piece of ice had come in a little off course, and we were going to have to run the asteroid drive at maximum until the very last moment to get it into the proper trajectory. I didn't want to fumble it and have the berg sail off into the sun. Or worse, impact the planet at speed.

Guppy began applying course corrections, with the changes registering on the schematic in real time. I watched the display absently, while I weighed my options. If necessary, I was prepared to let the drive go down with the iceberg and just build a new one. For a smaller chunk of ice, I'd have just shrugged and let it sail on past the planet, but this baby was huge. I could lose every other incoming chunk for the next six months while I built a new drive, and still come out ahead.

But if I lost the drive, I'd have no control over the pieces following this one. If one came in dead center, I would have to watch it go splat.

We were shepherding chunks of ice from the Kuiper belt, spaced about a week apart. Garfield found them and sent them inwards using his asteroid-moving drive, and I caught them at this end with mine. In another ten years, we would have dropped enough ice on Ragnarök to connect its small seas into actual oceans. My long-term plan was to make the planet fit for humanity to colonize.

[Coming up on alignment. Two minutes to shutdown]

"Thanks, Guppy. How much time will I have to get the drive off the berg?"

[650 seconds]

Wow, that was tight. I reviewed the script that I'd written for the drones. Twelve minutes required for a clean retrieval. That was with some wiggle room, but still...

There were twelve separate structures that had to be released from their anchors and flown off the interplanetary iceberg before it hit atmosphere. I'd already written off the anchors – they would take far too long to extract. Hopefully they wouldn't do too much damage when they hit the ground.

Garfield popped into my VR. "How's it looking, Bill?"

He was watching the whole drama unfold, and thankfully hadn't tried kibitzing. There wasn't anything he could do, anyway, from his location in the outer system. Twice the number of drones wouldn't have been enough to save all the equipment.

I grinned at him. "Just another day at the office. Nothing to see here. Move along..."

[Shutdown. Begin retrieval]

I ordered the drones to start the retrieval process. From here on, it was up to the AMI artificial intelligences controlling the drones. All I could do was stay out of their way and not joggle their elbows. Either they'd save the equipment, or Ragnarök would have some new craters.

Six hundred and fifty seconds later, the ice asteroid hit atmosphere. We were out of time. If the berg was left to itself, it would skip through the upper atmosphere and sail on into the sunset. Quite literally. Instead, I activated a number of explosive devices, and the iceberg fractured into a huge number of chunks, small enough to be melted before they made it through the layer of atmosphere. As the air dragged at them, they separated into diverging trajectories. They would all melt at high altitude, and fall to the ground as rain over the next several days to weeks.

Except for a bunch of anchors, and two drive segments, which would suffer a slightly different fate. Nuts.

I looked at Garfield and shrugged.

"Well, I did warn you that could happen. Far be it for me to say I told you so..."

"No, of course not." I grimaced at the video. "The next chunk of ice is due in a week. It's going to go splat, I'm afraid. Nothing we can do about that one, but if you can fly a couple of segments here ASAP, I can catch the ones after that."

"And then build some spares?"

"Short term, yes. Longer term, Garfield, the whole anchoring thing bugs me. Slows down the installation, slows down the removal. Something was bound to go wrong, eventually. I've been thinking of ways to do this without actual ground contact."

Garfield looked surprised. "Seriously? Like, just position the segments in orbit around the ice chunk?"

"Mmm, hmm. It would require two separate drive channels, but there's nothing wrong in principle with the idea. It would speed things up a lot. And I need a break from the Android project. Working the bugs out of that thing has become a game of Whack-a-Mole."

Garfield laughed. "Okay, old man. I'll pull a couple of segments and head them your way."

* * *

Despite my comment to Garfield, as soon as I had parked the surviving drive segments, I opened up my Android Project file. A video window opened up, showing my current prototype, located over on one of the orbiting labs.

The android was currently powered down and draped on the support rack. Bullwinkle was a quadruped design, about the size of a moose, and every bit as pretty. The external comms array on its head was strangely reminiscent of a famous pair of antlers. Probably not coincidence. Did I mention I'm not very mature?

This was Bullwinkle version five kajillion or something. The basic concepts weren't that difficult. Artificial skeleton, made from carbon fiber matrix, muscles made from memory plastics that would contract when a current was applied, and sensors to replicate the normal five senses. Package the whole thing up with a remote control system, and a replicant—like yours truly—should be able to control it as if it was my own body.

Well, that was the theory. Getting it working was an ongoing exercise in frustration.

Bullwinkle was working fine, mechanically. The problem was with senses, reflexes, and communications. Wiring for touch, heat, and cold sensitivity required micro precision akin to neurosurgery. Printers could only help so much. And the more of the contextual processing I built into Bullwinkle, the bigger the required local computer system. The more of it I designed to be handled remotely, the greater the required bandwidth. And the more that light-speed latency screwed things up. FTL communications would alleviate that, but I was still nowhere near making a SCUT small enough to fit into the moose.

I ultimately wanted controlling the android to be an immersive experience. I wanted to *feel* myself running across the ground. I wanted to feel heat and cold and touch, and the wind on my face. This was a far cry from controlling a drone or buster, which was more like playing a video game. I was ninety percent there, but the last ten percent was turning out to be a real PITA.

With a sigh, I closed the folder, and re-opened the asteroid-mover project. Back to work.

57. Mario – August 2169 – Beta Hydri

Beta Hydri was 23.4 light years from Sol. Rather than argue and compete with the other new Bobs for the closer candidate stars, I had decided to head for the far reaches. "I love to sail forbidden seas," and all that Melvillish stuff. By the time everyone else worked their way out to this point, I hoped to have a working space station declaring, "Mario was here."

And let's face it, I really didn't want to be around the other Bobs. It still amazed me how oblivious they were to the differences between each clone. It was creepy—Not enough variation to make them separate people, but enough to give them different opinions. It was like seeing myself with brain damage. And yeah, Bob-1 had set the rule about senior Bob being in charge, but I didn't see that holding for long. Original Bob had never been much of a follower.

Well, whatever. I was here, they were there, and I liked it that way. Time to explore my domain.

I dropped into the system, decelerating at a leisurely 2 g. I could have come in a lot hotter, but on the off-chance that there was a Medeiros here, I didn't want him to know what I had under my hood. He'd see the 2 g, a fraction of the output of my heavily shielded reactor, and he'd get cocky. I hoped. I really wanted a chance to meet up and hand him another ass-whupping. I had a couple of busters with his name on them. No, really. There wasn't a lot to do between systems, so I'd had the roamers stencil his name on a couple of busters.

So far, though, there didn't seem to be anything Brazilian in the neighborhood. Actually, there didn't seem to be much of anything. It was a large, well-filled-out system, but so far, I'd found no metal ore. Seriously, nothing. This star's spectral lines showed about two-thirds Sol's metallicity. Generally, the composition of the system would follow the composition of the parent star.

Hands behind my back, I walked around the balcony of my tree house, enjoying the view and the thousand-meter drop to the forest floor. This forest had never existed except in literature, and even there, it was an amalgam of a lot of different books. Mostly it was from Foster's *Midworld*, but I'd thinned things out so there were good lines-of-sight. I'd added lots of earth-birds and deleted any large, hungry, dragony things.

I raised an eyebrow at Guppy. "Got an opinion?"

[Above my pay grade]

I chuckled. The version-2 Heavens had more core and memory space than Bob-1 had started out with. Guppy had a lot of room to expand in the standard design, and I'd given him even more. He was becoming a person in his own right. He was acerbic and flip, just this side of insolent. I loved it. And, of course, he wasn't a Bob clone.

"Okay, wise guy. Got an analysis?"

[Those I have. Analysis: there's no metal]

"Thank you, Captain Obvious. Any idea why?"

[No, but I note that all of the other elements are within expected ratios. Only metals are missing. And completely so]

And that was just not possible, not by any known theory of stellar or planetary formation. Guppy blinked once and turned to face me. I knew what was coming.

[Someone else was here first]

"Dammit. Medeiros. But shouldn't there still be an autofactory around?"

I cut off what I was about to say and thought for a few seconds. Something was fishy with that theory, beside the originator.

"Hold on. How *much* ore are we talking about? Based on how much we think this system should have, how long would it take Medeiros to turn it all into cute little Medeiri?"

Guppy thought for a moment. Or calculated. Whatever.

[1,732 years. Give or take]

"So we can rule that out. We've only come twenty-odd light years. And he would have had to travel for the same amount of time." I was belaboring the obvious, and I knew it, but I'd always found that talking something out helped to work through it in my mind.

[That does represent a flaw in the theory]

"Ya think?" I pointed to the inner planets on the system schematic. "We may end up having to do some planetary mining. Let's go take a look at some of the rocky planets and see what's available."

[Your wish is my command]

We took a few days to get to the fourth planet—I still didn't want to show all my cards in case someone was watching. GL19-4 was a brown ball of mud with gray oceans and a thick, murky atmosphere. It looked like the result of a lot of volcanic activity, but I didn't see any immediate candidates in the way of rings or chains of volcanoes.

I inserted myself into a polar orbit and began deep scans for, well, anything, really. Metal deposits, of course, but also volcanic activity, and anything else interesting.

It was one of those good news, bad news situations. Good news, I found lots that was interesting. Bad news, no metals. None. Not within reach of anything in my arsenal, anyway. The planet had a magnetic field, so it obviously had a metallic core. But next to nothing in the crust. Oh, a patch here and a patch there, but not worth grubbing for.

[Anomaly detected]

"And this isn't anomalous enough already?"

[Double-plus anomaly detected. Better?]

Not loving it quite so much. For a fleeting moment, I thought of reinitializing Guppy. Only for a moment.

Not that I needed to worry. One of our redesign items was to not allow GUPPI to read our thoughts. That was just too creepy. He now required voice commands, however you define *voice* in a computer system that talks to itself.

"Okay, Guppy, what is it?"

[Accumulation of refined metal detected. An artifact]

"Holy crap." I thought for a moment. "Deploy three of our exploration drones. Send them down to the location of the anomaly. Have them carry a couple of roamers too. Set one of the drones to spiral outward from the site, while the other two and the roamers investigate the site in detail."

[Aye]

Guppy was all business now. This was serious. Had Medeiros crashed? Was it a probe from one of the other nations?

The drones got there in record time—I think Guppy might have driven them a little aggressively—and settled around the anomaly. One started to circle, gradually getting farther from the center, while the other two landed and spit out twenty-centimeter roamers. The drones lifted off and started on close-up visual scans.

One thing was obvious right away: this wasn't one of the probes. In fact, this wasn't from Earth at all. I couldn't describe exactly what about it screamed *alien*, but no human mind designed that. The best metaphor I could come up with was the alien ship in *Prometheus*. It just didn't make sense.

I took a moment to savor the thought. I had just found the first intelligent life outside of Earth. Well, okay, looking at the wreck, I might have just found the corpses of the first intelligent life. But still...

It was obvious that this had been some kind of cargo carrier. The thing had crashed and split open. It had spilled out part of its contents, which seemed to consist of stacks and stacks of large metal ingots of various types. Each ingot was pure, all one element. Iron, titanium, copper, nickel, tons of the stuff. The carrier looked like it had only been a quarter full, though, unless some had been taken.

It appeared we had found our metal thieves. Well, one of them. And *thief* was probably too strong a word. But still...

[Anomaly]

"Oh, for—what now?"

[See for yourself]

I picked up the video that Guppy offered to me. And my jaw dropped. This planet wasn't lifeless. Well, it was now, but it hadn't been at some point in the past.

I was looking at a dead ecosystem, what you'd get if everything in the Amazon basin died all at once. It was dry, it was weathered, it was corroded. But it was trees, and bushes, and the occasional animal. And it went on forever.

* * *

I sent down some biological analysis drones to do some necropsies and try to figure out what had happened here. That wasn't quite what they were designed for, but I had all the accumulated biological and medical knowledge from Earth, and a very advanced piece of technology designed by, uh, me.

They poked and prodded and cut, and they got some suitable specimens. They had their orders, and the AMIs were entirely competent within the parameters they'd been assigned. I just had to stay out of the way and not joggle their mechanical elbows.

The drones and roamers continued to examine the wreckage. Without being able to say why, I sent a couple of busters down to hover menacingly. Things looked deader than dead, but I just had a spooky feeling.

The report from the biological drones arrived on my desktop with a *ding*. I hurried over and opened the file.

Oh, wow.

Based on cellular damage, everything had been killed by something along the lines of a gamma ray burst. Basically a huge surge of radiation, more than enough to kill instantly. I knew that because not only had the animals been killed but their intestinal flora (or the local equivalent) had been killed at the same time. There was no bloating, no rotting from the inside out. I had to make some assumptions, using terrestrial analogies, but I was pretty confident that they would be close enough.

I also noted *how few* carcasses we'd found. The specimens were all small, in odd, inconvenient places, or in poor condition, even for dead bodies. I was pretty sure that 99% of the fauna were unaccounted for.

Without decomposition to provide a clue, I couldn't immediately tell how long ago this had happened. But wear and erosion on the carcasses and dead trees gave me some indications, as did an analysis of the number of forest fire tracks with no new growth. I estimated somewhere between fifty and a hundred years ago.

I sent the biological drones off to check another couple of points on the planet, especially a point as close to antipodal to this location as possible.

[Emergency! Hostile activity!]

"What? What's happening?"

[One of the roamers is under attack]

"Get the drones to do point-focused SUDDAR pings. I want as much detail as you can get."

[Done]

I dissolved my VR and cranked up to maximum frame rate. The video feed was real-time. It showed a window from the perspective of the roamer that was under attack, and another from the perspective of the second roamer. The first roamer seemed to be infested with mechanical ants. As I watched, the roamer was being eaten—metal parts thinning and dissolving.

"Guppy! Blow both roamers. Self-destructs, now!"

Guppy didn't argue or question. The video feeds disappeared.

"And firewall our device comms. I doubt those things had time to finagle the encryption keys from the roamers, but why take chances?"

I turned to the SUDDAR analysis, which was just assembling over the desk. To one side, Guppy had brought up the video record received from the roamers.

I played back the video record first. The first roamer had opened a container or locker or something. It appeared to have activated the ants. Whether that was a defensive reaction, or the ants just considered the roamer to be a resource to be acquired, was anyone's guess. I doubted there was really much practical difference. Either way, the ants had started to disassemble the roamer. The SUDDAR point-scan showed that they were separating it by element. They didn't seem interested in the plastic and ceramic components.

I didn't regret blowing up the roamers. I certainly couldn't have brought them back with the possibility of one of those ants coming along for the ride. And, silly as it was, I'd read and seen enough science fiction in my day about advanced technologies taking over the communication system and getting into the computer. That's me we're talking about, after all.

I can build more roamers.

Where did the ants get their power from? I scanned the ship again and found that about half of the ants that had survived the roamer suicides were now still. I didn't know if they were dead or just on standby.

I decided to scan at five-second intervals to see what they were up to. Strangely, every time I scanned, more ants became active. *The hell?* I cut off the SUDDAR scans for a full minute. When I did another scan, about a quarter of the ants were inactive. *Oh, hell.* I stopped scanning for five minutes, then did a quick scan, with as low power as I could manage. Sure enough, most of the ants were inactive.

Dammit! They're powered by the SUDDAR beam. It was my scans that reactivated them.

Well, that was a fine pickle. Any attempt to find out what they were doing would power them up. But that meant that the aliens had found some way to beam power through subspace and use it at the receiving end. I needed to examine those ants.

I waited an hour, then sent a single one-centimeter roamer in. No way an ant could piggy-back undetected on a roamer only slightly bigger than itself. The roamer picked up a couple of ants and brought them out of the hulk. I had prepared a couple of small coffins for the ants, filled with a plastic goop. The roamer stuffed the ants into the goop, then added the hardener. I now had ants under glass, more or less. While they might be able to cut their way out of those, I hoped they couldn't do it before I completed a scan.

I brought my two drones in close, and they did the most intense and high-precision close-in scans of which they were capable. That would produce almost a molecular-level map of the ants. I watched in fascination as the ants both powered up and produced little cutters from their front appendages. Fortunately they couldn't move, so all they did was drill a couple of holes in the plastic. Good to know.

I detonated the roamer–can't be too careful–and retired to my treehouse to ruminate.

* * *

I had completed my survey. There was no sign of a civilization on this planet, so the wreck was definitely alien. The aliens had come in, presumably killed all life with some kind of radiation weapon, mined the star system, collected the carcasses, then left. There were a lot of assumptions in there, but it fit the evidence.

The scan of the ants had shown some interesting technology. I was already setting up simulations to test some of it.

The scans of the hulk didn't have any huge surprises. It appeared to be run by an A.I. or AMI of some kind. It had a fusion reactor. It had a SURGE drive. It had a SUDDAR transmitter. However, the SUDDAR unit seemed designed to transmit power to a tuned receiver as well as using the SUDDAR as radar. I'd taken detailed scans of that for further study.

Maybe the aliens had come and rescued the crew and left the hulk. I doubted that. There didn't really seem to be any accommodation for anything biological. It was probable that the ship was completely A.I. Was this civilization biological at all? The fact that they'd collected all the carcasses hinted at an answer, and not one that I liked at all. I could only think of one reason to bother collecting all that protein.

And was this a one-time event? Or were they raiding systems on an ongoing basis? If so, which way were they heading? I certainly wouldn't want this fate to befall the Solar System, even if there *weren't* any humans left. The dolphins and chimps still deserved their chance.

I felt a pang of disappointment as visions of meeting Vulcans or Asgardians evaporated. This was more like an Alien scenario. As first contact situations went, this one sucked.

Like it or not, I had to bring the other Bobs into this. Which brought up another problem. At this distance, I couldn't send a message back to Bill. I would need the space station for a transmission, and I would need the raw materials in order to build one. The ore contained in the hulk, even adding in the hulk itself, wasn't enough.

I would have to leave.

58. Riker – April 2171 – Sol

The big day had arrived. The colony ships had been checked out end to end, they'd been inspected by the USE delegation, and they'd done a shakedown cruise to Jupiter and back. Now they were parked in low Earth orbit, waiting for their occupants.

Homer was doing a kind of war dance around my captain's chair, and I was forcibly reminded of my lack of rhythm. The VR upgrades from Bill meant that we Bobs could interact physically instead of just talking to each other through video windows. It had its downsides.

I turned my attention back to the status vids, which showed people lining up for the ground-to-orbit shuttles. Each shuttle could handle five hundred people, packed in like rush-hour commuters.

I remembered my early days as a working stiff, taking the seabus across the harbor twice a day. Hard plastic benches, barely wider than one's shoulders, arranged in back-to-back rows so you spent the entire trip eye to eye with a total stranger. And that irritating recorded lecture, every single trip, telling you how to use the life jackets. Fun times.

The shuttles carried more people, and the commute to the ship would take a little longer than fifteen minutes, but it would be the same prosaic, boring ride. At the end of it, the passengers would be hustled along to stasis pods, given a sedative, then hooked up and locked into a box the size of a coffin. Hopefully to wake up in less than four years ship's time, at a new home.

That was the plan, anyway.

Ten shuttles made a total of forty trips to move the USE colonists to the ships. A percentage of the contents of the Svalbard Vaults were loaded onto each colony ship, and the shuttles were docked in the cargo holds.

Then came the inevitable ceremony. Everyone had to make a speech. You'd expect the USE bigwigs to make a speech, but why did the groups from the other side of the planet feel the need? By the time we were half-way through, I had turned off my proprioception emulation to avoid falling over, virtually asleep. I reanimated sandbox Bob to take over the video and try to look attentive.

Eventually, though, they were done. Howard, our newest Bob, was making the flight with them, acting as escort. And, just between Howard and me, to make sure that they behaved at the other end. I hoped that was just excessive paranoia on my part, but I'd loaded Howard's cargo hold with a few of Bill's recent inventions, just in case.

The colony ships had a maximum sustained acceleration of 1 g, so the trip would take slightly longer than it would have for a version 1 Bob. They would be on the road for a little over eighteen years. About six years would pass on-board, but no time at all for the colonists in their stasis pods.

The ships were crewed by a couple of Riker clones and a crapton of roamers. No need for humans to risk their DNA during the voyage. I had placed the replicant matrices in the ships as one of the final tasks, thereby giving no one time to pull anything underhanded. There had been no hacking attempts, so possibly whoever it was had given up.

The third ship, designated for the Spits and the FAITH enclave, would be leaving in four months. They would establish the first settlement on whichever planet the USE contingent didn't pick. The first settlement's job would be to establish sufficient infrastructure for future groups to be able to settle in without undue hardship. It was the price of being first.

Valter was philosophical about that. "Even second prize is still a magnificent gift," he said in his speech.

Three more vessels were already under construction. Between new builds and returning colony ships, we hoped to maintain a steady stream of exodus from Terra, as long as there were people who wanted to leave. Meanwhile, the resources left behind and the kudzu production would continue to feed an ever-shrinking populace for a long time to come.

I just hoped we'd find more colonizable worlds before people started shooting at each other again.

* * *

I found myself tearing up just a little as I watched the image in the holotank, which showed the colony ships passing the orbit of Mars. After more than a decade of work, of butting heads with, ahem, a bunch of buttheads, we had actually launched. It was an emotional moment. Even Homer was silent.

Finally, with a groan, I stood up and stretched. "Back to the salt mines."

Homer grinned at me and pulled up a list. "Stuff for today…"

59. Bill - May 2172 - Epsilon Eridani

I held an air-horn over my head and pressed the button. A loud *blaaaat* filled the room. All conversation ceased, as every head turned towards me.

"Hey, everyone. Welcome to the first Bob-moot. I've built a matrix here at the Skunk Works that is more than big enough to handle everyone in the bobiverse in VR."

"Bobiverse? Really?" Garfield gave me the stink-eye.

I laughed. "Just thought of it. I think it's pretty good, actually."

"Bobiverse. BobNet. This galaxy may not be big enough for our ego." Garfield tried his best to look disapproving, but it's hard to fool yourselves.

I looked around at my audience. Not a huge crowd at this point. I had Riker, Homer, and the other clones from Sol; Bart and his clones in Alpha Centauri; and the Bobs on the way to Omicron^2 Eridani with the colonists. That last group would be out of touch in another month or so, when their tau got too high for VR interfacing. Hopefully by then, a few other Bobs would have picked up the SCUT plans and linked in.

Homer cupped his hands around his mouth and gave me a loud *boo*.

I looked around the group. "Okay, guys. I'm hoping we can make this a regular thing. It helps to keep everyone up to date."

"Plus it'll give you an excuse to inflict baseball on us!" Bart yelled.

"I plead the fifth." I smiled at everyone. "Meanwhile, we have beer. And coffee. And a pub to sit in. Shall we?"

We all popped over to the pub VR and settled into chairs. Time to celebrate.

60. Khan – April 2185 – 82 Eridani

Do not engage an enemy more powerful than you.
And if it is unavoidable and you do have to engage,
then make sure you engage it on your terms, not on
your enemy's terms.
  ... Sun Tzu, <u>Art of War</u>

We slowed down to sub-relativistic speeds well short of 82 Eridani. We wanted plenty of time to scope out the situation, without alerting Medeiros to our presence.

Bill had made good on his promise to avenge Milo. Eight version-3 Bobs, including myself, were poised outside the system, just itching to give Medeiros a piece of our collective mind. But Medeiros had had thirty-five years now to establish himself. None of us thought we'd be able to simply waltz in and whup his butt like back at Epsilon Eridani or Alpha Centauri.

And because we have always been a cautious person, reconnaissance was going to be a major priority. We had two scout probes each, with heavily shielded reactors, three-light-hour-range SUDDARs, and SCUD communications. And booby traps. We didn't want Medeiros getting hold of any of that tech.

And we had a new weapon in reserve, courtesy of Bill's Skunk Works.

We deliberately came in from stellar north, at right angles to the plane of the ecliptic. While we didn't expect Medeiros to be a "two-dimensional thinker"—he was after all, military—we did expect his assets to be mostly along the ecliptic. Our probes should be able to fall through that plane before he could react.

We launched the scouts across a broad front, to get the best overall scan of the system. With no radio emissions and a heavily shielded reactor, there was a good chance most of them would go right through undetected. However, there was no way we were going to get away clean. Our hope was that if Medeiros detected only one or two probes, he would conclude that there was only one Bob out here.

I sent out a meeting invitation to the rest of the squad. Within milliseconds, seven Bobs popped into my VR.

I looked around the table. "Strategy session, boys."

Hannibal accepted a coffee from Jeeves as he popped up a system schematic. "We will watch for anything hiding behind moons or planets. Not falling for that trick twice. We've got a good idea of where things are, thanks to Milo's preliminary report. We'll—"

Abruptly, Hannibal disappeared from the VR. We looked at each other in shock, then as one we abandoned our VRs and went into frame-jack.

"Who's physically closest to Hannibal?" I posed the question in reflex, although I was already checking our deployment diagram. Hannibal was at the end of the line of Bobs, with Tom next to him. "Tom, got a SUDDAR reading?"

Tom's response came back after a millisecond. "I have a very diffuse SUDDAR reading, but no Hannibal. Hold on—"

We waited for an eternal four milliseconds for Tom to continue. "—The diffuse area is spreading and thinning. I'm guessing an explosion of some kind. Everyone might want to do a full sweep, and hang the surprise factor."

I decided that was a good idea, and I cranked my SUDDAR up to full power, going for a three-light-hour full-spherical ping. The response was negative, except for a vagueness—like a shadow seen out of the corner of your eye—in the direction of the system. I refocused and sent a tight-beam ping in that direction.

Paydirt. "*Something* is headed our way, guys, at very high speed. And it's cloaked, or shielded, or something, to the point that I could only see it when I was pinging straight at it."

Grunts from a few of the others acknowledged the information.

"I've got one, too," Barney reported.

"Same," from Tom.

It took a few milliseconds to compare notes, and we realized that three unidentified objects were heading our way, and still accelerating. We launched three of our regular probes directly at them, to try to get a visual.

"They're dodging," Fred said. "I think they're expecting the probe to try to ram."

"Well, not a bad idea if we can manage it," I responded, "but first we want telemetry."

It took a little over fifteen minutes, at the combined velocities of the probes and the approaching objects, for them to pass each other. The incoming bogey was still dodging back and forth. The probes were only able to get a frame or two of poor images as they passed by, but they managed full SUDDAR scans.

As the results popped up over our desks, courtesy of SCUT instantaneous communications, there were gasps.

"Nuclear freaking bombs. He's built fission weapons."

"With shielded reactors and very, very large SURGE drives," Fred added.

"That jibes with the readings I've been getting. I think Hannibal is just a radioactive cloud, now," Tom said. "We are screwed."

"My ass," I retorted. "How long do we have until they're close enough to be able to take us out? Tom, do you have a feel for the megatonnage?"

There was a moment of silence, before Tom popped up a sensor readout in our VRs. Because we were still in frame-jack, it wasn't even paper—just a raw window with a data listing. "Here's the minmax analysis. We've got four minutes—an eternity. No chance to dodge, given their speed and spread. We don't have time to get outside the blast radii."

"So," Kyle said. "Medeiros seems to have set this up well. He probably thinks he's outflanked us, but good."

I smiled at Kyle's dry delivery. "Mmm-hmm. Okay, let's melt them down. Two Bobs per bomb, and I'll add a follow-up shot if needed. Everyone acknowledge when charged."

We were about to roll out *our* secret weapon. Bill had taken the light-saber tech, which was essentially a high-temperature ionized plasma in a magnetic bottle, and used it to build something new. He found a way to project the plasma, and the magnetic field with it, like a torpedo. The result was a million-degree, highly-charged spear that splashed against whatever it ran into and generally melted right through it, while delivering a very localized EMP. The weapon had been tested extensively at Epsilon Eridani, but this would be the first real-world use.

When everyone indicated a full charge, I said, "Fire."

Six plasma spikes shot out at close to light-speed. One of the biggest advantages to this weapon was that it was invisible to SUDDAR, since there was very little actual mass involved. And any other form of detection was limited by light-speed. The plasma spikes couldn't follow a dodging target, but the target wouldn't know they were coming until they arrived.

It took only moments for the spikes to cross the distance, and all three shadows disappeared. Full-on SUDDAR pings, at the narrowest and most intense setting, detected nothing but small fragmentary blips.

Ned spoke for all of us. "Well, that was unsettling."

Fred added, "We were barely able to detect those things at all, and even that only because of Bill's SUDDAR improvements. Did Medeiros invent some kind of SUDDAR cloaking?"

"I doubt it," I answered. "He never struck us as anything but career military. I think it's more likely that the Brazilian Empire had this tech developed back on Earth. They may have uploaded *all* their top-secret military tech to him before sending him out. That would explain the nukes, too."

"So this might not be the last surprise."

A round of curses and grunts answered that statement.

There was silence for a few moments before Ned spoke up again. "I guess we need to have another strategy session."

* * *

"Cloaking?" Bill's face was a study in surprised interest.

"Yup. That's the only explanation we can come up with." I replayed the entire sequence for him in a window, including popups of the sensor readings of the bombs.

"Well, crap. See if you can grab a sample or something. Meanwhile, I'll work on it from this end. I guess the element of surprise is gone, though." Bill gave me an informal salute and disappeared.

Great. Eight of us—no, seven, now—against an unknown number and disposition of Medeiri. I did *not* like the odds.

"Meeting!" I called out.

Six other Bobs popped into my VR.

"Bill didn't have much for us. He pointed out, quite correctly, that if we leave now with the intention of coming back, Medeiros will be even *more* prepared for us. He suggests we get our backups up to date and dive in."

"Easy for him to say." That was from Elmer, who had never been particularly enthusiastic about this venture. I think maybe quantum differences had left him a little light in the spine department. I was reminded of Bill Paxton's character in *Aliens*.

I glared at Elmer for a second, then continued. "We have the plasma spikes, and we have the busters, with the new controlled fusion detonation. It's not a lot. Best we can do, I think, is raise some hell before he takes us out. Make sure your dead-mans are in order, do a differential, and kiss your asses goodbye. We're going in."

With that, the Bobs disappeared from my VR, seven ships turned toward the center of the system, and we began to accelerate in at 10 g.

* * *

The first part of our dive into the inner system was relatively easy. Medeiros was still working on the assumption that we all had the same SUDDAR, and that he could see anything we launched at him. By the time we'd destroyed a half-dozen of his flying bombs, I guess he finally got the memo.

SUDDAR area pings showed everything with a SURGE drive scattering in all directions. At the same time, over a hundred fusion sources lit up the area and started to move. Decoys, I guess. Effective, too. We had no way to know which ones were real targets.

"Meeting!"

As soon as the other Bobs showed up, I started. "Okay, some of these fusions sources are decoys. Probably most. But some will be Medeiri, and some will be weapons. And there will be cloaked bombs as well. Suggestions?"

Elmer spoke up first, which surprised me.

"The bombs need to be within a certain distance to do any harm. If we move as a unit and assign certain Bobs to watching for the cloaked devices, we should be able to prevent any from getting too close."

"And," Fred cut in, "if we destroy any decoys that get within that range as well, we might be okay."

"Certainly better than splitting up," I conceded. "But the plasma spikes are only useful until Medeiros figures it out and starts jinking around. Plus, recharging the spike cannons takes time. They aren't like Hollywood six-shooters."

"Then we need to do as much damage as possible before he figures it out," Tom said decisively. "Let's just start blasting. Maybe *no* plan will throw him off a bit."

That was just stupid enough to be brilliant. We looked at each other wordlessly, nodded, and got to work.

It became a game of cat and mouse. Medeiros knew that we had something that could destroy his units without warning. He may have thought it was a cloaked missile. He reacted by scattering his units and using the decoys to distract us. We destroyed many units, but had no idea if we were destroying anything useful.

Finally came the moment we'd been dreading. One of Medeiros's units dodged several plasma spikes and managed to get within detonation range. Barely. The resulting EMP and blast of radiation played hell with internal systems for a few moments. Fortunately the version-3 Heavens had multiple redundancies. Five of us were able to continue. The other two must have lost too much functionality. Their dead-mans activated and they disappeared in reactor overload. I hoped Fred and Jackson's backups were recent and complete.

But Medeiros must have twigged to the fact that our weapon didn't chase its target. In the time that it took him to send out commands at light-speed, every Medeiros-controlled unit in the system was bearing down on us, jinking like crazy.

"Plan B, guys. Split up and do as much damage as possible."

We headed off in random directions, jinking as well.

While we ran, I did an analysis from the recorded telemetry of Medeiros's change in tactics. His units were given orders via radio. The ones closest to Medeiros would have started the new tactic first, followed by units farther away as the signal spread from the center. The center, of course, was Medeiros.

It took about forty milliseconds to determine where he must be, to within a few thousand km. That was too large an area for random plasma spike shots, but not too large for intelligent busters on a mission. I transmitted the coordinates to the other Bobs, and we simultaneously launched every buster we had. At the same time, we all activated SUDDAR jamming at maximum intensity. Everyone in the system was now blind, except for traditional visual and radar. The trick would be to keep it going until—

Hector and Tom's SCUT signals cut off without warning. I felt a pang of sorrow. They'd almost certainly been caught by a nuke. That left three of us, plus whatever busters were still going. I kept spiking fusion sources as best I could. The AMI pilots tended to be a little predictable. Many of them settled into a pattern of dodges that I could predict after several iterations.

Then Barney dropped out. That left just Elmer and me. I had to give him credit. Now that things had hit the fan, he was no longer whining about the danger. I mentally upgraded him to Michael Biehn.

Two nukes went off around me almost at the same time. They must have been a little impatient, or saw their solution deteriorating, because the distance was a little too great for annihilation. Not too great for damage, though. I was dead in the water for several minutes while Guppy scrambled the roamers to replace or reroute systems.

"You okay, Khan?" It was Elmer, checking up on me.

"A little damage. Roamers are on it. Don't try to cover me. We don't want to present a single target."

"No problem, dude. Having some fun of my own over here..."

[SURGE drive online]

That's what I wanted to hear.

I jammed the gas pedal all the way down to emergency level, and shot away at 15 g. I wasn't able to keep that up long, but it saved my bacon, as another nuke went off behind me, just out of range.

Finally, just when I had about decided I'd had enough excitement for the century, the busters converged on the point in space where we believed Medeiros to be. Remote telemetry showed forty-four busters bearing down on three Brazilian probes. The Medeiri must have finally gotten a visual warning, because they turned and scattered. But it was far too late. At least half of the busters made contact of some kind before there wasn't anything left that was big enough to register as a target.

Just one small problem. Destroying Medeiros didn't deactivate his units. We were still being chased by dozens of fusion signatures, at least some of which were real threats.

"Got any ideas, Elmer?"

"How's your equipment, Khan?"

"Well, I'm going to need new underwear, but I'm still running."

"I'm not so good. My SURGE has gone intermittent, and I don't have time or parts to fix it."

Elmer was silent for a moment, and sympathy and sadness washed over me. He was screwed, and we both knew it.

"I've updated a differential to Bill, so to quote the Celine Dion song—"

"Oh, please don't, Elmer."

He laughed. "Gotcha. So you turn off your SUDDAR jamming and run silent out of here. I'll keep blinding everyone until the last moment. Give Bill my regards."

"Will do, buddy. Sayonara."

"Hasta la vista, baby."

I did as he said. Once my SUDDAR emitter went silent, the Brazilian units locked onto the only bright source of SUDDAR in the area. As I ran from the area, Elmer's relayed telemetry showed close to fifty units converging. Then he was gone.

* * *

I coasted for two weeks to get far enough away from 82 Eridani before I reactivated all systems. I had given a full report to Bill, and I spent the time doing more thorough repairs. The last thing I needed was equipment failure halfway between stars.

Of the eight Bobs that went to 82 Eridani, I was the only one left. I think we took the Medeiri out, so I guess it was a success from that point of view. But I couldn't convince myself that the whuppin' had all been one-way.

I popped into Bill's VR. "Hey, Bill."

"Hi, Khan." Bill gave a flash of a smile. "I still can't say that without wanting to yell it."

We shared the standard laugh. Good names were getting a little scarce, and I was glad to have picked one that had some nerd lore behind it.

"Did we get all the backups?"

Bill shook his head, looking unhappy. "Three didn't complete. SCUT bandwidth just isn't dependable enough. Lots of dropped packets and re-sends. I've added them to the *In Memoriam* list."

"Elmer?"

Bill smiled, a small sad smile. "He made it. Guess he surprised all of us, right?"

I nodded, and let the silence extend for a few milliseconds.

"We're going to have to go back, you know."

Bill nodded. "We don't know for sure that we got all the Medeiri, even if we got all the *active* ones. And those AMI units will still be wandering around, looking for things to blow up." Bill waved a hand. "*And*, not to put too fine a point on it, I have to find out how he's doing that cloaking. That's a real danger to us."

I rubbed my chin in thought for a second, then looked at my hand in amusement. We Bobs were so used to VR now that we felt fully human most of the time. But once in a while the incongruousness of an action would jerk one of us back to reality.

"Bill, I want to be in on the next wave. I owe that to the guys we lost. It will take me thirteen years to get back, so load my backup into one of the new ships. I'll send you a full, and let me know if it comes through, okay?"

Bill nodded.

I gave him a salute and disappeared from his VR.

Medeiros, I'm coming back for you.

61. Howard – Sept 2188 – Omicron^2 Eridani

We'd arrived.

I can't even begin to describe the feelings of joy and relief as I passed the Kuiper belt and officially entered the Omicron^2 Eridani system. No Vulcan cruisers flew up to intercept us, so I added a few to my VR. Just because.

I did a quick scan of the system to confirm Milo's survey results and verify our orientation to the ecliptic plane. The two colony ships, Bert and Ernie—yeah, they named themselves that, yes, voluntarily—came into the system at a much more sedate 1 g deceleration. They would arrive at Vulcan and Romulus a week or two behind me.

I'd been thinking off and on about what it would be like to be a colony ship. The guys would be essentially running a shuttle service for up to a couple of centuries. Fly to Earth, fly to Vulcan. Fly to Earth, fly somewhere else. Rinse, repeat. On the other hand, they were doing a very valuable service for humanity. Any Bob could appreciate that.

And with our arrival, humanity now officially no longer had all its eggs in one basket. Now perhaps we could start to think about breathing a little easier. But just a little.

I dropped into the L4 point between Vulcan and Romulus and dropped a beacon. We would set up there to do initial recon and to give Colonel Butterworth and his people a chance to make a decision. Since I had ten days or so to kill, I send some exploration drones to each planet to expand on Milo's survey information. Then I settled back with a cup of coffee to relax.

DENNIS E. TAYLOR

Milo had left a couple of AMIs and a bunch of autofactory drones behind to continue mining the system. The drones put the refined metals into bundles of ingots and set beacons on them. With a couple of decades of peace and quiet, the automation had accumulated several hundred thousand tons of ready-to-use material, all in orbit inside the asteroid belt. Riker had started the AMI on building a farming donut a decade ago, to provide a backup food source. It would need only to be seeded from the stocks we'd brought with us. I hoped we wouldn't need it. Of course, I didn't hope that anything like as strongly as the colonists would. Kudzu was apparently not the food of the gods, although deities were often invoked when describing it.

I had quick conversations with Bill and Riker, just to let them know we'd made it. Full reports would follow. Riker gave me a list of colony ships that were already launched and on their way.

Hmm, but no pressure, right?

* * *

Exodus-1 and Exodus-2 settled into orbit without a hitch. We had a brief flurry of SCUT exchanges, then Bert and Ernie shut down the drives and went to station-keeping.

"Welcome to the home of Spock, boys." I popped into the common VR and grinned at them. They were grinning back, of course. After all, *Bob.* Bert and Ernie had adopted Battlestar Galactica-style uniforms and command deck VRs. I was a little surprised by that, as it hadn't been one of my favorite shows. Although the Cylons were definitely bad-ass.

"I was seriously considering putting up a couple of Vulcan cruisers to escort us in," Ernie said.

I felt my face turn red, and Bert started laughing so hard he almost lost his seat.

We took a minute to enjoy the joke—belly laughs are one of the best things about being sentient, and you should never miss a chance for one. We wiped the tears from our eyes, and I pulled up a holo of the system, with Vulcan and Romulus showing in an inset window.

"We'll want to push Butterworth to make a decision as quickly as possible. I want the colonists offloaded at the earliest possible date, and you guys on your way back to Earth." I gestured toward the holo. "Butterworth already has Milo's survey results, and I've been adding to the data. This isn't going to be a negotiation. He picks A or B, and we move."

Ernie nodded. "Guppy advises me that Butterworth has come out of stasis, and he'll be ready to talk within an hour. I'll package it up for him, let him have some quiet time to study it. Meeting in, say, three hours?"

Bert and I nodded, and we moved on to the next item.

* * *

"There really was never much doubt," Colonel Butterworth said with a smile. The video showed him sitting in the Exodus-1's common room. "Barring significant new information coming up at this end, Vulcan makes much more sense. We will need time to establish our own food production, so a robust ecosystem will bridge that gap for us." He nodded to the camera. "Thank you for confirming biocompatibility of the local ecosystem. It settles a lot of uncertainties."

I smiled in acknowledgement. Colonel Butterworth had become much more relaxed now that his civilian population seemed to have a future.

He continued in a distracted voice, "We'll hopefully be in a position to help out the Spits when they show up, until they have their food production set up." He arched an eyebrow at me. "Farm-1 won't be producing yet, right?"

"Not yet, Colonel. But since most of the colonists will stay in stasis until we're ready for them, ships stores will be sufficient for the first month."

Colonel Butterworth grunted. "Still tighter than I like."

The Colonel stared, rapt, at the virtual bulletin board that Bert had provided. The board showed real-time status of all current, upcoming, and completed colony setup activities. Video windows showed a constant rotation of views.

Setup crews were awake and had begun shuttling printers down to Vulcan. On the surface, roamers were printing out modular residential units and assembling them. AMI-controlled bobcats and backhoes stayed just ahead of the construction, preparing the ground for the houses.

In two days, we would start waking the first wave of civilians and shuttling them down to their new homes. And the universe would have actual Vulcans.

Roddenberry would be proud.